Want You Dead

STEVE FRECH

ONE PLACE. MANY STORIES

HQ
An imprint of HarperCollins*Publishers* Ltd
1 London Bridge Street
London SE1 9GF

www.harpercollins.co.uk

HarperCollins*Publishers*
1st Floor, Watermarque Building, Ringsend Road
Dublin 4, Ireland

This paperback edition 2022

1
First published in Great Britain by
HQ, an imprint of HarperCollins*Publishers* Ltd 2022

Copyright © Steve Frech 2022

Steve Frech asserts the moral right to be
identified as the author of this work.
A catalogue record for this book is
available from the British Library.

ISBN: 9780008471057

MIX
Paper from
responsible sources
FSC™ C007454

This book is produced from independently certified FSC™ paper
to ensure responsible forest management.

For more information visit: www.harpercollins.co.uk/green

Printed and Bound in the UK
using 100% Renewable Electricity at CPI Group (UK) Ltd

Thank you, Janice Hearon

"Go back inside, kids! Quickly! Get back inside!"

There was chaos and confusion as people stormed back into the kitchen, away from the horror lying under the pirate piñata in the backyard. Parents swept their children into their arms and held their faces to their chests so they couldn't see.

Jessica witnessed the shock in one father's face as he carried his daughter back down the hall while whispering, "Oh God … oh God … oh God …"

Chapter 1

"What is it?"

Jessica Hammond turned in the passenger seat of the Tesla to see her eight-year-old daughter, Daniella, staring at the gift-wrapped box sitting next to her.

"It's a remote-controlled car, sweetheart."

"Oh." Daniella turned back to the window. The passing trees cast momentary shadows as they drove.

Just looking at the present gave Jessica a sense of confidence and superiority. The other presents Dougie would receive at this party would be wrapped in thin paper with gaudy prints that had been purchased years ago at Target or Walmart and then thrown into the back of a closet with the rest of the Christmas wrapping paper.

That was not how Jessica Hammond operated.

This remote-controlled car had been wrapped in cream-toned paper that had the feel of soft parchment and tied with a red velvet bow with gold trim. If Jessica was being honest, the wrapping paper had probably cost more than a lot of the other presents that would be at the party. It only made sense. The remote-controlled car would easily be the most expensive gift, as well.

"How long are we staying at this thing?" her husband, James, asked as he navigated a corner.

James was in his early fifties. He was filling out at the waist but was still undeniably handsome with a strong chin, deep-brown eyes, and a full head of graying hair. The women at the Kensington Country Club openly called him a "silver fox."

"A couple of hours."

James rolled his eyes.

"Don't do that," Jessica said. "It's important for Kristi and Nick."

Dougie Sanders's birthday had actually been four months ago, but he had been undergoing another round of chemo at the time. Kristi, Dougie's mother and Jessica's friend, had said that they probably should have postponed his birthday party, again, but they wanted to give Dougie something positive after the months of suffering he had endured. He had been diagnosed with leukemia years ago, and it had been a constant game of whack-a-mole—remission, resurgence, remission, resurgence—but it was finally over. Kristi gave everyone updates at the company functions. Jessica received more updates than most. Kristi Sanders had been one of James's first employees in his company, CashFlo, which designed payment systems for online retailers, and over the years, she and Jessica had become friends.

"You know that Harold's going to be at this thing, too, right?" Jessica asked.

"Yeah," James replied with a heavy sigh.

She studied the lines in her husband's face, knowing he was already plotting their escape, but she wasn't so eager.

Most of the people at the party worked for her husband, and while they were all friendly, Jessica never missed a chance to show off. The Hammonds would have the nicest car there. They would be giving the nicest present in the nicest wrapping paper. Jessica had grown up poor, and she enjoyed demonstrating that she was now at the top of the food chain.

But that was only partly the reason she didn't share in her husband's desire to make their stay at the party brief. She had spent so much time in front of the mirror back at their home, getting ready, choosing the blouse, and leaving an extra button open at the top. If anyone wondered, they would assume it was the August heat in Georgia.

And that ravishing shade of lipstick?

Let them wonder.

James hadn't touched her in a while. Jessica was certain that he was fulfilling his needs elsewhere, maybe even going back to his ex-wife, and Jessica knew the only way to get under his skin was to go all out. She had never met anyone so jealous and insecure as James. On one hand, it drove him mad when other men looked at her. Ironically, it was that same jealousy and insecurity that would drive him mad if men *didn't* look at her. This beauty was his, and he viewed it as an expression of the fact that James Hammond got whatever he wanted.

When she had realized the extent of his jealousy and insecurity, she'd tried to talk to him about it. Of course, he didn't see himself as jealous or insecure, at all. That would imply that he had a weakness, but he did make it very clear: if she ever cheated on him, he would leave her in the cold. She tried to argue by bringing up his infidelities. He flatly denied them, which was almost comical, until he made the ultimatum that if she ever slept with another man, he would ruin her life.

She said she understood. The sex, which still happened from time to time, became less frequent, and then stopped all together. By then, Jessica had realized that she had grown accustomed to the house, the cars, the fashion, the food, and the social events, all while sticking to their arrangement, but recently, she had—

"Can I have a Moto-Tyke?" Dani suddenly chimed from the back seat.

"A what?" Jessica asked.

"A Moto-Tyke. Like Ashley has."

Ashley Wembley was Dani's friend from a few doors down and had recently received a Moto-Tyke from her parents. It was a miniature, motorized version of a white convertible.

3

"Sure, sweetie."

"Can it be pink?"

"Of course," Jessica answered.

Dani went back to looking out the window, a victorious smile on her face.

Jessica knew she spoiled Dani, and she didn't care.

"There it is," James said as a bouncy castle came into view.

The helium balloons tied to the mailbox gently bobbed in the faint breeze. Closer still, they could see the black-cloth-covered table on the lawn with a sign that read, "THE AMAZING PRESTO!" All of it was lorded over by the inflatable spires of the bouncy castle. The sides of the castle were bending and flexing from the kids inside.

James pulled the Tesla to the curb and threw it into park.

"Let's get this over with," he said, opening his door.

Jessica turned and pointed at the present. "Can you grab that for me, please?"

Dani obeyed.

"Now, remember," Jessica said as they exited the car. "Dougie's been through a lot, so you need to be super nice to him, okay?"

Dani nodded.

Jessica knew that Dani could do that if it meant the acquisition of a Moto-Tyke.

They walked across the front yard, through heavy, humid air—which was laced with the sounds of kids screaming and laughing in the castle, along with pleas from parents to be careful—to the open front door. The air-conditioning was fighting a losing battle against the heat that followed them down the hallway, past the living room, and into the kitchen. There, they found Dougie's parents, Kristi and Nick. Kristi was putting the final sprinkles on a tray of ice cream sundaes in little plastic cups. Nick was standing by to put the tray in the freezer. They looked up as the Hammonds entered.

"Hey! You made it!" Kristi cried.

Jessica smiled. "Yep."

Kristi quickly tapped a few sprinkles onto the last sundae. "Okay. We're good."

Nick picked up the tray. Kristi went to the freezer and opened the door, allowing Nick to slide the tray onto a shelf. She closed the door, breathed a sigh of relief, and stepped over to Jessica.

"Thank you so much for coming," she said, embracing her.

"Wouldn't miss it for the world," Jessica replied, returning the hug before turning to Nick. "Hi, Nick."

"Hey."

They hugged. As they pulled away, Jessica saw his eyes flit upward for a split second as James and Kristi awkwardly embraced.

Jessica mimicked his signal before turning back to Kristi.

"Quite the party you've got going," Jessica said.

"Yeah," Kristi concurred. "It's a little crazy."

"Where should I put this?" the momentarily forgotten Dani asked, still holding Dougie's gift.

"Oh, here, let me show you," Kristi said, leading her to the door to the backyard.

"If you've got things to do, just tell us where it goes and we'll take care of it," Jessica said.

Nick held up a hand. "Please. It'll get us out of this damn kitchen."

Everyone followed Kristi out the door.

The backyard was a birthday wonderland. Several folding tables were adorned with balloons, colorful paper plates, and plastic cutlery, with another dedicated to presents. Jessica took secret satisfaction in being proven correct that their present would stand out against the others, and when Dougie opened it, it would stand out even more. The backyard was dotted with trees. One in the back corner had a piñata hanging from a branch. A wooden softball bat rested below it against the trunk of the tree.

"We'll do the piñata and cake out here after the magician," Kristi said.

"You two went all out," James said.

"We wanted to give Dougie something special," Nick said.

"Is that a pirate?" Dani asked, pointing at the piñata.

"Yeah," Kristi answered. "Dougie read *Treasure Island* while doing his chemo and got really into pirates."

Jessica quickly cycled through Dani's recent accomplishments to see if there was any she could offer to match Dougie's, but quickly realized that this was not the time for parental competitiveness. Besides, Kristi was a friend, and she knew how much this all meant to Kristi and Nick.

"We thought about doing a piñata for the grown-ups," Nick added. "Let them work out some aggressions, and instead of candy, it would have been filled with little liquor bottles."

"We really should have," Kristi said with genuine regret.

"Mom?"

Everyone turned back toward the house. Dougie was standing at the open door to the kitchen. He was shockingly thin, and his hair was only just starting to grow back. His face was drawn, and his eyes sunken.

"There's the birthday boy!" Jessica sang.

"You remember the Hammonds and their daughter, Dani, right?" Kristi asked.

"Hi," Dougie said.

Jessica couldn't tell if he actually remembered them. He had been over to their house and played with Dani, but that was a while ago and he had been through so much, she didn't care if he remembered.

"Happy birthday," Dani said, handing him the present.

The beautiful wrapping paper and bow had already caught his eye, and he gauged the weight of the present with his hands.

"Do not shake it," Nick said. "Put it with the others, and we'll open it after the magician and cake, okay?"

"Okay," Dougie said, slightly dejected, and he put it on the table with the others.

"Did you need something, sweetie?" Kristi asked.

"Sarah Ferguson hurt herself in the castle."

Kristi snapped into action. "How bad?"

"She hurt her ankle, but she's not crying or nothing."

"I told you that castle was a mistake," Nick muttered.

Kristi shot him a look before returning to Dougie. "I'll be out there in a second. Are you okay, sweetie?"

"I'm tired."

"We'll have you sit down and rest for a while." Kristi turned to the Hammonds. "I'm going to go deal with this. If you need something to drink, there's booze in the garage. I've told all the parents to help themselves and that kids aren't allowed in there. It's the adult safe space."

"Brilliant," James said without sarcasm.

"Enjoy yourselves," Kristi added. "The magician will go on in a little bit, and we'll get everyone out front."

"I'll help you," Jessica offered. "Come on, Dani. You boys can look after yourselves, right?"

"I think we'll manage," Nick answered.

The women and two kids went back into the house. Once they had disappeared, James and Nick looked at one another.

"The garage?" Nick asked.

"The garage," James confirmed.

Chapter 2

They made their way back inside, turned left out of the kitchen, and headed down the hall. Nick opened the door at the end of the hall, and they entered the garage.

Inside, a handful of dads were chatting, beers in hand. They looked over as Nick and James approached. Pleasantries were exchanged. A few of the employees of CashFlo suddenly appeared nervous to be drinking around their boss, but James gave them a smile to let them know all was well.

Nick led them to the fridge and opened it.

"Bud Light? Corona?"

"Corona's great."

Nick pulled out two bottles along with two lime wedges that had been pre-cut for the occasion. He used the wall-mounted opener to pry off the caps, pushed a lime wedge into each of the bottles, and handed one to James.

"Cheers," Nick said.

"To Dougie," James replied and tapped his bottle against Nick's.

Nick smiled. "To Dougie."

They each took a sip.

"How is he doing?" James asked.

"It's been rough, but it looks like he's finally out of the woods.

He'll be able to go back to school in another month or two, which means I can finally start looking for a job." Someone awkwardly stepped over and stood off to their side. They both noticed, but Nick tried to continue. "Thank God for Kristi's insurance, because I don't know what we would have done with th—"

James couldn't take the eavesdropper anymore and turned to him.

"Hello, Harold."

"Mr. Hammond. Hello," Harold replied, nervously.

Harold Mantelli was a short, pudgy, balding man with glasses, and a face that always wore a sheen of sweat. He also lacked any and all sense of social etiquette.

"It's good to see you," James said, perfunctorily. He couldn't stand Harold, but he was trying to be on his best behavior. He couldn't stand a lot of the people around him, and soon, they'd be out of his life forever, but he couldn't let them know that.

"I, uh, I just wanted to say hi," Harold stammered.

"Is your daughter running around here somewhere?"

"Uh, no. She's over at her mother's."

"Oh. That's a shame," James said. There was an awkward silence. "But you came, anyway?"

"Yeah. I, uh, I felt I should be here." Harold caught a glimpse of Nick and quickly added, "For Dougie. I wanted to be here for Dougie."

"Kristi and I really appreciate it," Nick said.

Harold nodded and turned back to James. "But I did want to talk to you, Mr. Hammond."

"Of course. I'm going to mingle with everyone first, but find me later, okay?" James held up his Corona. "After I've had a few more of these."

"Okay," Harold said.

James lightly clapped him on the arm. "Great. We'll catch up."

Nick and James walked away, leaving the awkward Harold standing alone in the midst of the other dads.

"Sorry about that," Nick said as they stepped back into the hallway of the house. "Kristi wasn't sure if he would come or not."

"Jessica warned me that he would be here."

"Speaking of which, let's go see how they're doing out front."

"Lead the way."

*

They exited out the front door and into the bright sunshine.

Children raced across the grass. Parents stood in pairs or small circles. Some of the dads held beers in their hands, while the moms held glasses of white wine that sweated with them in the heat.

Jessica and Kristi were off to one side. Kristi was scanning the yard, while Jessica was staring daggers at a man with a square jaw and dark eyes. She shook her head and broke eye contact as their husbands approached.

"Everything okay with ankle girl?" James asked.

"She's fine," Kristi said. "Just a little sprain. More scared than hurt. Now, I'm trying to find the magician."

Jessica smiled. "The only person who can never really enjoy a party is the host."

Kristi rolled her eyes. "Tell me about it."

"Well, he's not in the garage. We were just there," Nick said. "You want us to look for him?"

"Would you please?"

"I'll check out the rest of the house. James, can you check the sides and the backyard?" Nick asked.

"Sure."

Nick went back through the front door, while James followed the path off the driveway to the right side of the house, toward the backyard.

*

James approached the gate in the tall fence leading to the backyard. To his left were equally tall, evenly spaced bushes. He checked between the bushes and found no sign of The Amazing Presto.

He reached the fence and pulled on the little rope that had been strung through a hole, lifting the latch on the other side, and opened the gate. The pirate piñata twisted slowly on the string and the softball bat rested against the tree as the gate closed behind him.

He checked behind the trees and bushes.

"Um … Mr. Presto?" he called out, feeling a little foolish, but there was no reply.

James continued through the yard to the other side of the house where there was an identical gate in the fence. He opened it and walked through.

It was a mirror image of the other side of the house down to the walkway and evenly spaced bushes.

A movement caught his eye.

The back of a cape was slightly protruding from the space between two bushes, accompanied by the unmistakable beeps and chimes of a video game.

James silently stepped up behind the wearer of the cape. He couldn't see the man's face, but he could see the phone in his hand, and that he was playing Candy Crush. In his other hand, he held a flask.

This could only be The Amazing Presto.

His phone sent up a series of bells and chimes as he completed a level. Suddenly, The Amazing Presto threw his head back. He brought the flask to his lips and took a long pull. He lowered the flask, coughed, and wiped his lips with the back of his sleeve.

James cleared his throat. "Excuse me?"

The Amazing Presto gasped and turned to face him.

"You startled me, mate." He had a British accent, beard, glasses, and he quickly tried to place the flask in his pocket.

"Are you the magician?"

"Yes. Uh, yes, I am," he stuttered and finally succeeded in getting the flask out of sight. "I was just, um, I was just warming up."

"The host is looking for you in the front yard."

"Right ... right," The Amazing Presto said, looking around the ground at his feet. "I'll be right there."

"I'll go tell her," James said and walked away.

He continued up the pathway, which took him around the side of the house to the driveway. He walked up to Kristi, who was now standing alone, watching over the proceedings.

"Found him."

"Where was he?"

"Around the side of the house, getting ... loose."

She gave him an odd look. "I don't like the sound of that."

"I told him you wanted to see him."

"Good. I may have to move things up. Dougie's really tired." James looked around. "Where's my wife?"

"I don't know. She was here a second ago."

*

Jessica reached the top of the stairs.

She had timed her escape perfectly and slipped back into the house without anyone noticing.

She quietly walked down the hall to the master bedroom. The room appeared empty. The sound of the kids playing outside crept in through the open window. She made her way around the bed toward the bathroom, the door to which was partially closed.

"Hello?" she whispered.

Nothing.

She inched closer toward the bathroom. The walk-in closet was on her left.

"Hello?" she whispered again, and began to reach for the door.

Suddenly, a pair of hands shot out from the closet, grabbed her, and roughly pulled her inside.

12

She nearly cried out until she felt lips pressed against her neck. She instantly responded by gripping his hair and pulling it back so his face was tilted toward her. She forcefully pushed her lips against his. Their tongues began savagely dancing. She bit down on his lip. His hand slid up her shirt, while she fumbled with the zipper on his jeans.

*

The Amazing Presto stepped around the side of the house, placing a silk top hat on his head, and walked up to Kristi.

"We ready?" she asked, eyeing him up and down.

"Yes, ma'am," he replied.

"Great. Now, that's the birthday boy, Dougie, right over there," she said, pointing to her son, who was standing outside the bouncy castle. "He's getting really tired, so I think I may have you go on a little earlier than planned. That okay?"

"Have no fear, madam. It shall be done."

The Amazing Presto bowed. When he straightened up, he held a flower in his hand that had seemingly come from nowhere and presented it to Kristi.

Kristi took the flower, and The Amazing Presto went over to the covered table.

She looked at the flower, unsure of what to make of it, and then at James.

"Whatever," she mumbled and dropped it. "Okay, everyone! Who wants to see some magic?"

There were cheers from the kids around the yard.

*

The sound of Kristi's announcement could be heard in the closet of the master bedroom, where Jessica was on her knees.

She took him out of her mouth and looked up.

"We should probably get back before someone notices we're not there," she said, teasing him with her tongue.

Through the faint sunlight that drifted through the small opening of the closet door, she could see the frustrated smile on Nick's face as he breathlessly sighed.

"You're probably right," he said.

"To be continued," she said, and gave one last kiss before standing.

"To be continued," he replied greedily as he zipped and buttoned his jeans. "We shouldn't walk out together."

"Good idea. You go first. I'm going to use your bathroom to put myself back together."

Nick was about to protest but stopped.

"Okay." He kissed her lips. "I'll see you out there."

Nick opened the closet door and walked out.

Jessica leaned back against the wall of the closet, a smile playing across her face as she listened to Nick's footsteps descend the stairs.

Chapter 3

"Good afternoon, ladies and gentlemen! Boys and girls! I am THE AMAZING PRESTO!"

The magician performed a flourish and threw something at the ground near his feet. It erupted in a puff of smoke that drifted back up into his face. The Amazing Presto coughed and tried to wave away the smoke with his cape.

The children didn't know what to make of this inauspicious start from the guy with the funny accent. Worried glances were exchanged among the adults.

"Oh no …" Kristi whispered.

James's phone vibrated in his pocket.

He took it out, checked the screen, and creased his brow. He scanned the surrounding parents and then looked at the open front door.

"Everything okay?" Kristi asked.

"Yeah. I'll be right back."

James tried to take a wide arc to avoid The Amazing Presto as he made his way back to the house.

"I understand that it is someone's birthday today!" The Amazing Presto proclaimed as James disappeared through the front door. The Amazing Presto pointed at Dougie. "You, sir!

15

Please join me!"

Dougie stood up from his seat on the grass with the other kids and took his spot at The Amazing Presto's side.

"It is your birthday, is it not?" The Amazing Presto asked in a theatrical tone.

"Yes," Dougie answered.

"Do you know how I knew that?"

"My mom told you?"

"No!" The Amazing Presto quickly cried. "It's because when it is someone's birthday, they are suddenly filled with money!" The Amazing Presto deftly placed his hands against Dougie's ears and appeared to pull a coin from each one.

Really? I'm paying three hundred dollars for this? Kristi thought, but as she watched, The Amazing Presto continued pulling more and more coins from everywhere around Dougie's head, who laughed as the coins began piling up on the ground near his feet. Every time it appeared that the trick was over, The Amazing Presto would pull another coin.

"You, my boy, are a regular piggy bank!" The Amazing Presto declared.

Kristi began to smile.

Okay, she thought. *That's kind of fun. Maybe he's not—*

The Amazing Presto's hand slipped and a mass of coins fell from his sleeve down to the grass.

"Shit," he said quietly, but in such close proximity, everyone heard it. He made a move to grab them, but instead threw up his hands and shouted, "Dougie! The Human Piggy Bank!"

There was applause from the kids, and Dougie seemed to love it.

Kristi took stock of the reactions of the parents. She was relieved that nearly everyone was chuckling, except for Sean Winston, who wore a scowl, checked his watch, and then began walking toward the house. The Amazing Presto shot him a disapproving side-eye as he passed.

Kristi caught sight of Harold Mantelli, who was nervously

watching Sean head for the door. He hesitated and then followed, once again drawing the ire of The Amazing Presto.

*

Jessica checked her hair and smoothed her clothes one last time as she approached the front door to join the crowd.

Yes, she and Nick were having an affair.

She had abided by James's rules long enough. She needed passion, she needed desire, and Nick gave them to her.

It had started a few months ago, when they found themselves chatting at the CashFlo Christmas party. They had known each other for years. Jessica had always found Nick attractive and him, likewise. They would flirt as friends, using the firewall of marriage as justification that it was harmless. Then, they started talking without their spouses' knowledge. It was innocent enough, at first. Eventually, they started venting to each other about their marriages. James had lost interest in her, sexually, and was fulfilling his needs elsewhere. She wasn't sure what to do and accepted the circumstances, but over time, she saw them as absurd. She was fifteen years his junior. She was vibrant, sensual, and she knew it.

Since Kristi's health insurance through CashFlo was better than his, Nick quit his job to take care of Dougie. That, combined with the constant demands on Kristi's time from working at a start-up, had Nick feeling like he had been left by the wayside. He and Kristi hadn't made love in over a year. There were always excuses; Kristi was too tired, too distracted. Or there was no excuse, only a simple "not now."

Then, at the Christmas party, after too many glasses of the punch that everyone was sure had been spiked multiple times, Jessica and Nick found themselves alone in one of the offices. They had their first kiss. As soon as it was over, Nick hurried to the door and locked it while Jessica cleared off the desk.

That was that.

It was supposed to be harmless, a one-time thing; but one time became two, then three, then they lost count. Before they knew it, they had confessed that they had feelings for each other. The affair was supposed to be for fun, but they both knew at some point in the not-too-distant future, they had a decision to make. Until then, they were going to have as much fun as possible.

Why would she risk such a thing when James made it clear what he would do if he ever found out? Because after years of living in fear, but craving affection, she had convinced herself that James would never find out.

She did feel terrible about Kristi. They were friends, but this ... *thing* ... had happened. They had tried to stop out of respect for her, but it never worked. They would stop for a week or two, trying to talk and act as if it had never happened, all the while their hunger for each other would begin building, and culminate in an explosive night or afternoon at a hotel while Kristi and James were at work.

Jessica was so preoccupied with making sure that she was acting normal, that she almost collided with Sean Winston as he entered the house.

"Sorry, Sean," she said, her expression hardening.

"Pardon me, Jessica," he replied and walked past her into the hallway.

Jessica watched him go, turned, and was about step outside once more when Harold Mantelli entered, obstructing her path.

"Oh ... hi, Jessica."

"Harold."

"I was just going to talk to Sean. I saw him come inside."

"He went down the hall, toward the garage."

"Thank you."

Harold quickly shuffled off down the hallway.

Jessica double-checked to make sure no one else was coming inside and went through the door.

*

"And I believe this is your card!" The Amazing Presto announced, holding out the queen of diamonds for the kids to see.

Sarah Ferguson, the eight-year-old "ankle girl," laughed. "No."

The other kids were laughing as well because her card, the four of clubs, was stuck to The Amazing Presto's forehead, a fact to which he appeared oblivious.

"Well, where is it?" he asked, shuffling through the deck.

"Your head!" came the cry from the children.

The Amazing Presto made a show of surprise as he discovered there was a card stuck to his forehead.

There was applause, but many people had been distracted by Jessica walking around to join the crowd. The Amazing Presto tried to hide his evident frustration.

"What did I miss?" Jessica asked, stopping at Kristi's side.

"A rocky start, but he's redeeming himself," Kristi said, and finished her half-full glass of chardonnay in one gulp.

The Amazing Presto collected the wallet of a nearby parent. He held it in his hand, placed a black silk cloth over it, waved his wand, and pulled the cloth away to reveal that the wallet was gone.

"One minute, good sir, while I memorize all of your credit card numbers," he said, closing his eyes and mumbling to himself. Then, he went to a small box on the table. The Amazing Presto lifted the box to reveal the man's wallet to the applause of the crowd.

"Where's Nick?" Jessica asked, then quickly added, "And James?"

The Amazing Presto handed back the man's wallet, who comically checked to see if there was still money inside. The Amazing Presto laughed, grateful to have someone playing along.

"Thank you, good sir!" he cried.

"He got a text message and went inside a few minutes ago," Kristi said.

Jessica nodded. That was nothing new. As the founder and CEO of a successful start-up, James was always getting texts, phone calls, and emails that interrupted family gatherings and other social functions. Jessica had learned to roll with the punches. It was part of the territory and demonstrated his importance.

"Here comes Nick," Kristi said, motioning to the door with her empty wine glass.

The Amazing Presto was in the middle of another trick involving metal rings, but had to pause to allow Nick to come around and stand with Jessica and Kristi.

"Where were you?" Kristi asked.

"I had to use the restroom."

"Now that you mention it," Kristi said and held out her empty wine glass to Nick, "can you two hold down the fort? I'm going to hit the restroom before we head to the backyard. My bladder is about to pop."

"We got this," Jessica said.

"Thanks."

Kristi hustled to the door.

The Amazing Presto tried to hide his exasperation as she slipped past the table and through the front door.

"And as a bonus, I shall make this woman disappear! Poof!" he said, with another flourish of his hand as Kristi entered the house.

"Seriously, where were you?" Jessica quietly asked.

"You said that you were going to check and make sure that you were presentable before coming back outside," Nick whispered out of the side of his mouth. "I decided to do the same and stop in the bathroom. Good thing I did, because your lipstick was all over me."

Jessica stifled a giggle. "I'm sorry. It was dark in the closet. I didn't see it."

"It's all right. Crisis averted."

"For my final trick," The Amazing Presto shouted, "I shall once again require the assistance of the birthday boy!"

An energized Dougie got to his feet and joined the magician.

"Uh oh," Jessica breathed. "Should I run and grab Kristi?"

"It'll be fine. I'm sure she'll be back in a second."

"Now, my boy, I need you to stand here," The Amazing Presto said, situating Dougie in front of the table. He then pulled out a sheet of newspaper. "In my hand is part of today's newspaper." He went over to one of the mothers standing nearby. "Can you verify that fact for me, ma'am?" He held the paper out to her but then pulled it back. "You can read, can't you?"

She laughed and nodded.

The Amazing Presto looked down at the smiling little girl who was sitting in front of the woman.

"Is this your mum?"

"Yes," the girl answered, giggling.

"Can she read?"

"I don't know."

"I guess we shall see," The Amazing Presto said and handed the woman the paper. "Madam, is this today's paper?"

The woman laughed as she read the date on the paper. "I think so."

"Wonderful! Thank you for being so honest!" he cried, and shaped the sheet of newspaper into a cone. "Dougie! I'm going to ask you to hold this right here," he said, placing the cone point down, just over Dougie's head.

Dougie reached up and held it while The Amazing Presto went back to the table.

"And this ..." he said, reaching under the table and pulling out another object, "is a pitcher of milk!"

He stepped around to one of the fathers closest to the table. "Sir, will you please taste that to prove that it is indeed milk?"

The dad reached for the milk, but The Amazing Presto stopped him.

"What are you doing, mate? This milk has been sitting out in the sun for hours."

That got another laugh, mostly from the parents.

The Amazing Presto stepped back over to Dougie just as Kristi hustled out of the front door and back into the yard, drawing everyone's attention.

"Sorry!" she said, jostling back to her spot with Jessica and Nick. "Sorry, sorry, sorry."

The Amazing Presto turned and addressed Dougie loud enough for all to hear. "Actually, it's a good thing she came out when she did, because if she had broken my concentration in the middle of the trick, it would have made this a very bad birthday for you, chum."

Dougie laughed uncontrollably. The newspaper cone trembled above his head.

Kristi stopped next to Jessica and Nick.

"Much better," she said. "What is he going to do?"

"Hopefully not screw up," Nick answered.

"Now, Dougie! It's important that you remain perfectly still because as I said, this milk has been sitting out here for hours!" The Amazing Presto declared, holding up the milk.

Dougie continued to shake with laughter.

"I shall require help from all of you!" The Amazing Presto swept his hand toward the audience. "I'm going to count to three, and I need you to shout, 'PRESTO!' Ready?"

"Yeah!" the children cried.

The Amazing Presto held the pitcher over Dougie's head.

"One! … Two! … THREE!"

"PRESTO!" the kids shrieked.

He tipped the pitcher and began pouring the milk into the newspaper cone.

Dougie was screaming with pure joy.

The Amazing Presto emptied the pitcher, placed it on the table, grabbed the newspaper off Dougie's head, and unfolded it to reveal it was bone dry and the milk was gone.

"PRESTO!!!" he shouted to the applause of parents and children, alike. He shook Dougie's hand. "Happy birthday, Dougie! Thank you so much for your help and for letting me celebrate with you." He turned to the crowd. "Ladies and gentlemen, let's hear it for Dougie, the birthday boy! I am The Amazing Presto! I hope you enjoyed the show. If any of you parents are looking to book some entertainment for a party or corporate gig, please come see me. I have business cards. Thank you again for having me and enjoy the rest of the party!"

There was a final round of applause, and Kristi exhaled with relief before holding up her arms and addressing everyone.

"Thank you, Amazing Presto! That was great. Now, we're going to head to the backyard for cake, presents, and the piñata!"

The kids all stood, and everyone began following Kristi to the front door.

Nick and Jessica hung back, allowing most of the crowd to get ahead of them.

"I'll be more careful with the lipstick next time," Jessica whispered as they walked, side by side.

"I don't want you to be careful," he whispered back. He glanced around to make sure they weren't overheard. "What I want to know is when are you going to finish what we started?"

She slyly smiled. "How long is this party?"

They entered the house. The partygoers were bottlenecked around them.

They finally stepped into the kitchen, but something was wrong.

The door to the backyard was open, but everyone had stopped instead of continuing on. A crush began to form, and the excited voices of the children tapered off into silence.

"Stay here, everyone," Jessica heard Kristi say.

She could see the top of Kristi's head as she walked across the backyard.

Parents and children craned their necks to watch.

"What's happening?" she asked Nick.

Kristi's voice suddenly erupted.

"Go back inside, kids! Quickly! Get back inside!"

There was chaos and confusion as people stormed back into the kitchen, away from the horror lying under the pirate piñata in the backyard. Parents swept their children into their arms and held their faces to their chests so they couldn't see.

Jessica witnessed the shock in one father's face as he carried his daughter back down the hall while whispering, "Oh God … oh God … oh God …"

Nick and Jessica stayed rooted to the spot as the mass of people moved past them back toward the living room.

Jessica turned to Kristi's panicked face. "What's wrong?" she asked.

"You can't go out there," Kristi said forcefully and turned to Nick. "Call the police."

"What are you talking about?" Jessica asked. "What's going on?"

"Jessica, please, go back out to the front yard," Kristi pleaded.

"Why? What's happened?" Jessica insisted as the last of the partygoers fled back down the hall, leaving her, Kristi, and Nick.

Jessica began to understand. "Where's James?" she asked.

"Jessica, please—"

"James!" Jessica cried.

She moved around Kristi, who tried to stop her, but Jessica threw off her arm and ran out the door into the backyard.

Hot, muggy air filled her lungs as she stepped on the patio and immediately recoiled.

A body was lying in the grass under a blue paper tablecloth. Blood soaked through the part of the tablecloth that covered the head.

In a daze, Jessica walked over, knelt down, and pulled back the tablecloth to reveal the body of her husband, James.

His face was a pink, frothy pulp.

Chapter 4

"'Sup. The name's Tyler. I'm an addict."

"Hi, Tyler," came the response from around the room.

"Most of you know me, but I see a lot of new faces, so I will give the abridged version of the story: In my younger days, I was a dealer. Like a lot of dealers, I started tasting my own product. I got hooked. Things looked bad, but I caught a break. Someone I looked up to gave me a chance to be something more, and I went for it. The only problem was that I took my addiction with me. I thought I could keep it under wraps, but we all know how that goes."

There were amused mutterings and nods of acknowledgment.

"Thankfully, I had a friend who cared enough about me to lay it on the line." Tyler, who was standing, looked down and gently bumped his hip against Meredith's shoulder. She was sitting next to him in one of the uncomfortable plastic chairs. "She let me know that I could either have all the things I had worked for, or I could have the junk. I couldn't have both. She saved my life. And thanks to her, I've been clean for over a year."

There was applause and whistles.

"I appreciate that," Tyler continued. "But it wasn't just her. There are a lot of people in this room who have kept me on the straight and narrow, and I want to say something to all you 'newbies.' Some of you are here against your will. Court order. You need to get those slips signed. There's no shame in that, but for those of you who want to stop using, no court order is going to make you get clean. You gotta want it, and you've gotta be willing to work for it. You can get there. I'm proof of that, but I'm here to tell you, it doesn't get easier. Some days, everything in me is screaming for one more hit. Just one. Even half a rail would do it. I hear people on diets talk about their 'cheat day' when they get to have a donut, and I'm like, 'Yeah. I want a cheat day. Where's my powdered donut?'"

There were more laughs.

"But we don't get cheat days, no matter how bad those cravings hit, and even though I've been clean for a year, odds are I'm gonna slip. But my odds are better, and so are yours, if you keep coming to these meetings. Last week, I was going out of my mind, and I was sure that I was gonna step out and try to score. So, I called up Darren." Tyler gestured to the old-timer who was heading the meeting. "I said, 'Darren, I need help, man.' The dude picked me up at one in the morning, bought me a cup of coffee and a plate of waffles, and we just talked. We talked football. We talked politics, and we talked about what I'd be throwing away if I took one more hit. He got me through it. It got me one more day of sobriety, and that shit is priceless.

"So, newbies, if you really want this, but you're too nervous or shy or embarrassed to stand up during these meetings and ask for that help, that's cool. You come find me or one of these other veterans when we're done. There's no judgment. We've been there. We know how hard it is. If you want to be sober, we want you to be sober, too. And I'll just leave you with this; I have more pride in my year of burning clean than I ever had in my time as a user."

The room was silent.

Tyler shrugged. "That's it. That's all I've got."

The room broke into another round of applause and whistles, even louder than before.

Tyler sat down, and Meredith bumped him back.

*

Once they had all held hands and recited the serenity prayer, most of the participants in the NarcAnon meeting amassed in the parking lot, just outside the door, smoking cigarettes. A few held small cups of coffee, even though it was stifling in the late afternoon sun.

Meredith was leaning against her car, watching, as Tyler spoke to a young guy with tattoos and buzzed hair. He had sought out Tyler as soon as the meeting broke. Even from across the parking lot, Meredith could see that the guy was upset. Tyler gently guided him away from the group. He offered him a cigarette and listened as he spoke. Tyler would nod and occasionally speak. She had no idea what they were saying. She was never a part of the conversations Tyler had with the other members, especially the newbies. Those conversations had to be private. She kept her distance, but she loved watching Tyler help people.

Meredith had made the NarcAnon meetings mandatory for Tyler if he wanted to continue as a detective after the case on Willow Lane.

Those first few months were hell. No matter how badly Tyler wanted to stay sober, the cravings didn't care. She and Tyler would have shouting matches. Sometimes he would cry. Sometimes she would cry. Sometimes they both cried. There were times that she was the recipient of his phone calls at one in the morning.

Little by little, Tyler had gotten himself under control. He made peace with the fact that he would never be able to subdue his cravings. He could only manage them, outlast them until he could bring himself down. The meetings helped. At first, he was reluctant to speak. Then Darren asked him to stand up and share. Tyler used his laid-back style to overcome his frustration, embarrassment, and vulnerability.

It was like a door opening.

Tyler talked to everyone. He liked listening to the stories of others who were further along on their path to sobriety. Meredith had experience with her father's alcoholism, but he had never tried to fight it. Her father had surrendered to it.

Tyler was fighting it with everything he had and shared a common bond with so many people in those rooms, and they came from every walk of life: mothers, fathers, young, old, CEOs, unemployed, artists, office workers, etc., all trying to achieve the same thing. Tyler was happy to talk to them all. He wanted to help. He knew that asking was the most terrifying and the most necessary step to take.

Which was why Meredith waited by the car as Tyler spoke to the newbies who approached him.

Tyler said something, and the guy laughed, even though moments ago, he was in tears.

That was the effect Tyler had on people.

Her phone buzzed in her pocket. She checked the caller ID.

"… Shit …"

She hit the answer button.

"Well, this can't be good."

"Sorry to interrupt your Saturday," Jackson from dispatch replied. "But I got one for you."

*

"I was using almost every day, and the Falcons were terrible that year, which I think made it worse," Tyler joked.

The guy with the tattoos and buzzed hair laughed and ashed his cigarette.

Tyler caught Meredith's approach over the guy's shoulder and grimaced. There was only one reason she would interrupt.

The guy turned to face her. His eyes were still red and puffy from before, but he was smiling.

"I'm really sorry to cut in—" Meredith began, but Tyler held up his hand.

"Gabriel, this is my friend, Meredith. Meredith, this is Gabriel. This was his first meeting."

"It's nice to meet you," Meredith said, shaking Gabriel's rough and calloused hand.

"You, too."

"And don't worry," Tyler said. "I told Gabriel that we might have to end our conversation if there was an emergency."

Meredith nodded. "There is."

"All right. Gotta run." Tyler reached into his pocket. "I'm here every Saturday, sometimes more, and I want to see you here again, Gabriel." Tyler pulled a card with his name and number from his pocket. He had had them printed when more and more people approached him at the meetings. They conveniently left out the fact that he was a cop. "If you feel like you're gonna step out, you call me, okay? We'll pick up where we left off with how terrible the Falcons are."

"Thank you," Gabriel said, his voice cracking and his face tightening.

"Hey."

Gabriel looked up from the card at Tyler.

Tyler shook his hand and pulled him in for a bro hug, which Gabriel returned.

"Glad you're here, brother," Tyler said, slapping his back. "I'll see you at the next meeting."

"Okay," Gabriel replied, tucking the card into his pocket.

Tyler and Meredith began walking across the parking lot back to her car.

"Sorry I had to break things up," she said.

"All good. Got him talking. Gave him a card. Told him to come back. Pretty much all I can do."

Meredith hit the button on the keychain fob to pop the locks on her car.

They climbed in, and Tyler dramatically flinched.

"Aw, come on, Somerset! It's boiling in here. All this time you were waiting, you couldn't crack a window?"

"Pipe down, you big baby," she said with a laugh and turned the air-conditioning to full blast.

As they pulled out of the parking lot, a few of the people waved to Tyler, who waved back and made a point to acknowledge Gabriel.

"Think he'll be back?" Meredith asked.

"Really hope so," Tyler answered. "All right. Game mode. Where are we heading? Where's the body?"

Meredith bit her lower lip.

"Somerset?"

"You're not going to believe it."

Chapter 5

"No, no, no, no, no …" Tyler muttered as Meredith parked next to the curb across from the Sanders home. "No way, Somerset."

A handful of police cars lined the street. The front yard was littered with parents and children. Some were talking among themselves. Others were arguing with the cops. The rest were sitting or standing on the grass in shock.

"This is a nightmare," Tyler said.

"Yup," Meredith agreed.

They stepped out of the car and crossed the street into the yard.

Sheriff Howell was standing at the edge of the grass, trying to coordinate his officers, while a father was in his face, angrily waving his finger.

As Meredith and Tyler made their way toward Sheriff Howell, they passed a man in a button-down shirt, cape, and top hat, sitting on the grass, openly drinking from a flask.

"You have no idea what this has done to my daughter!" the man yelled at Sheriff Howell while a little girl cowered at his side. "You have to let us leave!"

"Sir, I understand—"

"No, I don't think you do—"

"I need you to lower your voice."

31

"Oh really? You need me to lower my voice?" the man replied, seemingly oblivious to the fact that Sheriff Howell had a good seven inches in height and a couple dozen pounds of bone-crushing muscle on him. "Well, what *we* need is to leave."

"Sir, everyone has to sit tight for a little while longer until my detectives arrive."

"Sheriff?" Meredith said.

Sheriff Howell began to angrily turn toward them. "I will be with you in one damn min—"

Upon seeing Meredith and Tyler, he stopped and exhaled.

"Thank God."

"Give us the rundown, and we'll get things moving," Meredith said.

Sheriff Howell began to consult his notes.

"Hey!" the irate father seethed. "I'm not done."

"For the moment, you are," Sheriff Howell said.

The man stepped closer to Sheriff Howell. "Now, you listen to me. I pay your salary, so I expect you—"

Meredith knew Sheriff Howell to be extremely professional and capable under pressure, but there was a limit and Sheriff Howell had reached it. His shirt struggled to hold itself together as he tensed and spun back to face the father. The little girl shuddered, on the verge of tears.

Meredith quickly got between the two men and held up her hands to address the crowd.

"Okay, everybody, listen up!"

All heads turned in her direction.

"I'm Detective Meredith Somerset with the Cobb County Police Department. This is my partner, Detective Tyler Foles."

Tyler awkwardly waved.

"We understand that your families have been through a terrible ordeal this afternoon," Meredith continued. "Many of you want to go home, and we respect that. We're going to have you on your way as soon as possible, but we need you to sit tight for a few more minutes. My partner and I are going to check out the backyard. Once we've finished there, we'll start conducting our interviews."

"Who are you going to interview first?" a mother asked. "Because I need to leave."

"We need to go, too," another said. "Our son—"

A swell of voices began to grow, all presenting their arguments as to why they should be interviewed first so they could leave.

Meredith held up her hands, once again, silencing the crowd.

"There's a lot we don't know, and we'll cross that bridge when we get there, but for right now, it will help us out and speed up the interviews if you start going over in your heads everything you saw once you came to the party. All right?"

While no one was happy, they appeared placated by the fact that there was a plan for their release.

Meredith turned to the father who had been in Sheriff Howell's face. "We appreciate your understanding."

Meredith's intervention had delivered a little bit of clarity. He finally recognized just how easily Sheriff Howell could have dispatched him and decided to save some face.

"Come on, Chloe," he said, grasping his daughter's hand, and retreating to the far side of the yard.

"Appreciate you, Somerset," Sheriff Howell said.

"You good?"

"Yeah. Don't take this personally, but I can't wait to dump this mess in your lap."

Meredith nodded. "Let's get started."

*

"The victim is one James Hammond," Sheriff Howell said over his shoulder as he led Meredith and Tyler through the front door, past the living room, and toward the kitchen. "Age: fifty-three. Wife is Jessica and their daughter, Daniella."

"Where are they?" Meredith asked.

"They're upstairs in the master bedroom with Emma Kinson, a social worker who specializes in trauma."

"Thank you, Sheriff," Meredith said.

"Kristi and Nick Sanders, the hosts of the party and owners of the house, are in another bedroom upstairs with their son, Dougie," Sheriff Howell continued. "He's recovering from cancer. This was his birthday party."

"Damn ..." Tyler sighed.

"Yeah."

"Can you give us an outline of events?" Meredith asked.

"I'll give you what I got. My officers are still taking statements." Sheriff Howell consulted his notes as they continued walking. "The party started at noon. The Hammonds arrived around twelve-thirty. They mingled with the Sanderses and a couple of others."

"Anyone notice anything strange?"

"Nope. From all accounts, everything appeared normal." He flipped a page. "At 1 p.m., The Amazing Presto began his show. So, everyone was in the front yard. According to Mrs. Sanders, who was standing next to James Hammond, he got a text message a few minutes after the magic show started and excused himself. He walked back inside the house. That was the last time anyone saw him alive, as far as we know."

They entered the kitchen.

"Once the magic show finished, Mrs. Sanders corralled everyone and led them back through the house and into the backyard," Sheriff Howell said, leading them through the door and onto the patio. "Where they found this."

Meredith and Tyler froze.

The backyard, which had been decorated to the nines in balloons and streamers, was crawling with cops.

In the rear corner of the yard lay the body of James Hammond. The blood seeping from what was left of his face had begun to dry. Lewis, the forensic tech examining the body, was forced to occasionally shoo away the flies. The blood-stained paper table-cloth was in an evidence bag, lying on the grass. Eddie, another tech, was circling the body, snapping photos on a digital camera.

"Jesus …" Tyler whispered.

"The kids saw this?" Meredith asked.

"When she saw the blood soaking through the tablecloth, Mrs. Sanders hustled everyone back into the house. Mrs. Hammond was the one to remove the tablecloth. So, thankfully, no. The kids didn't see this."

"Witnesses said he got a text. Do we have his phone?" Meredith asked.

"Yeah, but by the time we got it, it was locked up. I asked the wife, but she doesn't know the PIN."

"It was worth a shot," Meredith said. "Thank you, Sheriff."

Sheriff Howell motioned to the body. "He's all yours."

Meredith grimaced as she and Tyler made their way across the grass.

Lewis was inspecting the corpse's hands. His kit was off to the side, next to the bloody bat and bagged tablecloth.

"Hey, Lewis," Meredith said, as they crouched down to join him. "What can you tell us, so far?"

"I think, and I'm just guessing here, that the cause of death was trauma to the head," he sarcastically said, pointing to the carnage that had once been James Hammond's face. "I'll let Mike in the Morgue make the definitive call on that one, but at least our killer was polite enough to leave the murder weapon."

"What's with the tablecloth?" Tyler asked.

"This is going to sound messed up, but I'm pretty sure the killer put it over the face as they went to town to keep the blood from splattering on them."

Tyler whistled.

Meredith stared at the flattened remains of the nose. Mangled teeth protruded from what had been the mouth, but the lips were unrecognizable. The most prominent feature that was still distinguishable was the one intact eye that bulged from the socket.

"And this is how he was found?" Meredith asked in Sheriff Howell's direction. "No one touched him?"

"His face had been covered by the tablecloth, which the wife removed when she found him," he replied. "Other than that, he was found exactly as you see him, along with the bat."

"Did you find any other injuries?" Tyler asked.

"Funny you should mention that. Take a look." Lewis pointed to the arm, where a vicious bruise was peeking out from under the short sleeve. "That's a fresh one. Almost certain it was part of the attack."

Meredith peered intently at the bruise and then at the body in total, the gears in her head turning.

"No one heard anything?" she asked Sheriff Howell. "No one heard him cry out?"

"No."

Meredith brought her face closer to the dead man's hands. "Any bruises on the hands?"

"Nope," Lewis replied.

"What's on your mind, Somerset?" Tyler asked, noting Meredith's expression.

"If he was still alive, and someone had hit him on the arm with that much force, he would have cried out. People in the front yard would have heard it."

Tyler immediately picked up her train of thought. "Which means that the hit on the arm most likely came after he was dead."

Meredith nodded. "But that makes even less sense. Who does a number like that to someone's face and then takes one last swing at the arm?"

"Best guess, Lewis. You think this hit on the arm happened postmortem?" Tyler asked.

"No way to tell. It would have had to happen soon after he was dead for the body to still bruise."

Meredith was suddenly gripped by an idea. "And you didn't find any bruises on the hands? No defensive wounds?"

"Nope. Just the face and that one shot to the arm."

Meredith turned to Eddie, who continued to snap photos.

"Have you gotten everything you need, Eddie?"

"Yeah," he said, lowering his camera. "I'm good."

"I want to see something," Meredith said and turned her attention to Sheriff Howell. "Can you and one or two of your officers give us a hand?"

Sheriff Howell nodded to two officers, who stopped their search of the surrounding bushes and came over to the body. Lewis pulled a couple pairs of gloves from his kit and handed them to the officers, who put them on.

"What I want to do," Meredith began, "is to get him onto his side so that we can get a look at the back of his head."

The officers crouched next to the body as Tyler and Lewis joined Meredith on the other side.

The two officers positioned themselves at the shoulders and waist, while Sheriff Howell cradled the neck and nodded to Meredith.

"On three," Meredith said. "One … two … three …"

The officers gently pulled the body onto its side, while Sheriff Howell supported and rotated the head.

"I'll be damned …" Lewis said.

There was an obvious strike to the back of the skull.

"My guess is this is what killed him, and everything else came after," Meredith said.

"And I would agree," Lewis confirmed.

"Thank you, officers," Meredith said.

They gently lowered the body onto its back, once more.

"How'd you know?" one of the officers asked.

"He didn't cry out, and he didn't try to stop his murderer from hitting him. We know the hit on the arm was most likely after he was dead, but if someone is about to swing a bat at your face, you're going to scream or at least put up your hands to try to defend yourself. There are no defensive wounds on his hands, which means he didn't know it was coming, and he didn't try to stop his fall. So, the odds are that he was struck from behind, and he was dead before he hit the ground."

Lewis, Sheriff Howell, and the other officers were impressed, but Meredith didn't seem to share in their enthusiasm. Neither did Tyler.

"That was a good catch," Sheriff Howell said. "What's got you two so worried?"

"You want to tell them, Detective Foles?" Meredith asked.

Everyone looked at Tyler.

"If our guy was killed by a home run to the back of his dome, he probably fell forward. That means that whoever did this was worked up enough that they felt the need to turn him over and bash his face in, even though he was already dead, but they also had the presence of mind to cover him with the tablecloth to prevent any blood splatter getting on their clothes."

Lewis, Sheriff Howell, and the officers' appreciative expressions slowly sank at the realization of the savagery of this new take.

"Detectives?" an officer called from the bushes next to the fence. "Got something."

Meredith and Tyler left the body to join the officer.

Tall, scraggly bushes formed a perimeter around the yard and extended a few feet above the fence just beyond.

"What's up?" Tyler asked.

"Right here," she said, pointing at the branches near the top of the fence. Some of them had been bent or snapped, revealing the green wood underneath. "Looks like the killer may have climbed the fence."

"Nice spot, officer. Thank you," Tyler said. He traded a suspicious glance with Meredith before addressing the other officers. "Okay. Need everyone to keep this section of the fence clear. Have forensics dust for prints."

The officers got to work, while Meredith and Tyler moved a few yards away to be alone.

There was an awkward pause before Tyler finally spoke.

"All right, Somerset, do you want to call bullshit or should I?"

"We're both calling bullshit. That's a vanity fence. There's no way it would support the weight of someone climbing over it without serious damage."

"And why climb the fence at all?" Tyler argued. "Just use the side gate. It's secluded enough that no one in the front yard is going to see you and even if you argue about not wanting to be seen going through the gates, are they really being less sneaky by climbing the fence in broad daylight? In this neighborhood? No way I'm buying that."

"Me neither, but someone wants us to." She looked back at the body.

Tyler shook his head. "Nah. No way some random guy is walking along and decides to hop the fence, bashes the guy's head in with a weapon that happens to be there, uses the tablecloth, smashes his face, and then hops back over. Someone tried to stage this, which means premeditation. Howell said our victim got a text during the magic show. Someone tell him to come to the backyard?"

"It's possible, but he also may have wanted to make a phone call in private," Meredith countered. "Or maybe someone did tell him to come to the backyard. They argued, it got out of hand, Hammond turns his back on them, killer grabs the bat and swings. Not premeditated. Just opportunistic."

"But it's too opportunistic, right, Somerset? They waited until everyone was in the front yard and then lured him back here. And the tablecloth to protect their clothing as they went to town?"

"That could have been in the moment. I think there's a chance it wasn't premeditated, but point taken."

Tyler shook his head, again. "I'm at a loss, Somerset. The text, someone making it look like someone hopped the fence? That's premeditated … but the guy's face? That's rage."

"And the hit on his arm?" Meredith asked, equally at a loss.

"I don't know what that is. It's like our killer was angry, smart, and confused all at the same time." Tyler paused and looked around the yard. He was about to say something but glanced down at the ground, instead.

"Tyler?"

Tyler continued to stare at the ground.

"Talk to me," Meredith said. "What's on your mind?"

"You know I hate asking, Somerset, but I gotta."

"Ask away."

"Is Alice here?"

In past cases, Meredith had seen the image of her missing sister, Alice, at crime scenes. Alice appeared just as she had the day she disappeared over twenty years ago. It was a secret that Meredith had kept hidden from Tyler, but after the events of their first case involving a strangled girl found in the middle of the street, which had almost cost them their lives, Meredith told Tyler about her visions. It was the only way to trust one another. They had to share any vulnerabilities that might affect their work if they were going to put their lives in each other's hands.

Meredith scanned the bushes and the windows of the house.

"No," she answered, honestly.

"I'm just checking in, Somerset," Tyler said, apologetically.

"It's fine."

"You know I'm only looking out f—"

There was a sudden commotion of growing voices coming from the kitchen.

"No, you don't understand," a man with a British accent was arguing.

"Sir, I need you to go back out to—"

"But I can prove to the inspectors that it couldn't have been me, and then I can go."

"Sir—"

The man in the cape and top hat spilled through the open

kitchen door and onto the patio but locked up at the sight of James Hammond's decimated face.

"Oh, fuck me," he groaned and rested his hands on his knees like he was about to vomit.

A breathless officer appeared in the door behind him.

"I'm sorry, detectives. He said he needed to go to the bathroom and then ran out here."

"Take him back to the front yard," Tyler said, while he and some of the officers tried to obstruct the view of the body.

Sheriff Howell moved toward him, but the man straightened up and put out his hands.

"No, listen. It's fine. Everything's fine. I was a little twisted by the sight of … that," he said, with a wave toward the body. "I only wanted to prove to your inspectors that it couldn't have been me."

Sheriff Howell leaned in toward The Amazing Presto's face and sniffed.

"You been drinking?"

The magician sputtered. "I may have had a nip."

Sheriff Howell looked at Meredith and Tyler for guidance.

Tyler spoke quietly into Meredith's ear. "If we send him back out front, he might cause a scene and upset everyone else. Let's hear what he has to say, but make it quick."

Meredith nodded.

"What's your name?" she asked.

The magician straightened up. "The Amazing Presto," he replied. "I mean … Randy … well, Randall. Randall Langstrom."

"And you said you can prove that you didn't do it?"

"Yes. Yes, I can."

"That's fine," Meredith said, "but you still might be a witness—"

"Just hear me out, all right?"

Meredith motioned for him to continue.

"Right. When I started my performance, the man was alive. He was in the crowd, watching. A few minutes in, he walked past me and went inside. I was outside, doing my show, the entire

41

time. Everyone saw it, so it couldn't have been me. Everyone at this party is my alibi ..." He nodded toward the body of James Hammond. "... except him."

"You remember seeing him walk inside?" Meredith asked.

"Yeah," the magician said with a tinge of annoyance. "People kept going in and out during my performance. It got so distracting that I made a joke that I was causing them to disappear. When they walked inside, I would say, 'Poof!'" He demonstrated with a flourish of his hand.

There was an awkward silence.

"That's it?" Meredith asked.

"Well ... yes ..."

"Listen, Mr. Langstrom, that's all well and good, but you could still be a witn—"

"Hold up," Tyler said. "You noticed the people coming in and out of the house while you were doing your thing?"

"Yes," the magician said, a little worried at Tyler's sudden enthusiasm. "Only because it was incredibly rude."

"You remember them?"

"... Yes ..."

Tyler stepped forward and turned him back toward the house.

"Come with me," he said.

"Uh ... Where are we going?"

"We're going to a lineup."

Chapter 6

Meredith trailed Tyler and The Amazing Presto back down the hall and into the living room.

"What I'm gonna have you do," Tyler explained, "is kinda stroll through the crowd and point out anyone you remember going in or out of the house during your performance."

The Amazing Presto stopped just as Tyler reached for the front door.

"Sorry, mate, but I can't do that."

Tyler stared at him. "What?"

"I can't go out there and start pointing at people."

"... Why?"

"Because the job."

"The job? What job? What are you talking about?"

"Most of the work I get is by word of mouth or from the cards I pass out at my shows, and I passed out a lot of cards before everything went under. If I go out there and say, 'This person might be a murderer or that person might be a murderer,' I'm done for."

Tyler's mouth fell open. "This is a joke. This is one of those awkward British humor things, right?"

"Mr. Langstrom," Meredith said, "we need your help in

43

identifying who killed Mr. Hammond, and it's possible that one of the people you saw go inside the house was the killer."

"Yes, but even if they are, that means the others aren't, and if I go out there pointing fingers, my career might be over in this town."

Tyler's eyebrows shot upwards. "*Career?* That's what you're going to say to protect a murderer?"

"Detective Foles?" Meredith cautioned.

Tyler took the cue and stepped away, allowing Meredith to take over.

"We understand that you've got some business interests to look after, Mr. Langstrom, but Detective Foles is right. We need you to help us identify possible suspects … and you might have some legal problems if you refuse."

"And she's putting it lightly," Tyler quietly added.

The Amazing Presto searched for a rebuttal. "I want to help, inspectors. Really, I do, but when you said a 'lineup,' I was thinking of that thing on telly with the one-way mirror, where I can see them but they can't see me."

"Buddy," Tyler said. "We ain't got that."

Meredith glanced to her right.

"Actually …"

*

"That one, there. Blue shirt. Good-looking chap," The Amazing Presto said, pointing to Sean Winston. "He walked in while I was performing."

"You sure?"

"Of course I'm sure. Then that one over there, the short, chubby fella." The Amazing Presto pointed at Harold Mantelli, who was sitting on the grass. "He went in right after."

Meredith, Tyler, and The Amazing Presto were kneeling on the couch, facing the window, and peeking out through the partially closed blinds to the front yard, where parents and children were wilting in the heat.

"And that's it? That's everyone you saw go in or out?" Tyler asked.

The Amazing Presto surveyed the yard, once again. "The host went in and out toward the end, but I don't see her. Her husband came out at one point. So did a woman with red hair, but I don't see either of them out there."

"The red-haired woman is the victim's wife. She's upstairs with her daughter, as well as the host and her husband."

"Right," The Amazing Presto said, leaning back from the window. "That's it."

"You're sure?" Tyler asked.

"As sure as I'm ever going to be, mate."

"Okay. Thank you," Meredith said. "We'll need your contact information, and you'll need to give a statement to one of our officers."

The Amazing Presto got off the couch, turned to the nearest officer, and resumed his stage persona. "Lead the way, good sir."

The officer rolled his eyes and led him back down the hall toward the kitchen.

Meredith addressed Sheriff Howell. "If you could please have your team collect those two gentlemen and bring them inside. Keep an officer with them so that they don't disturb anything that might be evidence. Make sure you've got the contact info for everyone else, ask them about their movements and if they saw anything, and then you can send them on their way."

"You got it."

"Let's head upstairs to talk to the wife," Meredith said.

"You mispronounced 'widow,'" Tyler replied.

*

Meredith and Tyler found Officer Hawthorne in the upstairs hall keeping an eye on the Sanderses, who were waiting in Dougie's

45

bedroom. Officer Hawthorne left his post to meet them and spoke in a quiet voice while consulting his notes.

"So, I've got Jessica Hammond and her daughter, Daniella, in the master bedroom with Mrs. Kinson, the social worker Sheriff Howell called in." He then pointed with his pen to a door behind them. "The birthday boy, Dougie, and his parents are in his bedroom. He's recovering from cancer and is, understandably, worn out."

"Hell of a birthday present," Tyler mumbled.

"Okay," Meredith said. "We'd like to speak to Jessica Hammond, first."

Officer Hawthorne went to the master bedroom door and gently knocked before opening it. Jessica Hammond was holding Daniella while sitting on the bed. Next to her, with a comforting hand on Jessica's back, was Emma Kinson.

"Mrs. Kinson?" Meredith asked.

Emma stood and joined them in the hall. Officer Hawthorne pulled the door shut behind her.

"Has Mrs. Hammond said anything?" Meredith asked.

"She gave me a general rundown of what time they got here and what she saw, but she wasn't very detailed," Emma said.

"Did she mention anything about being inside during the start of the magic show?"

"No. Like I said, she wasn't very detailed. She's in a deep state of shock."

"I can imagine," Meredith said. "Thank you, Mrs. Kinson." Meredith went to the door and looked back at Tyler. "Ready?"

Tyler nodded.

Chapter 7

Emma and Tyler followed Meredith into the master bedroom.

Jessica Hammond was still sitting on the bed, holding Daniella and gently rocking back and forth.

"Mrs. Hammond? I'm Detective Meredith Somerset with the Cobb County Police Department. This is my partner, Detective Tyler Foles. We want to begin by saying how sorry we are for your loss."

Jessica's gaze remained straight ahead.

"Would it be okay to ask you some questions?"

Jessica nodded.

Emma stepped forward and gave Daniella a warm smile. "Come with me, sweetheart. We'll go see how Dougie is doing, okay?"

Jessica slowly released Daniella and helped her off her lap. Emma took Daniella's hand and led her out the door.

"We'll be down the hall if you need us," Emma said.

Thank you, Meredith mouthed to her.

Officer Hawthorne followed them out into the hall and closed the door, leaving Meredith and Tyler alone with Jessica.

Meredith sat next to Jessica on the bed.

"Again, we're very sorry for your loss, Mrs. Hammond."

Jessica continued to stare.

Meredith wondered how many times she had seen that stare, that far-off gaze, trying to comprehend that nothing would be the same.

"Can you tell us everything you remember about the party, leading up to the backyard?"

Jessica's voice trembled. "We, um … We arrived, I don't know, around twelve, I think … We met Kristi and Nick in the kitchen. They showed us to the backyard. A girl got hurt in the … uh, bouncy thing … and Kristi went to help. She was okay, and Kristi and I started chatting and had a glass of wine."

"Do you know where your husband was during that time?"

"I didn't see him for a while, but he and Nick came out to the yard with drinks. Then, Kristi wanted the magic show to start, so she asked Nick and James to go find the magician."

"We understand that you came out of the house during the performance," Meredith said.

Jessica appeared to focus for a moment. "I got a little warm outside and decided to cool off for a bit. I came up here to lie down. We've been friends with Kristi and Nick for a long time, and I didn't think they would mind."

Meredith nodded, but she noticed that Jessica had begun to slightly wring her hands. A glimpse toward Tyler confirmed that he had caught it, too.

"What happened then?" Meredith asked.

"I could hear that the show was about to start, so I went back outside."

"Did you happen to see anyone else in the house?"

Jessica searched her memory. "As I was walking out, I ran into Harold Mantelli and Sean Winston."

"Who are they?" Meredith asked as she wrote in her notepad.

"Harold was James's partner when he started the business."

"Can you describe him for us?"

"He's, uh, short … bald …"

Meredith nodded to Tyler. They had him downstairs.

"And Sean Winston?"

"He's the vice president of my husband's company."

"What does he look like?"

"He's tall, um … dark hair. Glasses."

Meredith nodded, again. He was downstairs, as well.

"You're doing great, Mrs. Hammond. Can you tell us what happened next?"

"I went outside and joined Kristi to watch the rest of the magic show."

"Was your husband there?"

"No. Kristi said that he had gone inside to take a call or something."

"Then, what happened?"

"The magic show finished, and Kristi wanted everyone to go to the backyard for cake and presents, but people started screaming and running back inside. James was lying in the grass with the tablecloth over his f-face. Kristi told me to go back out front, but I had to see. I lifted up the tablecloth, and I saw— … I sa—"

Jessica suddenly leaped from the bed and ran to the bathroom.

"Mrs. Hammond, are you—?"

Meredith was cut off by the sound of the toilet lid being thrown open and Jessica Hammond vomiting. Her wretches were interspersed with sobs.

Jessica emerged from the bathroom a few minutes later with tear-streaked cheeks, bloodshot eyes, and a handful of tissues.

"I'm sorry."

"Perfectly all right," Tyler replied.

Jessica walked back into the room and sat next to Meredith. She appeared more alert and less stunned.

"Mrs. Hammond?" Meredith asked once Jessica seemed ready. "Do you know of anybody who would want to harm your husband?"

"No. Almost everyone at the party works at CashFlo. His

ex-wife harassed him for a time, but that was a while ago. I can't imagine anyone wanting to do this."

"Had your husband mentioned any trouble at work?"

Fresh tears began spilling down Jessica's cheeks.

"No."

"I'm sorry if this question seems delicate, Mrs. Hammond, but I have to ask: has there been any trouble between you and your husband, recently?"

"No. Everything has been great," Jessica said, her throat constricting. "He said that soon he was going to be spending more time with me and Dani. Everything was going to be f—"

She suddenly stood up again and ran for the bathroom.

*

Meredith closed the door behind them as she and Tyler stepped out into the hall.

"Thoughts?" she asked, keeping her voice low.

"Not too much to say. She's pretty shook up, but who wouldn't be?"

"What do you think of her story?"

"Checks out ..."

"But?"

"Coming back inside and lying down because she overheated? I get it, it's miserable out there, but she'd only been here, what? Less than an hour? ... I don't know. Maybe I'm being heartless."

"No. You're right. It's a little weird. We'll follow up with her later, but she's pretty fried right now."

"You think it's guilt?"

"We can't rule it out," Meredith said, reluctantly. "James Hammond went into the house while she was upstairs, cooling off. Maybe she sends him a text, telling him to meet her in the backyard, and does a number on him. He's not surprised to see her, which is why he doesn't scream."

"So, she flips him over, covers him with the tablecloth, goes to town on his face, stages the fence thing, calmly walks out to enjoy the rest of the magic show, and then gives an Oscar-winning performance when they find the body?" Tyler asked, doubtfully.

"Is it unlikely? Oh my God, yes, but is it impossible?"

Tyler thought it over. "No. We need to find out if she has a motive … But someone at this party has to be involved, right?"

"Someone at this party knows something," Meredith agreed. "But who does that? With kids around?"

"Time to talk to the Sanderses?"

"Yeah."

Chapter 8

"Mr. and Mrs. Sanders?" Meredith asked as she opened the door.

The spindly frame of Dougie Sanders was asleep in his bed. Kristi was sitting on the floor, holding Daniella Hammond, while Nick paced the floor near the window, quietly talking on his phone, and Emma waited in the corner.

"I have to go," Nick said upon seeing Meredith and Tyler and quickly ended his call.

Meredith crouched next to Kristi and Daniella.

"Hi, Dani. Mrs. Kinson is going to take you back to your mom, okay?"

Emma smiled and reached out her hand. Dani shuffled over to her, and they walked out into the hall.

Kristi stood, and Nick stepped up behind her.

"How is Jessica doing?" she asked.

"About as well as can be expected," Meredith answered. "Would it be okay to ask you some questions?"

"Sure," Nick said. "But let's go across the hall to the guest bedroom. I don't want to wake up Dougie."

*

"I just can't believe it," Kristi said, sitting on the edge of the bed in the guest room. Nick was sitting by her side.

"It's new territory for us, too," Tyler said.

"Can you tell us everything you remember about your movements during the party?" Meredith asked.

"I was all over the place," Kristi said, "from the moment people started showing up."

"How about from when the Hammonds arrived?"

"The first time we saw them was in the kitchen when they got here. Then, we showed them to the backyard," Kristi said, turning to Nick to make sure her recollections were correct. "Then ... I'm sorry. It's all kind of a blur."

"Mrs. Hammond mentioned something about someone getting hurt," Meredith said. "In the bouncy castle?"

"Yes. Jessica and I went out front to take care of it. It was just a little sprain."

"That's when James and I went to the garage to grab a beer," Nick said.

"How did Mr. Hammond seem to you? Was he nervous? Did he appear to be on the lookout for anyone?"

"No. He was ... James."

"Did you see anyone else in the garage?"

"A lot of the dads were there."

"Did you talk to anyone?"

"Uh ... We had a brief conversation with Harold Mantelli."

"Mr. Hammond's former business partner?"

"Yeah."

"What did you talk about?"

"Harold said he wanted to talk to James about something, but James blew him off."

Meredith wrote it down and made a mental note to ask Harold Mantelli about it.

"Then what happened?"

"James and I made our way into the front yard to join the rest of the crowd."

"And did you go back inside at any time before the body was found?"

"Yes," Nick said, glancing at Kristi. "We couldn't find the magician. So, Kristi asked James and I to look around. I looked inside the house. James looked around outside."

"James found him on the side of the house and had him come to the front yard to start the show," Kristi said.

"I came back outside when I heard Kristi announce that the show was about to begin, but I really needed to use the restroom first," Nick added.

"When you were inside the house, did you see anyone else?" Meredith asked.

"No. I searched upstairs and down. Everyone was out front. I came out a few minutes into the show after taking the bathroom break."

Meredith shifted her attention to Kristi. "Sheriff Howell said that you were standing next to James Hammond during the show, and he received a call or a text?"

Kristi nodded. "He excused himself and went back inside."

Meredith's pen scratched across her notepad. "Do you remember the approximate time he went back inside?"

"I didn't check the time, but it was toward the start of the show."

"Did he say who the text was from?"

"No, but he seemed confused."

"And did you, yourself, go back inside at any time during the magic act?"

"Yes. Toward the end. I had been running around all day and had a few glasses of wine to settle down. After Nick mentioned the bathroom, I couldn't hold it in any longer. I wanted to go to the bathroom before we opened presents in the backyard."

"Did you see anyone inside the house?"

Kristi shook her head.

"Did you happen to look in the backyard?"

"I didn't. I was in a bit of a rush."

"Can you tell us about your relationship with Mr. Hammond?" Meredith asked, changing gears.

"I've been with CashFlo almost since the beginning. Nearly eight years, now."

"And would you say you had a good working relationship with Mr. Hammond?"

"Wouldn't have stayed with the company for so long if I didn't. I was in line to be VP, but …"

Nick took her hand in support.

"Dougie got sick," she continued. "Building a company from scratch is grueling, and I couldn't focus. He needed a lot of care, but I couldn't quit the job."

"Kristi's insurance was a lot better than mine," Nick jumped in. "Dougie was too sick to go to school and needed to be home-schooled. I worked freelance as a graphic designer, so I stayed home with him. It just made sense."

Meredith made a note on her pad. "Is there anything else you remember? Anything leading up to the backyard that stands out?"

"Nothing really strikes me," Nick said.

"No. Nothing," Kristi added.

Meredith turned to Tyler, giving him the chance to ask any questions he might have.

Tyler scratched his chin. "What can you tell us about the bat that was used?"

"It's an old softball bat. I've played in a league every Sunday for the past few years."

"Where do you normally keep it?"

"In the garage."

"A lot of people like to use that bat in your league?"

"Yes," Nick answered, confused.

"Any chance you cleaned it, recently?"

"I'm sorry, detective," Nick said, helplessly. "I don't understand what any of this has to do with—"

"You'll have to excuse Detective Foles," Meredith said. "He's trying to figure out if we'll be able to get any usable fingerprints off the bat."

"Sorry. That's what I was driving at," Tyler said. "And it sounds like we won't."

*

Once they were back in the hallway, Tyler headed for the stairs to continue their interviews, but Meredith stopped and took out her phone.

"What's up, Somerset?" he asked.

"Getting a jump on who sent that text to James Hammond," Meredith said, bringing the phone to her ear.

After the third ring, Meredith was worried that it would go to voicemail. It was Sunday, after all, but she was relieved when it was answered by Kelly Yamara, the assistant district attorney.

"Detective Somerset?" Kelly asked, the voices of her two children in the background.

"Hey, Kelly. How's your Sunday going?"

"You tell me."

"I'm with Detectives Foles at the scene of a pretty brutal homicide. It appears that the victim was lured to the crime scene by a text message. I wanted to get a start on the warrant for the phone records."

There was some commotion on the other end.

"Yes. Thank you, sweetheart," Kelly said, away from the phone. "Can you and your brother take the plates to the kitchen? ... Thank you." She returned her attention to Meredith. "You're saying that the victim got a text message before they died, and you want to know who the message was from?"

"Yeah. Top of your head, how hard will it be to get the records?"

56

Kelly spoke away from the phone, again. "Yes. Just take them to the sink, Luke. No— Stop. Just stop ... Sorry, detective. I'm trying to teach the kids the value of doing chores. To answer your question, it might take some time. The phone companies tend to fight these tooth and nail, but give me the number and I'll get started."

*

After relaying James Hammond's number to Kelly, Meredith and Tyler made their way downstairs to question the two remaining guests who had been inside the house during the magic show.

"I've got an officer with Harold Mantelli in the garage and an officer with Sean Winston in the office," Sheriff Howell said.

"Thanks, Sheriff," Meredith said and turned to Tyler. "Let's go find out what Harold Mantelli wanted to talk to James Hammond about."

Chapter 9

An officer was watching Harold Mantelli talking nervously into his phone on the far side of the garage when Meredith and Tyler opened the door.

At the sight of the detectives, Harold hung up and shoved the phone in his pocket.

"Harold Mantelli?" Meredith asked.

"Yes, uh … Yes. I'm Harold Mantelli," he affirmed, his face glistening with a layer of sweat.

"I'm Detective Meredith Somerset. This is my partner, Detective Tyler Foles."

"Hi. Hi. How are you?" Harold sputtered, extending his hand and tightly smiling.

After shaking his hand, Meredith discreetly wiped her palm on her pants.

"We won't keep you much longer," she said, taking out her notepad. "We're trying to put together a picture of everything that happened today, and we were wondering if you could tell us about your relationship with James Hammond."

"Okay. Well, ten years ago, Mr. Hammond and I started CashFlo together. I designed the software, and he came up with the business model."

Meredith didn't need to turn around to know that Tyler also found it weird that Harold was referring to James Hammond as "Mr. Hammond."

"You've been with the company from the start?"

"I'm no longer with CashFlo."

Meredith's pen stopped.

"What happened?"

Harold fidgeted. "I guess I wasn't exactly cut out for the ruthlessness of a start-up. Mr. Hammond brought in a team of designers to handle the software updates. He cut me a settlement, and I moved on."

"How long ago was that?"

"About five years ago."

"And you still came to the party even though it's pretty much nothing but CashFlo people?" Tyler asked.

"I'm still friends with Mr. and Mrs. Sanders. And I wanted to support Dougie."

"Nick Sanders said that you wanted to talk to Ja— Mr. Hammond about something," Meredith corrected herself. "Could you tell us what that was about?"

"I— … I had an idea for a new program, something to add to CashFlo. He wanted to wait until later to talk about it."

Meredith nodded while continuing to write on her notepad. "We understand that you entered the house during the magic show?"

"Yes."

"Were you looking for James Hammond?"

"No. I came back inside to grab another beer. I was trying to build up some, uh, you know, liquid courage?"

Harold laughed at his own joke, but it was awkward and forced, as though he felt it was something he was supposed to do, rather than being genuinely pleased with himself.

"Did you happen to see anyone when you came back inside?"

Harold's mouth twisted as he tried to remember. "Uh, yes. I ran into Mrs. Hammond as she was coming outside."

"Did you speak to one another?"

"Not really." He leaned in conspiratorially. "To be honest, she was acting a little strange."

"How so?" Meredith asked, aware of the irony.

"You know, just *strange*." Harold smiled. "Like I had caught her doing something."

"Okay …" Meredith said, still writing. "Did you happen to see anyone else?"

"I ran into Mr. Winston. He came in just a few moments before me."

"Did you speak to him?"

"Yes. He's the vice president at CashFlo. I thought it was the perfect chance to run my idea by him as sort of a warm-up for when I spoke to Mr. Hammond."

"Where were you?"

"We were here, in the garage."

"Do you have a rough idea how long you were talking?"

"I don't remember exactly, but it was a couple of minutes. We stopped when we heard the screaming. We went back out into the house and saw all the commotion. Someone told us what happened, and we waited for the police."

"We really appreciate it," Meredith said. "I want to make sure I have everything; what time did you arrive at the party?"

"Around twelve."

"Was anyone with you?"

"No. My daughter, Cybil, would have come with me, but her mother has custody this weekend."

"Did you happen to see or hear anything that felt out of place before or after the Hammonds arrived?"

"No, but I was in the garage for most of it." He smiled, again. "You know, liquid courage?"

Harold laughed, even more awkwardly than before.

"Right," Meredith said, forcing a smile and turning to Tyler. "Detective Foles? Anything?"

Tyler thought it over. "You came up with CashFlo?"

"The software for it, yes."

"What was the add-on you wanted to pitch to James Hammond?"

Harold playfully wagged his finger. "Ah-ah-ah. Trade secrets."

*

Meredith and Tyler watched Harold Mantelli walk down the hallway and out the door to the front yard.

"What the hell was that?" Tyler asked, once they were alone.

"I have a feeling Harold Mantelli is not very good at social interactions."

"You can say it: the dude is kind of a freak show."

"Not going to go that far."

"He's a grown man. What was with the 'Mr. Hammond' and 'Mr. Winston'?"

"Maybe it's a weird respect thing." Meredith turned to Sheriff Howell, who was still standing in the hall. "Sean Winston in there?" she asked, motioning to the closed office door.

Sheriff Howell nodded.

"Okay," she said. "Last one."

Chapter 10

Sean Winston was sitting behind the desk with his phone pressed to his ear, as if it was his own office, while an officer waited just inside the door.

"Sean Winston?" Meredith asked.

Sean held up a finger for her to wait as he continued speaking on his phone.

"Okay. Got it … Yes, that's fine." He hung up the phone and motioned for them to come in.

Sean Winston was intimidating, commanding, and behaving as though Meredith and Tyler had scheduled this meeting through his secretary.

Despite her mild annoyance, Meredith remained unfazed. Tyler, on the other hand, was radiating his dislike.

"Thank you for waiting to speak to us, Mr. Winston. I'm Detective Meredith Somerset. This is my partner, Detective Tyler Foles."

Sean nodded to each of them. "I would offer you a seat, but it looks as though they don't have very many meetings in here."

"We were wondering if you could tell us about your movements at the party," Meredith said, jumping into the questioning.

Sean frowned. "I'm not entirely sure why I was singled out.

There were a lot of people at the party who were allowed to leave after you arrived."

"Mr. Hammond was killed during the magic show. Everyone was in the front yard, but from what we understand, you reentered the house during the performance."

"Is that it? I went back inside, so that makes me a suspect?"

"We only want to know if you saw anything," Meredith replied.

"Unfortunately, I didn't see anything," Sean said.

"But you did come back inside during the magic show?"

"Yes," he answered with a sigh. "I came back inside during the magic show."

"Why did you do that?"

"If I'm being totally honest, it's because I was bored. I'm the vice president of CashFlo, and while I appreciate what Nick and Kristi are doing for their ailing son, I'm here more out of obligation than friendship, which was fine until we were all forced to stand out there in the heat to watch some insipid magic tricks. I came back inside to be a little more comfortable. In hindsight, I wish I would have just suffered through the show."

"Why is that?"

"For one, I could have been on my way by now. Two, I wouldn't have had to listen to Harold babble on about some idea he had for CashFlo. I figured no one would be in the garage, but there he was. I was trapped. He went on and on. I was almost grateful for the commotion when it came, until we discovered what it was about."

Meredith took a moment to write it down before continuing. "You're the vice president of CashFlo?"

"Yes."

"How long have you worked there?"

"Almost five years. I was brought in early when James did a bit of a shake-up and restructure."

"What was your relationship like with James Hammond?"

"Not good," Sean replied, his voice steady and matter-of-fact. Meredith looked up from her notes.

"Could you tell us a little more about that?" she asked.

"We butted heads from the start. I wanted to get CashFlo under control. James was throwing around money the company didn't have." He straightened up in his chair. "But I want to be clear, we recognized that we needed each other. We complemented one another. There were areas that we agreed upon, like getting rid of Harold."

"He was fired?" Tyler asked.

"Yes and no. 'Pushed out' is more like it. His initial idea and software were good, but he was a stone around our necks moving forward. James cut him loose as he was bringing me on board. We talked about it, and I agreed. Harold was given a settlement and was no longer part of CashFlo."

Meredith seized on the subject of co-workers. "What about Kristi Sanders? How is your relationship with her?"

"She's fine. She had a very good career in front of her until her son became ill."

"And Jessica Hammond?"

"I have no opinion of her. She knew that James and I didn't get along, but I don't find her particularly interesting."

"I see ..." Meredith said, finishing in her notepad. "Detective Foles?"

Tyler, who had been leaning against the wall, stood upright. "I hope you don't read too much into this, Mr. Winston, but you don't seem too emotional about your boss's face getting caved in with a softball bat."

"I'm not an emotional man, Detective Foles. Emotions solve nothing in a crisis. Am I saddened for his wife and daughter? Of course, but I'm already trying to navigate what this will do to CashFlo for the sake of our employees."

Tyler held up his hands. "So, again, don't read too much into this question, but James Hammond's death means you're in charge of CashFlo now, right?"

"Yes," Sean answered confidently. "And please don't read too much into this answer, but if I wanted to be in charge of CashFlo, I wouldn't need a softball bat."

Chapter 11

Since it was Sunday, Meredith and Tyler had the bullpen at the precinct almost entirely to themselves.

She was standing at the whiteboard, studying the crude diagram they had drawn of the Sanders home and the locations of their suspects. Their notes from the interviews rested on the table before them.

Tyler swiveled in a chair with his head back.

"I could be home watching preseason football right now," he groaned. "Falcons versus the Bears. I should have a bag of potato chips, right here," he said, indicating his right hip. "And some sweet tea, here," he said, indicating the other hip.

"Sorry that our murderer isn't more respectful of your Sunday night," Meredith said, smiling.

"You know I'm messing around, Somerset, but let's call it a day. We'll know more tomorrow after Mike in the Morgue does the autopsy."

"We can spitball some ideas," Meredith countered and cast a glance toward Sergeant Wheaton's open door. "Besides, he came in. He'll want a preliminary update."

"He gets paid the big bucks to come in on Sundays. Besides, we don't have anything to tell him."

"Unless we come up with something, right now," Meredith said and beckoned him to the board. "Let's go."

"Fine." Tyler stood with a huff and walked over to her. "What do you want to focus on? I mean, it's possible that our killer isn't one of the people on our list."

"What do you mean?"

"What if our killer stayed inside while everyone gathered in the front yard for the magic show, bashed James Hammond's head in, and then stayed inside the house, and only joined the chaos when the body was discovered? Our eyewitness magician would have never seen them."

"What about Nick Sanders's statement that he didn't see anyone while searching the house?"

"Could be lying. Also, there are plenty of places to hide in the house."

Meredith smiled. "See? We're already coming up with ideas, and you wanted to go home."

"Falcons versus the Bears, Somerset," Tyler pleaded.

"I think you're right," Meredith said, ignoring his last statement. "But for right now, these names are all we have to go on, and even if they didn't do it, maybe they saw something in the house or were in on the murder."

"Still feels like a dead end."

"Okay. Then let's talk about motive. Why would someone savagely beat this guy's face in at a kid's birthday party?"

"I'm stuck," Tyler said. "And you've got something on your mind, so walk me through it."

"We're both leaning toward the idea that it had to be someone at the party. The text message he got, the tablecloth, the staged fence-jumping. A random killer doesn't make any sense."

"I'd say that's a safe bet."

"And almost everybody at the party worked at CashFlo."

"You think it's tied to the company?"

"Can't say for certain, but I'd say it's a good place to start,"

Meredith said, staring at the X that designated the spot in the backyard where the body had been found. "We need to find out more about James Hammond; see if anyone in his past or present had a beef with him."

"The guy was an entrepreneur. All I know about that world is that it's pretty cutthroat. Might be a long list." Tyler looked at the board. "Jessica Hammond also mentioned an ex-wife. She's probably got insights to his personal and his business life."

"Agreed."

Tyler scoffed. "This is all going to be cake when we find out who sent him that text that made him go inside."

"I hope so," Meredith said. "But we have to assume that it's going to take a while to get the phone records—"

Sergeant Wheaton popped his head out of his office. "All right, you two, get in here and make it quick. The Falcons–Bears game is on." He disappeared back into his office.

Tyler pointed and gave Meredith a stare as if to say, *See?*

Meredith rolled her eyes and began walking.

Chapter 12

Sergeant Wheaton winced as he stared at the photos of James Hammond's shattered face on the screen of his computer.

"Christ. You're telling me this happened at a kid's birthday party?"

"Yes, sir," Meredith replied. "A kid whose mother works for the victim's company, CashFlo."

"And you think it was someone at the party?"

"Hard to see it being anyone else," Tyler said. "He was killed in the backyard. There's a tall fence and an even taller hedge surrounding the property. Someone tried to make it look as if someone jumped the fence, but it's made of pretty thin wood. No way someone goes over it without causing a bunch of damage."

"The murder took place during a magic act that was held in the front yard," Meredith said, picking up the narrative. "There were five people who were unaccounted for at the time of the murder: the two owners of the house, the vice president of the company, the man who started the company with the victim, and the victim's wife."

"The victim's wife?" Sergeant Wheaton pointed at the screen. "You think she might have done this?"

"I know it's unlikely, but we have to include her."

"Braining someone at a kid's birthday party. Unreal," Sergeant Wheaton said, clicking the mouse to banish the image from the screen. "And we don't know if this was premeditated or not?"

"There were multiple strikes to the victim's body. The blows to the face indicate the killer was worked up, but they had the presence of mind to cover the body with a tablecloth to avoid blood splatter. We'll know more tomorrow after Mike in the Morgue performs the autopsy."

"Anything else to go on?"

"If we're acting on the assumption that it was someone at the party, then it might have something to do with his company. We figured it's a good place to start," Meredith said. "But according to witnesses, the victim received a text message that caused him to head to the backyard. I've already got Kelly working on the warrant to see who sent the text."

Sergeant Wheaton was already reaching for the phone. "Let's see if we can speed things up." He punched in some numbers and put it on speakerphone.

The office was filled with the purr of the phone on the other end.

"Hey, Sarge," Kelly Yamara chimed.

"Kelly! My favorite assistant district attorney!"

"Okay. Pretty sure that means you need something."

"I'm with Detectives Somerset and Foles. They got called to a homicide this afternoon. Detective Somerset said that you were already working on—"

"The detectives are with you?" Kelly asked, suddenly full of energy.

"Yes, we're here," Meredith said in the direction of the speaker.

"Detectives, I'm so sorry. I was distracted this afternoon when I spoke to you, and I totally forgot to ask: was the victim married?"

Meredith and Tyler exchanged a confused glance.

"Yes, he was. Why?"

"Well, like I said, the phone companies usually fight these

things like hell, but if the victim was married and the spouse was on the phone plan, it makes our lives a whole lot easier."

*

"Mrs. Hammond?"

"Yes?" Jessica's voice came through the speakerphone on Meredith's desk. Tyler had pulled up a chair to listen to the conversation.

"It's Detective Somerset. I'm here with Detective Foles. How are you holding up?"

"I'm okay," she replied, though her tone said otherwise.

"We're sorry to bother you, but we need to ask a favor."

"A favor?"

"Yes. Are you and your husband on the same phone plan? I only ask because it appears that James received a text before going to the backyard. It might be crucial to the investigation. We could get a warrant, but that will take time. If you are on the same phone plan, you would have the authority to show us all his text messages."

There was a long pause.

"... Mrs. Hammond?" Meredith asked.

"I'm here."

"Would it be all right to look at the phone records?"

Silence.

"I'm sorry. I'll have to speak with our lawyer," Jessica finally answered.

Tyler's eyes went wide.

"Mrs. Hammond, whoever sent that text could very well be the person who—"

"I'm sorry, detective. I just want to make sure this is handled properly. I'll have her get in touch as soon as possible."

Meredith looked at Tyler, who threw up his hands in bafflement.

"Okay. Thank you, Mrs. Hammond."

The line clicked off.

"What the hell is she doing?" Tyler asked.

"I have no idea."

*

Holding her phone to her ear in one hand, Meredith pushed open the door of the precinct with the other, and stepped into the stuffy twilight air. Tyler was waiting by the curb.

"Tomorrow is perfect," she said into the phone. "We'll be at your office at eleven … Okay … Have a good evening."

Meredith hung up and put the phone in her pocket as she came even with Tyler.

"We're on for tomorrow with James Hammond's ex-wife," she said as they began walking.

"How did she sound?"

"Surprisingly calm."

"You don't think she had anything to do with it, do you?"

"No. She wasn't happy or anything like that. I just got the feeling that there wasn't a lot of love lost between them."

"All right. Hopefully Mrs. Hammond gets her head together and lets us see the phone records. Autopsy and interview with the ex tomorrow. I'd say that's a good start."

"What are you going to do with your evening?" Meredith asked as they arrived at their cars.

"Since the game is over, I'll probably kick back with a drink and do a couple lines of coke."

"Come on, Tyler. Don't joke about that."

Tyler smiled. "Gotta joke, Somerset. Otherwise, it's all tears."

"Seriously, though, I know we were at the meeting this afternoon, but I feel like I haven't checked in with you for a while. How are you doing?"

"I'm good."

"You don't want to use?"

72

"Shit. I always want to use. I'd love to do a rail right here off the roof of my car. That's what being an addict is like … but I want to hold on to what I've worked for more than I want that bump."

Meredith nodded. "I just wanted to know."

"We all got our addictions, Somerset, but you know I appreciate you."

"… I'm proud of you, Tyler."

"Thanks. Proud of me, too."

They shared a moment.

"All right," Tyler finally said. "Gonna get out of here before you make me blush."

He climbed into his car.

"See you tomorrow, Tyler," Meredith said.

Tyler gave her a salute from the driver's seat, started the car, and pulled out of the parking lot.

"We all got our addictions," Meredith whispered to herself as she watched him drive away.

Chapter 13

Meredith entered her apartment.

Her brain on autopilot, she walked to her bedroom and opened the closet. She placed her Sig Sauer 9mm in the gun safe and locked it. Once she heard the small bolt slide home behind the metal door, she went back out into the kitchen, poured herself a glass of water, and carried it, along with her laptop, into the spare bedroom—a bedroom that contained no bed, no nightstand, no dresser, nothing that would accommodate a guest.

There was only a chair in the middle of the room.

Meredith set the laptop on the floor, calmly sat in the chair, leaned forward, resting her elbow on her knees, and stared at the wall, which was covered in maps, photos, police reports, newspaper clippings, and Post-It notes—all the details of her sister's kidnapping.

Pinned to the wall, in the center of all the theories and evidence, was a dirty, light purple child's bathing suit, the bathing suit Meredith's sister, Alice, had been wearing when she disappeared over twenty years ago. The suit had been left on her doorstep after the case on Willow Lane, along with a handwritten note, which Meredith had pinned to the bathing suit as it hung on the wall.

She still misses you, Meredith.

Meredith hadn't taken it to the police. Alice's kidnapper wouldn't have left a thing on it as evidence. He was too smart for that. This was a game, a game that the person who took Alice had been playing for two decades. He had sent her the suit as an invitation, and Meredith was going to play.

Upon finding the bathing suit, Meredith immediately dove back into a world she thought she had left behind—an obsession that she once feared would devour her—but now, she had given it free rein. Before, she had been a fifteen-year-old girl whose life had been decimated in a single afternoon. Now, she was a detective who had mastered the skills she needed to find this guy, and he had opened the door.

She got her hands on every scrap of evidence from the old case file. She combed through the potential suspect list, which painfully included nearly every adult male in her life, even her high school history teacher, Mr. Lloyd, who had been so nice after Alice's disappearance. There was also their next-door neighbor, Mr. Bartlett, who let her and Alice play in his backyard and would sometimes babysit the two of them when their parents wanted a date night. There was also Wallace Hogan, a loner who lived deep in the woods behind the pool. When interviewed, he'd talked about seeing a man and a little girl walking through the woods, but when asked for more detail, he'd said he couldn't say anymore because the "shiny birdie" told him not to. He also mentioned the monsters and dragons that came out at night. The detectives on her sister's case eventually thought that Wallace Hogan was their man, but didn't have enough to charge him. They claimed that he took Alice to fulfill a sick need, but as Meredith worked her way through law enforcement, she believed that as the case hit one dead end after another, the detectives just wanted to pin the crime on someone.

Meredith picked up the laptop and set it in her lap. She clicked through a series of folders and finally got to the one labeled "WALLACE_HOGAN_INTERVIEW" and double-clicked.

The footage was grainy, first recorded on VHS, and then digitized a couple years later, when the technology still couldn't provide the pristine clarity found today.

The video started with Wallace Hogan's confused, fearful face. He was sitting at a table in an interrogation room.

"It is August eighth," a voice said off screen, whom Meredith knew to be Detective Reed, the lead detective on her sister's case. "I am interviewing Wallace Hogan on the disappearance of Alice Somerset."

Wallace looked like he was about to cry. It was painful to watch.

"Now, Mr. Hogan, why don't you tell me why you took that girl?"

"I didn't take nobody," Wallace said in his thick accent. "It was the man with the shiny birdie. He said that the shiny birdie would hurt me if I told anyone."

"Yeah, yeah, yeah." Detective Reed sighed. "You told me all about how scared you are of the shiny birdie."

"He did! The shiny birdie said he would—"

"Mr. Hogan. I'm trying to help you. If you don't help me, I can't help you. If you just tell me why you took the girl and where she is, I promise, no one will hurt you."

Watching the video, Meredith shook her head. She had seen it dozens of times. She knew every word, every one of Wallace Hogan's flinches and protestations of innocence. He should have had a lawyer, or at least a social worker, and Detective Reed had to have known it. He was looking for a scapegoat.

Meredith cursed herself for even starting the video.

Wallace Hogan hadn't taken her sister.

Twenty years later, the swimsuit confirmed it.

Wallace Hogan had died six years ago. They found him in his shack in the woods. He had been dead for months. Suspected heart attack.

Whoever had taken Alice was still out there, watching, toying with Meredith, or maybe they thought they were helping her, inspiring her with that cryptic message.

She still misses you, Meredith.

Was Alice still alive?

It was cruel and twisted, but it propelled Meredith into action.

Meredith thought she could solve it quickly, that Alice's abductor had made a critical mistake. She converted her spare bedroom into her "case room" and went to work with an intensity that surprised even her. She obsessed over every photo and transcript, but after that initial fire, her investigation had gone cold. She no longer seized upon every shred of evidence on her wall.

Instead, she merely sat in the chair, staring at the mosaic of evidence that pointed nowhere, with the bathing suit in the middle.

At some point, Meredith's gaze had drifted to the floor.

"I miss you, Meredith."

Meredith looked up.

Alice was there, standing right in front of her. Water dripped from her hair down to the floor. Her expression was the same as it had been that afternoon when she had spoken those last words to Meredith.

This was what she had kept from Tyler. She had been keeping it from Sergeant Wheaton, from her therapist, Dr. Kaplan. She had been keeping it from her ex-husband, Pete, and Heather, Pete's fiancée and Meredith's friend. Like the bathing suit, she had been keeping the fact that she was still seeing Alice from everyone.

Meredith no longer saw her at crime scenes, but she saw her in this room. Here, among the scattered puzzle of her disappearance, Alice still haunted Meredith, but that she only saw her in this room allowed Meredith to feel like she had some control. It was not a ghost she was seeing, only a manifestation of her guilt, but that didn't make the visions any less disturbing.

Meredith was jolted back to the present by the ringing of her phone.

Her daughter, Allison, was calling.

Meredith looked again, but Alice was gone.

Before answering, she stood and walked out of the room, carrying her laptop.

It was a mental trick of compartmentalization. That room was her dark obsession, and Meredith didn't want anyone else inside, even if it was on the phone. Only Meredith was allowed in that room; Meredith and whoever had taken her sister.

"Hey, baby," she said, closing the door behind her and setting her laptop on the kitchen table.

"Hey, Mom. Just calling to say good night. What are you up to?"

"Work stuff," Meredith said.

"You have a case?"

"Yeah. Had a homicide this afternoon—"

"Oooooh. Where?"

Allison had developed a strange curiosity about Meredith's work. Meredith would normally relish a chance to be closer to her daughter, and it made sense, since Meredith's past had influenced Allison's life; she was even named after Meredith's lost sister. After the divorce, Pete insisted that Allison keep Meredith's last name as a way to comfort Meredith after she gave up custody. It had been profoundly helpful to Meredith's state of mind at the time, a way of reassuring her that Allison was, and always would be, her daughter, and they had done an amazing job raising her together while no longer married. They had watched her grow into an intelligent and inquisitive teen, but Allison's enthusiasm about murders and crimes felt a bit much.

"Baby, I'm not sure that this is something—"

"Allison?" Pete's voice called out in the background.

"What?" Allison asked in that clipped, defiant teenage tone.

"We've talked about this, sweetheart. Mom's work is Mom's work."

"Ugh," Allison groaned. "It's fine. I can handle it."

"Baby," Meredith said. "It's not that your dad and I and Heather don't think you can handle it. It's just that—"

"I want to know about it," Allison said. "I'm thinking of starting a podcast."

"… A podcast?"

"Yeah. A true-crime podcast. They're huge right now, and I've got Mr. Beisner for English this year. He lets us choose our own finals project. I thought it would be cool with your job and the stuff about your sister."

Pete was closer now. "Allison, I told you not to—"

"It's for school," Allison said, annoyed. "And I'm asking *Mom*."

There was a pause.

"So can I, Mom?" Allison asked.

Meredith pinched the bridge of her nose. "We'll talk about it this weekend when we hang out, okay?"

"Okay."

"I'm not saying yes," Meredith clarified.

"Fine. Are we still doing a driving lesson?"

"Yep," Meredith said. It was a thought that terrified her, but she was happy to move on. "Are you done with homework?"

"It's the first week of school, Mom. There's almost no homework, yet."

"I'm going to assume that means you have *some* homework left."

"… Some history stuff."

"Get on with that and we'll talk more later, okay?"

"Okay."

"Good night, baby. I love you," Meredith said.

"Love you, too, Mom," Allison replied.

"Let me talk to your dad really quick."

"Here, Dad. Mom wants to talk to you."

The phone changed hands.

"Hey, Meredith." Pete sounded tired.

"How are you and Heather holding up?" Meredith asked.

"I know you gave me custody, but do you want to take her back for the last two years before we can kick her out?"

"That bad, huh?"

"She's sixteen. You know how it is."

"Yeah."

Actually, Meredith didn't. Fifteen was the age when her life had fallen apart.

"Is it getting worse?" Meredith asked.

"Nah. Still the same. She thinks as long as she keeps her grades up, she should be able to do whatever she wants."

"Any more parties?"

"No. Just the one."

A few weeks earlier, Allison had been at a party where some of the kids were drinking. Meredith and Pete found out because one of the kids had posted on Facebook while the party was happening. A parent saw it and gave them a call. The three of them, Meredith, Pete, and Heather, went to get her. Most of Allison's ire had been aimed at Pete and Heather, since she lived with them. When Allison tried to appeal to Meredith, Meredith had their back. Since Allison hadn't been drinking, they decided not to ground her, but there were new rules on her social life.

"How are she and Heather getting along?" Meredith asked.

"They're doing fi— … No. I'm not going to lie. Allison's taking things out on Heather."

"Shit." Meredith sighed. "I'll talk to Allison."

"I think Heather wants to handle this herself. Actually, I'm pretty sure I wasn't supposed to say anything."

Meredith gritted her teeth.

Pete was right. Allison and Heather needed to work it out between themselves.

"Okay, but if Heather needs me to tap in, all she has to do is say the word."

"Thanks. I'll let her know."

"How are you doing? How's the job hunt?"

Two months ago, Pete had lost his job as an English professor due to budget cuts at Georgia Tech.

"It's going," he said, unconvincingly.

"Good," Meredith said, taking the hint. "Well, I should get back to work."

"Yeah. I'm going to check and make sure the monster is doing her homework."

"I'm sure she is. Like you said, she thinks if she keeps her grades up, she can do anything."

"I guess it's better than her just thinking she can do whatever she wants … Good night, Meredith."

"Good night, Pete."

"I love you."

"I love you, too. Give my love to Heather, too, and let her know I'm here if she needs some help laying the smack down."

"I will," Pete said with a chuckle and hung up.

Meredith lowered the phone and stared at the laptop on the kitchen table, then at the closed door to the spare bedroom.

She had a choice: fire the laptop back up and work on the murder of James Hammond or dive back into the past and hope that she was only one small detail away from solving her sister's disappearance.

Chapter 14

The Jaguar's 5.0 liter, V8 supercharged engine purred as Sean Winston navigated the darkened streets.

He pulled into the parking lot that bordered the massive park and stopped in one of the dozens of empty spaces underneath a light post. He cut the engine and stepped out of the car.

As he approached the softball fields, he glanced up at the glowing lights. During the day, the fields would be alive with the sound of pinging aluminum bats and softballs slamming into leather mitts, but at night, the fields were eerily quiet. The only noise was the faint hiss of the distant interstate through the trees.

As he drew nearer, a figure stepped out of the shadows cast by the bleachers.

He was younger, late thirties, with a nest of copper hair and dark eyes. Sean was used to others being intimidated by his presence. Not this guy.

The man regarded Sean with barely contained contempt as they sized each other up.

"What did you want to talk about?"

"I'll keep it brief," Sean said. "James Hammond is dead. In the next forty-eight hours, I'll be named head of the company."

The copper-haired man's impassive expression briefly conveyed an air of surprise.

"He's dead?"

"Yes."

"How?"

"Does it matter?"

The man was about to reply, but thought better of it.

"I simply wanted to let you know that the deal is off," Sean said.

The man nodded, taking it in, and then asked, "And we couldn't do this over the phone or with a text?"

"No. From here on out, there can be no link between us. No phone calls. No texts. No emails. This is the last time you and I will meet privately."

"Shame," the man said, insincerely.

"And you need to get rid of all traces of our communications," Sean added.

"I could do that … I could also hold on to them in case you try to fuck me over."

Sean studied him and cracked a leering smile. "I'm sorry. It was rude of me not to answer your question about James Hammond's death. After all, you were only expressing your concern, right?"

The man blinked. "Of course."

"Someone smashed in his face with a softball bat."

The man's shock was accentuated by the hard swallow of the lump that had formed in his throat. He was suddenly more aware of the fact that he was alone with this man in a darkened park.

"Have a pleasant night, Graham," Sean said as he turned and walked away, leaving the man alone among the shadows.

*

"How are you doing?" Nick softly asked into the phone.

"I'm still in shock," Jessica replied. "I can't believe he's gone."

"How's Dani?"

83

"She's asleep … She still doesn't understand that—" Jessica's throat caught.

"Jess. I don't know what to say."

"… I really wish you were here."

"I wish I was there, too, but we can't right now. Not for a little while."

"I know," Jessica said with a sniff. "Where's Kristi?"

"She's upstairs in the bedroom."

"I need you, Nick. I really need you."

"It'll be okay. They'll catch whoever did this."

"I don't know what to do. The police know I was inside the house … and they asked for my phone records."

Nick froze. "Why?"

"They think James received a text that lured him to the backyard. Because we're on the same phone plan, I can let them see our records without a warrant."

"What are you going to do?"

"My lawyer's working on it … Nick, do you know what would happen if anyone found out about us? … About what we were doing?"

"Hey. Hey, hey, hey. Jess, listen to me, no one knows about us and no one is going to find out, all right? You need to focus on yourself and Dani and helping the police get whoever did this to James. Then, we'll get back to us."

"I know … I know …" She let out a light laugh of disbelief. "Listen to me, this happened at your house and at Dougie's birthday party, and all I can think about is myself."

"It's okay, Jess. No one can tell you what you should be feeling."

"How is Dougie?"

"He's asleep. He's been asleep most of the day."

"I'm sorry, Nick."

"Stop. This isn't your fault, and they're going to catch who did it, but for now, the best thing to do would be to get some sleep. Kristi will be at work tomorrow. With all of this going on, she's going to be really busy over the next couple days, and you can call me whenever you need, okay?"

"Okay … I love you, Nick."

"I love you, too."

"Good night."

"Good night," he said and waited for Jessica to hang up before ending the call himself.

Nick exited the den and trudged up the stairs and into the bedroom where he found Kristi sitting up in bed, scrolling through her phone.

"Anything in the news, yet?" he asked.

"Not yet," she answered. "Not even sure there will be. After all, James wasn't a celebrity or anything."

"Might be right," he said, pulling off his shirt to get ready for bed.

"How's Jessica doing?" Kristi asked as she continued to scroll.

"As good as can be expected, I guess. The police asked for her phone records."

Kristi looked up. "Why?"

"The police want to see James's texts. They're on the same plan, so she can give them permission to look but she doesn't want to. She said her lawyer's working on it."

Kristi thought it over, shrugged, and went back to her phone.

Nick crawled into bed next to her and began kissing her shoulder, working his way upwards.

"More importantly, is she still in love with you?" Kristi asked.

"Yep," Nick said, finally arriving at her mouth.

Kristi put down her phone and kissed him deeply on the lips. "Good."

*

Miles away, Harold Mantelli was sitting in the recliner in his living room.

The house was silent.

A strange smile played across his face.

He just sat there … smiling.

*

Tyler checked the address again and walked up to the door.

He steadied himself and knocked.

There was no answer, but he could see a light on inside.

He knocked, again.

"Gabriel?"

No answer.

"Gabriel, you called me. Open up. Let's talk."

Tyler was about to knock again, but stopped when he heard the rattle of the doorknob and the fidgeting of the deadbolt being thrown back.

The door opened, and Tyler saw the tortured face of the new guy he had been speaking to after the meeting that afternoon.

Gabriel wiped his nose on the back of his wrist.

"How you doin', man?" Tyler asked.

Gabriel didn't answer.

"You use anything, yet?"

Gabriel shook his head.

Tyler glanced past him into the apartment. Like a lot of addicts' apartments, it was populated with second-hand furniture.

"Any drugs in there?" Tyler asked.

"No."

"You sure? This is all a waste of time if you shoot up after I leave."

"I don't have anything," Gabriel said. "But I was about to go out and find a score."

"Okay," Tyler said. "Good. Calling someone for help is the hardest part, and now, it's done."

Gabriel nodded.

"Come on, man," Tyler said. "Let's get you out of here."

Gabriel stepped out of his apartment and locked the door behind him.

"You did good," Tyler said, leading him away. "Let's go grab some waffles and talk shit out."

*

Meredith continued to stare between the laptop and the door to the spare bedroom, where she could feel Alice waiting.

Work on the murder of James Hammond or Alice's disappearance?

She took a small step toward the laptop before quickly going to the door to the spare bedroom.

Somewhere in the back of her mind, she could hear Tyler's words echo as she went inside.

"We all got our addictions, Somerset."

Chapter 15

A cup of coffee in each hand, Meredith opened the door to the morgue with a hip-check.

Tyler and Mike, whom everyone referred to as Mike in the Morgue, were standing by one of the metal slabs, upon which rested the body of James Hammond covered by a sheet.

"Sorry, sorry, sorry," Meredith said, approaching the pair. "Long night. Got a late start this morning."

"Me, too," Tyler said, accepting the cup from her. "Had to go talk a guy down. What were you up to?"

"… Couldn't sleep."

They took a sip from their coffees and turned to Mike, who regarded them coldly.

"Where's mine?" he asked.

Meredith and Tyler shifted awkwardly.

"Unbelievable," Mike snorted. "I'm the one who was here at six to do the autopsy on the human piñata."

Tyler held out his cup. "You want mine? I ain't got cooties or nothing."

Mike smiled. "I'm just giving you shit. I've already had three cups. Shall we?"

He turned, walked to the head of the table, took a breath, and removed the sheet.

Tyler flinched.

Meredith had spent the drive to work preparing herself. She had already seen James Hammond's shattered face in the yard, but this was infinitely worse.

Now that Mike had cleaned the corpse, the inner workings of Hammond's face were on display. One eye had been obliterated, while the other bulged and had taken on a milky quality. The nose was flattened, almost concave. There was nothing that could be called a mouth, just a jagged hole with teeth.

Meredith took a series of slow, deep breaths through her mouth, avoiding the use of her nose. While the morgue was well ventilated, the slight stench of decay was enough to make her stomach consider her breakfast as "return to sender."

"Yeah," Mike said, noting their reactions. "It took me a couple minutes, too. I've seen a lot of traumas in my time down here, but nothing like this …"

His foot found the pedal under the table that activated the recording microphone overhead.

"It is eight-oh-nine on the morning of August twenty-third. My name is Mike Redden, forensic pathologist with the Cobb County Police Department. I am joined by Detectives Meredith Somerset and Tyler Foles. I am presenting my preliminary findings on case …" He checked the notes that were clipped to the raised lip of the table. "Four-seven-six-one-seven. The deceased is James Hammond. Age: fifty-three. Height: six-foot-one. Weight: two hundred and ten pounds. The cause of death is blunt force trauma to the left side of the occipital bone, just above the external occipital protuberance. The blow was severe enough that death was most likely instantaneous or shortly thereafter. There are no injuries on the deceased's hands or wrists to indicate a struggle or that he attempted to stop himself from falling after receiving the blow. This is of note because the initial blow to the back of the skull would have caused the victim to fall forward, which means that once he was on the ground, he was turned over so that the blows could be administered to the face. Again, there are no defensive wounds on the hands, so the victim was already dead or at least, incapacitated. The trauma to the face is severe. The frontal bone, glabella, supraorbital former and margin, the nasal bone, zygomatic bone, palatine, maxilla, and mandible are fractured in several places. Multiple teeth have been knocked out. The nasal cavity is collapsed, as well as the right ocular orbit. The bruising around the face and the bone fractures indicate that the person was moving around the victim as they struck the face. The killer placed a paper tablecloth over the victim before striking the face to avoid the blood spatter. I found paper fibers in the wounds that matched the color of the tablecloth found at the scene."

Mike moved down the table. Meredith and Tyler followed his hands as he pointed out the bruises.

"There are further strikes over the body, such as the left shoulder and chest. However, they appear to be of lesser intensity, causing only mild bruising."

Tyler held up a finger, and Mike took his foot off the recording pedal.

"Your opinion, Mike," Tyler said. "You think our guy got tired after doing a number on his face, and that's why the love taps on the body aren't as bad?"

"It's possible, but I am not going to make any guesses as to the motivation or reasoning of anyone who would do that," he said, motioning to Hammond's face.

Tyler nodded, and Mike put his foot back on the pedal to continue recording.

"The murder weapon is most likely a softball bat that was found at the scene. There was blood on it, and the injuries are consistent with a softball bat. Blood collected from the bat is currently being tested to confirm, and the bat is also being studied for fingerprints. My conclusion is that James Hammond was struck from behind. Death was instantaneous. The perpetrator then turned Mr. Hammond over onto his back and covered him with the tablecloth so that they could repeatedly strike him about the face and the rest of his body and avoid the blood splatter. In my opinion, this was an incredibly sick individual."

Mike took his foot off the pedal.

Meredith nearly choked on her coffee. Mike was always careful to keep his recordings professional, never deviating from his professional analysis and never including his own opinion.

"Mike. You recorded that," she said.

"Yeah. I know."

*

"I've never seen Mike shook up like that," Meredith said once the doors of the elevator had closed.

"Can you blame him? I mean, I saw plenty of messed-up shit in narco and vice, but that? That was something else."

Neither of them spoke until the doors slid open and they stepped out into the hall.

"I'm still trying to figure out those secondary hits," Tyler said. "You think our guy figured he had done enough damage to Hammond's face but wasn't finished?"

Meredith tried to reason it through. "Maybe the killer was tired. Maybe the killer was interrupted. Maybe there were two killers. I have no idea. None of it makes sense. It was over after that first hit to the back of his head. To turn him over and do that to his face … The killer hated him."

"All right. Let's go find out who hated James Hammond."

Chapter 16

And where better to start? Meredith thought as she and Tyler took their seats across the desk from Anna Hewitt, James Hammond's ex-wife.

Her ultra-modern office overlooked Centennial Park. Her desk was made of glass and white plastic. The drawers were clear, so that the orderly contents were on subtle display.

Anna's stylish white suit matched the décor and caused her raven-dark hair to stand out. She carried herself with an easy confidence, secure that she was running the show around her.

"Thank you for seeing us today," Meredith began. "We understand this may be a difficult time for you."

"Not really," Anna said, sliding into her own chair, the logo of her company on the wall behind her. "I'm sorry. That sounded crass. Of course, I feel for his wife and daughter, and I will absolutely do whatever I can to help you catch who killed him, but I won't lie and say that I'm particularly broken up about his passing."

"... Thank you," Tyler said, in a tone that was almost a question.

"How long were you two married?" Meredith asked, getting out her notepad.

"Seven years. We married in two thousand three and separated in two thousand ten."

"How did you meet?"

"We ran in the same circles. Entrepreneurs are a little bit of a social club in this city. Doesn't matter the field you're in; the cocktail parties are all the same. I think we first met at some angel investor thing. Then, at an art gallery function. Before we knew it, we were having dinner around town, then having sex at his place, then getting married at a church, and then on opposite ends of a table with our attorneys."

"Was the divorce amicable?"

"I didn't kill him, if that's what you're asking," Anna said with ease, and caught herself. "Again, I'm sorry. I can't help it. Building and running your own company can toughen you up a little bit. I wouldn't describe our divorce as amicable, but I wouldn't say it was hostile. I would call it 'indifferent.' I only want to make it clear that I had nothing to do with his death."

"We're only trying to get a better understanding of your ex-husband's life and who might want to do something like this," Meredith said.

"And you think I might know?"

"Not necessarily. It's a starting point for us to find out what kind of person he was."

Anna seemed satisfied.

"When was the last time you spoke with him?" Meredith asked.

"A few weeks ago."

"What did you talk about?"

A strange smile played across Anna's face. "He was talking trash, like he always did."

"Talking trash?"

"Yeah. When James and I started dating, it wasn't just physical attraction between us. Ambition is attracted to ambition. We were both extremely competitive, even with each other. I was trying to get seed money for this place," she said with a gesture to the logo behind her. "He was trying to start a new cell phone company. At the time, we were both going after the same money." She got a little bit of a far-off look. "It was incredibly sexy, and we were hot and heavy for a while. Even when we fought, it was sexy. We thought we were in love and got married, but I discovered that competitiveness is great for sex but horrible for a relationship."

"What happened?" Meredith asked.

"I won. I got my start-up money, built my company, which allows you to plug your phone into any computer and automatically download your social media or any other apps to your phone with the login information so you don't have to reset all the passwords you've forgotten."

"Damn smart," Tyler said, under his breath.

"Yes, it is. Anyway, once everything was getting off the ground, I offered James the chance to come on board as CFO. Big mistake."

"He didn't take the job?" Meredith asked.

"It pissed him off that I even offered it. He said that I was asking for his balls and that he was still going to start his own company. I told him to have at it. I had plenty of work to do." She lost that far-off look and came back down to earth. "As I said, the competitive stuff was fun and sexy in the short term, but you can't do it if you're trying to have an honest relationship."

"Is that what led to the divorce?"

"Yes, but not right away. We were a little bit of a 'power couple' for a while. It was good for business and good for him, but it got old. He kept bouncing around from idea to idea for a business, but nothing stuck. All the while, my business kept growing. He got so frustrated and resentful ... That's when the affairs started."

"He started seeing other women?" Meredith asked.

"Fucking other women," Anna corrected her without a hint of anger or embarrassment. "He would say it was because they were so attracted to him, but he was really doing it to try to get back at me for my success. That's how competitive he was."

"Sounds kind of complicated," Tyler said.

"It's not. James always had a roving eye. I think he was sleeping around the whole time we were together. He didn't tell me about it until he wanted to hurt me."

"What did you do?" Meredith asked.

"By that time, I didn't care. I didn't have time for his bullshit, and eventually, I called the marriage off."

"How did he take it?"

"It sent him over the edge. I had gotten my company off the ground while he couldn't get anywhere. He felt neglected while I was pouring everything I had into this business. He slept around to hurt me, and I didn't care. I showed him the door. No woman had ever done that to him before, and you have no idea what that does to a man like James."

"Could you give us an idea?" Meredith asked.

Anna's tone darkened. "He was furious. He said that I wouldn't be anywhere without him and that he was going to start a company that would be bigger than anything I could ever hope to create."

"And what did you do?"

"Ignored him. I had other things to do, which only made it worse. He started seeing Jessica and really tried to rub it in my face, telling me how young and gorgeous she was. I still ignored him ... Then he started sending me pictures of them having sex. He told Jessica they were just for him, but all the while he was sending them to me."

"Did you respond?"

"Yep."

"How?"

Anna smiled. "I sent him photos of my company's quarterly earnings reports. That kicked him into high gear, and he set to work on CashFlo. He kept me apprised of his progress. It was like we were flirting, again ... Then, their daughter came ... That's when things got weird."

"Really?" Tyler said. "*That's* when things got weird?"

"How so?" Meredith asked, cutting him off.

"The competitiveness was fine when it came to matters of business but … he tried to use his daughter to goad me. He would send photos of him with her and tell me I would never have that kind of love or fulfillment in my life … That's when I told him he had to stop. I know how screwed up our little games can look to people who don't understand, but using his daughter to try to hurt me was a step too far, even for me. I told him that I was happy about CashFlo and his family, which I truly was, but he needed to stop being so petty and focus on raising his daughter instead of using her as a chip."

"How did he take it?"

"He thought he had won, that he had finally gotten to me and started stepping up the bullshit. I tried to ignore it at first but got fed up and told him that if he didn't stop, I would show the photos he had sent me to Jessica."

"Did that work?"

"Oh, yeah. Jessica could have filed for divorce and taken everything, including CashFlo. He stopped … for a while."

"What happened?"

"A few months ago, he got back in touch. It was just a couple of text messages. He really eased into it, saying he was sorry and wanted to know how I was doing. Like an idiot, I believed him."

"He started harassing you, again?"

"Nothing like before. There were no photos of him and Jessica having sex, or of their daughter. He was back on CashFlo."

"What did he say?"

"He said something big was coming with CashFlo, something that would make my company look like 'the insignificant piece of shit it was' … That was James," Anna said, sarcastically. "Always the romantic."

"Did he say what it was?" Meredith asked.

"No," Anna answered. "This was about two weeks ago. I guess he never got the chance."

Chapter 17

The street cart vendor holding the cup of freshly sliced pineapple waited as Meredith spoke into her phone.

"Okay … Okay … Got it … No. We expected as much. Thanks, Mike."

Meredith hung up, pocketed her phone, and accepted the cup and plastic fork.

"Thank you," she said, before joining Tyler on the bench over-looking Centennial Park. "That was Mike in the Morgue," she said, plopping down next to him.

"And?" Tyler asked through a mouthful of watermelon.

"Got the preliminary findings back from the softball bat. It's definitely the murder weapon." Meredith stabbed a chunk of pineapple and brought it to her lips.

"Fingerprints?"

"Only a few dozen. Partials, mostly, but it's just as we thought: essentially worthless."

"I'm sorry?" Tyler smirked. "*We?* I think I was the one who called that."

"I knew where you were going."

"You're just riding my coattails, ain't you, Somerset?"

Meredith flicked her plastic fork in his direction, splattering a few drops of pineapple juice on him.

Tyler laughed.

"Okay," he said, wiping a napkin across his cheek. "How do you want to play it, knowing what we know from the ex-Mrs. Hammond?"

"In addition to asking why she's slow-walking the text message, we'll ask her what she knows about her husband's … habits."

"Like, if she knew her husband was creeping around?"

"She knew," Meredith said, popping another bit of pineapple into her mouth as they watched a guy throw a frisbee for his dog.

"What makes you so sure?"

"A hunch. Anna Hewitt made it clear what kind of man he was, and men like that don't change. If he was sleeping around, Jessica had to have known, even if she tried to turn a blind eye."

"You're that certain?"

"Mmm-hmm," Meredith answered.

"Your man sleep around on you when you were married? … Or vice versa?" Tyler asked.

"Nope," Meredith confidently answered. "What about you? You ever cheat in a relationship?"

Tyler paused with a bite of watermelon a few inches from his lips and smirked.

Meredith's mouth dropped open in amusement. "Tyler. Did you cheat on someone?"

"I refuse to answer on the grounds that it may incriminate me."

They continued to stare out at the park.

"Can I ask you something?"

"I took a bullet for you, Somerset, and you've helped me stay clean. Ain't no secrets between us."

"You did cheat on someone?"

"Yep."

"Why?"

Tyler pushed around the remaining pieces of watermelon in the cup with his fork.

Meredith shook her head. "I'm sorry. You don't have to—"

"No, no, no. It's an interesting question. Guess I've never really thought about it, before."

Meredith waited. If Tyler seemed embarrassed or ashamed, she would have dropped it, but he appeared to be genuinely intrigued. She had never cheated on Pete or in any of her other relationships. She was also certain that Pete hadn't cheated on her, no matter how badly things deteriorated toward the end of their marriage. Heather had come along a year after they split … hadn't she?

Tyler snapped her out of it with his answer. "I was young. Stupid. I think, at first, it was exciting to not get caught. Then, as it went on, it was almost as exciting *to* get caught until … you know, you get caught."

"Are you sorry that you cheated?"

"Every day … But now we've got a problem, right? One of propriety. Yesterday, we couldn't rule her out but thought it was unlikely because there was no motive. Now, she might have one, but if we ask her about her husband's affairs and she really didn't know about it, we're adding insult to injury."

"We'll be gentle," Meredith said.

Chapter 18

"Thank you, Rosella," Jessica said, as the elderly Hispanic woman led Daniella out of the living room.

Situated in the ritzy neighborhood of Buckhead, the Hammond household was everything Meredith had expected. It was California mission style, with stucco walls, red tiled roof, and a heavy front door. The living room had a vaulted ceiling and tiled floor. Jessica was sitting on an oversized, cabernet-colored couch. Meredith and Tyler were on its twin, across the coffee table, which looked as if it had been built with the same timbers used in the ceiling overhead.

"We appreciate you seeing us, Mrs. Hammond," Meredith said. "We know that you and your daughter are still coping with a tragic loss, but there are some things that we needed to discuss."

Jessica nodded.

"The first thing we'd like to talk about is a text message that witnesses observed your husband receiving moments before he went back inside."

"Okay …"

Meredith and Tyler waited for a response, but Jessica remained silent.

"As we said before," Meredith said, "it might be the key to finding out—"

"My lawyer is still working on it," Jessica said. "I want to make sure that it's all handled properly."

The air in the room changed.

Meredith had been giving Jessica the benefit of the doubt, hoping her reluctance was down to confusion and grief. Now, there was no question that Jessica Hammond was hiding something.

Meredith decided to press further.

"I apologize, but we have to ask; did your husband have life insurance?"

"He did, but I can assure you that Dani and I had everything we needed without the life insurance."

There was a brief standoff, and Meredith decided to move on.

"There's also something else we needed to talk to you about."

"Of course," Jessica replied, seemingly relieved to move on.

"How would you describe your relationship with your husband?"

"What do you mean?"

"We've been conducting some interviews, trying to find any motive for your husband's murder. I'm sorry if this is uncomfortable, but it is important; has there been any infidelity in your marriage?"

Jessica's eyes narrowed.

"You've been talking to Anna, haven't you?"

"Yes, ma'am."

Jessica scoffed. "What did she tell you?"

"I'm afraid we can't speak to that."

Jessica's nervousness and awkwardness evaporated and was replaced with sardonic disdain. "She's been obsessed with James ever since they separated. She wouldn't leave him alone. James told me all about her and how she was jealous of our marriage and our family."

"Getting back to my question; do you know if your husband was ever unfaithful?"

Jessica cocked her head in disbelief at such a question.

"We're trying to find a motive for his murder, Mrs. Hammond," Meredith said.

Jessica considered before answering.

"James was a very successful, driven, and attractive man. He told me when women made advances, but he never reciprocated. He was a loving, faithful husband and father."

Meredith nodded.

"Thank you, and I'm sorry for this last question, but I have to ask; were you faithful to your husband?"

Jessica stared coldly at Meredith.

"Always."

*

"That was super interesting," Tyler said, once they were back in the car and Meredith started the engine.

"Putting it mildly."

"This could be over in five minutes if she would just let us see those phone records."

"Why do you think she's stalling?"

"Don't be coy with me, Somerset. You and I both know the reason; she doesn't want us seeing *her* records. She doesn't want us knowing who she's talking to, which makes me think her last answer was a lie."

"Great minds, Tyler," Meredith replied, taking her foot off the brake. "Great minds."

*

They spent the rest of the day back at the precinct, going over notes from the autopsy and crime scene, hoping to catch a break from the photos but were forced to call it a day.

"All right," Meredith said, pushing open the door and stepping out into the parking lot with Tyler close behind. "Tomorrow, we start the follow-up interviews. I want to see if James Hammond or any of our suspects have more skeletons in their closets."

They arrived at their cars.

"You heading home?" Meredith asked.

"Going to a meeting."

"Everything okay?"

"Oh, yeah. I'm good. Darren asked me to lead tonight's meeting a while ago. You want to come? Always like having you there."

"I would," Meredith replied. "But tonight's the night."

Tyler's face fell. "Oh no."

"Yeah ..."

"Listen, Somerset, you be super careful and go easy on her, okay?"

"That's all going to depend on her."

Tyler whistled. "I would not want you as my instructor."

Chapter 19

"No, baby, you have to—"

"I got it, Mom."

"No. You don't. You can't be timid with—"

"I said I got it!"

"Baby, listen to me—"

"Mom!"

The clutch let out a pleading *crrrrrk!* and Meredith and Allison were pressed against the seat belts as the car lurched forward and abruptly stopped.

Meredith had pleaded with Allison to learn on Pete's Civic with its automatic transmission, but Allison insisted that she was going to learn how to drive a stick shift. She didn't want to learn driving in stages.

They sat silently under one of the lights in the Walmart parking lot. Meredith thought it was an ideal location. Most of the shoppers were gone, and Allison would be driving primarily in straight lines. If she was going to learn to drive stick, Meredith wanted her to get the feel of the timing of the gearshift, and the parking lot guaranteed that they would never get out of second gear, but even getting out of first gear was proving difficult.

"Baby, I know it's tough because you're just starting, but you can't be timid with changing gears."

"Yeah. I know. You've told me a million times."

"That's a little dramatic."

It was true that Meredith had told her multiple times, and instead of grasping it, her daughter had become more frustrated.

Allison stared straight ahead, tightening her lips and breathing heavily.

You really are just like me, Meredith thought.

"Baby, do you want me to—?"

"No. I can do it."

Meredith twisted in her seat to look out the side window. "Okay, well, this guy needs to get out of his space, and we're blocking him in, so …"

Allison huffed and wrenched the key.

"Baby, you have to—"

"I *know!*"

Allison was successful in starting the car, but overthought the clutch, again, which caused the car to lurch and stall.

The man waiting to back out of his space tapped his horn.

"I know, asshole!" Allison shouted.

"Watch it," Meredith said.

"Sorry," Allison said, more in frustration than sincerity. She took a breath, started the car, and managed to sync up her feet between the clutch and the gas, allowing the car to move forward.

"There you go," Meredith said with cautious encouragement.

They proceeded to the end of the aisle, near the entrance of the store, where Allison had to stop to allow a man in overalls and a woman in Daisy Duke shorts to cross.

Once they passed, Allison tried to ease off the clutch and press on the gas.

Meredith grimaced as they lurched. The transmission cried out in agony. The tires let out a short squeal, drawing the attention of everyone around them.

Allison groaned and leaned forward to rest her head on the steering wheel, which brought a short blast from the horn, adding insult to injury.

Meredith looked at Allison as if she were a bomb whose timer had hit zero a while ago.

"You okay?" she asked.

"I'm fine," Allison replied, close to tears.

Meredith nodded to the Wendy's in the far corner of the expansive parking lot. "Want to call it a night? Grab a Frosty?"

Allison remained motionless, then yanked up on the parking brake, unclipped her seat belt, and got out so that she and Meredith could switch places.

Thank God, Meredith thought.

*

Allison looked like she was about to crack a rib as she tried to get the Frosty up through the straw.

"It takes a little bit of time," Meredith said. "Then, it's like riding a bike."

She tried to sound confident, but Meredith would be fine if Allison didn't drive for a while. The thought of her daughter going sixty-five miles an hour down the interstate in a four-thousand-pound machine terrified her, even more than the thought of Allison dating.

"How long did it take you?" Allison asked after finally succeeding in gulping down some Frosty, only to be rewarded with an ice cream headache.

"It took me a little bit, but I learned on an automatic, which was much easier."

Meredith prayed that Allison would take the hint.

"What made you want to learn how to drive stick?" Allison asked.

"I could only afford a stick shift car. They were cheaper than automatics back then."

It was a bald-faced lie.

Meredith learned stick because she wanted to feel more like a badass, because it was more fun, but she wasn't going to tell Allison that.

"How's school going?" Meredith asked, changing the subject.

Allison shrugged. "It's easy."

"Are you going to run for student council, again?"

"Maybe. Have you thought any more about that thing I asked you?"

"What thing?"

"The podcast thing."

"Oh … that."

"Mr. Beisner thinks it's a cool idea. He says it would be a great way to get into media studies or even production, if that's what I want to do in college."

"Does he?"

"Yeah," Allison continued, eagerly. "And what makes it even more cool is that it could be successful on its own, you know? Not just some school project. So, what do you think?"

Meredith glanced around, trying to find some way to stall or even get back on the subject of driving, but it was hopeless.

"What exactly is it that you want to do, again?"

"I just want to talk to you. I think it would be cool for everyone to hear about what you do and what it's like to be a homicide detective."

"That might be tricky."

"Why?"

"Because I wouldn't be able to talk about ongoing investigations."

"Yeah, but you've been a detective for like, what, thirty years?"

"Okay, not even cl—"

"And you've done a ton of murder investigations, right?"

"Yes."

"See? It's perfect. You can tell me about the really gruesome ones and what it's like and what made you get into police work. People would love it. I told you, true crime is so huge, right now."

Meredith paused.

She genuinely loved her daughter's enthusiasm, but there was a line she didn't want to cross. She didn't want to bring her work to Allison, nor did she really want Allison stepping into her work. Even though Allison was maturing, Meredith wanted to keep her away from the things she had seen, like the pulverized face of James Hammond.

"I'm not so sure that's a good idea."

Allison sighed. "Why not?"

"Baby, there's some stuff that I don't think you or anyone would—"

"Is it because of the thing with your sister?"

Meredith stared at her.

For Allison to reduce the most devastating event in her life, and that which shaped everything that came after, as "the thing with your sister" caused Meredith's blood to run cold.

Allison sensed it and shrank back.

Allison knew vague bits and pieces about it. It had shaped her life, too. It was the reason she lived with her father and soon-to-be stepmother. Through no fault of her own, Allison was a part of it, but Meredith hadn't told her everything, nor was she in a rush to do so.

"I'm not sure I'm ready to talk about it," Meredith said.

Allison pushed her straw up and down through the plastic lid, emitting a sound like a mournful kazoo.

"I'm sorry," Allison said, not meeting her eyes. "I didn't mean to make you mad. I know it messed up a lot of stuff, but I think people would find it interesting … and I'd like to know."

The anger slowly flowed from Meredith. Allison's apology was ineloquent but sincere.

"It's okay. You didn't do anything wrong," Meredith said. "I think I just need a little more time."

Allison continued to play the sad kazoo with her straw.

*

"Jessica, why did you tell them th—?"

"What was I supposed to do, Nick?" Jessica asked into the phone. "I was trying to protect you. I was trying to protect us."

"But you know the kind of guy James was. You know he was sleeping around."

"Yes. I don't need you to remind me." Jessica composed herself. "What good would it have done to tell them I knew about James? It would have made me look bad. They might have wondered if I had something to do with his death. And do you think I should have told them about us when they asked?"

"No. Of course not … What are you going to do about the phone records?"

"I spoke with Grace, and I think I've found a way through."

*

After dropping Allison off at Heather and Pete's, a weary Meredith returned to her apartment.

The hour-long assault on her nerves from Allison's hour-long assault on her car's transmission, followed by the uneasy conversation surrounding her podcast proposal, had exhausted her.

Why? Meredith wondered. *Why couldn't she want to connect about anything other than this?*

Meredith glanced at the closed door to the spare bedroom, unable to shake the feeling that there was a live beast locked away in there.

Did Meredith owe it to her? Allison was becoming an adult. She was intelligent and hard-working, and Alice's disappearance had shaped the contours of her life before she had even been born. Meredith wondered if it was only fair to let Allison in.

Meredith went into the spare bedroom. The air was different in that room. It was cold and stale. She shut the door, as if afraid that the beast might escape.

She walked to the chair, sat, and stared at the photos, reports, and clippings that radiated from Alice's swimsuit and accompanying note.

She still misses you, Meredith.

Why am I doing this to myself? Meredith thought.

She let her head hang and stared at the floor in contemplation.

She wondered if letting Allison see this would help her move on. Would talking to her about the pain of that day and every day since help free her and bring her and Allison closer? Or would it just be more pain and suffering? Not to mention having to disclose that the man who had taken Alice was still out there, knew where Meredith was, and continued to taunt her. Could she count on Allison to keep such a secret? If Allison couldn't, Meredith's career would be in jeopardy.

Droplets of water landed on the hardwood floor and rivulets began slowly running down the drywall.

Meredith looked up.

Alice was there, suspended against the wall, wearing the bathing suit with the note still attached. Her hair and bathing suit were soaked, as if she had just been pulled from the water. Her eyes were open, staring down at Meredith.

Meredith inhaled, looked back down at the floor, and made her decision; she could never let Allison, or anyone else, ever see this room.

Chapter 20

"Good morning, sunshine," Tyler chimed as Meredith entered the office and made her way to the desk across from him.

Tyler's good-natured ribbing was born from the fact that she normally arrived before him.

"Hey," she replied, gruffer than she had intended. Her foul mood was the result of falling asleep in the spare bedroom the night before.

"Did I say sunshine?" Tyler asked. "I meant 'downer.'"

Meredith smiled in spite of herself. Tyler had his charms.

She fired up her computer and opened her email. There was a message waiting from Jessica Hammond's attorney.

"We've got the text messages."

Meredith clicked on the attachment and creased her brow.

"Why are we not happy?" Tyler asked.

*

"Hello?"

"Hello. Is this Grace Ormond?"

"Yes, it is."

"Good morning, Mrs. Ormond. This is Detective Meredith

Somerset with the Cobb County Police Department. I'm here with my partner, Detective Tyler Foles."

"Good morning, detectives. What can I do for you?"

Grace Ormond's cheerful tone was a little too forced for Meredith and Tyler's liking.

"We're conducting the investigation into the murder of James Hammond."

"Did you receive Mrs. Hammond's phone records?" Grace asked.

Meredith stared at the sheet of paper in her hand. Tyler, who was listening in on the call at his desk across from Meredith, held his own copy in his hand.

"We did," Meredith said. "But we have some questions."

The printout of the Hammonds' text and phone records had their names and numbers printed at the top of the page, but the rest of the records were black lines, save for the one text message that James had received at 1:03 p.m. the day of the party.

Meet me in the backyard.

The text was from a 770 area code, putting it in northern Atlanta.

"That is the text you were inquiring about, correct?" Grace asked.

"It is and it's a great help, but it might be even more helpful if we could see if there were any other messages from that number on any other occasions."

"Oh. It was my client's understanding that this was the text you were concerned with."

"It is, but it would help us to know more."

There was a pause that stretched to the point where Tyler and Meredith exchanged knowing glances.

Here it comes, Tyler mouthed.

"I see … I'll have to discuss it with my client."

"Okay," Meredith said. "Let us know, and please convey it again to your client that it'll help us catch her husband's killer. Thank you for your help."

"Thank you, detective." Grace hung up.

Tyler put down the phone and ran his fingers through his hair. "Our mourning widow isn't doing a whole lot to ease our suspicions."

"No, but at least we have a number."

"I'll get on the phone to Kelly Yamara and have her start tracking it down."

Meredith nodded. "In the meantime, let's find out about CashFlo."

Chapter 21

As she took in the furnishings, it was hard for Meredith to conceive that this man could have been a multimillionaire like James Hammond. Harold Mantelli's living room and kitchen reminded Meredith of her grandparents' home.

Harold's short, squat form busied about in the kitchen.

"Would you like a drink? Water or coffee?" he asked.

"Water would be great," Tyler said.

Harold opened a cabinet and pulled down a glass that resembled a mason jar. He filled it to the brim with water from the sink and brought it into the living room, walking very slowly so as to not spill any.

"There you are," he said, handing the glass to Tyler, who accepted with both hands, trying to avoid spilling any into his lap. He immediately brought it to his lips, sucked some off the top, and made a face.

"Mmmm … warm tap water. Just the way I like it. Thanks."

Harold smiled and sat in his recliner.

"You have a lovely home," Meredith said, attempting to break the ice.

"It's my castle," Harold said with forced confidence.

Meredith assumed he was making a reference to the saying that a man's home is his castle but didn't ask for clarification.

"Do you live by yourself?"

"Yes. I bought the house with the money I received from my settlement with CashFlo."

"CashFlo is actually what we wanted to talk to you about," Meredith said, while Tyler set down his mason jar of warm tap water on the coffee table.

"My settlement from CashFlo was perfectly agreeable, and there was no wrongdoing on the part of CashFlo or their executives," Harold added with a cadence that suggested he had said the words numerous times before.

"That's … That's fine," Meredith said, "but I was wondering—"

"I'm supposed to say that, according to the agreement we came to when I left the company."

"I see …"

Meredith had prided herself on her interview techniques. Over time, she had learned how to read subtle clues, such as tone and posture, but Harold Mantelli was like an alien inhabiting human form who hadn't worked out the finer details.

"Can you tell us about your time at CashFlo and how you came up with the idea for the company?"

"Sure," he said, settling back in his recliner. "Back in April two thousand seven, I was shopping online for a new chessboard. I found one on the site of a small store in Sackets Harbor in Upstate New York. The pieces were hand carved to resemble historical figures from the War of the Roses, the English civil war. Not the movie from nineteen eighty-nine."

Meredith nodded as if she had heard of the film. Tyler was listening in rapt silence.

"I tried to purchase the board with a credit card, but there were several hoops to jump through and my card was declined, even though I had excellent credit. I really wanted the chessboard, so I got in touch with the owner of the store. He apologized and explained that it was the credit card company. Because he was such a small retailer that sold more expensive items, credit card companies were quick to red-flag many of his transactions as possible fraud. It was because he was so specialized, and his products were expensive. I was working as a computer programmer for a medical supply company called Medtech. I also liked building contraptions and writing programs for them. I've got a workstation in my basement. I had the idea to write a program that would provide an authentication code for each retailer upon each transaction. That way, the credit card company would know the transaction was legitimate and speed things up and help out smaller retailers. It was simple, really. I tried out the beta with the retailer to buy the chessboard. It worked." Harold waved to a table in the corner, upon which sat the chessboard with the red and white carved wooden pieces. "The retailer was so happy, he refunded me the money."

"And how did you get in touch with James Hammond?" Meredith asked.

"My ex-wife encouraged me to sell my idea. I talked to an IP lawyer, and he set up a meeting with Mr. Hammond. I told him about my program, and he loved it. He put together the capital to start the company, and we worked out an agreement."

"What was the agreement?"

"I received five percent," Harold said, still smiling.

Meredith blinked. "Five percent? That doesn't seem like much, considering it was your idea."

"Mr. Hammond explained that it would take a while for the company to become solvent, and when it did, we would work out a new agreement."

Tyler sat up. "Hold on. Didn't your lawyer have a problem with that? I mean, he's supposed to be looking out for you and I'm no fan of lawyers, but he had to be getting screwed too, right?"

For the first time, Harold's smiled cracked a degree. "Yes, but he told me that it was a good arrangement and that was how these sorts of things worked."

"Then what happened?" Meredith asked.

"The company got off the ground. I thought things were going well, but three years in, Mr. Hammond said we needed to restructure. He wasn't very happy with me. He said I wasn't adding anything. He brought in some more people and felt it would be best if I was no longer part of the company. I received a settlement and was no longer a part of CashFlo."

"What was your share?"

"Three percent."

Meredith and Tyler were speechless.

"And how did you feel about that?" she asked.

"My settlement from CashFlo was perfectly agreeable, and there was no wrongdoing on the part of CashFlo or their executives," Harold repeated, word for word as before.

"But you had to be a little salty, right?" Tyler asked. "I know I would be."

"My settlement with CashFlo was perfectly agreeable, and there was no wrongdoing on the part of CashFlo or their executives."

"I know you have to say that as part of your settlement," Meredith said, "but what did your lawyer think?"

That fissure suddenly reappeared in Harold's cheery demeanor. "I only found out later that he was also Mr. Hammond's lawyer. I guess Mr. Hammond paid him a lot of money. My wife was furious. She wanted me to sue, but I wouldn't."

"Why not?"

"Mr. Hammond said that he would take care of me when the company took off."

"And you believed him?"

"… Yes," he answered, uncomfortable. "My wife left me and got custody of our newborn daughter. I didn't put up much of a fight."

Tyler leaned forward. "If I had found out that I'd been screwed out of a company I had founded, I'd want to light someone up."

Harold squirmed. "I'm very averse to confrontations, but the

117

settlement was enough to buy this house and I could pay child support for Cybil."

"Were you still on good terms with James Hammond?" Meredith asked.

"Yes," Harold replied and then quickly added, "My settlement from CashFlo was perfectly agreeable, and there was no wrong-doing on the part of CashFlo or their executives."

*

"First Jessica Hammond, now this guy. Normally people try to move down the suspect list in an interview," Tyler said as they climbed into Meredith's car.

"I don't think he knew he was doing it," she replied, twisting the key in the ignition. "We need to find out some more about him."

"You want to bring him up to Sean Winston and Kristi Sanders this afternoon?"

"They might be able to tell us about his dealings with CashFlo, but I want to know more about the kind of person he is."

"We got a lot about James Hammond from his ex-wife." Tyler shrugged. "Harold Mantelli's got an ex-wife."

Meredith nodded. "Give her a call and let's see if we can set up something after our meeting at CashFlo."

*

Harold watched them go through the small separation in the curtains in his living-room window.

That ever-present sense of worry that resided in his stomach was fluttering. He had done his best, walking the line between being honest and being cautious.

He picked up his phone and dialed, following the instructions he had been given.

Chapter 22

The CashFlo offices were situated on the seventh floor of a building north of downtown, just off Interstate 285. The area was peppered with buildings that were the home of telecommunications companies, web developers, and other cutting-edge fields. Unfortunately, due to the nature of those industries, the sleekly designed structures were revolving doors of companies that promised the future, only to go bust long before it arrived.

Meredith and Tyler parked in the structure adjacent to a pair of mirrored-glass, pillar-shaped buildings that sat side by side and were topped by giant shapes—one a cube, the other a sphere.

As they walked across the pedestrian bridge that connected the parking structure to the raised plaza between the buildings, the windows reflected the harsh sunlight at them as if they were ants under a magnifying glass.

Tyler shielded his eyes as they passed through the most intense spot on their way to the doors of the building topped by the sphere.

"These things are filled with science and technology whizzes, and no one thought of this?"

"They're in the buildings. They didn't design them," Meredith said.

"All they got to do is cover the walkway," Tyler jeered. "There. I'm smarter than the people who designed these things." They came out of the sunspot, and Tyler lowered his hand. "Okay, before we get up there, you want to start with Kristi Sanders or Sean Winston? I got a coin."

"Let's start with Kristi. She was still rattled at the party, more so than him, so she might have remembered more details."

"Copy that," Tyler said, holding open the door for her to go inside.

The CashFlo logo was etched into the glass wall behind the reception desk. Through the glass wall, Meredith and Tyler could see the hustle and bustle taking place as employees, all appearing to be in their mid-twenties to early thirties, moved through rows and columns of open workstations.

The receptionist, a young woman who looked fresh out of high school, looked up and smiled at them.

"Are you the detectives?" she asked.

"Yes," Meredith finally said. "I'm Detectiv—"

The receptionist picked up the phone from the cradle on her desk.

"Mr. Winston? They're here," she chirped, waited a moment for an answer, and hung up. "He's on his way."

Seconds later, through the glass wall, Sean Winston emerged from a hallway at the back of the main room. As he passed by the open workstations, people gave him space, like a shark passing through a school of fish.

Sean opened the glass door and stepped into the lobby.

"Detectives." He shook each of their hands with a firm, single up-and-down motion. A power handshake. The practiced move of someone attempting to establish dominance.

"I thought we might conduct the interview in my office. Then, I'll show you to Mrs. Sanders. I feel the need to say again that I would have preferred to do this somewhere else, away from my team. They're pretty upset."

Meredith glanced toward the main office through the glass wall. If these people were upset, they weren't showing it.

Sean was already turning back to lead them through the door. "Right this way, please."

"Actually," Meredith said, "we'd like to speak to Mrs. Sanders, first."

Sean stopped. As good as his poker face was, he couldn't hide a momentary flash of annoyance.

It was exactly what Meredith wanted to see.

Sean was a guy who wanted control, to set the rules to maintain any advantage he could get. It could have just been his personality, but she wanted to throw him off his game.

"I think she's on a call," Sean said.

"We'll wait," Meredith said. "Then, once we're done with Mrs. Sanders, we'll talk in your office—"

"I might be busy. There are a lot of things happening right now, and I really don't have the time—"

"You'll wait," Tyler said.

Sean regarded them coldly.

"Very well," he said, opening the door.

*

Sean led them past the rows of cubicles toward the hall from which he had emerged. CashFlo employees continued giving him a wide berth as he walked by, but many couldn't help taking a glance at Meredith and Tyler.

They reached the hallway, which held three doors, one on either side and one at the end. Sean knocked on the door to the right.

"Come in," Kristi Sanders replied, but Sean was already opening the door.

Kristi was sitting at her desk in the plush suite. Her face was pensive as she stared out the curved window that overlooked the plaza.

"Kristi," Sean said. "I believe you've met Detectives Somerset and Foles."

"Yes," she said, rising from her chair.

Meredith stepped over and shook her hand.

"Thank you for taking the time to speak with—"

"They wanted to talk to you first," Sean interjected. "Once you're finished, detectives, my office is down the hall."

Tyler was about to sarcastically thank him, but Sean was already out the door.

"He's always like that," Kristi said and motioned for them to have a seat in the two chairs across from her desk. "As you can imagine, things are a little chaotic. Everyone's pretty shook up."

Tyler shrugged. "The people out there don't seem too shook up."

"I know what it looks like, but people who work at companies like this are a different breed. We process things differently. CashFlo needs to keep moving."

"We wanted to start out by asking if there was anything else you remember about the party," Meredith said.

Kristi shook her head. "I've been racking my brain, but nothing comes to mind. I went inside to go to the bathroom, didn't see anything, came back out, led everyone into the backyard, and that's when the nightmare started."

Meredith nodded. "Okay. Then we'd like to ask you some questions about your relationship with James Hammond and your time at CashFlo."

"By all means."

"If you could please start at the beginning and tell us how you came to be here," Meredith said, casting her eyes around the suite.

"Well, once upon a time," Kristi said with a little laugh, attempting to lighten the mood, "I was head of marketing for a company downtown. I was good, but I wanted more. Nick and I became pregnant with Dougie. I quit my job and took the last few months of my pregnancy off, as well as the few months after

122

Dougie was born. The whole time, I knew that I was going to get back into business. Nick was one hundred percent behind me, too. He was still a freelance graphic designer. I had built a reputation at my old job, so we both agreed that I was going to be the best shot at being the family's moneymaker. When I was ready, I put out some feelers, and that's when James found me. He recruited me for CashFlo. When he offered me the job, Nick and I knew it wasn't going to be easy—the hours, the stress—but it was a once-in-a-lifetime opportunity. Nothing was certain, but if CashFlo was a success, with the stock options and bonuses James was offering, it was possible that in ten, fifteen years, I could retire, or at least downshift into a less stressful position when we went public. Nick and I decided to go for it. He continued freelancing, which allowed him to stay at home with Dougie. CashFlo turned out to be a lot more difficult than we had anticipated, which meant the bonuses and stock options weren't paying out, but we were all in. I worked my way up, then Dougie got sick … I couldn't concentrate. Nick couldn't handle it, alone. The business started flagging. I decided that it was best for Dougie and my marriage, and for CashFlo, if I stepped down. James agreed. I became the company director. He brought in Sean. Even with less responsibility, it was a nightmare. Dougie's cancer kept coming back. If I could have quit, I would, but we needed the insurance … I think that's everything up until now."

"What happens to your position in the company now that James Hammond is gone?" Tyler asked.

"Sean is moving up to president and CEO. We haven't made a formal announcement, but everyone assumes it's a given. He's already setting up in James's office. As for me, I'll have to step back up to vice president. It could be temporary, but at this point, it might be easier than the company director role. Sean and I make a decent team. He's a little bit of an automaton, and I'm the one with some compassion."

"Were you aware of anything big on the horizon for CashFlo?" Meredith asked, recalling their conversation with Anna Hewitt.

Kristi's brow creased. "What?"

"James Hammond told someone that something big was about to happen at CashFlo. We were wondering what it was."

Kristi shook her head. "I don't know anything about it."

"Would he have shared that kind of information with you?"

"He damned well should have." Kristi leaned back in her chair. "But I wouldn't put it past him. He liked being in charge. He could be ruthless like that."

"Can you think of any reason why he wouldn't tell you?" Meredith asked.

"Depends on what it was. Do you think it had something to do with his death?"

"We don't know," Tyler said with a shrug.

"What about your personal relationship with James Hammond?" Meredith asked. "How would you describe it?"

"A working one. I wouldn't call us friends. I'm friends with Jessica, but as far as James? We had our jobs to do. I didn't always approve of his conduct, but for me, it was all about what I wanted to build this company into and what I could take out of it."

"What about his conduct did you disapprove of?" Meredith asked.

Kristi hesitated. "It's going to come out, so I'll just tell you; he could be inappropriate with some of the employees. He liked to hit on our younger, attractive staff. He could also be hot-headed if he didn't get his way. Sometimes even cruel."

"Was he ever inappropriate with you?" Tyler asked.

"Early on," Kristi admitted with a sigh. "I stopped him before he even got going. He would ask me to stay late at the office or invite me out for drinks. I told him that I was married. I swear, it made it worse, but eventually, he got the message. I had no more problems with him after that. I was also the one who would rein him in if he was harassing an employee. That could have led to some huge problems. He was an asshole, but CashFlo needed him."

"Why?"

"It was his company. His connections. He was the public face. If James Hammond went, so did CashFlo."

"What about now?"

Kristi measured her words. "This is going to sound incredibly dark, but there's a huge difference between him getting taken down for sexual harassment and him being murdered. If he had been brought down by someone suing him for sexual harassment, he would have taken CashFlo down with him. Him being murdered is different. Sean and I think we can steer CashFlo through something like this. I just feel horrible for Jessica and Dani. I may not have had much love for James, but Jessica has been a great friend to Nick and me."

Chapter 23

Kristi led them out of the office and down the hall to the executive suite. The plaque next to the door still read "James Hammond, President & CEO."

"Come in," was the authoritative reply to Kristi's knock.

It was easily double the size of Kristi's office. Wood-paneling covered the walls, save for the one that was a floor-to-ceiling window and offered an impressive view of the Atlanta skyline in the distance. Sean was sitting behind the desk, talking into the phone. The office was devoid of any personal effects, but there were a couple boxes stacked in the corner with "Hammond" written in black marker on the sides.

"I'll call you back," Sean barely got out before hanging up.

"They're all yours," Kristi said.

"Thanks." Sean stood and walked around the desk, while Kristi closed the door, leaving them alone.

Meredith noted that this would have been the customary time to offer a seat, but the chairs were on the far side of the office, against the wall, as if waiting to be summoned.

Sean leaned back slightly on the desk as he stood and folded his arms across his formidable chest.

Meredith immediately picked up on what he was doing. He

didn't want her and Tyler getting comfortable, in the hopes of bringing the interview to a swift end.

"Moving in pretty quickly," Tyler said with a nod toward the boxes.

"We need people to know that CashFlo is still operating. James will be missed, of course, but pausing to mourn in the business world accomplishes nothing … But I'm making sure those boxes get to Jessica."

"We were wondering if you remembered any additional details from the party," Meredith began.

"I'm sorry, detectives. I haven't been able to recall anything else that might be useful."

"That's fine. Our main purpose in talking to you today was to ask you some more about your relationship with James Hammond."

"Of course," Sean answered, while also making a point to check the time on his watch. "What would you like to know?"

"Can you start at the beginning?"

"Sure. A couple years ago, I was the president of a company called Heliosphere. It was a tech firm with offices in Midtown. When I started, it was a nightmarish mess. I turned it around in six years. James had taken notice and lured me away with an offer of VP of CashFlo."

"President of one company to VP of another?" Tyler asked. "That sounds like a bit of a step down."

"It was, but James offered a lot. Kristi was stepping down from the VP position, and CashFlo was in trouble. James needed me and made it sound like he would make it worth my while."

"Made it *sound* like?" Meredith asked. "What was the reality?"

"The company was in a lot more trouble than James had let on. It had started with a good idea and a solid product, but it had stagnated, and it was all down to James. He was arrogant and unfocused. He was treating this company like a vanity project. I told him all of this before I signed on. He convinced me by saying he would be a figurehead while I ran the company, but when I started, his ego wouldn't let him give up the title. One year in and I was still putting out fires and butting heads with him on almost everything. I've never seen anyone so sure of themselves when the evidence of their incompetence was all around them ... But he did have flare. He had a way of connecting with clients and staff. They fed off his enthusiasm, until he offended them somehow, and Kristi and I had to come in to clean up the mess."

"Such as?"

"It usually happened at some sort of function with a client. James would get a few drinks in him and tell them how poorly they were running their own business, which was incredibly ironic. Occasionally, he would make a pass at someone's wife ... or their daughter. If something like that happened, I'd step in and reassure the client that they would only be dealing with me from that point on to avoid any more unpleasantries."

"This doesn't sound like the deal he offered," Tyler remarked.

"It wasn't."

"So, why stick around this long?"

"For the same reason Kristi has: the opportunity. I made a name for myself with Heliosphere. If I could pull CashFlo out of its James Hammond–inspired tailspin, I could cash in on my stock and write my ticket for whatever I wanted."

"It sounds like James Hammond getting bumped ain't a bad thing for CashFlo or your career prospects. How much is that stock worth?"

"I don't have to answer that question, and I can see where you're going with this, detective."

"I'm making it pretty obvious," Tyler said with a wink.

"And you're correct. I already told you this after the party. It'll be easier to implement the ideas I have for CashFlo with James out of the way, but I'm only acknowledging the reality of CashFlo's situation and doing what's best. Besides, wouldn't it be ridiculous to kill him with such an obvious motive? And why would I put my 'career prospects' at risk like that?"

Tyler didn't have an immediate answer.

Meredith chimed in. "Mr. Winston, are you aware of any major changes that were on the horizon at CashFlo?"

Try as he might, Sean couldn't maintain his icy demeanor.

"I … It's a fast-moving company. There are developments all the time."

"But do you know of something major coming up that James Hammond may have told someone about?"

Sean looked between them. "No … Who did you hear this from?"

Tyler smirked. "We don't have to answer that question."

*

"Yes … We can be there in twenty minutes … Great … See you in a bit." Meredith hung up the phone as they walked back through the plaza toward the parking structure. "That was the ex-Mrs. Mantelli. She says she's got a couple minutes to speak to us, but we need to hustle."

"You really think both Kristi Sanders and Sean Winston had no idea that something big was coming for the company?" Tyler asked as they once again passed through the spot of concentrated sunshine.

"I'm having a hard time buying it, especially after his reaction. But who can we talk to? Who else besides them would know about it if they're not going to admit it?"

Tyler was struck by an idea. "Maybe we can kill two birds with one stone."

"Yeah?"

"We can ask Jessica Hammond if we can see more of her husband's texts. We might be able to see who he was talking to about CashFlo and if he asked anyone about his wife's infidelities."

Meredith gave him a sideways glance.

"What?" Tyler asked.

"You're just full of good ideas, aren't you?"

"I have my moments."

"One day, you might even be a detective."

"Couldn't just let me have that one, could you, Somerset?"

*

Before the doors of the elevator had closed on Meredith and Tyler, Sean was striding quickly back through the main office to the executive hallway. Instead of continuing to his new digs, he stopped at Kristi's door and opened it without bothering to knock.

She looked up from her computer in mild shock.

"What are you doing?" she asked.

"Did you tell them about the Blackstone deal?"

"No. They asked me if I knew about something big coming for the company. I told them no, but I didn't have a chance to warn you."

Sean studied her, trying to decide if she was lying.

Kristi was alarmed. This was the closest she had ever seen Sean Winston to losing it.

"Sean, I didn't say anything about the deal," she said.

"Then how could they possibly know?"

"I have no idea."

He stared at her for a moment longer and then left, not bothering to close the door behind him.

Once back inside his office, he dropped into the chair behind the desk, looked out the window, and steepled his fingers below his chin.

Who could have told them about the deal? There were only a small number of people who knew and one of them was dead. Did he believe Kristi? Maybe. Harold? Would he really be that stupid? Sean had meant it when he told the detective that his motive would be too obvious, but the Blackstone deal getting out would be a huge problem.

It was obvious.

Someone talked.

Someone was trying to throw him under the bus, and that was not something you tried to do to Sean Winston.

Chapter 24

"We appreciate you seeing us on such short notice, Mrs. Mantelli."

"Lochmore, actually. Tammy Lochmore. I haven't gone by my married name in a long time."

"Lochmore. Got it. Sorry," Meredith said, getting out her notebook as she and Tyler sat at the kitchen table.

Tammy Lochmore was short and heavyset with straight chestnut hair, but what struck Meredith the most was her demeanor of resignation, as if Meredith and Tyler walking through her door was somehow sadly inevitable.

"I guess I should have called you before it came to this."

"Why do you say that?" Meredith asked.

She looked at them in confusion. "I … I just assumed that's why you were here. She was acting so weird when she got back from Harold's. I asked her what was wrong, and she said she wasn't supposed to tell."

"Hold on," Meredith said, sitting forward. "Who was acting weird?"

"Our daughter. Cybil. A few weeks ago, after she came back from spending time with Harold, she was acting—"

Tammy froze, as though she had made a horrible miscalculation. Her manner instantly changed, and her defenses went up.

"Mrs. Lochmore, do you believe that Harold did something to your daughter?" Meredith asked.

"I … No. No, of course not," she stammered.

"You just said—"

"No, that's not what I meant."

Tyler appeared just as baffled as Meredith. "Mrs. Lochmore, why do you think—?"

"You contacted me. I thought— … What are you doing here?"

"We wanted to ask you about your ex-husband," Tyler said, trying to be truthful, but noncommittal.

"Let's back up and start at the beginning," Meredith said, trying to sort out the crossed wires. "Can you tell us about your relationship with your ex-husband?"

Tammy tried to wrangle her confusion before answering. "We were a hookup. A mistake. We met at a speed-dating thing. Afterwards, we went on a date … I'll be totally honest; I was lonely and wanted some companionship. We got drunk and had sex. Later, I found out that I was pregnant. I called him to let him know that I wasn't expecting anything from him, but he didn't hesitate. Not for a moment. He said he wanted to be there. We got married and had Cybil. It wasn't ideal, but we tried. He cared for her and for me, but he was just so awkward. I tried. I supported him through the CashFlo thing, but it turned into a disaster. I told him he was being taken advantage of, but he gave away everything. That was the last straw. We agreed to split but that he would still be a part of Cybil's life. That's why it didn't make sense that after all this time, he would do something that made her feel that way."

"Gonna hit pause, here," Tyler said. "Mrs. Lochmore, what do you think Harold did to your daughter?"

"You said you were here because of what he did to Cybil, right?"

"We're here because your husband's former business partner at CashFlo, James Hammond, was murdered," Meredith said.

"… What?"

133

"Someone took a softball bat to his face at a kid's birthday party," Tyler followed up.

Tammy's mouth hung open.

"Now, please, tell us, what do you think Harold did to your daughter?" Meredith asked.

"I— ... Nothing. He's not allowed to say it, but Harold was always upset with James for shutting him out of CashFlo ... You think he killed him?" Tammy asked, incredulously.

"We have multiple suspects," Tyler said. "But Harold is unaccounted for at the time of the murder at the party."

Tammy looked around, uncertain of herself, but suddenly snapped her gaze back to Meredith. "But Harold ... there's no way he could possibly ..."

Meredith leaned in. "One more time, Mrs. Lochmore, what do you think Harold did to your daughter?"

Tammy's posture stiffened. "I don't know what you mean."

Chapter 25

"Hello?"

"Mrs. Hammond? It's Detective Somerset."

"Oh. Hello, detective."

Meredith looked across the desk to Tyler, who was listening in on the call. Jessica Hammond sounded exhausted, which Meredith thought was understandable, given the circumstances.

"I'm sorry to trouble you, again, but Detective Foles and I were wondering if you could do us another small favor."

"What is it?"

"We wanted to look at more of your husband's phone records. We'd like to know who he was talking to, recently."

"I don't understand. What about the number that sent the text?"

"Our assistant DA tracked it down. It's a burner cell phone, and it's going to take a while to find out where it came from. It might be a dead end, and in the meantime, we can start developing other leads."

"Do you think he was talking with the person who killed him?"

"It's possible. The answer might be in your husband's phone records. Would it be all right to take a look at them?"

There was a pause. Tyler and Meredith once again glanced at each other in confusion.

"I'll have to speak to my lawyer, again."

Tyler threw up his hands.

"That's fine," Meredith replied, while sharing in Tyler's frustration. "Please have her get back to us as soon as possible. And if you remember anything else, Mrs. Hammo—"

The line went dead.

Meredith and Tyler hung up their phones.

"I'm not even sure she wants us to find who killed her husband," Tyler said. "What do you think she's hiding?"

"Whatever it is, I hope it's worth it."

*

A naked Jessica Hammond returned her phone to the bedside table, rested her head on the pillow, and stared up at the ceiling.

"What was that about?" an equally naked Nick Sanders asked as he lay beside her, kissing her shoulder.

"They want to look at James's phone records."

He raised his head to look at her. "Why?"

"They think he may have been talking with whoever killed him."

Nick lay back on the bed and joined her in looking at the ceiling. "I thought they already had the number from the text message."

"They do, but it's a disposable phone that might take a while to trace. They want to see all of James's communications."

"Are you going to let them?"

"I should, but it's a joint account and our texts and phone calls are on there, too."

Nick turned to her, draped his arm across her breasts, and held her. "You could tell them it's none of their business."

She pulled away and looked at him. "I still want them to catch whoever killed James."

"Of course," he said, pulling her closer. "I'm sorry, Jess."

She went back to staring at the ceiling.

"What are you going to do?" he asked.

"I'll talk it over with Grace. Maybe I can black out all of my records and let them see only James's." She turned to him, again. "Is that okay?"

"This is your call. Of course, you should help the police catch whoever did this."

"I'm just worried that even if I black out all our calls and texts, James may have mentioned in a text to someone that he had suspicions about us."

Nick thought it over. "Even if he did, it's only suspicion. He didn't have any proof … You're right, though. Letting them see the records is the right thing to do."

Jessica sighed.

He kissed her shoulder, again, but the air in the hotel room had changed. They had had their two hours of blissful fun, forgetting their complicated situation, but now the outside world had intruded, bursting their bubble.

"I need to get back," Nick said. "It's almost time to pick up Dougie."

He got out of bed and dressed while Jessica called her lawyer. Before he left, he interrupted her phone call to grab one last kiss.

I love you, he mouthed.

Love you, too, she mouthed back before returning to her call.

"I'll go over the phone bill tonight, cross out my calls and texts, scan it, and email it to you in the morning, okay, Grace?" Jessica asked as Nick stepped out the door and into the hallway.

Instead of going to the elevator, Nick ducked into the stairwell, went down a flight, and began furiously texting while mumbling, "Shit … shit … *shit* …"

Chapter 26

"So, how are things? How are Allison and Pete and Heather?" Dr. Kaplan asked.

"Allison's acting up a little bit," Meredith replied from the couch across from her in Dr. Kaplan's office. "A few weeks ago, we picked her up at a party where some kids were drinking. She wasn't drinking, but still ..."

"Are you worried about her?"

Meredith chuckled. "Always. I'm trying to teach her how to drive but she's sixteen, headstrong, and getting a little rebellious. That, and she wants to interview me about my work for a podcast she wants to start."

Dr. Kaplans ears pricked up. "Really?"

Part of Meredith felt like she had stumbled into a trap. She wasn't sure if she wanted to talk to Dr. Kaplan about it until she had a better idea of what Allison wanted.

But what else am I here for? Meredith thought.

"Yeah. She wants to do a podcast about, I don't know, homicide detectives, their cases. Some true-crime thing. She wants me to be her guinea pig."

"And you're reluctant?"

"I just … I don't know how I feel about letting her into my work. I'm worried what it might do to her."

"Like what?"

"Like the case I'm working on right now. A guy's face was pulverized with a bat at a kid's birthday party. Technically, I'm not supposed to discuss an ongoing investigation, but I can't think of any case that I'd like to casually discuss with my daughter."

"Is there a way you could discuss things in general?"

"I don't know … and she wants to know about how I became a detective, which means she'll want to know about my sister and the family history. I don't know if I want to share all of that with her."

"Would it make you more comfortable if someone else asked you those types of questions?"

"What do you mean?"

"What if someone else, some other podcaster or whatever, wanted you to tell them about how you became a homicide detective and what it's like. Would you talk to them?"

Meredith thought it over. "Maybe … Yeah, I think so." She looked over and saw Dr. Kaplan's expression. "What?"

"It's interesting that you feel more comfortable telling these things to a complete stranger than your daughter."

Now, Meredith really felt like she had stumbled into a trap.

"I'm not sure Allison's mature enough to hear it," Meredith said. "I mean, it's not like she's a passive observer. It's affected her, too."

"That might be all the more reason to do the interview. Meredith, you know it's not my job to tell you what to do. That's not what these sessions are for. My job is to help you see what's troubling you and your options clearly. Allison is a very intelligent girl. She's also very strong. You and Pete have done a remarkable job in raising her, but she's also been patient in accepting your arrangement in not talking about your past until now. And as you said, she's a part of it, your sister, your parents.

She wants to know more about you, and I think by avoiding the interview, you have to ask yourself: are you protecting her or are you protecting yourself?"

Meredith squirmed and looked down at the floor. "Is this new carpet?"

The joke died somewhere between her and Dr. Kaplan.

Meredith sat back in resignation, knowing that Dr. Kaplan was right.

"I just wish I knew what kind of questions she would be asking, but that kind of defeats the purpose of the interview. I don't like the idea of being her guinea pig."

Dr. Kaplan's eyes lit up behind her delicate spectacles. "Okay. Is there someone else she can interview? Someone who might be more comfortable talking to her about sensitive subjects. You could watch and see how she handles herself and then make a decision."

The answer came to Meredith in a flash and a weight flew from her shoulders. "Yeah," she said with a laugh. "There is someone. I've got someone who is perfect. Oh my God, it's *too* perfect. I can't believe I didn't think of it."

"There you go," Dr. Kaplan said, sharing in Meredith's relief. "Is there anything else you wanted to discuss? Have you had any more instances of seeing Alice?"

"Nope," Meredith lied. "Everything else is good."

Chapter 27

Around the same time Meredith was wrapping up her session with Dr. Kaplan, Sean Winston was experiencing a sensation that was relatively alien to him.

Sean Winston was freaking out.

He was still in his office at CashFlo. He didn't think of it as James's old office. It was the executive office. James had been the executive. Now, Sean was the executive. It was his office, as it should have been long ago.

He had spent the late afternoon and into the early evening working the phones, calling clients and partners to reassure them that while the death of James Hammond had been tragic, CashFlo was in capable hands. Sean had made subtle hints that it was actually in better hands, but ever since the detectives had left, uncertainty and paranoia had begun festering inside him.

They were feelings that were anathema to his entire being. In business, you made a decision and you made it boldly. Even if it turned out to be the wrong decision, you still tried to course-correct without losing face or admitting you were wrong, but this wasn't business. This was new territory altogether.

From the start, he knew that he appeared to be the one who would most immediately profit from James Hammond's death.

There was nothing he could do about that, but now it appeared that someone was leaking the Blackstone deal to make Sean Winston the prime suspect.

But who?

He believed Kristi, even though he didn't entirely trust her. Her husband might be trying to protect his wife by pointing the police away from her, and it made sense with the history between James and Kristi, but if that's what Nick was up to, he would have told her, and there was no way she could hide it from Sean.

A bolt of rage and frustration shot through him, and Sean slammed his fist into the desk.

This was pointless. He knew exactly who had talked.

Harold. Fucking. Mantelli.

The weakling had probably been terrified after being interviewed by the detectives and panicked. It made perfect sense. Of course, Harold would try to point them toward Sean to protect his own skin.

Sean seethed behind the desk. Everyone else at CashFlo was gone for the night. He had been left alone to make his calls, which had only allowed his uncertainty and paranoia to grow. He stared at the boxes of James's belongings in the corner. He was filled with the sudden urge to throw them away. This was his office, his company. James Hammond no longer had a place here. There no longer was a "James Hammond." Sean had gone to unfathomable lengths to get here.

And Harold Mantelli was going to fuck it all up, and not just CashFlo. He was going to fuck up *everything*.

Sean had to get out in front of this. He had to get control of the situation, and most of all, he had to get Harold Mantelli back in line.

Shaking with rage, Sean grabbed his phone and dialed Harold's number.

"Mr. Winston?" Harold answered. His voice was scared and weak, which wasn't out of the ordinary, but it only confirmed Sean's suspicions.

"Harold, what the fuck do you think you're doing?"

"Mr. Winston, I … I don't know what you mean."

"You told the police about the Blackstone deal."

"No! No, I didn't, Mr. Winston. I swear. I didn't tell anyone—"

Sean laughed. "You're such a pathetic liar."

"I swear!" Harold repeated, his voice cracking.

"You listen to me, you little shit. Keep your mouth shut. I know you think you have leverage on me, but if you keep talking and try to save your own ass at my expense, I will fucking deal with you. Do you understand me?"

"Mr. Winston—"

"Do you understand me?!"

"… Yes, but—"

"Good, because you know what I'm capable of, you weak, simpering piece of shit."

Sean hung up and sat back in his chair.

While it felt good in the moment, he immediately recognized that threatening Harold hadn't been the best play. It was emotional, impulsive, and therefore, a sign of weakness.

He had slipped. He had given in to impulse because while he was used to high stakes, he had never been in a situation like this. How could he regain the advantage? The answer was simple. He had to stop thinking of this situation as new. He needed to think of this as a business transaction, a hostile takeover.

How would he go about that?

The first thing he would do is find out everything about the players in the game. *Everything*. It was the only way to see the board clearly, strategize, and start making his moves. He would do it quietly, and once he had everything he needed, he would do what he had always done, the very thing that had defined his success.

He would do whatever was best for Sean Winston.

*

As Harold stared at his phone, something changed inside him.

He had done everything he was supposed to do. He had kept his end of the deal, and now, Mr. Winston was threatening his life. He had seen Mr. Winston upset, but it was always a cold, controlled rage that he would then focus like a laser on whatever had crossed him and then quietly crush it. Harold had never heard Mr. Winston speak like that.

Harold knew that he, himself, was different. He knew that he didn't process emotions like other people. Nor could he interpret social norms and cues like other people, but Mr. Winston had been clear; he had threatened to kill him. Harold had told him the truth. He had done what he was supposed to do, and it didn't matter. Mr. Winston didn't believe him. Harold couldn't persuade him. He was helpless to stop whatever was causing Mr. Winston to suspect him, which led Harold to the only logical conclusion.

No matter what Harold did, Mr. Winston would try to kill him.

Something inside Harold shifted.

For fifty years, he had been pushed around. He had done what other people told him to do because they told him that they were trying to do what was best for everyone, including Harold, only to take advantage of him, and then toss him aside. Harold was great with building things and programming because the answers were simple, straightforward. He understood them. He didn't understand people because people were irrational, unpredictable, and liars.

He was scared, and for the first time, Harold was facing a threat to his life. He had to take Mr. Winston at his word. Other times, Harold would cower and wait for the threat to pass, but his life was now in danger and waiting was not an option.

It was time to start thinking like all the people who had taken advantage of him his whole life.

Harold Mantelli wasn't going to be taken advantage of anymore.

Not by James Hammond.

Not by Sean Winston.

Not by anyone, ever again.

Chapter 28

"So, what is she gonna do?" Kristi asked from the bed to the open door of the bathroom.

"She's going to have her lawyer black out all of our calls and texts and then hand them over to the police," Nick called back through a mouthful of toothpaste.

"Wait. We don't know what's in James's texts."

"Yeah. I know."

"Did you try to stop her?"

"I did, but I didn't want to try too hard."

"Why not?"

There was the sound of spitting and rinsing, and then Nick appeared in the doorway.

"Because I didn't want it to sound like I didn't want her to help the police catch James's killer."

Kristi sighed. "You're right. I'm just worried about Jessica missing something and all of this coming out."

Nick crawled into bed next to her. "She'll be careful. It would be a hell of a lot worse for Jessica than it would be for us." He kissed her lightly on the nape of her neck, sending goosebumps down her arm.

"Dougie's asleep?" she asked, as he began working his way down her body.

"Mmm-hmm …"

"She didn't wear you out, did she?"

"Nope."

"Good."

*

"So, you'll do it?" Meredith asked.

"Sure. You know me. I ain't got no problems sharing my experiences, and it'll give me a chance to hang with Little Somerset."

That was Tyler's nickname for Allison.

"I haven't asked her if you're an okay substitute, but I wanted to know if it was okay with you first."

"Yeah. I'm down," Tyler said, leaning back on his couch, while speaking into his phone.

"Tyler, I really can't thank you enough."

"No sweat, Somerset. Just let me know when, but now, I'm gonna shut it down for the evening."

"Me, too. Jessica Hammond's lawyer should have those phone records for us tomorrow morning."

"Been thinking about those, and I'm more convinced than ever that she's trying to hide the fact that she's bangin' someone on the side."

"Really, Tyler? Bangin'?"

"*Bangin'*."

Meredith lightly laughed. "Good night, Tyler."

"Good night, Somerset."

*

"You were too afraid, so you asked your partner to do it?" Allison asked, annoyed.

"Hey. Watch the tone, okay?"

Meredith had been so excited that when she called Allison to

146

say good night, she immediately led with what she thought was her perfect solution. Allison didn't see it that way.

"I wanted to talk to you, Mom."

"And I'm not saying you won't. I just want to see how it goes. You'll like interviewing Tyler. His stories are way more interesting than mine. You'll be able to—"

Meredith turned in her kitchen and stopped.

She had left the door to the guest room open just a few inches, and now, through the crack, she saw Alice standing there, watching her.

Meredith shut her eyes and took a deep breath.

"Mom? … Are you there?"

Meredith opened her eyes.

Alice was gone.

"Yeah. Yeah, baby. I'm here." She turned away from the guest room and rubbed her eyes. "What do you want me to tell Tyler?"

Allison thought it over. "Tell him okay."

"I'll also tell him you said thank you."

"Yes. And tell him I said thank you."

"Okay. Finish up your homework and start coming up with interview questions."

"I will. Good night, Mom."

"Good night, baby. I love you."

"Love you, too."

*

"Thank you, Grace."

Jessica hung up with her lawyer.

It was done. She had done her best to cooperate with the police to find James's killer while protecting her relationship with Nick.

She looked around the massive bedroom and up into the vaulted ceiling. She stared at James's empty side of the bed before turning off the light and nestling into the soft mattress and pillow under the luxurious sheets, but her eyes stayed open.

She tossed and turned, searching for that perfectly comfortable position, but it wasn't her body that denied rest.

It was her thoughts.

Her guilt.

After a few more attempts to force herself into dreams, she threw off the sheets and swung her feet onto the floor. She stood, placed her feet into her slippers, and went out into the hall.

She stopped outside Dani's bedroom door and quietly pushed it open.

The star-shaped nightlight in the socket near the floor cast a soft glow across Dani's sleeping face. Her hair was fanned out across the pillow.

Jessica felt that swelling in her chest.

Her marriage to James had never been perfect. Toward the end, until she connected with Nick, it was almost unbearable, but she wouldn't trade it for anything, because it had given her Dani.

In addition to the privileged life her marriage had given her, another reason she stuck with it, despite James's demands and hypocrisy, was to protect Dani. If she had tried to divorce James, he would have hurt her as much as possible in any way he could, and she was sure that he would have used Dani to that end. She couldn't imagine what that would do to her.

Jessica once dreamed of all the things James Hammond could provide for Dani. Now, she wanted to protect Dani from the James Hammonds of the world, from those who would rob her of her happiness for their own amusements.

And now, James was gone.

Jessica had to ride this out, and then there was the possibility of happiness at the end of the dark tunnel.

For Dani, and herself.

Chapter 29

The next morning, Harold Mantelli stepped into the Atlanta Exposition North Building and found himself extraordinarily out of place, which was not uncommon in his life.

Unaware of the proper dress code for gun shows, he decided to play it safe and wore a tie and short-sleeved shirt. It was eighty-seven degrees outside, after all. The result was a comical juxtaposition. There was the squat Harold in his shirt and tie that he always knotted too short, surrounded by men with weathered faces, some with beards, and wearing T-shirts with slogans declaring their masculinity, daring you to mock them. Some wore fatigues. Some looked like they were part of a SWAT team.

Harold stood out to the point that more than a few of the other attendees took note of him with an amused grin, but he couldn't care less.

Harold looked around in wonder. Upon the endless tables and booths were guns of every kind. Some dealers dealt specifically in handguns. Every inch of their table or booth was covered in pistols and revolvers with small handwritten tags dangling from the trigger guards describing the gun's make, model, and price. Other dealers only sold shotguns. Others dealt exclusively in antique guns, displaying rifles straight out of a western. Harold wondered if they were real Winchesters. He didn't know if there were other guns in the Old West. "Winchester" was a name he had heard. Some dealers displayed rifles that looked like they belonged in a video game. Their gleaming metal barrels were topped with laser sights. Then there were the dealers who didn't have guns at all, but knives of every kind: cheap folding knives, knives with ornately carved wooden handles, and knives with black carbon blades and serrated backs.

There were even dealers who sold neither guns nor knives, but food rations, radios, and other items to help you prepare for the impending breakdown of society.

To the new, more assertive Harold, it was Disneyland.

His whole life, he had been weak and timid. He shriveled at the first sign of a confrontation, but just being here, surrounded by the firepower and trappings of self-reliance, filled him with a new confidence.

He didn't know where to begin, so he joined the established flow that slowly worked its way around the massive floor, drifting from table to table.

He very quickly established a hierarchy for his interests. He didn't care for the dealers who sold radios, flashlights, and rations. He could appreciate the knives but wasn't sure if he would ever be able to use one effectively. He liked the antique rifles. They were the real deal, and being a fan of history, he was fascinated by the stories they might tell. This one may have been used to hunt wolves on the Oregon Trail. That one might have been hidden under the bar of some saloon in a Nevada silver-mining town. The next step up on Harold's ladder was the tricked-out assault rifles. As someone with a passion for mechanical engineering, he marveled at their design, which was intended to inflict as much damage as possible while also being an aesthetically pleasing work of art.

But the items he was most drawn to were the handguns. They boasted the same beautiful but powerful designs as the assault rifles, but were more practical. He felt that he could quickly become proficient in their use in the shortest amount of time.

After he scouted a few tables, his heart was set on a handgun.

Since most of the tables and stalls dealt in handguns, Harold had an ample selection. Almost too ample. No sooner did he see the gun he thought he wanted when another gleaming barrel on the next table called his name.

"You gonna stare all day or you gonna buy something?" the dealer asked with a sigh after watching Harold fondle one too many of the grips and price tags.

While Harold had felt a swell of confidence upon entering the gun show, he was still Harold, and the slight rebuke caused him to slink away.

Old Harold was back. He was painfully aware of how out of step he was with those around him and noticed their mocking smirks. He was about to turn and walk to the exit and forget the whole thing, until his eyes latched on to a booth halfway across the floor. Instead of being surrounded by tables, it stood alone and contained plexiglass display cases where the overhead lights glinted off the barrels, hammers, and triggers.

Harold was immediately drawn to it.

He cut across the flow of traffic. A few times, a fellow attendant had to alter their course to keep from running into him, but Harold had become oblivious to them.

The closer he got, the more transfixed Harold became. He sidled up to the booth and stared into the case at a gun that held him fast.

The black anodized metal didn't reflect the light like the other guns. It absorbed it, giving it a menacing look. The hammer and the sight at the other end of the barrel looked like horns. The Picatinny rail atop the barrel resembled a spine.

"Good morning, sir," the man working the booth said, snapping Harold out of his trance. He was tall and exceedingly thin with a pointed nose and a bowl haircut. He looked nothing like all the other dealers, which immediately won Harold's approval.

"Good morning," Harold said.

"If you have any questions or want to get a feel for any of them, you let me know," the dealer said.

"Thank you."

Harold was at ease. There had been no push, no hustling. He had received permission to browse.

He continued to stare at the gun, finding more and more to admire.

Harold finally screwed up his courage and turned back to the dealer.

"Can I see that one?" he asked, pointing.

The dealer smiled. "Ah. The Desert Eagle. L5 357." He produced a small key and opened the case. He lifted the gun from its mount and handed it to Harold as if it were a diamond necklace.

Upon feeling the weight in his hands, Harold knew that he had to have it. His fingers curled around the designated grooves on the handle as if it had been tailored to his grip. He couldn't help himself. He raised the gun and aimed, like he had seen people do on television.

"Oh, no, no, no," the dealer said, gently placing his hand on the barrel and slowly pushing it down. "Even though it's empty and the safety is on, I recommend that you don't do that."

"Sorry."

"Quite all right. It is a beautiful weapon."

"It is," Harold agreed, still mesmerized.

"Are you a collector?"

"Um, no. Not really."

"Sportsman?"

"No."

"Enthusiast?" the dealer asked, running out of categories in which to place him.

"I guess so. As of about an hour ago."

The dealer laughed, a real honest laugh, making Harold feel like a million bucks.

"Well, you picked the perfect starter," the dealer said.

Harold inspected the price tag and blanched.

$2,995.00.

"She's worth every penny," the dealer said, noting Harold's reaction. "The first time you fire it at the range, you'll know that it's one of the best purchases you've ever made."

The dealer didn't have to work too hard. Harold was already getting over his shock. This was going to be his gun.

"I'll take it," he said.

The dealer's face split into a wide grin. "Excellent."

Harold handed the gun back and eagerly reached for his wallet.

"Now," the dealer said, producing a packet of paperwork, "I just need your ID for the background check. Once that's cleared, you can come back in a few hours to pick up the firearm."

Harold stopped, his bulging wallet in his hand. He had withdrawn the money earlier that day, hoping to pay cash and leave no trail. He had a healthy suspicion of submitting personal information. Harold felt the most secure when he was unnoticed. He also knew how easy it was for someone to steal your Social Security or credit card number. It had been one of the biggest hurdles in writing the programming for CashFlo.

"A background check?" Harold asked.

"... Yes," the dealer answered awkwardly, confused by Harold's ignorance at such a standard practice. He then noticed Harold's cash-laden wallet. "And we only take credit."

"I, uh, I didn't know that," Harold stammered. A background check meant giving his Social Security number. Credit only? They would take his credit card number. Double whammy. "I thought I could just buy it."

The dealer's face fell at the realization that he was about to lose his biggest sale of the day, but he tried to remain upbeat.

"I know there are a lot of guys here who would take the money, no questions asked, but we're one of the bigger retailers. We do things by the book to keep ourselves out of trouble."

"I understand," Harold said.

The dealer put the gun back in the case.

"Have a good day, sir," he said, locking the case. He was being sincere in wishing Harold a good day, but there was a finality to it that carried a message of "move along."

Once more, a dejected Harold turned to the exit. He could have tried to find a dealer who would take his money, no questions asked, but he didn't want to feel out which ones would play along and which ones would call security.

He would pass a background check. Of course, he would. He just didn't want to register. If things in his life went bad over the next few weeks, it would be too obvious.

Harold was mere steps away from going through the door and back out into the stifling heat when he heard a voice behind him.

"Hey, friend."

Harold turned.

The voice belonged to a man in his forties with long, shaggy hair. He wore a yellow T-shirt and a hat with the Confederate flag.

"Saw what happened back there," he said with a nod toward the booth. "I can help you out. Your money's good with me."

Harold blinked. "I'm-I'm sorry?"

"That Desert Eagle you fell in love with back there? I got one I can sell you. Not as pretty as that one, but it'll do the job if you're okay with an older sister."

Harold nervously looked around. "Do you operate one of the tables?"

The man laughed. "You could say that. Just not one of the tables in here."

"I'm afraid I don't understand."

"What I'm saying is that I can sell you a Desert Eagle, like the one you were just holding, for fifteen hundred. I don't need a signature. I don't need an ID. I don't even need to know your name. Is that something that interests you?"

Harold hesitated but couldn't figure out why. Wasn't this exactly what he was looking for? Well, not entirely. He wanted the transaction to be legal, but that wasn't an option. He didn't like the idea, but he recalled the feeling of power and assuredness at the weight of that black beauty in his hands.

"Yes. I'm interested."

*

The man grabbed the handle and opened the sliding door to the rusted Ford Aerostar extended minivan.

"Step into my office," he said, motioning inside, but Harold paused.

He wasn't sure what he had been expecting this man's "office" to be, but it certainly wasn't the interior of a minivan.

"Look, friend, it's not stylish, I know, but I got what you need, and I don't want people to see us like this. So, hop inside or we'll go our separate ways."

"New Harold," Harold said to himself.

"What?"

Harold climbed into the van.

The man shrugged and followed.

It was sweltering. The seats had been removed so that there was enough space for them to sit on the floor while the rest of the area was filled with a dozen or so Pelican cases with hand-written labels on the side.

Harold sat as the man pulled the sliding door shut.

"Hot as shit in here," the man mumbled as he opened the windows. Then, he clapped his hands. "All right. Let's get you set up. You liked that Desert Eagle, right?"

"Yes."

"Great. Let's see …" He began inspecting the labels on the

cases. "Here we go." He set one on the floor, flipped the latches, and opened the lid.

Inside, nestled into foam cutouts, were four pistols. He extracted one, closed the case, and handed the gun to Harold.

The chrome barrel was scratched and scuffed. The grip was worn, and it didn't have the finger grooves.

The man saw the disappointment in Harold's expression. "Don't get me wrong, I know she ain't as pretty as the prom queen back there, but this is a slightly older model of the same gun. The L5. It's lighter, and other than a little wear and tear, all the bells and whistles are the same, and it'll put any punk in their place if they try to fuck with you."

Harold studied the gun.

It didn't look as menacing, but he felt that same sensation of power and control.

"Same five-inch barrel," the man continued. "Same gas-operated ejection, which lets you use larger slugs. Also, not entirely sure how it happened, but the serial number on this one has been scratched off," he said with a wink.

Just like the guy at the booth, Harold didn't need a sales pitch. This was his gun.

"How much, again?" Harold asked.

"For you, my friend, fifteen hundred."

Old Harold would have eagerly nodded and forked over the cash, but New Harold came to play.

"I'll give you a thousand."

The man cocked his head.

*

Harold held the gun in his hand as he drove home, savoring the weight.

He knew it was dangerous, so he kept it low, out of sight from the cars that passed him.

156

He had gotten what he wanted. Not only that, he had also talked the guy down to twelve hundred and some ammunition to boot.

He liked New Harold. New Harold was going to be different. New Harold was going to get what he wanted.

His grip tightened on the gun.

New Harold wasn't going to be threatened.

Chapter 30

Tyler casually tossed the papers in his hand onto his desk.

"I can't deal with this."

They were printouts of the Hammonds' phone records, sent by Grace Ormond. There were easily two dozen pages, and even though a good portion of the calls and texts had been blacked out, that still left hundreds of calls and texts to sift through.

In addition to discovering what was on the horizon for CashFlo, they had hoped James Hammond's records would tip them off to what Jessica Hammond may have been hiding, but reading his texts, you wouldn't even know he was married. There were no mentions of Jessica or his daughter, save for the sneering texts he had sent to his ex-wife.

Although they weren't able to find out more about Jessica Hammond from her husband's texts, they both agreed that she was still hiding something. Why go through the trouble to black out her own texts? Her lawyer claimed she had done it to help the detectives know which calls and texts came from James's number, but it made no sense. They could have easily figured it out. The only reason to obscure Jessica's records was because she was hiding something. Although it might not be nefarious, it certainly was suspicious. But with nothing else to go on, they had to focus on CashFlo.

"All right," Tyler said. "How do you want to go about this?"

"Let's just start cold-calling."

Tyler groaned. "It's gonna take hours, and we're still not sure what we're looking for is in here."

"Nope. And the sooner we start, the sooner we'll know."

*

It took them an hour to whittle down the phone records to a list of numbers James Hammond had called or texted at least once in the past two months. They had also eliminated the numbers they already knew, such as those of his wife, Kristi Sanders, Sean Winston, and his ex-wife. That still left easily over a hundred numbers they had to sift through.

After the first dozen or so calls, Tyler had his spiel down. He would ask about their relationship with James Hammond while avoiding telling them he had been murdered. Some knew that he was dead. Others, especially the calls that had taken place further in the past, didn't.

The worst were the calls that were answered by a journalist. James Hammond was by no means a celebrity, so these were D-list reporters who had interviewed him for some puff pieces. When Tyler identified himself as a detective with the Cobb County Police Department, the reporters would do everything they could to keep him on the line, but Tyler knew better and simply hung up. They could find out he was murdered on their own. If they considered themselves journalists and weren't aware of that information by now, they could stay on the D-list.

There were also the handful of women James Hammond had given his number to by way of drunken text. They were the easiest. As soon as they voiced their frustration that James Hammond hadn't texted them back, Tyler hung up. Piece of cake.

Meredith wasn't having any better luck, but she was much better at handling people than Tyler.

After three hours, Tyler was going through the motions while still dutifully writing down the information. Each call had him more convinced that the whole exercise was a wild, but reluctantly necessary, goose chase.

Tyler moved on to the next number and dialed. He was resting his chin in his hand when the phone was answered.

"Who is this?" the terse voice of an older man asked.

"Hello. My name is Tyler Foles. I'm a detective with the Cobb County Police Department. How are you doing today?"

"What do you want?"

"I was wondering if you knew a man named James Hammond."

The line suddenly went dead. Tyler briefly stared at the phone in confusion. Then, he sat up and got Meredith's attention as he hit redial. Meredith ended her call and watched.

Tyler waited as the line rang. There was a click, and the ringing stopped. Tyler could hear breathing.

"… Sir? Are you there?" Tyler asked.

"This is my private line. How did you get this number?"

"We found your number in James Hammond's phone records. I'm not sure if you were aware but he was murdered, and I'm assuming that you didn't hear me when I said that I was a detective with the Cobb County Police Department or you wouldn't have hung up on me."

"… I'm sorry, detective. I was startled when you asked about James Hammond. Yes, I'm aware that he's dead."

"May I ask whom I'm speaking with?"

"My name is Raymond Savita."

"And how did you know James Hammond?"

Again, there was a long silence.

"Is that relevant?" Raymond asked.

"That's what we're trying to find out."

"Mr. Hammond and I discussed some business matters."

"And can I ask what you do for a living, Mr. Savita?"

"I'm the president of a company called Blackstone."

"And what sort of business is Blackstone?"

"We're a software engineering company that specializes in point-of-sale systems."

Tyler began typing on his computer, searching for "Blackstone."

"Cool. Cool. Listen, Mr. Savita, my partner and I need to come talk to you at your earliest convenience."

"I really don't have a convenience."

"Then we're just gonna drop by."

"No. No, it's fine, detective," Raymond said, folding like a card table. "Are you available this afternoon? I'd like to clear this up as soon as possible."

"No problem. I'm looking at your website, right now. Are your offices still on Peachtree Plaza?"

"Yes."

"What time works for you?"

"As I said, I'd like to have this cleared up as quickly as possible."

"We can be there in thirty minutes."

"That will be fine."

"Thank you, Mr. Savita." Tyler hung up and looked at Meredith. "See? I knew we'd find something."

Meredith rolled her eyes.

*

Raymond Savita put down the phone and rubbed his liver-spotted scalp, a nervous tic that he performed when he was uncomfortable and didn't know what to do.

He needed to think and only had a short time to do it. He hadn't done anything wrong. He wasn't the one who had taken a softball bat to James Hammond's face, but if word of the deal they were about to execute got out under these circumstances, it would be a public relations black eye for Blackstone.

Still, he wanted the deal to happen.

He quickly had to come up with a strategy. Raymond Savita

161

knew that he was too old for the game, and this business with CashFlo had become one more situation that he couldn't navigate, another mess his old style of thinking couldn't grasp. Not that he would ever admit it, but he needed help.

Not help, he corrected himself.

Raymond Savita never needed help. He needed "perspective."

He lifted the phone on his desk and punched a button.

"Yes, Mr. Savita?"

"Get in here," he said and hung up.

A few moments later, there was a knock on his door.

"I said get in here," he spat.

The door opened, and a man with a nest of coppery hair stepped in.

"Graham," Raymond began, "James Hammond, the president of CashFlo, was killed a few days ago."

"What? I had no idea," Graham lied.

"The police are heading over very shortly to ask some questions. I already know what I want to say, but I wanted your input."

"What are you planning to tell them?" Graham asked.

Raymond expelled a wheezy breath through his nostrils. "I just told you, I know what I'm going to say, but I thought it would be a good learning experience to hear your thoughts."

"I think, at this point, that honesty is the best policy," Graham offered.

Raymond shook his head. "No. That would ruin the deal with CashFlo. We can still salvage it."

"Mr. Savita, with James Hammond dead, the deal with CashFlo is off, or at the very least delayed, and in the meantime, it will get out, which will be a whole other problem."

"Can they do that?" Raymond asked. "Can the police disclose that type of stuff?"

"I'm not a legal expert, but it'll definitely get out. That's why I think you should come clean. It'll protect Blackstone."

Raymond nodded. "Yes. That's exactly what I was going to do."

"Do you want me to sit in when the police arrive?"

"Yes. I think it would be a further learning experience to see how to handle these types of situations. I'll have Erin in here, too."

"Very good, Mr. Savita," Graham said as he stood, and walked out of the office.

*

None of the employees who passed Graham as he walked back to his office would have known that he was frustrated and tired.

After so many years of working with Raymond, Graham was a master at hiding his annoyance with the only person who was higher on the ladder of Blackstone. Raymond was a dinosaur who long ago had lost the ability to understand the business he was in. Technology was developing rapidly, and he was still in awe when it came to the internet. That's why he had leaped at the chance to acquire CashFlo from James Hammond with no real plan of how to fold it into Blackstone, and Graham knew it.

Raymond tried to hide his indecisiveness with bluster and bravado, but Graham saw right through it, like a poker player reading an opponent's obvious tell.

It was fine. He could handle Raymond Savita. Graham was the real driving force behind Blackstone. He only had to wait for Raymond Sativa to die, and then he would publicly take the helm that he had been guiding behind the scenes for the past few years. He was ready. He had no problem rafting the treacherous rapids of the business world, as he was about to demonstrate with a phone call that he knew would send someone over the edge.

*

"I only want to reassure you that CashFlo is moving forward," Sean Winston said over his roasted pepper chicken salad to the client as they sat on the patio of Soirée, one of the swankiest restaurants in Midtown.

His phone, sitting on the table, began to vibrate. Sean's face hardened when he saw the number on the caller ID.

"I'm sorry," he said. "Excuse me for just a second."

The client, who was on the fence about his company's continued business with CashFlo, nodded.

Sean smiled, picked up the phone, left the table, and headed toward the short hallway at the back of the restaurant.

He hit answer as he neared the door marked "Gents."

"Are you out of your goddamn mind?" he asked, shoving open the door and entering the restroom. "I told you never to contact me again."

"I just thought you'd like to know that the police are on their way here to talk to Mr. Savita about his business dealings with James Hammond."

Sean froze next to the sink. "What?"

"Oh. Do you need me to repeat myself?" Graham asked.

"How did they find out about Blackstone?"

"I have no idea, and I honestly don't care. It doesn't matter to me."

Sean hung up.

It did indeed matter. It mattered to Sean Winston, because yesterday, the police didn't know the name of Blackstone. Now, they did, and there was only one way that could have happened.

Harold. Fucking. Mantelli.

Chapter 31

"Detectives. Welcome to Blackstone."

Meredith and Tyler shook hands with Raymond as well as the vice president, Graham Donovan, and Raymond's assistant, a young woman named Erin.

Blackstone occupied the top several floors of a building in downtown, and Raymond Savita's office dwarfed anything Meredith and Tyler had seen at CashFlo. There were couches, chairs, a wet bar, and two walls of floor-to-ceiling windows.

Erin had met them in the lobby and gave them the introductory speech on the elevator ride up. Mr. Savita had started Blackstone in the 1980s as Savita Industries. He began by designing cash registers and then moved into credit card technologies, and finally into online retail POS systems as the internet took off in the late nineties. In the early aughts, he changed the name to Blackstone to better fit in with the bold, striking one-word business names of the time. Meredith and Tyler dutifully listened as she rattled off statistics, the number of employees, daily transactions, and revenue before exiting the elevator and entering the suite.

"I understand you have some questions about my communications with James Hammond," Raymond said as they all settled into the couches and chairs.

"Yes," Meredith began. "As you know, James Hammond was murdered last Sunday. We were able to obtain his phone records for the past few months and saw that he called you on several occasions."

"Yes. We spoke."

"Could you tell us about those conversations?"

"Am I under any legal obligation to do so?"

"No, but we would take note of your help instead of making us get a warrant."

"It's just that it's a privileged matter, and I don't see how it could be relevant to your investigation."

"We'd like to be the judge of that," Tyler said.

Raymond rubbed his scalp. "Can we count on your discretion?"

"Absolutely," Meredith assured him.

Raymond still couldn't help himself and turned to Graham, who nodded.

"Very well," Raymond said. "James Hammond came to me a few months ago. I knew who he was, and I knew CashFlo. I had had my eye on it for a while. He asked me if I was interested in purchasing the company."

"And were you?" Meredith asked, trying to mask her surprise.

"Of course. CashFlo was a mess, thanks to James, but they had a good product and that's what I wanted. We have plenty of programmers here at Blackstone who could take over the property. I told him all of this, that we wanted the product but not the company, and he was fine with that. We decided to be as quiet as possible because it wasn't going to be the prettiest of purchases."

"What do you mean by that?"

"We didn't need the CashFlo team."

Tyler leaned forward. "So, what would happen to the employees at CashFlo after you purchased the company?"

"I ... well ... I'm not sure if I sho—"

Graham finally spoke up. "That was going to be James Hammond's problem. Not ours."

Meredith looked between Raymond and Graham. "So, every employee at CashFlo was going to be left out in the cold?"

"Again, that would have been James Hammond's problem," Graham reiterated.

"How close were you on the deal?"

"A few more weeks would have sealed it," Graham continued, since Raymond was still rubbing his scalp in uncertainty. "James Hammond was in the process of getting the financials together, but he had to be hush-hush about it or he would have had a revolt on his hands."

"But the CashFlo employees would have benefited from the buyout, even if they didn't approve of it, right?" Meredith asked.

Raymond's expression soured. "They were promised stocks when the company went public, but it wasn't public, yet. James Hammond controlled virtually everything, since it was still a private company, so … he … well—"

Graham appeared tired of his boss's wavering and once again stepped in.

"James Hammond wasn't planning on compensating any of his employees at CashFlo. He was going to pocket all the money from the deal. At least, that's what he told us one night after we set up the preliminaries and he had drunk half a bottle of scotch. I believe his words regarding the employees at CashFlo was 'fuck 'em.'"

"Graham, please," Raymond said, finally taking his hand away from his scalp. "Let the dead rest in peace."

Chapter 32

"My money is now squarely on Mr. Sean Winston," Tyler said, collecting the ammo and earphones from the rangemaster behind the counter.

Even though they were deep in the Cobb County Public Safety Police Academy, which held the indoor firing range, the thunder from the storm raging outside still shook the cinderblock walls. Meredith and Tyler had just beaten the storm inside and hoped it would end the ridiculous heat.

"I'm still leaning toward Harold Mantelli," Meredith said, ready to enter the firing range.

"How can you say that after what we just heard? James Hammond was about to royally screw over everyone at CashFlo, and I don't buy for one second that Sean Winston had no idea it was coming. So, he stopped him the only way he could think of. I ain't sayin' Mantelli's clean. His wife definitely thinks he did something to his daughter, and she's trying to point the finger at him for Hammond's death, because, I don't know, maybe she wants her ex-husband to go away, but she doesn't want to subject their daughter to a police investigation. Mantelli might have some pervy dirt under his nails, but I don't think he could pulverize Hammond's face."

"Okay, but doesn't your reasoning also apply to Kristi Sanders, as well? Wouldn't she know about the Blackstone deal?" Meredith asked as they walked to the plexiglass door leading to the range. She held it open for Tyler as they entered.

They were the only ones there, meaning their conversation wasn't drowned out by constant gunfire as they made their way down the stalls.

"Sure, but Sean Winston benefits the most. He gets bumped up to president and takes the deal for himself."

"You really think he'd be that obvious?" Meredith asked as they took their positions in side-by-side stalls.

Tyler shrugged. "Sounds like there was a lot of money up for grabs. Maybe he's trying to pull some reverse psychology on us. Besides, why are you still leaning toward Mantelli? He's not even a part of CashFlo anymore. The sale wouldn't affect him."

"Maybe it does," Meredith said. "Maybe it was a last straw for him. Hammond stole his idea and screwed him over by forcing him out of the company, and maybe Mantelli felt that Hammond was screwing him over again by selling the company to Blackstone."

"My theory is less of a stretch," Tyler said, clipping his paper target onto the wire overhead. He turned the dial to send it down-range.

Meredith did the same but was struck by an idea.

"What if it was both of them?"

"What are you talking about?"

"They said that they were both in the garage, having a drink. They're each other's alibis. What if they killed him together and agreed to vouch for each other?"

"I like that, but it's hard to see them working as a team. Sean Winston doesn't seem to have much patience for Harold Mantelli."

Another rumble of thunder rattled the building.

"It could be an act."

"How do we find out?"

169

"We keep the pressure on them. It's all we can do. You ready?"

"Ready," Tyler answered.

They took aim at their respective targets and began firing, warming up for their biweekly competition. Once they had fired a few rounds, they would each fire three shots at a target twenty feet away. They had thirty seconds from their first shot to complete their turn. The loser bought drinks afterwards, which meant Tyler was normally the one picking up the tab, although Meredith had to admit that he was getting better.

After a few dozen shots apiece, Tyler turned the dial to reel in the spent paper target.

"Let's do this," he said enthusiastically over the headphones and seemingly continuous thunder.

Meredith nodded.

They took down the bullet-ridden targets and replaced them with new ones. They turned their dials to twenty feet. The two targets zipped away from them and came to a stop, side by side.

"Ladies first," Tyler said, motioning to the targets.

"I think you mean winner from last time goes first."

"Yeah, yeah, yeah."

Meredith set her feet and calmly raised her Sig Sauer. She sighted down the barrel and slowly squeezed the trigger. The gun kicked. The paper target twitched, but the bullet had passed through two inches to the right of the bullseye. Meredith steadied herself, again.

"Twenty seconds left," Tyler called out.

"Shut up," Meredith replied, good-naturedly.

She fired again, but had overcompensated to the left, a rare miscalculation on her part. She shook out her shoulders a little, raised the gun, aimed, exhaled, and slowly pulled the trigger. Just as she was about to reach the breaking point, a booming crack of thunder swept through the building, startling her and causing the lights to flicker. The gun fired, but she had been thrown off and the hole created by the bullet was easily five inches above the bullseye.

"Damn," she hissed. "I should get one more shot."

"Absolutely not. It'll be nice having you pick up the tab for a change." Tyler set himself up to fire. "Get ready to start timing."

"Fine," Meredith huffed.

Tyler braced himself, aimed, and fired. His first shot had gone south of the bullseye by a few inches. He grunted and set up, again, but as he was aiming, the lights blinked and went out, which was immediately followed by a deafening concussion of thunder. Lightning had to have hit the building.

"Holy shit ..." Tyler said.

A weak light kicked on overhead, powered by the building's backup generator and the rangemaster's voice called out, "Hold fire!"

"Twenty seconds ..." Meredith said.

"What?"

"Eighteen ..."

Tyler looked down-range. The dim light overhead allowed them to barely see each other, but the target was wrapped in darkness.

"This is bullshit, Somerset."

"Sixteen ..."

"Somerset, I can't see the target ..."

"Fifteen ..."

Tyler stared at her as she continued to count. Even in the dimness, he could see the smile on her face. He turned and stared down-range into the blackness.

"Ten ... nine ... eight ..."

Meredith was relishing the fact that Tyler was going to be cheated out of victory, but suddenly, Tyler raised his weapon, aimed, and fired.

The muzzle flash illuminated just far enough to see the outline of the target. There was a brief pause as Tyler adjusted his aim, and fired, again.

"Hold fire, goddammit!" the rangemaster raged.

They waited, Meredith's jaw hanging open in disbelief.

The lights kicked on.

The rangemaster came barreling through the plexiglass door. His face was burning red, and a vein throbbed in his forehead.

"Who fired those shots?!" he demanded.

Tyler put up his hands. "That was my bad, man. I was kind of already in the process, you know?"

"Those shots came way after I called 'hold fire' and there were two of them!"

"Yeah," Tyler said, looking at his gun. "This thing's got a hair trigger."

"Very funny, asshole. You can be cute all you want, but I'm reporting this to your superior."

"I'm sorry, man. Really, I am."

The rangemaster turned and stormed off.

"You're busted," Meredith said as Tyler retrieved his target.

"I was hoping to use the muzzle flash to see the target."

"How'd that work out for you?" Meredith asked, mockingly.

"It was too far away. You win, Somerset," Tyler said, ripping the paper target in half, "but I'm only buying the cheap stuff."

Chapter 33

Meredith slashed her hands through the muggy air. Water had seeped through her shoes and socks from the puddles she had encountered on her nightly jog. The hopes that the evening's cloudburst would bring an end to the heatwave had been dashed. The air was still thick, and the heat had only lessened a few degrees. Now, the moisture in her shoes only added to the buckets of sweat that were pouring out of her.

The night sky was still a blanket of low-hanging clouds that reflected the lights of the city. A strobe of heat lightning occasionally flashed above. The storm had driven everyone inside to wait for tomorrow, and Meredith was left alone with her thoughts as her shoes slapped the pavement.

She and Tyler had continued to go back and forth over her victory beers. She had to admit that Tyler's theory that Sean Winston was their guy made more sense. In fact, it didn't just make more sense, it was painfully obvious. Meredith couldn't articulate why she still suspected Harold so strongly. Maybe it was his ex-wife's suspicions. Maybe it was Harold's past with James Hammond. Maybe it was his demeanor she couldn't get around.

Was Harold Mantelli capable of doing that to James Hammond? she wondered as she rounded the corner onto her street.

She believed that he could conceive the plan. Despite his awkwardness, Harold Mantelli was intelligent, a problem-solving engineer. Nearly everyone had at some point wanted to kill someone and wondered how they would do it, but it normally stayed in the abstract. She had more difficulty believing that he would go through with it. Harold was weak, submissive. He did what he was told. He didn't act on i—

Meredith abruptly stopped and turned back to look down the street, forgetting Harold Mantelli, Sean Winston, Kristi Sanders, or anything else that had to do with James Hammond.

She had seen something, something out of place. She couldn't put her finger on it, but she was certain. It was instinct, subliminal.

Every one of her senses was heightened. The smell of wet pavement filled her nostrils. She cast her eyes up and down the endless line of cars parked by the curb. She peered into every windshield and into the windows of the surrounding buildings. She strained to hear any footsteps in the humid stillness. The only sound was that of distant cars.

She remained motionless, searching for whatever had triggered the sensation, but the street was quiet and still.

Finally, she walked the remaining twenty yards to the pathway leading to her apartment.

Meredith's new neighbor, Mildred Johnson, was out on her porch, smoking a clove cigarette.

Mildred was in her seventies and had recently moved from Maine. In addition to her clove cigarettes, she enjoyed her scotch, coffee, and gossip, and was constantly trying to feed Meredith or set her up on a date.

"Good evening, Mrs. Johnson," Meredith said with a smile.

"Evenin', Meredith, and please, call me Mildred," she said, exhaling a plume of purplish smoke. "You need to rehydrate? Want some scotch?"

Meredith laughed. "No. Thank you."

"Your loss," Mildred said. "Knock on my door if you want a nightcap."

"I will."

Opening the door to her apartment, Meredith was greeted by a blast of cool air. She stepped over to the sink, poured herself a glass of water, and greedily chugged it. She looked down to see that her soaked shoes had left a trail from the door. She quickly slid them off, along with her socks, which did nothing other than allow her wet feet to leave more defined footprints. Beads of sweat were also falling from her arms and hair.

Just get to the shower, she told herself.

She started going for the bathroom but stopped. Something was pulling her toward the guest room. Meredith slowly pushed open the door and stepped inside.

Alice was standing by the window, her was back to Meredith and her arms hung at her side. She was peering out toward the street through the small space between the blinds.

Meredith silently crossed the room and stood behind her, trying to see what she was looking at, but the street appeared unchanged from moments ago.

"He's here," Alice whispered.

Chapter 34

Meredith didn't bother bringing the mug over to the table, sitting down, and taking her time. As soon as she poured the insanely strong brew into her cup, she brought it to her lips. It was acrid, bitter, and scalding hot, but Meredith needed that hit of caffeine.

It had been a sleepless night.

She hadn't stayed long in the guest room, but her thoughts had remained there until the sun came up. She knew she wasn't really seeing or hearing the ghost of Alice. It was her own subconscious talking to her, a darkness within. It wasn't healthy, she was perfectly aware of that, but the irony of ironies was that Meredith knew the only way to eradicate it was to find the person who had sent her Alice's bathing suit, and the only way to do that was to indulge the darkness.

She took another sip of coffee and bit off the corner of a slice of dry toast from the plate by the coffee pot. She turned to the closed door of the guest room as she chewed.

If she could keep Alice in that room, Meredith believed she would be okay, that she had control, but the paranoia of last night wouldn't go away.

She had seen something on her street. A shadow? A face? She couldn't pin it down, and it had been eating away at her all night.

Alice may not have really been in that room, but whoever had taken her really was out there, somewhere.

*

The distractedness and paranoia followed Meredith to work. Even Tyler picked up on her demeanor as they sifted through the last of the numbers on James Hammond's call log. They were certain that they had their winner in Blackstone, but wanted to be thorough.

Tyler finished calling the last number on his list, which turned out to be a woman James Hammond had met at a bar in Miami. Once he hung up, he looked over to see Meredith staring down at her desk, her mind a million miles away.

"Somerset?"

She neither moved nor blinked.

"Yo, Somerset?"

Meredith inhaled sharply as she was brought back to reality.

"Hi. Welcome back," Tyler said. "What's goin' on?"

"Nothing."

"Bullshit."

"It's nothing."

"There's an 'it's,' which means it's something."

"I'm fine," she snapped, causing Tyler to lean back.

"Cool," Tyler said. "Let me pick my skull off the ground from where you bit it off, just there."

Meredith normally would have rolled with Tyler's jokes, but she was sleep deprived. Her blood flash-boiled, and she was about to snap, again, when Sergeant Wheaton poked his head out of his office.

"Got Kelly Yamara on the line for you two," he said.

Meredith and Tyler stood and followed him into the office.

"Okay," Sergeant Wheaton said into the speakerphone as he rounded the desk to his chair. "They're here, Kelly."

"Detectives?" Kelly asked.

177

"Yes?" Meredith answered.

"How much do you love me?"

They both looked at Sergeant Wheaton, who smiled.

"I don't know," Tyler said. "I have a feeling it depends on what you're about to tell us."

"I've got some info on the burner phone used to text James Hammond."

"You found who it belonged to?" Meredith asked.

"No, but I did a little bit of detective work myself. It was easy to find the service provider from the number. Burner phone manufacturers usually have deals with service providers. The service provider is a company called NexTalk. They have a deal with a burner phone manufacturer called Zing in Seattle. The SIM card and the phone were shipped as a bundle. Zing were able to track it down because the number in the SIM card and the phone were listed under the same UPC code in Zing's inventory."

"Wait," Meredith said. "They were okay with telling you all of this?"

"Not at first, but I told them if they didn't, then we'd go the warrant-subpoena route. I didn't tell them that I'd be on shaky ground, but both NexTalk and Zing are fairly small companies that didn't want the headache and decided to kick the can down the road to the vendor who sold the phone. We might run into trouble if the vendor is stubborn or if they sold it to someone who then sold it to someone else, but it's a start."

"Is the vendor in Atlanta?"

"Yep. The phone was sent to a shop in Alpharetta called Cellular Depot."

"That is outstanding work," Meredith said. "Thank you, Kelly."

"My pleasure, detectives."

"And Kelly?" Tyler asked.

"Yes?"

"We love you very much."

Chapter 35

Thad Harris was nursing one hell of a hangover.

The four Advil he had popped on the drive to his office had barely made a dent. Sitting behind his battered wooden desk, he rubbed his eyes, opened a drawer, and took out two more aspirin from the reserves he kept on hand. He hadn't been at a bachelor party or a ball game. It had been a standard evening of polishing off the better part of a bottle of Jack while watching television. He placed the pills on his tongue and stared at the guns and photos on the wall as he worked up some spit to swallow the pills.

The lights were off, and the thick walls slightly muffled the sound of gunfire. It was only a footnote to his pulse, which rhythmically hammered against his temples.

His gaze rested on the framed photo sitting on his desk. Thad's own eyes stared back, but they were filled with the excitement and pride of youth. His crisp military dress uniform accentuated his toned nineteen-year-old frame.

A long time ago, Thad thought as he scratched his gut.

There was an unwelcomed knock on the door, and Josh Demato, the young guy who worked the front desk at the firing range, opened it. The sound of gunfire became louder.

"Thad?"

"Yeah?"

"They're waiting for you."

Thad acknowledged him with a grunt, and Josh exited.

Thad stood with a groan.

Time to pay the bills.

His gun safety course was a way to educate people so they wouldn't do something stupid, like accidentally shoot themselves or leave their gun out for the kids to find, but it was also a prerequisite for anyone wanting to use the firing range. Not everyone needed it. He had customers who were ex-military or current police who knew what they were doing. The Line of Fire Indoor Range brought in all types. It was even neutral ground for cops and gang members. Thad had seen seasoned police officers have friendly marksmanship competitions with a guy sporting colors in the stall next to him. The safety courses were for the weekend warriors, the soccer moms, the wannabes, and the gun-curious. They all paid the two-hundred-dollar registration fee, and everyone's money was the same color. Thad taught the class three times a week, and the revenue generated by the classes rivaled that of the firing range itself.

Thad stepped out of the office and walked past the front desk, behind which was a wall of bulletproof plexiglass offering a view of the firing range. Even at that early hour, nearly half the stalls were occupied by men and women, young and old, short and tall, firing at paper targets. The bullets tore through the paper and buried themselves in the mound of shredded rubber that reached to the ceiling behind the targets. He had purchased the rubber from a manufacturing plant that had gone under and sold him their old conveyor belts.

Thad stopped in front of the door marked "Class in Progress."

No, it wasn't. Not until he got in there.

He took a breath and opened it.

The room was laid out like a high school classroom with rows of plastic chairs with small desk attachments. Nearly every seat was filled. The thought of each one as a couple hundred bucks helped distract Thad from the sour taste in his mouth.

There were the usuals: the people who were there to get it over with and spent most of the class on their phones. There were others who would be polite and listen to his instructions, maybe ask a question or two. But today Thad was immediately drawn to the guy sitting dead-center in the front row, crammed behind the desk, which struggled to contain him. He couldn't be comfortable, but the guy didn't seem to mind. He had a spiral notebook open on the desk in front of him and a pen in his hand, ready to go. A gun case rested on the floor by his feet.

Thad mumbled a "good morning" and got a few replies in return. Thankfully, his hangover-induced gruffness added to his hardened ex-Marine persona. He had taught this class so many times, he was already slipping into autopilot.

Thad took a clipboard from the desk at the head of the room and did a roll call.

Each name was answered with a "here" or a raised hand.

"Harold Mantelli?"

The hand of the guy in the front row shot up.

"Present, Mr. Harris."

*

Thad had worried that this Mantelli guy was going to be an over-eager pain in the ass, but by the end of the course, he had changed his mind. He was a little enthusiastic, but he was respectful, inquisitive, and appeared to have a genuine interest in his instructions.

At the very least, he had made the three-hour class go much faster. He took notes and asked questions. It was a little much when he clapped at the end, but it was entertaining.

Once the class was over, all the attendees were welcome to rent a gun from the front desk if they didn't already have one, purchase some ammunition and paper targets at ridiculous markups, and try their hand on the firing range. Some people saved it for another day after sitting through the three hours of tutorials, but not Harold.

He grabbed his gun case and walked straight from the classroom to the front desk, purchased fifty rounds of .357 ammo from Josh, along with four paper targets, and rented a set of noise-reducing headphones.

Thad could have gone back to his office, closed the door, and sat through the rest of his fading-but-still-formidable hangover, but there was something about this Harold Mantelli. Out of curiosity, Thad wanted to see how well his instructions settled in with someone who was really paying attention.

Harold carried his case, ammo, targets, and headphones through the door and into the firing range. His grin threatened to burst. Now that it was later in the day, the stalls were almost full. The only one that was unoccupied was the last stall against the wall. Harold eagerly made his way past the other shooters.

Thad and Josh watched him through the plexiglass wall. Josh gave Thad a slightly worried side-eye.

The stall next to the wall was not where you wanted a first-time shooter to be. One errant shot could ricochet off the wall. They had seen it happen, and even though everything was designed to keep bullets going down-range, a ricochet was still bad news.

It was when Harold opened his case and Thad saw the Desert Eagle that he began to really worry. That wasn't a beginner's gun. Thad grew more worried as he watched Harold load the clip with such eagerness, he dropped two bullets.

Josh made a move to go to the door.

"I got this," Thad said and went around him.

He normally would let Josh handle it, but he wasn't sure about Harold Mantelli. Sometimes the most well-meaning, enthusiastic amateurs were the ones who had the worst accidents, and Harold Mantelli, despite being affable, seemed a little off. Thad felt that he had a rapport going with Harold from the safety class and worried that Josh could set him off.

Thad grabbed a set of headphones and put them on before entering the range.

He made his way down to the last stall, where Harold had finished loading his clip and inserted it into the Desert Eagle.

Harold set the gun down on the shelf in front of him, safety on, and barrel pointed down-range, just as Thad had taught him. Harold clipped his target to the wire overhead and pressed the button on the shelf, sending the target toward the mountain of shredded rubber at the back of the room.

As Harold reached for his gun, he must have sensed Thad standing behind him because he turned and smiled.

Thad wanted him to remain calm and confident and gave him a thumbs-up. Despite those two bullets he had dropped while loading the clip, he had done everything else by the book.

Harold turned back toward the range, picked up his gun, and checked his feet: left foot forward, just as Thad had demonstrated. Thad thought it was a little too forward, but not disastrously so. Harold centered himself, raised the gun, positioned his shoulders, stared down at the target, and squeezed the trigger.

Nothing.

He tried again, squeezing harder.

Still nothing.

He looked at the gun and saw he had forgotten to disengage the safety.

Harold looked over his shoulder at Thad and sheepishly smiled.

"Believe me," Thad shouted over the gunfire. "That's one mistake I'm okay with you making."

Harold was embarrassed but grateful for the support. He looked back toward the target, aimed, thumbed off the safety, and slowly pulled the trigger.

It took so long, Thad wondered if he was okay, but he wasn't going to interrupt someone aiming a loaded weapon.

Suddenly, the Desert Eagle roared.

Harold was barely able to control the recoil, but his feet remained planted. He blinked, caught his breath, and stared at the target, which was wholly intact.

A total miss.

Thad wasn't entirely surprised. His form was fine, but that gun was not right for a novice.

Undaunted, Harold set up, again.

He aimed and squeezed.

The gun fired. Harold was more prepared and had braced himself. He looked down at the target.

Still intact.

Harold couldn't hide his frustration.

Thad stepped over to him before he aimed, again.

"Harold? Right?"

Harold nodded.

"You're looking good but let me help you." Thad gently kicked at Harold's shoes. "Let's close up those feet a little."

Harold allowed Thad to pose him like a doll, all the while keeping the gun pointed toward the target.

"Turn your shoulders a bit. Relax, but not too much. What's happening is that when you're slowly pulling that trigger, you're tensing up, anticipating the kickback, and it's causing the barrel to rise. Don't think of the shot starting and ending when you pull the trigger. It starts when you aim. The shot is already beginning, and you're using your whole body. You're focusing the energy of the gun toward the target. See the shot. Take your time and don't tense up when you pull the trigger. It's only the end of the process, okay?"

Harold nodded.

"You got this," Thad said, stepping back. "Go again."

Thad watched as Harold prepared to fire again. He thought he could already see the difference as Harold aimed down the barrel. He appeared more focused and steady.

Harold's finger coiled around the trigger, and he slowly began to apply the pressure …

BAM!

Harold's arms and shoulders absorbed the recoil, and it dissipated throughout his body.

Harold blinked and looked down-range.

"There you go!" Thad called out.

Harold squinted.

There was a hole in the target six inches off-center of the bullseye. It wasn't exactly where he had been aiming, but had it been a person, there was no doubt his shot would have been fatal.

Harold's triumphant grin split his face from ear to ear.

Chapter 36

Johnny Masten, the owner and sole employee of Cellular Depot, threw up his hands in exasperation on the other side of the counter. "I'm telling you, detectives, if they paid cash for the phone, there's not a whole lot I can do."

He was in his thirties with a self-assured swagger and a smart tongue. From the moment Meredith and Tyler had identified themselves as detectives, he had assumed a permanent sneer.

His little shop was in one of the seemingly endless strip malls in Alpharetta and was far too small to be called a depot. It was one display room with a small office and storeroom. The window advertised repairs, cheap phone plans, and disposable phones, all in hand-painted letters.

"We've got the UPC code," Tyler said. "We're not asking a whole lot. We just need you to check your sales log and tell us who bought the phone."

"I sell a lot of burner phones, man. If they paid cash, it won't matter, and besides, I don't use the manufacturer's UPC codes."

"What?" Meredith asked.

"I put new bar codes on all my products to do my own inventory."

"Why?"

"I like my method better, and I'm going to keep telling you this until you get it: almost everyone who buys a burner phone pays in cash. That's kind of the point. They don't want anyone to know they've got it."

"Trust me, my partner and I know the advantages of burner phones," Tyler said. "This one was purchased sometime in the last three months. It arrived at your store in a shipment with forty-nine other phones."

"Zing sold me out?" Johnny asked.

"They didn't sell you out. They are within their rights to tell us where the shipment went. It's up to you whether you decide to tell us who bought the phone or not," Meredith said.

"Even if I wanted to, you expect me to remember everyone who paid cash for a burner phone in the last three months? I've sold dozens of them. And besides, what if I don't want to help you?"

"We looked into your shop on the way over," Meredith said. "You reported that you had been robbed three times in the past year and a half. Police haven't been able to make any arrests."

"Yeah? So what?"

"Maybe we could talk to someone in the Alpharetta PD to get some more eyes on your case."

Instead of appearing grateful, Johnny's sneer only grew. "Don't worry about that."

Meredith eyed him and then looked around at the metal shelves of haphazard boxes of burner phones, chargers, screen protectors, etc.

"Come on," Tyler said, reaching into his pocket and extracting a folded printout they had made at the station. He flattened it on the counter. There were five pictures on it. Kristi Sanders's and Sean Winston's pictures had been pulled from the CashFlo website. Nick Sanders's photo was from his freelance graphic designer page. Jessica Hammond's photo was from Instagram. Harold Mantelli's photo had been a little more difficult to get a hold of, but Meredith had found one in a tech magazine that

187

had run a story online about CashFlo. "Any of these people buy a burner phone from you?"

Johnny shook his head. "I'm not going to remember."

"Give it a shot."

Johnny glanced at the sheet. "I don't recognize any of them."

"You're sure?"

"Dude, I'm not saying they didn't buy a phone from me. I'm saying I'm not going to remember."

Tyler hung his head and turned to Meredith, who was looking at the corner of the ceiling.

"How long have you had that?" she asked, pointing to the dark plastic bubble mounted on the wall.

Johnny's lips tightened. "I had those installed after the last time my store got hit."

"Have you been robbed since?" Meredith asked.

"No."

Meredith's smile completely confused both Johnny and Tyler.

"Is your merchandise insured, Mr. Masten?" she asked.

Tyler looked back at Johnny, who squirmed uncomfortably.

"Yeah. Gotta protect my—"

"You weren't getting robbed, were you?"

"That's a pretty bold accusation to make," Johnny said, more nervous than offended.

"That's why you don't use the manufacturer's UPC codes, right?" Meredith asked, enjoying Johnny shift from wiseass to worried. "You can sell some of them for cash under the table and then claim they were stolen and collect the insurance. Not all of them. Just when you need a little extra cash, right?"

Tyler turned back to Johnny with raised eyebrows and joined in Meredith's fun. "My partner's good, right? No wonder they never found who was hitting your store, but don't worry, we can get them to dig a little harder."

Johnny shook his head. "Fine. Whatever. What the hell do you want me to do? There's no way to find out who bought it."

"You do keep a daily record of your sales, right?" Meredith asked.

"Yeah."

"Do you have any more models of that phone left?"

"I think I've got a few."

Johnny went over to a shelf and pulled down two small boxes with "Zing!" printed on the side in lightning-shaped letters. There were large stickers with barcodes obscuring the original barcodes on the packaging. He brought the boxes back and placed them on the counter.

"How much are they?" Meredith asked.

Johnny pointed a scanner at the barcode on one of the boxes, and a number popped up on the register's display.

"They're forty-seven eighty-one."

"Okay. This is what you're going to do for us: you're going to go through your daily sales for the past three months, and anytime you find a transaction for that amount, you're going to pull up the security footage for that time and see who bought it."

"I only keep the footage for two months."

"Fine. We'll take it. We'll leave those photos with you. You tell us if you recognize any of them." Meredith reconsidered. "Nah. You know what? Just to be sure, send us an image from your footage of everyone who bought that phone model in the past two months."

"It's gonna take me a few days."

Tyler looked around the empty store. "You don't look too busy."

"Give me your email," Johnny said in defeat.

Chapter 37

Thad had rarely seen anything like it.

Hours later, this guy, Harold Mantelli, was still at it. He had purchased and fired well over two hundred rounds. In addition to the safety course, he had spent hundreds of dollars on the ammo and targets, and in that time, his improvement had been remarkable. He would never be the next Annie Oakley, but he had grown more comfortable in handling the Desert Eagle. He was confident in his stance and more fluid in his movements, which was reflected in his enhanced marksmanship.

Thad had been coaching him almost the whole time. His interest in Harold Mantelli was twofold. He was genuinely intrigued by the guy. It was rare to see someone go so hardcore. Most people took the course only because they had to if they wanted to use the range. They didn't pay attention in the class, and it showed when they stepped into the firing range. More than once, Thad had told someone to stop firing and explained that they had to take the safety course, again, at full price, since they wasted his time, and he would not allow them to take up a free seat that someone else would pay for.

That wasn't the case with Harold Mantelli. He had a bug up

his ass to get good at shooting, and that's where Thad's more selfish interests came into play.

He wasn't sure why Harold seemed hell-bent on becoming a good shot in one afternoon. He was unreadable, his emotions locked away somewhere in his short, rotund body. Thad assumed that Harold fell into the category of Mid-Life Crisis Rambo. Those were the guys who woke up one morning, sat at their desk in their office, and suddenly questioned everything about their manhood. They had a nice car, a house, a stable job, but they were never going to be the badass alpha male they thought they would be. They were never going to be their own boss. They didn't want to put in the pain and commitment at the gym to get jacked. So, they turned to the "manly" image that required very little knowledge, could easily be bought, and gave them an air of danger: guns. The Mid-Life Crisis Rambos always became obsessed and poured money into buying weapons and gear so they could tell the womenfolk around them that when the inevitable shit hit the fan, they would protect them.

That had to be Harold's motivation, and Thad hoped that he might be able to use it to get a few more bucks out of him.

One corner of the lobby of The Line of Fire was devoted to survival gear. There were night-vision goggles, small recording devices, security cameras, and tactical flashlights that shined so bright, they could practically see through walls. There were also tactical sunglasses, which reduced glare so you could see the sun flash on a sniper's scope in the desert, never mind that these guys would never come close to anything like that scenario. None of the stuff was military grade, but Thad found that if you slapped the word "tactical" on something, guys who never served a day in uniform would pay way more to feel like they were "operators." That's not to say that things like the tactical scalpels weren't sharp. They were razor-sharp, but they were nothing more than scalpels made with black steel that Thad had bought for seven dollars each and sold for fifty.

He had started stocking the gear two years ago, hoping to make a killing, but the merchandise ran a distant third in the revenue race after the range and the safety classes. It had been expensive to stock the gear, and it wasn't selling. Every few weeks, he'd have one guy come in and spend a couple hundred bucks in one afternoon, but most of the inventory remained on the shelves, collecting dust.

He had stopped placing orders for new stock, and he wanted to get this stuff off his hands. Harold Mantelli just might be the sucker to do it.

He watched as Harold fired the final bullet from his latest round of ammo. Following Thad's instructions from the safety course, Harold ejected the clip, thumbed the safety on, and locked out the barrel, all while keeping the gun pointed down-range.

He walked behind the row of stalls, opened the door, and stepped into the lobby, where he took off his earphones and went to Josh, who waited behind the counter.

"I'd like fifty more rounds of ammunition, please."

Thad sidled up next to Josh. "I got this one."

Thad opened a drawer in the counter and made a show of selecting the right kind of ammo for his new favorite customer.

"You're getting pretty good in there," he said in an admiring tone. "I wouldn't have recognized you from the man who came in this morning."

Harold smiled, but it was forced. He wasn't used to processing flattery.

"What's your goal?" Thad asked.

"Goal?"

"Yeah. Is this a hobby? Are you only looking to become a good marksman? Is this a personal defense thing?"

"It's a personal defense thing."

Jackpot, Thad thought.

"Are you worried about someone breaking into your house?"

"Maybe."

"Well, you've got the right weapon and you are doing the right thing in knowing how to handle it, but the weapon can only protect you at close range. What I mean is, it'll only protect you after an intruder has broken into your house and is in your bedroom. The gun is one step in self-protection. You need to protect your house, too, and we've got some equipment that will make your house a castle." Thad motioned toward the shelves in the corner.

Harold followed his gesture but said nothing. His face was unreadable.

Thad worried that he may have been too obvious in his pitch, and maybe he hadn't given Harold enough credit.

Harold's phone began to ring in his pocket. He took it out, and his face dropped. He abruptly turned and headed for the door.

"Excuse me. I have a phone call," he said, just loud enough for Thad to hear it.

"Sure," Thad called after him. "I'll keep an eye on your firearm."

It was the first time since that morning that he had seen Harold break a safety rule. You never left a gun unattended, loaded or not, but whoever was calling had caused him to forget that he had left his Desert Eagle on the counter.

*

Harold pushed open the door and walked into the blazing sun and muggy air of the parking lot.

He thought about not answering, but what good would that do? He couldn't avoid the caller forever.

Harold hit the answer button. "Mr. Winston?"

"Hello, Harold. Where are you?" Sean asked. His voice was cool, congenial.

"I'm running errands." It took effort to lie, but New Harold was in charge and deemed it necessary.

"Good. Good. Listen, I just need to ask you a question, okay?"

193

"... All right."

"Do you know why the police would go to a place called Cellular Depot and show photos of me to the clerk, asking if I bought a disposable phone there?"

Harold felt the ground tilt below him.

"Harold? ... Are you there?"

Harold abruptly hung up, which was something he had never done to Mr. Winston before. He stared at the screen, expecting him to immediately call back. Instead, the screen remained dark, which was infinitely worse.

Harold turned and went back inside.

Thad was waiting. He had placed Harold's gun behind the counter but returned it as Harold approached.

"Everything all right?" he asked.

Harold nodded, but his expression said otherwise.

"Here's the fifty more rounds of ammo you wanted," Thad said, placing the box on the counter next to the Desert Eagle. "Anything else I can get for you?"

Harold turned to the shelves of tactical gear.

Chapter 38

Jessica stared at the spot where James had been found. She couldn't picture it as real. It was something out of a nightmare, and tomorrow, she hoped a chapter in that nightmare would end.

"Are you ready for tomorrow?"

"No, but I don't have much of a choice, do I?" Jessica said, exhaling a column of smoke while she and Nick sat on the back patio of his house. It was surreal to be only a few yards from where her husband had been beaten to death, but she had wanted to see Nick. She needed to see him, but he had Dougie, so a meetup at a hotel was out of the question. She had to come to him. They had had sex at his house before, in the bed that he and Kristi shared, while Dougie was asleep down the hall. Jessica had found it irresistible, but it had been a one-time thing, and tonight, Nick wasn't in the mood. He was quiet, pensive, and unresponsive to her advances, hence the cigarette, and since Nick wasn't going to let her smoke inside, the patio was all that was left.

"How many people are you expecting?" Nick asked.

"Not many. I want to keep it small. Most people will probably be there out of obligation. You'll be there, right?"

"I'm going to try."

"Nick, I need you there—"

"It depends on how Dougie's feeling."

"Please, Nick."

"Kristi will be there, for sure."

"But you're the one I want—"

Nick bristled. "I said I'll try."

"James would want you to be there."

The moment Jessica said it, she wanted to take it back, especially when she saw the look on Nick's face.

"Do you really think I'd care what James wanted? After what he did?"

"I'm sorry. I didn't mean—"

"You know the kind of man he was."

"Yes. Of course, I know what kind of man James was. That doesn't mean—"

"And you know that he—"

Jessica stood from her chair and began working her way toward him. "Nick, I'm sorry."

"I really can't believe you would try to use James to make me do anything."

Jessica knelt in front of him and softly kissed his lips. "Let me make it up to you …"

"You don't seem all that upset about tomorrow … or this whole thing."

"I am, Nick. I really am. I just want to forget about it for a while," she said, fumbling with his belt buckle and then whispering in his ear, "Now, please, let me make it up to you …"

Jessica playfully bit his earlobe as she finally opened his belt.

"Nick?" Kristi's voice called out from inside the house.

Jessica shot to her feet and went back to her chair as Nick quickly refastened his belt.

"Out here," he called.

By the time Kristi appeared at the door to the kitchen, Nick and Jessica were back in their places, just two friends talking.

"Hey, Jess," Kristi said. "Saw your car out front."

"I was having a rough time thinking about tomorrow and needed a shoulder to cry on ... and a cigarette," she added, guiltily.

"Don't worry about that." Kristi stepped out onto the patio. She and Jessica embraced. "How are you feeling?"

"I really want all this to be over."

"I'll bet. Did Nick at least offer you a drink?"

"No," Jessica said, making a pouty face in Nick's direction. "He's being very rude."

"Let me get you something. We've got wine or something stronger if you need it."

"Thanks, but I should be going. I've taken up enough of Nick's time."

"Are you sure?" Kristi asked.

"Yeah. You've had a long day. You shouldn't have to play host."

"Fine," Kristi said and laughed. "I'll drink the glass of wine I was going to offer you, but first, we'll walk you out."

*

"Thanks for letting me chew your ear off, Nick," Jessica said as they reached her car, which was parked in the street.

"No trouble at all."

"So, I'll see you both tomorrow?" Jessica said to Kristi, but somehow managed to send her energy toward Nick.

"Of course, we'll be there," Kristi answered.

Nick forced a smile.

"It'll be short," Jessica said. "Like I said, I want it over with. I think James would want that, too."

"If you need anything, let us know," Kristi offered as Jessica got in the car.

"Thank you, guys. Have a good night."

"You, too."

Jessica started the car and drove off.

Kristi continued to smile and wave as she spoke through

clenched teeth. "We agreed, Nick. Never in our home when Dougie's here."

The contrast between her tone and her smile unnerved him.

"Nothing happened. She wanted to see me, and I thought it was best to keep an eye on her … I feel like she's up to something."

"Let's go inside," Kristi said. "We've got some stuff to talk about."

*

"Hey, baby. How was schoo—"

"I want to come stay with you." Allison's voice was quivering.

"What?" Meredith asked.

"I want to come stay with you for a while."

"Whoa. Slow down. What happened?"

"Heather and I got into a fight. She and Dad are talking right now, but I wanted to talk to you before she tried to lie about—"

"Allison. Stop. I'll listen to what you have to say, but don't call Heather a liar."

"You're already taking her side," Allison moaned.

"Baby, I'm not taking anyone's side. You shouldn't call people liars, especially when you're living under their roof."

"That's why I want to come stay with you."

A knot of pain was forming behind Meredith's eyes.

"Baby, just tell me what happened."

"Talia Shepherd is having a back-to-school party tonight at her house and she invited me, but Heather won't let me go."

"Allison, you know why. You're grounded from parties for three more weeks."

"This isn't that type of party! These are nerds. Not cool kids."

"Baby, that other party wasn't *that* type of party until we found out that it was."

"But I didn't do anything."

"You lied about Ricky's parents being there, and you stayed when you knew you should have left."

"But I didn't do anything! You're a cop. Aren't I, like, innocent until proven guilty or something?"

"Parenting is a dictatorship, baby. Laws don't apply."

Meredith thought her joke was genuinely funny but should have known better in the face of a teenager who felt she was being wronged.

"Mom?"

"Baby, no parties, but it's only for a few more weeks. There'll be other parties."

Allison grew quiet.

"Can I come and stay with you for a while, anyway?" Allison asked, again. "Heather and Dad are fighting a lot more. I think Dad not having a job is stressing them out."

"Oh …"

Meredith knew Pete was the kind of guy who bottled up his stress to maintain his cool, laid-back demeanor, but if he held it in too long, it tended to boil over. He was never violent, and Meredith didn't worry about the safety of Allison or Heather, but he could get heated, and it might relieve some of the tension if she took Allison off their hands for a while. She loved spending time with her, but there was a problem.

She didn't have a spare bedroom. She had a spare conspiracy room.

The deciding factor was the feeling that she was being watched. She couldn't bring Allison into that and decided to punt.

"We'll talk about it tomorrow when you come over for the podcast thing, okay?"

"… Okay."

There was a faint knocking on Allison's end.

"I'll be out in a minute," Allison said. "I'm talking to Mom."

Meredith shut her eyes. The knot was growing. She would have preferred to be the one to tell Heather and Pete that she had spoken to Allison.

Meredith could hear Pete's muffled voice.

"Dad wants to talk to you," Allison said.

"Okay. Put him on."

"It's my phone. He should call you on his—"

"Put him on, Allison."

"Ugh. Fine."

There were the pops and thuds as the phone changed hands.

"Meredith?"

"Hey, Pete."

"Where are you going with my phone?" Allison protested in the background, her voice trailing away.

"I'm going to talk to your mother in the bedroom," Pete called back.

He was breathing heavily through his nose. A door opened and then closed.

"Rough night?" Meredith asked.

"Yeah. There seem to be a lot of those, lately."

"You okay?"

"I'm fine."

"And Heather?"

"It's getting to her, but only because Allison has a huge chip on her shoulder … She stopped calling Heather 'Mom.'"

"Shit."

It had been a major hurdle in the past to get to that point. Meredith's ego had been stung when the subject was brought up, but Heather really was another mom to Allison. She was raising her, too. Heather loved Allison and cared for her deeply. Due to a medical condition from her teens, Heather would never have children, and when Allison started calling her Mom, it meant the world to Heather.

"You want me to talk to Allison about it?" Meredith asked.

"No. Heather doesn't want you to talk to Allison about it, either."

"Why not?"

"Heather said that we all agreed that we would let Allison

decide what she wanted to call her. She wants us to keep our promise, even if Allison changes her mind."

"Wow ... Good for her ... I think."

"Yeah. I don't know."

"How's the job hunt?"

"Why? Did Allison say something about it?"

"No," Meredith lied. "I was just asking."

"It's fine. Still sending out feelers. A few nibbles but no bites. You know how it is."

"Yeah ..."

"Listen, I'm gonna go and talk to everyone here and deal with this. You're backing us up, right? No parties?"

"One hundred percent. No parties, and if you need me to come over there to talk to Allison, I will."

"No. We've got it. I'm sure you've got work to do."

"Pete. Come on. Don't—"

"Good night, Meredith."

Pete hung up.

There was a flash of anger at the fact that Pete had hung up on her, but she took a breath and relaxed. He was tired and frustrated, but it was still troubling.

She thought about calling back, but it wouldn't help. She had their back if they needed her. She would let them talk to Allison.

But Meredith wanted to be there. She wanted to be a part of it, even if it was drama.

*

Nick pulled a cigarette from the pack that Jessica had accidentally left, along with the lighter. He stuck it in his mouth, flicked the wheel, and touched the flame to the end of the cigarette. He hadn't smoked in years. Not since Dougie was born.

"What do we do?" he asked.

"I'm not sure there's anything we can do," Kristi said. She had

201

laid out everything she knew. Nick had listened in silence, his sense of horror growing to the point that Kristi didn't begrudge him the cigarette. She sat down next to him on the step of the patio and held out her hand. Nick passed the cigarette. She took a long drag, causing the tip to glow. She hadn't smoked since college. It was an acknowledgment of how screwed up their situation was. She blew the smoke through her nose as they both stared out to the spot where James Hammond had been discovered.

"We'll be fine," she said.

Chapter 39

Jessica Hammond silenced the alarm on her phone.

5 a.m.

She was up.

She turned on the light and looked once more at the empty side of the bed next to her. Last night, she had tried to shift more toward the middle, but it felt wrong to encroach on the other side of the bed, which had always been James's side.

No, she told herself.

She had to stop thinking like that. It wasn't their bed anymore. It was *her* bed … just as it was now *her* house.

Jessica got up and immediately changed into her workout clothes, just as she had always done, and went downstairs. On her way to the basement door, she poked her head into the kitchen, where Rosella was starting breakfast.

"Good morning, Rosella."

"Good morning, Mrs. Hammond."

Jessica continued to the basement door and descended the stairs.

The small gym they had in the basement was nothing fancy. There were a few weight machines, a treadmill, elliptical, rowing machine, free weights, resistance bands, and an area covered with mats for yoga and aerobics. She had been the only one to use the mini-gym. James preferred to go to the "real" gym downtown, which cost hundreds of dollars a month and counted many of Atlanta's elite among its members. He told her that it was to network, but Jessica knew James met women there, other trophy wives whose full-time job was to stay fit.

Jessica fired up the television mounted to the wall and logged into her fitness app on the Apple TV console. She found a kick-boxing class that she had meant to do yesterday but had hit the weights instead. She tapped "play" and tossed the remote aside.

The session opened with the camera on the straight-out-of-a-fitness-magazine instructor in front of a room full of equally beautiful people. Playing to the camera, the instructor welcomed everyone to the workout and outlined the exercises they would be doing. Jessica knew the class so well that she didn't need the reminders.

Then came the stretching. Jessica followed along, bending down to grab her ankles, and felt the slow burning in her hamstrings. She sat down, spread her legs, and pulled her torso toward her feet, then pulled back on her toes, prepping her calves. She then reached over and loosened up her lats. From there, she pulled her elbow behind her head, stretching her triceps.

After a few more stretches, the insanity began.

As always, Jessica kept up, throwing quick jabs with her fists. In perfect unison with the instructor, she raised her foot to the level of her chin, striking the air.

With every twist, uppercut, and bob, droplets of sweat flew from her body. She was hitting her stride, the endorphins cheering her on.

She suddenly stopped, snatched up the remote, and hit "pause."

In the silence, the enormity hit her.

They were holding the funeral service for her murdered husband in a few hours, the father of her daughter, and she was going through the motions as if it were any other day. Today was the day that she hoped to take one more step toward that happiness she sought for herself and for Dani, and she was doing the exact same thing she would be doing if James were still alive.

It was as if James's absence made no difference, which, on its face was heartless, but Jessica didn't know how to feel.

She hadn't cried since the party, and that may have been more due to shock.

Was that why she felt this way? Had the realization that James was gone not truly set in? Is that why she was feeling so unforgivably normal?

But that wasn't it, because here she was, contemplating what had happened, processing, understanding that nothing would ever be the same, and she wasn't crying, she wasn't hyperventilating.

She was working out.

Not only was she working out, but she had also *paused* the workout. If she was so overwhelmed, why would she pause the workout like she was afraid of missing something. As if all she needed was a moment, and when it passed, she was just going to hit "play" and continue her workout.

Jessica finally understood an unavoidable truth: the death of her husband hadn't affected her that much. It had been shocking, and of course, she wouldn't wish it on anyone, but she had grown up poor and from a young age, had adopted a mindset to not dwell on the things you couldn't change. When things didn't go your way, you had to find whatever you could in the situation that worked to your advantage. She had never dreamed she would have to apply that mindset to the death of her husband, but she was doing it automatically. She had lost a husband. Daniella had lost a father, but he was an absent father, and Jessica would have every resource she needed to raise her daughter.

Maybe this mindset had been why she had been trying to see Nick more often. Maybe she wasn't trying to escape what was going on around her. Maybe she wanted to see Nick more because she subconsciously realized that she no longer had to worry about James finding out about the affair.

Jessica felt … fine.

She pressed her hands against her hips and hung her head.

It wasn't right to feel this way, but she knew that she couldn't force herself to be sad when she wasn't. She wanted to be, but it wasn't there.

However, Jessica also understood that everyone expected her to be upset.

Grieving for her murdered husband was the proper thing to do, even if she didn't necessarily feel it. Observing the rituals of society would earn her the freedom to do whatever she wanted after society stopped watching.

Very well.

If she wanted this to be over, then she had a part to play, and in a few hours, she would play it to the hilt.

Chapter 40

"We're still in agreement; no one jumped that fence, right?"

"Yeah," Meredith agreed, standing at the whiteboard in the bullpen, where she had drawn a rough diagram of the house with the front and back yards. An X marked the spot of James Hammond's body. Post-It notes were stuck to the board with each of the suspect's names at their general locations and bullet points of their statements written on them. "The person would have to know James Hammond would be there, while everyone would be in the front yard, know that the softball bat would be there …" She trailed off. The point had been made.

Tyler's eyes narrowed. "Wait a sec. Even if it was one of our partygoers, would they know that the softball bat would be there? The only ones who would know for sure are Kristi and Nick Sanders, yeah?"

"It's not a bad idea, but the invitations they sent mentioned there would be a piñata."

"But if I got that invitation, I would assume that we'd be using a whiffle ball bat or something similar around the kids. Not a Louisville Slugger."

"It's something to keep in mind, but let's get back to the question of premeditated verses spur of the moment."

"Premeditated," Tyler said.

"Maybe it was a hybrid."

"Meaning?"

"The killer lures James Hammond to the backyard to confront him. It gets out of hand. The killer grabs the bat and kills him. They realize what they've done and try to make it look like someone climbed the fence."

Tyler scowled at the rudimentary diagram.

"What?" Meredith asked.

"I guess it makes sense."

"But?"

"It's really convoluted."

"No offense taken, and I agree."

"There's gotta be a simpler explanation. Hookum's razor and all."

"You mean Occam's razor?"

"Who?"

Meredith shook her head. "Never mind," she said and went back to the board. "We're in agreement that it had to be one of our suspects at the party. So, who's lying?"

"There's still the possibility it was two people."

"It's possible."

"Okay. How about this: We've got Jessica Hammond resting upstairs," Tyler said, "which still sounds suspect to me. We've got Kristi Sanders heading inside during the magic show to take a piss, which I get. Chardonnay will do that to you, and we have Nick Sanders searching for the magician that our victim finds on the side of the house. I know it still seems messed up, but out of all of these, the story I have the most trouble with is Jessica Hammond's. Leaving the motive aside, let's focus on her."

Meredith stepped away from the board to allow Tyler to present his theory.

"Now, let's say that Jessica Hammond really is upstairs like she said, but she ain't resting. The window in the master bedroom looks down over the front yard, yeah?"

Meredith nodded.

"Maybe it was Jessica Hammond's plan to be alone in that room. She watches from the window to make sure that everyone is out front when the magic show starts. She then sends the text from the burner phone, watches her husband receive it, and goes to wait for him in the backyard. They meet by themselves, he lets her get behind him, because she's his wife, and he suspects nothing. She grabs the bat, clocks him, stages the scene, and then goes out to enjoy the party to play the grieving widow when the body is found."

Meredith stared unflinchingly at the board, as if she hadn't heard a word Tyler had said.

"Where'd you go, Somerset?"

"Wait a sec …"

Tyler stepped aside as Meredith approached the board.

"Can you grab Nick Sanders's statement for me?" Meredith asked, eyes still locked on the board.

Tyler quickly moved to the table and sifted through the documents.

"Got it."

"What did he say about searching the house for the magician?" Meredith asked.

"Uh … here. You asked, 'When you were inside the house, did you see anyone else?' He replied, 'No. I searched upstairs and down … Everyone … was out front.'" Tyler slowed as he caught up to Meredith's train of thought.

"If he searched upstairs and down, how did he not see Jessica Hammond lying in his bed?"

Tyler smiled. "That's it, Somerset. That's the lie."

"Yeah, but from who? Is he lying about not seeing her or is she lying about being in that room?"

"Maybe they're in it together, the same way we thought Sean

Winston and Harold Mantelli were working together … and maybe Nick Sanders is what's hidden in Jessica Hammond's texts."

"Maybe … but if they were working together, wouldn't their stories match, which would establish an alibi for both of them? And how would we even find out? If they are working together, when we ask one of them, they'll call the other right away to work out their stories before we get a chance to question them. We need to question them at the same time."

Tyler sported a wicked grin. "They're together, right now."

"Are you suggesting that we …?"

"Crash a funeral? I'm down."

Chapter 41

"How you doing, buddy?"

"I'm okay," Dougie said, leaning against his father's side on the verge of sleep, as they sat in the lobby of Arden Funeral Home.

"This will be over really quick, and we'll get you back home," Nick said comfortingly, but inside, he was seething.

Dougie shouldn't be here, but Kristi had said they both would attend and Nick couldn't leave Dougie at home alone. So, they'd got him ready in his best attire, which hung off his frail frame. They needed to get his weight back up. He was getting better, but he was far from well, and more importantly, getting ready had drained Dougie. Nick felt terrible dragging him to this hastily put together farewell for someone so loathed.

White flowers filled every vase, pot, and basket, complementing the black-and-white marble of the lobby and the heavy black doors leading to the main viewing room. The funeral home coordinator waited by the doors.

As Nick sat with Dougie, patting his shoulder, he watched Kristi quietly mingle with the two dozen or so attendees discussing the future of CashFlo. Almost everyone there was a business associate and not necessarily a friend of James Hammond.

Sean Winston was there, too, staying within Kristi's orbit so they could tag-team any VIP with their confidence in CashFlo. They were the new face of the company. The new leadership. Proof that CashFlo would go on, even though James Hammond wouldn't.

There was also Harold Mantelli.

He had started to approach Nick, but he waved him off, indicating Dougie. He felt terrible about using his son as an excuse, but he couldn't talk to Harold. Not right now.

Instead, Harold stood off to the side in a shirt that had to have been purchased years ago, when he was twenty pounds lighter, and even though it was cool in the lobby, Harold's face shone like the surrounding marble due to his sweat.

The one person who wasn't there was the only person they couldn't start without: Jessica Hammond.

Nick checked the time on his phone, again. Jessica was twenty minutes late.

How could she be late for this? he wondered. *How can she be late to her own husband's funeral? How could she—?*

Heads turned toward the smoked-glass entry doors, which offered a view of the parking lot, as the Tesla pulled in and parked in the space with a printed sign that read "Jessica Hammond."

Jessica stepped out of the Tesla, followed by Rosella and Dani, and nearly everyone in the lobby forgot to breathe.

She was strikingly beautiful in a simple, understated way. Her rich red hair was pulled into a tight bun. Her black dress was modest, tasteful, and still somehow stunning. Her makeup was minimal. Her expression was solemn.

The coordinator went to open the door for her. She nodded to him as she stepped inside and addressed the attendees.

"I'm sorry for running late," she said with a melancholy smile.

There was a muted chorus of "it's okay," "don't worry about it," and "not at all."

Nick was in awe. The way she carried herself. The way she spoke. It was like a different woman.

212

Jessica continued to smile and began thanking everyone individually for coming, while Dani and Rosella stood off to the side. The coordinator discreetly came to her side and whispered something in her ear. She answered softly, something to the effect of "a few minutes." Jessica made her way around the room, continuing to thank everyone, keeping it brief but respectful.

However, Jessica's spell over Nick began to wear off as she worked her way around to him and Dougie. She was carrying herself differently, speaking differently, but he knew her well enough to spot that it was an act. A good act, but an act nonetheless.

Finally, after completing the circuit around the room, she arrived at Nick and Dougie.

Nick stood, and they formally embraced.

"Thank you so much for coming, Nick."

"Of course."

"And you, too, Dougie. It means a lot to me."

Nick was having a hard time keeping his frustration under wraps, but caught a glimpse of Kristi over Jessica's shoulder. She was staring at him with a look that said, *Get with the program.*

Nick gently took Jessica's hand. "I'm glad we could be here."

"Thank you," Jessica replied. She then turned to the coordinator and nodded.

*

The main viewing room at Arden Funeral Home resembled a cavernous chapel in a modern church. There was a raised section at the head of the room in front of rows of chairs. Upon the raised section rested a closed coffin on a cloth-covered stand. Next to the coffin was a large framed photo of a smiling James Hammond.

While there were enough chairs for a hundred people, only a third were occupied. Since James had been an only child and his parents had died long ago, Jessica and Dani were the only family members in attendance.

Jessica and Dani sat in the front row, along with Kristi, Nick, Dougie, and Sean. Kristi and Nick held hands. Rosella was a row behind. Harold sat alone toward the back.

The coordinator stepped up to the front of the room, next to the coffin. He thanked everyone for coming on Jessica's behalf. He gave them a brief outline of how the next half-hour would go and reminded them that the day was about remembering the joy that James Hammond brought into the world.

At the conclusion of his speech, he motioned to Jessica.

She stood and walked the few steps to stand next to the photo of her murdered husband. She thanked the coordinator, who nodded and slunk away to the back of the room. Jessica turned to the small group of mourners.

"Thank you all again for coming. It means so much to me, and it would mean so much to James, who was the greatest man I've ever met. He was a loving husband and a caring father ..."

As Jessica rattled off accolades about her late husband, Kristi's grip tightened and her fingernails dug into the skin on the back of Nick's hand.

Chapter 42

"I'm dying. I'm dying, Somerset, and it's all your fault," Tyler groaned as he pulled at his sweat-soaked shirt while he and Meredith waited in the parking lot of Arden Funeral Home.

"They'll be out any minute now," Meredith said, hiding the fact that she was also miserable.

The parking lot had been the compromise.

Tyler wanted to wait in the lobby and talk to them as soon as they exited the viewing. It was sure to catch them off guard and had the added benefit of air-conditioning. Meredith didn't want to confront Nick and Jessica inside the funeral home. They would still question them at the same time, without warning, to see if either changed their story. They would just do it outside.

"You owe me a snow cone after this," Tyler said.

"You want a Happy Meal, too?"

"If you're buying …"

They could make out faint movement through the smoked-glass doors as shapes began to emerge into the lobby.

"Here we go," Tyler said.

*

Sean Winston stood from his chair and stretched, as did the other attendees, relieved that the service had been short, tasteful, and relatively painless, aside from Jessica laying the praise on a little thick about her ex-husband. In his estimate, Jessica Hammond had performed admirably.

Sean had stood before everyone and given a few words. The hardest part had been "thanking" James for choosing him to come aboard CashFlo. Kristi spoke after him and echoed his sentiments. Sean had felt that she had performed admirably, too.

Now, it was over, and there was work to do.

As everyone stood and let out a collective sigh, Sean stepped into the aisle and approached Harold.

"Harold?" Sean began. "Could you do me a huge favor?"

"Uh … okay …"

"Can you wait by the door, please? I want to talk to you, but I have to shake some hands, first."

"What did you want to talk about?" Harold asked, his voice fluttering between octaves.

"It's all right, Harold. I wanted to apologize. I've been really stressed, as you can imagine, and I shouldn't have gone off on you like I did the other night. I was out of line."

"Oh …"

"There's more, but I want to catch everyone before they leave. Is that okay?"

"… Yeah."

"Great. I'll only be a second."

Sean turned to glad-hand with some of the executives as they moved toward the lobby. Harold turned and went across the row of chairs to avoid the stream of people and stopped a few feet away from the door.

The last to leave were Jessica, Dani, Rosella, Kristi, Nick, and Dougie. Sean whispered something to Kristi and then broke off to rejoin Harold with an apologetic look.

"So, how have you been holding up, Harold?"

"I'm fine."

"Good. Like I said, I wanted to apologize for going off on you. I hope you'll forgive me. The pressure of holding this all together got to me, and it won't happen again. I promise."

"… Thanks …"

Sean double-checked to make sure that they were alone. "But we do need to talk about what we're going to in regards to the phone."

"I told you, they won't be able to—"

"Shhh … We can't talk about it here. I don't want anyone overhearing us. Would it be okay to swing by your place tonight? Around eight?"

"Yes," Harold answered.

Sean patted him on the arm. "Good. We'll work it out, don't you worry, and afterwards, you can tell me about some of the ideas you've been having for CashFlo." Sean winked. "See you tonight."

He waited for a response, but Harold was too struck to reply. Sean nodded and smiled, again, but the moment he turned away from Harold to go for the door, the smile was gone.

Harold watched as Sean passed through the doors and into the lobby. Old Harold would have probably even thanked Sean for acknowledging his existence, but not this New Harold.

New Harold was thinking ahead.

And New Harold would be ready.

*

Sean joined the dwindling number of people in the lobby.

Nick was once again sitting on the bench seat against the wall with Dougie. Kristi was standing by Jessica's side, helping her thank the last of the attendees.

Sean sensed movement behind him. A split second later, Harold hurried past him and exited the lobby into the parking lot. He drew the attention of the room for a moment, but was soon forgotten as he reached his car, got in, and drove away.

Jessica Hammond thanked the last person to leave, an older Asian gentleman in a multi-thousand-dollar suit. He opened the door and left, allowing a puff of warm air into the lobby that was quickly conquered by the powerful air-conditioning.

The coordinator appeared seemingly out of nowhere next to Jessica's side.

"It really was lovely," Jessica said, shaking his hand. "Thank you for everything."

"Of course, Mrs. Hammond. Our pleasure." His tone softened even further. "Now, for the last step in all of this, we'll have the cremation in a few hours. Would you like to come back to collect the ashes, or would you like us to send them to you?"

Jessica's shoulders sagged as she looked at Kristi. "Is it horrible if I have them sent to me?"

"Not at all."

"Okay," Jessica said. "Let's do that."

"Very good," the coordinator said. "We'll take care of everything."

"Thank you."

The coordinator inclined his head and walked away.

Sean, who had been staying back, approached Jessica. "It was a lovely service."

"Thank you for coming, Sean. I know you and my husband didn't really see eye to eye, but I'm glad you were here."

"Of course." Sean turned to Kristi. "I'll see you back at the office." With that, Sean walked out of the lobby.

Jessica exhaled. "Okay. Let's get out of here."

*

"Where do you think he's going?" Meredith asked as they watched Harold Mantelli quickly waddle to his car.

"Don't know," Tyler said, "but he's late."

Sean Winston came out moments later, striding purposefully toward his Jag.

"Surprised he even showed up," Tyler quipped.

"Probably not his choice."

The doors to Arden Funeral Home opened once again, and Jessica, Dani, Rosella, Kristi, Nick, and Dougie walked out.

Meredith and Tyler went into action.

*

"What are you going to do now?" Kristi asked.

"Go home and take a long bath," Jessica answered.

Nick kissed Kristi. "I'll see you tonight after— … What the hell?"

Everyone followed Nick's stare to see Detectives Somerset and Foles walking toward them.

"Hi, Mrs. Hammond," Meredith began. "How was the service?"

"It was … fine," Jessica replied, utterly confused.

"Listen, we're very sorry to have to do this right now, but we need to clear up some things about the party."

"You can't be serious?" Nick huffed, angrily. "You're going to ask her questions now?"

"Sorry, but it can't wait," Tyler said. "But this is perfect because we need you to clear up some stuff, too."

"I can't believe this," Nick fumed.

"I know," Meredith said. "But it'll be really quick."

Nick, Kristi, and Jessica stared in disbelief.

"All we need is a minute or two, and everyone can be on their way," Meredith added.

"Ridiculous," Nick said, fuming. "Kristi, take Dougie to the car and get the AC going so he's not out in this heat while we take care of this."

Kristi nodded, took Dougie's hand, and led him across the scorching pavement, looking over her shoulder almost the whole time.

Jessica instructed Rosella to take Dani to the Tesla and wait.

"Okay, detectives," Nick said, once he and Jessica were alone with Meredith and Tyler. "What is so important that we have to do this now?"

"Actually, Mrs. Hammond," Meredith said, motioning with her arm, "could you step over here for a second?"

Jessica cast a glance toward Nick. "Uh … Okay."

They began walking away down the sidewalk next to the building.

"Where are they going?" Nick asked Tyler.

"My partner has some questions just for Mrs. Hammond. We've got some things we'd like you to clear up, as well. Cool?"

Nick shook his head. "Yeah. Fine."

Meredith and Jessica stopped about twenty yards away, out of earshot but still in plain sight of Tyler and Nick.

Tyler pulled out a notepad and consulted his writing. "Real quick, you said you were looking for the magician in the house, right?"

"That's right."

"And you searched upstairs and down?"

"Yes. I did."

"Every room?"

"Yes. I already told—"

"The master bedroom?"

"Yes."

"And you didn't see anyone?"

"No. Why are you—?"

"That's weird because Mrs. Hammond said she was resting on the bed in the master bedroom."

Nick inadvertently blinked.

*

"You said you were lying on the bed in the master bedroom, resting?" Meredith asked.

220

"Yes."

"Did you happen to see anyone?"

"No."

"I wanted to double-check because Mr. Sanders said that he was searching the house for the magician. He said he looked in the master bedroom. Did you happen to see him?"

Jessica couldn't help her eyes darting in Nick's direction.

He was looking at her but turned back to the detective.

She watched and saw him nod in the affirmative. Jessica's mind raced. She had to assume that they were asking Nick something along the same lines. Had he seen her? And she had just seen him nod and say yes. There was no time. She felt beads of sweat running down her spine.

"Yes," she said. "I did see him."

"Oh. Why didn't you mention that before?"

"Because it was really brief. Just for a moment."

*

"I did see her resting on the bed," Nick said.

"Why did you fail to mention that before?" Tyler asked.

"It was so quick, and I guess when you asked if I had seen anyone in the house, I was thinking 'anyone who might have killed James Hammond' and not Jessica."

"Ah," Tyler said. "Yeah. I get that. Still, it would have helped if you would have told us that, and we wouldn't be here, today."

"Are you really trying to blame me for the two of you ambushing us right after her murdered husband's viewing?"

"Nah. No, man. We didn't want to, but our sergeant is up our ass, wanting to wrap this up."

"Is there anything else?" Nick asked, impatiently.

"Yeah. Last one, you did see her?"

"Yes."

"Did you say anything to each other?"

Nick fought desperately to keep from looking at Jessica to gain some sort of hint, but he couldn't risk it.

"No. She was lying on the bed, resting, so I let her be," Nick said.

"You didn't say anything to her? She didn't see you?"

"No."

*

"So, did you see Mr. Sanders?" Meredith asked.

"Yes."

"Did you happen to say anything to one another?"

Jessica sputtered, froze, began to speak, then froze again. Finally, she collected herself enough to answer.

"Yes. We spoke very briefly. He asked if I was okay, and I said that I was and that I was resting. He asked if I had seen the magician and I said no."

Meredith wrote in her notebook. "Okay. I think that's it. Again, I'm really sorry to be bugging you today of all days, but my partner and I appreciate it. Thank you."

*

Meredith and Tyler reached her car.

In the half-hour or so since they had left it, the interior had become an oven. As they entered, Tyler rolled down the window and Meredith put the air-conditioning on high.

"Okay," Meredith said. "Jessica changed her story. She now says that she did see Nick upstairs in the master bedroom."

Tyler deflated. "Same here. Nick says that he saw her resting upstairs in the master bedroom but didn't say anything to her."

Meredith turned and smiled at him. "That's not what she said."

*

222

"You said you spoke to me?" Nick said, fighting to keep his expression on an even keel as they stood in the parking lot after their respective interviews.

"Yes."

"Why?"

"Because it would have been crazy to say that we saw each other but didn't say a thing."

"Shit," Nick hissed through clenched teeth.

Jessica's eyes were frantic. "What are we going to do?"

"Just look normal. They can still see us."

"But, Nick, they know we're—"

"Stop." Nick guided her back to her Tesla, where Rosella and Dani were waiting. "Go home. Don't talk to anyone. I'll figure something out."

"Okay. Okay. I'll call you," Jessica said, her mind in a daze. She climbed in the Tesla, started the whisper-quiet engine, and drove off.

Nick walked back to his car, where Kristi waited while Dougie sat in the back seat.

"What happened?" Kristi asked as they watched Meredith and Tyler exit the parking lot.

"Problems," Nick replied.

*

A few minutes later, Harold was sitting behind the wheel of his car with the windows rolled down, staring at his phone. A few of the men waiting at the entrance to the parking lot had approached his window, asking if he needed any work done. Harold waved them off.

He would occasionally check to make sure no one else was getting close to the car. He didn't want anyone to see what he was studying. He was so intent that he almost forgot to switch the browser on his phone to "private."

223

When he felt like he had gleaned enough information, he closed out the browser, and returned the phone to his pocket. Ideally, he would have liked more time, but it wasn't up to him. He started the car and found a spot closer to the building entrance.

Equipped with his mental shopping list, Harold got out of his car and began walking toward the sliding doors of the massive hardware store.

Chapter 43

Sergeant Wheaton held his glasses in one hand and pinched the bridge of his nose with the other.

"So, you've got James Hammond, who is … I'll just say it because we're all friends here, an asshole who couldn't keep it in his pants and was about to screw over everyone at his company. He gets his face pounded in, and the list of suspects just keeps growing?"

"Harold Mantelli and Sean Winston are still our prime suspects," Meredith said from her seat in Sergeant Wheaton's office. "But we can't eliminate Hammond's wife as a suspect. She's unaccounted for at the time of the murder, and her reluctance to help us doesn't look good."

"What reluctance?"

"She hesitated in showing us the phone records from their shared phone plan when it could have helped our investigation. She ultimately did but took pains to black out all of her communications. Most spouses of murder victims would agree right away to show us the records to see where that text came from."

"And get this," Tyler chimed in. "Nick Sanders said he was searching the house for the magician. According to his statement, he looked upstairs and down, but didn't see anyone. Jessica

Hammond said she was resting in the upstairs bedroom, and she didn't mention seeing him."

"Okay. It's getting weird," Sergeant Wheaton said.

"It gets weirder," Meredith said, picking it up. "We questioned them separately after the viewing, today. Both Nick Sanders and Jessica Hammond changed their stories to say that they did see one another but then contradicted themselves. Nick Sanders told Tyler that he saw her but didn't speak to her. Jessica Hammond told me that they did have a conversation."

Sergeant Wheaton sat up. "Wait. You're telling me you trapped them at James Hammond's viewing?"

Meredith and Tyler traded a guilty expression.

"That's heartless … and I kind of love it," Sergeant Wheaton said. "So, you think they're lying?"

Meredith nodded. "Yes, and we think they might be having an affair."

"We're pretty sure that's what Jessica Hammond is hiding in her phone records," Tyler said.

"… You're sure?" Sergeant Wheaton asked.

"… Yes."

"That's not the kind of yes I'd put money on, Detective Somerset."

"Jessica Hammond may have been tired of her husband's affairs and the way he controlled her," Meredith said.

"And what about Mr. Sanders?"

"If he and Jessica Hammond had a thing going, maybe he wanted to help her. We don't have concrete evidence they're having an affair, yet. All we're saying is that this might be a new piece of the puzzle," Tyler said.

"None of your pieces fit, yet."

"We're getting there," Meredith said.

"All right, then," Sergeant Wheaton said with a sigh and motioned toward the open office door. "Let me know when you get to wherever 'there' is."

*

226

The temperature had dropped a few merciful degrees that evening as Meredith and Tyler exited the station.

They had agreed to keep Sean Winston and Harold Mantelli as their prime suspects but would try to figure out a way to get to the bottom of whatever was happening between Nick Sanders and Jessica Hammond.

"What do you think?" Tyler asked as they walked down the steps. "You want to ask Kristi Sanders if she's got any suspicions about her husband?"

"Not yet. If there is something there, we can use it as leverage against him. Might shake him loose if we tell him that we're going to tell his wife if he doesn't come clean."

"You're kind of ruthless, Somerset. You know that, right?"

"You're the one who had the idea to ambush them at the viewing." Tyler smiled, thoroughly pleased with himself. "... Yeah."

"What are you up to tonight?"

"Gonna stop by and see Hannah. Then prep for my big debut tomorrow."

"I really can't thank you enough for doing this, Tyler, and neither can Allison. I'm letting you know just in case she forgets to say it tomorrow."

"I'm looking forward to it. Have a good night, Somerset."

"You, too, Tyler. Say hi to Hannah for me."

Tyler saluted, climbed into his car, and drove off.

*

"Maybe you should call the detectives and tell them that you did speak to me," Jessica said, her voice tight and wavering.

"Jess, I can't do that. They'd know I was lying."

"Then what do we do?"

"There's nothing we can do," Nick said. He was sitting on the bed, holding out the phone so that Kristi could hear the conversation on speakerphone as she silently paced.

"But Nick," Jessica said, unaware of Kristi's presence. "They'll know I was lying."

"Jess, they already know that we're both lying."

Kristi shook her head and continued to pace as she gnawed on her fingernail. Nick had only seen her chew her nails when she was beyond stressed, like when they were waiting on Dougie's diagnosis all those years ago.

"Maybe we should come clean," Jessica said.

Nick looked at Kristi, who shook her head.

"No," Nick said. "Not yet."

Jessica sniffed. "… I love you, Nick."

Kristi rolled her eyes.

"I love you, too," Nick replied, still looking to Kristi for guidance.

Kristi mouthed some words at him, which Nick repeated into the phone.

"But we have to wait."

Chapter 44

Tyler waved to the man at the reception desk as he stepped into the lobby of New Horizons Learning Center.

"Hey, Nate."

"Evening, detective."

"Okay to see her?"

Nate motioned to the hallway off to the right. "Head on back."

"Thanks."

Tyler was a regular at New Horizons. He came to see his sister, Hannah, who had Down syndrome and needed full-time care, whenever time would allow, and sometimes even when it wouldn't. Tyler hadn't told Meredith about Hannah straight away because she was somewhat of a secret. Not because he was ashamed of her. Far from it. He loved his younger sister, but Hannah needed constant care and she found it at New Horizons. The only way that Tyler could afford it was because his mentor, Doc McElwee, had risked his career to make Tyler's mother's overdose look like a botched robbery so that Tyler and Hannah could collect the insurance. Tyler worried that if it were to get out, it would stain the legacy of the man he had viewed as a father. Meredith became the only other living soul that he had told, confident that she would keep his secret.

Tyler walked down the hallway. All the doors were open, and inside the rooms were children with varying learning disabilities working with teachers and caregivers.

Tyler found Hannah's room and peeked inside.

She was sitting on the floor, drawing in a coloring book as a caregiver watched.

Tyler gently tapped on the door.

Hannah turned and instantly smiled.

"Tyler!" she cried, stood, and embraced him in a fierce hug.

*

Although it was still muggy outside, Hannah wanted to hit the playground next to the building, and Tyler was more than happy to oblige.

They played on the see-saw, and games of tag and hide-and-go-seek. Tyler would keep an eye on Hannah, even when he was "it," by watching her hide through the cracks in his fingers, feigning frustration when he couldn't find her. They finally ended up at Hannah's favorite, the swings.

Tyler pushed her, and she laughed hysterically while begging him to send her higher, which he declined. She didn't need to go any higher, but Tyler continued pushing her until his arms were sore. Finally, it was time to go, and Tyler slowly brought her to a stop. Hannah was still laughing, but Tyler noticed that she was short of breath. It wasn't the shortness of breath that came from laughing too hard. These were split seconds where she was fighting for air.

"Hannah? You okay?"

"Yeah," she said, still beaming. "Push me, again!"

Tyler sadly had to inform her that he had to leave.

He walked her back to her room, where they said their good-byes. It was rough on Hannah. It always was. Tyler didn't like it either, but he promised that he would be back soon.

On his way out, he stopped at the reception desk.

"Can you do me a favor, Nate?"

"Sure, Mr. Foles. What's up?"

"When Dr. Holland comes in tomorrow to work with Hannah, can you ask her to keep an eye on Hannah's breathing?"

"Of course."

"Thanks, Nate. Have a good night."

*

"Are you ready for the interview with Tyler tomorrow?" Meredith asked.

"Yeah. I've got my questions ready to go," Allison replied.

"Just remember that Tyler is doing you a favor, so don't be too rough on him."

"I won't."

"How are things with you and Heather?" Meredith asked.

"… We're not talking that much."

"You need to talk to her and you should apologize."

"For what?"

"For getting upset with her when she told you that you couldn't go to the party."

"Mom—"

"You should, Allison."

"… Okay … I still want to come stay with you for a while."

Meredith looked around the spare room, which was dimly lit by the light filtering through the window from the street. "We'll talk about that tomorrow."

"Okay. I have to go. I have to finish my homework."

"Okay. I'll pick you up tomorrow after school at your dad's and Heather's. Good night, baby."

"Good night, Mom."

"I love you."

"I love you, too."

Meredith hung up the phone and resumed sitting in the darkness of the spare room, staring out the window to the street, looking for whoever was watching her.

Alice was standing at her side.

Chapter 45

Sean Winston had no problem with making tough decisions.

In fact, he thrived on it.

Nothing ever really was a tough decision, not when you saw things clearly. That was the difference. That was the key to his success. While regular people hemmed and hawed over what they should do, considering pointless factors that only complicated their decisions, Sean weighed only one consideration: what was best for Sean Winston. Doing what was "right," by definition, put other factors before his own objectives and was a strategy designed for failure. He was a problem solver for the problems that applied to Sean Winston.

And that was what his trip to Harold Mantelli's had become, a problem-solving expedition.

There had been some reservations initially. He had been walking to his car in the parking garage, when he stopped and almost turned around, but once he applied his principles, the course of action was clear: Harold Mantelli needed to disappear.

The detectives would assume that he was responsible for James Hammond's death. Harold had wanted revenge on James for continually screwing him over; the Blackstone deal had been the last straw, and Harold had smashed in his face with the softball bat.

Now, he was on the run.

It was clean, neat, and tidy.

The physical act of taking a life was what concerned Sean the most. The planning had been interesting. Fascinating, in fact. The execution was altogether different.

Sean didn't own a gun, nor did he have the time to acquire one. A knife was also out of the question. He needed Harold to disappear without a trace, and if the police searched the house and found blood everywhere, they would know that Harold's disappearance was not of his own making.

That left one option: strangulation.

Harold might struggle, but Sean had eight inches of height on him and hundreds of hours of working out with his personal trainer.

In a few minutes, when Harold let him into his home, Sean would wait for the right moment, strangle him, open the garage, pull his car inside, put Harold in the trunk, drive up I-75 to the sprawling Allatoona Lake and dump the body from one of the many lonely bridges.

Harold Mantelli would be fish food. Problem solved.

As Sean approached Harold's house, he became focused.

He parked in the driveway, pulled up close to the garage, and walked to the front door.

Sean was wearing khakis and a polo. He wanted as much freedom of movement as possible. He was confident he could handle a struggle with Harold but didn't want to take anything for granted.

The lights inside burned as Sean stepped onto the porch and pressed the glowing button next to the door.

The chimes were answered seconds later by a smiling Harold.

"Evening, Harold," Sean said in a collegial tone.

"Hi."

Sean stepped through the door and was greeted by a mildly antiseptic smell.

"Thanks for seeing me on such short notice."

"Of course," Harold replied.

They stood awkwardly by the door. Sean was waiting for Harold to lead him to the living room or some other place he would have more room to subdue him. If he tried to strangle him in the hall, he might hit the wall, leaving evidence of a struggle. But Harold stood there, staring at him with an unreadable expression.

"Well," Sean said, "shall we have a seat and talk?"

Harold motioned down the hall. "I have a couch and a recliner in the living room."

Sean tried to hide his reaction to such an odd answer and began walking. He was in his head, preparing himself for a struggle, amping up his adrenaline. He had hoped that Harold would take the lead, but instead, Harold followed behind. Sean quickly recalculated his plan. Upon reaching the open space of the living room, he would turn, grab Harold's neck, and crush his windpipe.

"I really like your home," Sean lied, hoping to put Harold at ease.

"Thank you," Harold replied as they emerged into the kitchen. "The living room is to the right."

Sean obliged and walked into the dimly lit room.

He was so focused on Harold behind him, that he only noticed something out of the ordinary when he stepped onto the carpet, which was covered by a clear plastic tarp.

Sean stopped and looked down as it crunched under his weight.

"Harold, what the hell is th—?"

Sean Winston never heard the shot, nor did he particularly feel the bullet enter the back of his neck, and exit out the top of his skull.

Chapter 46

An energized Tyler walked into the bullpen the next morning to find Meredith at her desk.

"Okay. I've been going over it in my head all night. We're in agreement that Jessica Hammond and Nick Sanders are bumping uglies, right?"

"Did I just hear you say 'bumping uglies'?"

"You did, and if they are bumping uglies—"

"Having sex. Having an affair. Call it anything other than 'bumping uglies.'"

"Fine. If Jessica Hammond and Nick Sanders are naked friends—"

"Come on."

"—that gives us our clearest motive, right? They have feelings for one another. James Hammond isn't treating Jessica right. She and Nick want to be together. At the party, Jessica lures him into the backyard. She keeps his attention by telling him about the affair as Nick Sanders steps up behind him with the bat, takes him out, and goes a little overboard to the face because he's pissed about how he treated Jessica. Then, they rough up the bushes to make it look like someone climbed the fence, rejoin the party, and act like they're just as surprised as everyone else when the body is discovered."

"Then what?" Meredith asked. "They announce their relationship and ride off into the sunset, hoping that no one connects the big, blinking dots that maybe they killed her husband so that they could be together?"

"They wait it out. Once it all dies down, they make their move."

Meredith shook her head. "I still don't like it. That means Nick Sanders is leaving his wife and cancer-surviving son. I don't see that from him."

"People will do weird things when they're bumpin' uglies."

"Stop it." Meredith's phone began to ring. She picked it up off her desk. "This is Somerset …" Meredith cast a knowing expression at Tyler. "Mrs. Sanders, what can I do for you?"

Tyler watched as Meredith listened and creased her brow.

"When was the last time—? … Okay … Yeah? … We're on our way." Meredith hung up the phone and looked at Tyler. "I think your theory is already busted."

*

"Thank you for coming," Kristi said, closing her office door behind them. "I've worked with Sean Winston for years and never once has he been late or not gotten back to me when I called."

"When was the last time you tried calling him?"

"I've tried at least a dozen times this morning. He's usually the first one in the office."

Tyler held up his hand. "Whoa. You were so worried that you've called him a dozen times?"

"It's just so unlike him. Normally, I wouldn't be this freaked out, but after what happened to James …"

"Have you tried any family members? Friends?" Meredith asked.

"This is going to sound strange, but I don't know of any family members or even friends. CashFlo was Sean's life."

Tyler was still baffled, and Meredith couldn't blame him.

"We can swing by his place and see if he's there," Meredith offered. "Other than that, it might be best to wait until the end of the day to see if he checks in. If he doesn't, we'll start getting the word out."

"Thank you, detectives."

"Let us know if you hear anything from him."

"I will."

*

"I'm at a loss," Tyler said as they rode down in the elevator. "She seems way too worried about a grown-ass man not being on time this morning."

"I get it."

"What do you mean?"

"James Hammond was killed while he was president of CashFlo. Now, if something happened to Sean Winston, maybe she's worried that she's next."

*

"You aren't asking me to let you into his apartment, are you?" Keith Paxton, the manager of The Colonnade apartment building in downtown, asked. It was a shimmering glass structure filled with units that carried a price tag of over a million dollars, each. Keith's office was on the first floor and looked more like the office of an art collector than a property manager.

"No," Meredith assured him while Tyler fidgeted uncomfortably in the high-backed chair next to hers. "We would like to knock on the door to see if he's there."

"I can ring the phone in his apartment, if you'd like."

"That'd be great. Thank you, Mr. Paxton."

Keith grabbed the phone on his desk, punched in a few

numbers, and waited. Finally, he returned the phone to the cradle. "No answer. Is there anything else I can do for you?"

He meant it as an end to their meeting, but Tyler had an idea.

"Mr. Winston has a spot in the parking garage, yeah?"

"Yes."

"Would it be possible to see if his car is still here?"

"Of course," Keith said, rising from his chair. "Follow me."

*

The office of the parking garage was more subdued than Keith Paxton's stylish digs, but it was still nicer than a lot of offices Meredith and Tyler had been in.

A woman was sitting at a computer, scrolling through her phone, when Keith knocked.

"Debbie?"

"Mr. Paxton."

"How we doing?"

"Fine," she replied, trying to discreetly put her phone away. "What's up?"

"Can you bring up camera 4C, please?"

"Sure," Debbie said, swiveling her chair back to the keyboard.

A few clicks later and they were looking at a corner of the parking garage on the screen.

Keith pointed at the empty parking spot on the screen. "That's Mr. Winston's space, right there. Number two-eighty-seven."

"Would it be possible to see what time he left?" Meredith asked.

"Sure. Debbie?"

Debbie punched a few buttons, which brought up a scrollable timeline at the bottom of the screen. She moved the cursor across the timeline in reverse, causing cars to teleport in and out of the frame.

Suddenly, Sean Winston's Jaguar appeared in the picture.

"There," Meredith said.

Debbie hit the button to allow the image to play at normal speed.

The timestamp read 7:33 p.m. the previous night. After a few seconds, Sean Winston walked into frame. He approached his car, his eyes down toward the pavement. He stopped and turned, as if he was about to walk away. He was uncertain, hesitant, totally different from the Sean Winston they had known. He opened the door to the Jag, paused, and then got in. The headlights flared to life. The Jag backed out and drove away.

"There it is," Keith said. "He left around seven-thirty last night and hasn't been back."

"Thank you, Mr. Paxton," Meredith said. "We appreciate your help."

Afterwards, Meredith and Tyler walked toward her car, which was parked in the visitor's space.

"What do you think?"

"Ain't it obvious, Somerset? Our boy is guilty and did a runner. How do you want to play it?"

"We told Kristi Sanders that we would wait until the end of the day, but after seeing that, we need to start looking for Sean Winston, now."

"Copy that."

*

Once they were back on the road, Meredith put in a call to have the highway patrol keep a lookout for Sean Winston's Jaguar. Tyler called Kelly Yamara about contacting Sean Winston's bank and setting up an alert if he used his debit or credit cards.

No sooner had Tyler hung up with Kelly than he received a call.

"She get a hit already?" Meredith asked.

"No," Tyler said, looking at the caller ID. "Hold on a sec ..." Tyler hit the answer button and brought the phone to his hear. "Dr. Holland?"

Sean Winston was momentarily forgotten.

Meredith had met Dr. Holland when she had joined Tyler on visits to see Hannah, and she knew that if Dr. Holland was calling, it couldn't be good.

She watched as concern spread across Tyler's face.

"Yeah … Okay … How is she doing? … I'll be there as soon as I can," Tyler said and hung up the phone.

"Everything okay?" Meredith asked.

"We need to take a detour, Somerset."

*

Meredith waited in the lobby of New Horizons while Tyler went off down the hall.

Dr. Holland was waiting outside Hannah's room, sporting an expression that was equal parts assurance and worry.

"Where is she?" Tyler asked.

"She's in her room," she said quietly so Hannah wouldn't hear. "She's fine."

"What happened?"

"I kept an eye on her, like you asked me to. We were using cards to help improve her memory. She grew very frustrated and had difficulty breathing, again."

"But she's okay?"

"I tested her blood oxygen levels once she had calmed down, and it was fine. We played some other games and finished out her lessons, no problem, but I wanted to speak to you."

"Can I see her?"

"I don't think that's a good idea."

"Why not?"

"You know how empathetic she is. She'll pick up on the fact that you're worried, which will upset her. And since you're only stopping by, you know how she is when you leave."

Tyler wanted to argue, but he couldn't.

"So, what's going on with her?" he asked.

"I can't say for sure. There are several heart defects associated with Down syndrome. The most common is called AVSD, atrio-ventricular septal defect. It's when there are holes in the walls separating the chambers of the heart. It's usually diagnosed in infancy, but it can develop later."

Tyler bit his lip. "Okay. What do we do?"

"I've already scheduled an echocardiogram early tomorrow at Emory St. Joseph's. It would be great if you could be there to comfort her during the test."

"Absolutely," Tyler answered.

*

A few minutes later, they were back in Meredith's car, heading to the station. Dr. Holland made it clear that there was nothing they could do until tomorrow.

"I'll be in the office tomorrow no later than ten, tops."

"Tyler, knock it off. You need to take care of her, and I'll tell Allison that you can't do the interview tonight."

Tyler watched the world passing by outside the window. "Nah. I still want to do it."

"Tyler. You don't have to—"

"I kind of need to do it, Somerset."

"… Why?"

"'Cause if I don't, I'm going to go crazy, pacing around my apartment … That's when bad things happen."

Chapter 47

Harold Mantelli answered his phone sweating, out of breath, and without checking the caller ID.

"Hello?"

Silence.

"Is someone th—?"

"Harold. It's Kristi." She sounded more nervous than he had ever heard her.

"Oh. Hi."

"Harold … Have you seen Sean?"

"You mean Mr. Winston?" Harold asked, glancing over his shoulder.

"Yes. Have you seen him?"

"No, Kristi. I haven't." Harold caught himself. He had never addressed her by her first name. It felt good. He felt that surge of confidence, that he was leveling the playing field.

"When was the last time you heard from him?" she asked.

"Ummmm … I, uh, I spoke to him yesterday, at the service."

"What did he say?"

"He apologized for being rude to me."

"And that was all?"

"Uh, yes. Why? What's going on?" he asked, trying his best to sound in the dark.

"He didn't show up to work this morning, and he's not answering his phone."

"That's, uh, that's not like Sean at all." It was the first time he had called Mr. Winston Sean, and it felt even better than calling her Kristi.

"No … It's not," she said. There was another long silence. "If you hear from him, will you let me know?"

"Uh, sure."

"The police are looking for him, too."

"… Okay." Harold once again glanced behind him. "I, uh, I should be going."

"All right … Good-bye, Harold."

"Um, okay. Good-bye, Kristi."

Harold hung up the phone. The latex gloves made it difficult. The plastic suit made it even worse. Sitting on the carpeted floor of his basement, he turned back to the horror just visible in the small room down the short hallway and replayed the conversation with Kristi in his mind.

She had to suspect something. That's what the call was about, but how much did she suspect? Did she know?

And she said that the police were looking for Sean. Was that a warning? A threat?

Old Harold would have freaked out and asked what she meant and maybe even pleaded for help.

Not the New Harold.

Outwitting Sean Winston had been a revelation. Harold had never felt more fearless or self-assured.

The police were looking for Sean? Fine. It didn't matter if Kristi was trying to threaten or warn him. Harold knew that sooner or later, the police were going to come knocking on his door, anyway.

He cracked a smile at the surge of confidence that flowed through him.

Harold had been ready for Sean Winston.

He would be ready for them.

*

Miles away, Kristi stared at the phone.

That little change in Harold. That he had called her Kristi and Mr. Winston was now Sean.

She knew.

Kristi looked up at Nick.

"We have to get Dougie out of here."

Chapter 48

Allison double-checked the two microphones sitting on Meredith's kitchen table. She had purchased them with the money she'd saved while working at the grocery store over the summer. She tapped one of the microphones and peered intently at the levels on her laptop.

Meredith sat in a chair, off to the side, and watched in amusement. She knew that Allison was already thinking big, that this podcast was going to blow the lid off … something. It reminded Meredith of the time when Allison was ten and believed she was going to become not just a pop star, but a world-renowned singer and songwriter.

It was a phase that lasted all of two months, until she really got into dinosaurs.

Meredith didn't know if this was a phase for Allison, but she loved seeing her passion, even if she was wary of becoming a part of it.

"I think that should do it," Allison said. "Can you speak into the microphone, please?"

Tyler leaned forward in the chair across the table. "Test, test, test. Mic check. One, two, one, two."

"Hmmm … I'm picking up a lot of room tone, but I'll isolate

it and edit it out later. When I set up my studio, I'll have foam on the walls to dampen the sound," she said in her most professional voice.

While Allison continued to adjust the levels, Tyler winked at Meredith.

Allison tapped a button. "One more time, please?"

"Thank you, Atlanta! We love you. Good night!"

"Normally, please," Allison said, unamused.

"Sorry. Check, check. One, two, one, two."

"Thank you." She made one last adjustment. "And … we're recording." She closed her eyes, exhaled, and began speaking in a somber tone. "Hello and welcome to the first episode of Catching Evil, a podcast that pulls back the curtain on the darkest of crimes by interviewing the people who solve those crimes and catch the killers. I'm your host, Allison Somerset. Today, we'll be talking with someone who has been tasked with … catching evil."

Meredith fought back a smile. It was the pop-star phase all over again, for sure.

"Could you please tell us your name and your job title?"

Tyler leaned forward. "My name is Tyler Xavier Foles, and I am a homicide detective with the Cobb County Police Department."

Allison broke her podcasting persona. "You don't need to lean closer to the mic. I've got it set up where it'll pick up your voice clearly."

Tyler leaned forward, again. "My bad. Shit, I mean—" He leaned back and collected himself. "My bad … and sorry about the swearing."

"Can you do your intro, again?" Allison asked.

Tyler almost leaned forward but forced himself to stay upright. "My name is Tyler Xavier Foles. I'm a homicide detective with the Cobb County Police Department."

"Thank you for speaking with us today, Tyler." Allison was back in "serious" mode.

"It's a pleasure to be here. Thanks for having me."

Allison consulted the questions she had written in a notebook next to her laptop. "How long have you worked in homicide?"

"About two years."

"And how do you like it so far?"

"Well, on my first homicide case, I took a bullet to the chest. That was fun."

"That was the case of the strangled girl on Willow Lane?"

"Yep. It was quite an initiation, but nothing a couple of surgeries couldn't fix."

"And even though you almost lost your life, you still wanted to be a homicide detective?"

"More than ever."

"And why is that?"

"It's a job where you feel like you're doing something good."

"Are you still affected by murder scenes?"

"Sure, but I already saw a lot of dark stuff before I got my homicide badge when worked in narco and vice … and from when I was a drug dealer."

Allison froze. Even Meredith was caught off guard by Tyler's casual mention of his past.

"You dealt drugs?" Allison asked, her podcast demeanor slipping.

"In my youth."

"And now, you're a cop?"

"Yep."

"What did— … How did that happen?"

"Had it rough as a kid. Pops left when I was little. Mom couldn't even take care of herself. My younger sister had special needs. I got into the business when I was fourteen to keep a roof over our heads and food on the table. It was fine for a time. Then, I got busted when I was seventeen. While I was inside, waiting for my trial as a juvey, my mom was killed during a robbery at her apartment. Doc McElwee, the cop in charge of my bust, saw some potential in me and got me into the narcotics field of law enforcement. He was the father I never had. I did pretty good. Then, one night, Doc was shot and killed after walking into a 7-Eleven as it was getting hit. They never caught the guy who shot him. That's what made me want to be a homicide detective."

Allison's eyes were wide. She was about to consult her notebook for the next question, but stopped and tilted her head in genuine interest.

"So, it was Doc McElwee's murder that made you want to be a cop and not the murder of your mother?"

"Baby," Meredith said. She knew the truth that Tyler's mother had died of an overdose and Doc McElwee had staged the robbery so that Tyler and his sister could get the insurance payout.

"It's a legit question," Tyler said, smiling. "And you're an observer, Somerset. If you want to talk, you do an interview."

Meredith was a little irked, but she wanted to hear Tyler's answer.

Tyler turned back to Allison. "At the time of my mother's murder, I didn't know homicide detective was an option. I was following Doc's lead. He knew where my talents and knowledge could best be put to use, and he was right."

"Have you tried to find Doc's murderer on your own?" Allison's podcasting persona was gone. It was her and Tyler, just talking.

"No. I'd love to, but Doc's killer is long gone. Anyone robbing a convenience store isn't doing it to make a big score. Most likely, they were desperate for drug money. Someone making stupid decisions like that ain't gonna last long. Odds are he's probably dead."

"Could you ever forgive them?"

"Nope," Tyler answered without hesitation. "Working in narcotics, I saw a lot of people in pain. I get it. Drug addiction will drive people to do some incredibly stupid, self-destructive things, and I would know. I got hooked while I was dealing and had my own struggles. I still struggle with addiction every day, but even at my lowest point, no matter how badly I needed a hit, I knew that killing someone is wrong. So, I don't care how desperate that guy was for a fix, there's no forgiveness coming from me. The dude had two options: either get help or rob a 7-Eleven with a gun and shoot whoever came through the door. He chose the latter and took the man who I saw as my pops, and if I have to forgive him to get into heaven, I'll gladly check into hell."

"Do you think criminals are evil?" Allison asked, her prewritten questions totally forgotten.

Tyler considered it. "Good question. Some are. I mean, they're just people. Some of them do horrible things deliberately because they want something. Some make mistakes. Some feel they didn't have a choice. But whether a person who commits a crime is evil isn't my call. The court gets to decide that. I only catch them."

"But you have to have an opinion. What about the person who shot you? Were they evil?"

Tyler smiled at Meredith. "She's really good." He gave his focus back to Allison. "The person who shot me had some messed-up values, and that's as generous as I'm going to get. I would, however, like to take this opportunity to thank my union for the spectacular health insurance."

*

The interview, which was supposed to last an hour, stretched into two.

Allison and Tyler fell into an easy back and forth. Tyler provided thoughtful analysis of what it was like to be a detective, and Allison never missed a chance for a follow-up. Meredith watched from the sidelines, amazed at Allison's natural interview skills. Meredith was also blown away by Tyler's philosophical takes on law enforcement. She had seen him open up at NarcAnon meetings, but she had never seen him like this: thoughtful, introspective, with a demeanor that belied his drawl and easy swagger. And he seemed to be enjoying himself, giving Allison what she wanted while also occasionally jabbing back at presumptions about being a detective.

"So, Doc McElwee's murder is what made you want to become a homicide detective, but what is it that makes you stay a homicide detective?" Allison asked.

"Oh, man. Great question, Ms. Somerset … You know what? Doc's killer is why I became a detective, and it's why I stay a detective."

"Even though you said his killer was long gone?"

"See, that's the thing with detectives, or at least a lot of them I know. There are those who become detectives because of what they saw on television, but they give up because it's not romantic. They burn out from the slog of climbing the ranks. Then, the pay sucks. Sometimes, their partner is the worst," he said with a subtle nod in Meredith's direction. "I've found that the good detectives, the ones who stick around, have that one thing that drove them to it, and it's something they can never make right and they can never get over. The closest they'll ever get is to make it right for someone else. That's what makes them the best at what they do."

Allison sat back in appreciation. She then glanced at the recording time on the screen and realized how long they had been talking.

"Thank you for speaking with me today, Detective Foles," she said and reached across the table.

Tyler shook her hand. "It was my pleasure, Ms. Somerset."

Allison tapped a key, ending the recording, and shot out of her chair.

"Oh my God! Oh my God! Oh my God! That was so cool!"

Tyler stood and stretched. "That was great. You're a hell of an interviewer, Little Somerset."

Allison ran around the table and embraced him. "Thank you, so much!"

Tyler laughed. "I mean it, you're really good at this."

She released him and went back to her laptop. "Okay. Wow. Okay. I have to get home and start editing."

Meredith stood. "I'm going to walk Detective Foles out, and then I'll drive you back to your dad's."

Allison didn't look up from the screen.

*

"I really can't thank you enough for doing that," Meredith said as they approached his parked car on the street.

"My pleasure. It was very cathartic." Tyler opened the door and climbed in. "I recommend you give it a shot."

"We'll see," Meredith replied, noncommittally.

"She really is something special, Somerset."

"I know."

"All right. See you in the morning."

"Have a good night, Tyler."

Meredith waved at him as he drove away. He hit the horn once in reply before turning the corner.

Meredith put her hand down and turned to walk to the door, but she suddenly tensed.

As Tyler drove away, he had passed a blue Nissan Sentra parked down the street.

There was a shadow sitting in the driver's seat.

Maybe it was someone delaying going inside because they didn't want to deal with their spouse. Maybe they were finishing up a phone call. The odds were that it was nobody, but as Meredith walked back up the pathway to her front door, she glanced at the darkened window of the guest bedroom.

Alice was peeking through the space in the blinds, down the street, looking at the same blue car.

Chapter 49

"That was so cool!" Allison repeated for about the twentieth time from the passenger seat, as she skimmed through the audio on her open laptop.

Meredith alternated her gaze between the road and the rearview mirror, keeping an eye out for the blue Nissan.

"—you now, right?"

There. About twenty yards back.

It might have been the same Nissan, but it was dark and the glare from the headlights made it hard to tell.

"Mom?"

"I'm sorry, baby. What did you say?"

"I can interview you now, right?"

"We'll see. I'd like to hear the final product, but you did really well."

Allison grunted in frustration. "Fine. I can work on it tonight and have a rough edit by tomorrow."

"It's a school night. You probably shouldn't stay up too late. There's no rush on it."

Allison continued tapping the keys on her laptop. "I want to get it done."

Meredith navigated to Pete and Heather's house, just as she

had done hundreds of times before, but she continued to keep an eye on the rearview mirror. No one appeared to follow them into the subdivision.

Pete was waiting for them as they pulled into the drive.

"Hey, sweetheart," he said, anticipating a hug from Allison, but she raced past him, clutching her laptop and bag, and sprinted through the front door.

"Hey, Dad," she barely managed to get out before disappearing inside.

"What's with her?" Pete asked Meredith, who trailed in Allison's wake.

"She's really excited to get to work editing her podcast." She cast a glance back toward the street. "Listen, I know it's late, but can you do me a favor?"

"Sure. What's up?"

"If you don't hear from me later tonight, call Tyler, okay?"

"You okay?"

"Yeah. Just going to give you a call when I get home."

Meredith got back in her car before Pete could ask any more questions.

*

Meredith attempted to be casual as she drove back to her apartment. The odds were still in favor of it being nothing, but she wanted to be sure. If she wasn't being followed? Then no harm, no foul.

She parked in the designated spot outside of her apartment and discreetly scanned the street as she stepped out of her car. The Nissan was gone, or at least it wasn't in the same place.

Upon entering her apartment, she went straight to the guest bedroom and turned on the light, leaving the rest of the lights off. She then exited the room and closed the door. If anyone was watching, they would think that she was in there.

She kept low as she crept through her apartment and peered out the windows. She didn't spot the Nissan from her bedroom or the living room.

She snuck into the utility/laundry room and looked out the window toward the side street.

There it was.

Through the small window, she could see the Nissan parked by the curb.

It made sense. If this guy was following her, which Meredith had no doubt he was, he may have noticed that Meredith had clocked him earlier. He had to move, and the side street allowed him to keep an eye on the front door.

Meredith now had the advantage, but unfortunately, he was parallel parked and she couldn't see his plates.

She would have to go out there.

She slunk back to the guest room and turned off the light, as if she had just completed her nightly routine of staring at the wall. She went into her bedroom and changed into her jogging clothes with the addition of a baggy sweatshirt, which would be suspicious in the heat, but she had no choice. She went to the gun safe in the closet, punched in the code, removed her Sig Sauer, tucked it into the waistband of her leggings, and pulled her sweatshirt down over it. She put in her earbuds, like she normally did for her jogs, but didn't turn them on. The man who had taken Alice was possibly sitting outside her apartment, and she needed all of her senses.

She paused by the front door to steel herself and then stepped outside. She began stretching her hamstrings, just as she always did before a run. She loosened her quads and her calves and jogged in place, bringing her knees high to get the blood going.

Normally, she would head off to the right to start her run, but the Nissan was to the left. She could do her usual run and hope the Nissan would still be there when she returned, but he was there, now.

Screw it, she thought.

She wasn't going to take a chance at losing him.

She went down the pathway to the street, turned left, and began jogging. Upon reaching the side street, she turned again.

The moment she began advancing down the street, the Nissan came to life.

Meredith began sprinting.

The Nissan's tires screamed as it suddenly pulled away from the curb.

Meredith was closing the gap, but the Nissan hit the accelerator and shot down the street. Meredith continued sprinting after it. She didn't need to catch them. She only needed to keep the car in view for a few more seconds.

She got within five yards before the car pulled away, leaving the scent of scorched rubber in its wake.

Meredith slowed to a stop, breathing heavily, and rested her hands on her knees.

"Gotcha."

*

Meredith raced back inside and fired up her computer. She logged into the CCPD website and clicked the link to the department's DMV page.

She entered in the license plate number and hit "search."

The results were almost instantaneous.

Next to the laptop, her phone began to vibrate. Meredith picked it up.

"Hey, Pete."

"Meredith? I hadn't heard from you and was about to call Tyler. Are you okay?"

"Yeah. I'm fine."

"What's going on?"

"It's nothing. Everything's fine."

"Meredith? Tell me."

"It's fine."

"Okay," Pete said, obviously not believing her.

"Pete, it's okay. I promise."

"Okay. Good night, Meredith."

"Good night, Pete."

Meredith sat back and cursed.

The plates were registered to a Stephanie Dennison of Acworth for a 2004 Toyota Tacoma, which had been declared stolen.

In other words, this guy was using false plates.

He didn't want to be found.

Meredith was more certain than ever; whoever was in that car was the one who had sent her the swimsuit.

This was the man who had taken Alice.

Chapter 50

"Good morning, Nate," Tyler said, entering the lobby.

"Good morning, detective. How we doin'?"

"Good, man. How about yourself?"

"Can't complain. She's ready for you."

"Thanks."

Tyler moved off toward the hallway.

New Horizons was just waking up. Some of the residents, accompanied by caregivers, were making their way to the cafeteria for breakfast.

Tyler reached Hannah's room and poked his head inside.

Hannah and Dr. Holland were sitting on the bed, talking and laughing. Hannah was dressed and ready to go, wearing her favorite T-shirt with the blue horse on it.

"Good morning, munchkin," Tyler said.

Hannah smiled, raced over, and embraced him.

"Good morning, Tyler," Dr. Holland said.

"Good morning, doc. We all set?"

"Yep. She's ready to go. Are you sure you don't want me to come with you?"

"Thanks, but we'll be fine. Right, Hannah?" he asked, ruffling Hannah's hair.

"Yes," Hannah said.

Tyler felt a tinge of guilt. He knew that Hannah's enthusiasm came from the fact that normally, when he came to pick her up, they were going to the zoo, or a movie, or staying at Tyler's for Christmas. She didn't understand that this was different, but Tyler had plans to make it up to her with ice cream afterwards.

"All right," Tyler said, "let's get out of here."

*

"Where are we going?" Hannah asked as he started the car.

"First, we have to go see a doctor," Tyler said, trying to sound upbeat. "They're going to take a look at your heart. It's going to be really cool. Then, we're going to get ice cream."

Hannah didn't grasp the first part, but she knew ice cream.

They spent the drive over to Emory St. Joseph's singing along to Hannah's favorite songs, which Tyler had loaded into his phone the night before.

It was still early, and they were heading in the opposite direction to the morning rush hour, which meant they arrived with some time to spare.

Hannah held Tyler's hand as they walked across the parking lot to the building and didn't let go as they rode the elevator to the office of Dr. Rachel Tealman. They passed the minutes in the waiting room playing Rock, Paper, Scissors and Hot Hands. Tyler was deliberately slow in pulling his hands away, allowing Hannah to slap them, and then overdramatizing the severity of her strikes.

Finally, they were led by a nurse to a room with a bed and echocardiogram machine. The nurse talked them through the basics of how the test would go as she took Hannah's blood pressure and temperature. Hannah dutifully complied, holding out her arm when asked so the nurse could slide on the blood pressure cuff and lifting her tongue so the nurse could take her temperature.

"Okay," the nurse said, making one final note in Hannah's file, and patting the hospital gown on the bed. "We need you to put this on. Then, you can hop up here on the bed, and the doctor will be in shortly."

"Got it," Tyler said.

The nurse put Hannah's file in the plastic tray mounted to the door as she walked out into the hall.

"Okay, Hannah," Tyler said. "Let's do this so we can get ice cream."

Tyler helped Hannah out of her shirt and into the hospital gown. She didn't understand what was happening but her trust in Tyler was absolute.

"Now, I need you to climb up here and lie down," Tyler instructed, indicating the bed. He helped Hannah crawl onto the bed and lie back. "There. Comfortable?"

Hannah nodded, but he could see that she was starting to worry. Tyler had done his best to hide his concern because Hannah would catch on to it. He held out his hand with his fingers hooked and his thumb in the air. Hannah smiled and took his hand, mirroring his grasp.

"Ready?" he asked.

Hannah laughed.

"One, two, three, four, I declare a thumb war," Tyler said as they waved their thumbs back and forth.

Hannah continued laughing as their thumbs parried. Tyler allowed her to pin his thumb against his hand.

"One, two, three, four, I won the thumb war," Hannah counted out as Tyler "struggled."

"No!" he cried. "Rematch!"

After ten minutes and a dozen or so rematches, there was a knock at the door. It was quickly opened by a tall woman with black hair.

"Good morning," she chimed.

"Good morning," Tyler said.

260

"Good morning, Hannah," Dr. Tealman said to Hannah.

"Good morning."

"Are we ready?" Dr. Tealman asked.

"Yeah," Tyler said. "We want to get this over with so we can go have ice cream."

"Awwww. I want ice cream," Dr. Tealman mock-pouted.

"You can have ice cream with us," Hannah said.

"That's very sweet of you, Hannah, but I'm on a diet. So, let's get you out of here so that you can get that ice cream."

Dr. Tealman enlisted Tyler's help getting Hannah ready. He helped her lower her gown so Dr. Tealman could attach nodes across her chest. Hannah remained quiet, watching with interest as Dr. Tealman fired up the machine. The monitor glowed with different readouts. Dr. Tealman made some adjustments and seemed satisfied. She picked a tube of gel and squeezed a blob onto the end of the transducer.

"This is going to feel a little cold, Hannah, but it won't hurt, and I need you to breathe normally, okay?"

Hannah looked to Tyler, who nodded.

Dr. Tealman placed the transducer on Hannah's sternum. The monitor began displaying a blurry, black-and-white image, which synched up with a *wump-wump* sound emanating from the machine.

"Cold," Hannah said.

"Yeah, but do you hear that sound?" Tyler asked. "That's your heart. How cool is that?"

Hannah smiled and turned to watch the screen.

Dr. Tealman began moving the transducer. The blurry image moved with it.

"Okay, Hannah. I need you to lie on your side," Dr. Tealman said.

Hannah looked at Tyler for assistance.

"Gonna need you to move this way, Hannah," Tyler said.

Hannah allowed him to help her roll onto her side.

"If I could have you hold up her arms, please?" Dr. Tealman asked.

Tyler looked down at Hannah. "Give me those arms, you monster."

Hannah laughed and lifted her arms so Tyler could hold them as Dr. Tealman pressed the transducer against the side of her ribcage.

The *wump-wump* of Hannah's heart thudded from the machine.

Hannah looked up at Tyler, who stuck out his tongue, causing her to laugh.

Tyler chuckled and glanced over at Dr. Tealman and saw the concern on her face.

Hannah's heartbeat continued while Tyler's stopped.

*

"Sorry, sorry, sorry," Tyler said as he hustled into the office. "I know I said ten, but it went a little long."

"It's fine," Meredith replied. "How did it go?"

"She's all right. They just need to do some more tests."

"They didn't find anything?"

"No. Not yet."

Meredith tried to read him but couldn't.

"Any sightings of Mr. Winston?" Tyler asked, changing the subject.

"No, but since he doesn't appear to have any close friends or family, I tracked down the next best thing, his former assistant at CashFlo. I figured she would have some insight as to where he might have gone. And there's a bonus; she was Kristi Sanders's assistant before she was Sean Winston's assistant. She's going to meet us at a coffeeshop in Midtown in about an hour. Want to head over that way and grab some lunch?"

"Thanks," Tyler groaned. "But I already had lunch with Hannah."

"Nice. What did you guys have?"

"A lot of ice cream."

Chapter 51

"How long were you with CashFlo?"

Theresa Filmore stared up at the rotating fans in the half-full coffeeshop as she searched her memory.

"About four years. Moved on last March."

"Where are you, now?" Meredith asked.

"Telecom South. It's a fiber optic company just up the block."

"How are you liking it?"

"I'm doing a lot of the same stuff I was doing for CashFlo: running errands, answering phones, and scheduling for one of the executives."

"Do you like it?"

"It's a job."

"You like it more than working at CashFlo?"

Theresa hesitated, giving Meredith the opening she wanted.

"How was it, working at CashFlo? Any problems?"

"There are always problems at a start-up company. The constantly rotating bosses, the long hours. CashFlo always felt like it was hanging by a thread. Not for the executives, of course. They always had cash for their salaries and expense reports. It was us underlings that sometimes had to wait for our paychecks."

"They didn't pay you?"

"No. They would pay us eventually, but it would be a few days. I'm good with money, so it wasn't a problem, but for the others who were living paycheck to paycheck, it was a nightmare."

Tyler took a sip of his caramel frap. "You were there four years? That seems like a lot of time to put up with stuff like that."

"They kept promising that the benefits were coming soon. Stock options. Those sorts of things."

"Who promised?" Meredith asked.

"All of them. Mr. Hammond, Mr. Winston, Mrs. Sanders. Well, that was until she stepped back from her position because of her son."

"Did you and Mrs. Sanders get along while you worked for her?"

"We got along enough. I can handle myself around egos. She could be just as ruthless as Mr. Hammond or Mr. Winston, but once her son got sick, the fight left her. Kind of sad, really. When she stepped down, I became Mr. Winston's assistant."

"What was that like?" Tyler asked.

"My job description was pretty clear: do whatever was best for Mr. Winston."

"Did he and Mr. Hammond get along?"

Theresa shifted uncomfortably. "Yes and no. In public, they tried to come off as a 'united front,' if you know what I mean, but it could get ugly when it was just the two of them. Sometimes, even when it wasn't."

"What would they fight about?"

"Anything and everything, and when they went at it, everyone would clear the room, except me."

"They'd fight in front of you?" Tyler asked.

"That's the thing about being an assistant; we tend to become invisible after a while."

"So, their fights were intense?"

"Are you asking if I think Mr. Winston killed Mr. Hammond?"

"No," Meredith said. "But now that you mention it …"

The following silence and fidgeting from Theresa took Meredith and Tyler by surprise.

"I don't know," she finally said. "They could be intense, but I thought it was only because they had different styles of management. Mr. Winston was cold and, like, distant. He put up a wall between himself the employees. Mr. Hammond was heated and emotional. They were both self-centered control freaks, but Mr. Hammond wore it on his sleeve. I have no idea if that would be enough for Mr. Winston to kill him."

"Hold up," Tyler interjected. "You said that Mr. Winston put up a wall between himself and the employees. You're saying Mr. Hammond didn't show the same restraint?"

Theresa's eyes did a lap around the coffeeshop in an attempt to avoid their expectant gazes.

"Theresa?" Meredith asked.

"No. He didn't."

"Okay," Tyler said. "What happened? Was he abusive? Maybe a little too hands-on?"

"I don't ... I don't know if I should say anything."

"What made you finally leave CashFlo?" Meredith asked, taking the direct route.

Theresa slumped back in her chair.

"Listen, I've been in this business long enough to know that the bosses are going to make a pass at anything young and attractive. Most of them are rich, ego-maniac assholes who are used to getting whatever they want. People are kissing their asses every minute of every day. It's going to happen. Do I like it? No. Is it okay? Absolutely not, but it happens. You shoot them down the first time they try it. If you're good at your job, like I am, you make yourself too valuable to fire."

"We're sorry that happened to you," Tyler said, sincerely, "but you still haven't answered our question."

"Theresa, did Mr. Hammond sexually harass you?" Meredith asked.

"Of course he did. He tried it with almost every female employee at CashFlo. It was about a year after I started. He knew his game, too. He would start small. Little things, here and there, like compliments about how I looked or seemingly harmless questions about my dating life. He would take these little baby steps until he felt that you were comfortable with him. That's when he'd ask you to stay late to catch up on paperwork or invite you to meet up with him for drinks to 'discuss your career.' I saw him coming a mile away and cut him off early."

"Were you afraid for your job?" Meredith asked. "Was he mad?"

"I was Mrs. Sanders's assistant at the time, so it wasn't entirely his call to fire me, but no, he didn't seem mad. He just moved on to the next green hire. Another mark of a creep who knows what they're doing."

"And you stayed with the company?"

"I knew it was bad, but it was a start-up. You get in on the ground floor when your CEO pays you in stock options instead of cash and five years later, some tech giant acquires you? It's time to retire. Everyone working at CashFlo had their eyes on the prize. Ever hear of Bonnie Brown?"

Tyler shook his head. "Nope."

"She took a job as a part-time masseuse at Google in 2002. They could only pay her $450 a week and gave her a bunch of stock options, instead. When the company went public in 2004, those options made her a millionaire. It's stories like that that make you hold on to an opportunity like CashFlo for as long as you can."

"So, what was it that finally drove you away?"

"I became Mr. Winston's assistant after Mrs. Sanders stepped down. It was fine. I didn't particularly enjoy working for him, but I respected the guy. He never came close to doing something that could be considered inappropriate with me or anyone else in the office, as far as I knew. I still had to watch Mr. Hammond make his clumsy passes. Like a lot of start-ups, turnover was high and anytime we had a new, attractive hire, I always tried to give them a subtle heads-up. Sometimes it worked. Sometimes, it didn't, but I—"

"Theresa?" Meredith asked. "What happened?"

Unable to stall any longer, Theresa shook her head.

"It was the Christmas party two years ago. We had parties every year at the office, and I'm sure you know about the stereotypes of how employees behave at those things."

"We've got a pretty good idea," Tyler said.

"It's worse at places where the stress is high, like a start-up company. I attended the parties because it's good for comradery, but I stay away from the punch bowl and out of the supply closets, if you know what I mean. Anyway, I got a call from Mrs. Sanders's husband. I was Mr. Winston's assistant by then, but Mr. Sanders still had my number. He's a nice guy. I liked him. He was home with their son, and he needed to talk with Mrs. Sanders. Something about a doctor's appointment for the next day, and he couldn't get a hold of her. She wasn't answering her phone. So, I started checking around the party, which was being held in the lobby and conference rooms. She wasn't there. She wasn't in her office. I started checking other offices. I knocked on the door to the office at the far end of the hall. When I opened the door, there was Mr. Hammond, trying to get his dick back in his pants and a woman on the desk."

"He was sexually assaulting someone?" Meredith asked.

Theresa shook her head. "He wasn't assaulting anyone. It was explained to me later that it was consensual."

"And who did the explaining?" Tyler asked.

"The woman he was having sex with, Kristi Sanders."

Chapter 52

Meredith and Tyler exited the elevator and walked with purpose through the CashFlo lobby.

"Hi. Welcome to CashFlo." Tiffany, the receptionist, tried her best to convey warmth and welcomeness, but Meredith's frustration was plainly visible. "How may I help you?"

"We need to speak to Kristi Sanders," Meredith said.

"Do you have an appointment?"

Meredith flashed her badge. "Get her, now."

Tiffany grabbed the phone from her desk and pressed a button while keeping her eyes on Meredith and Tyler.

"Mrs. Sanders? It's Tiffany. The detectives are here to see you ..." Tiffany listened further and then hung up. "She'll be right out."

Meredith tucked her badge away and waited.

Moments later, Kristi Sanders emerged into the lobby, sporting a black suit and yellow shirt.

One look at Meredith and Tyler, and she knew.

"Dammit ..." she hissed under her breath.

"We need to talk," Meredith said.

"Fine. Follow me."

Not a word was spoken as they marched past the cubicles toward her office.

Once inside, as soon as Kristi closed the door, Meredith was out of the gate.

"Why did you fail to mention that you had an affair with James Hammond?"

"Because I didn't," Kristi said, closing the blinds.

"That's not what you told Theresa Filmore," Tyler said.

"I had to tell her that," Kristi spat, walking around her desk, but her temper wouldn't allow her to sit. "But an affair is consensual. This wasn't."

"I'm confused," Tyler said. "You're saying it wasn't consensual."

Kristi shook her head. "This is a disaster."

"It might not be if you would tell us what happened and why you lied," Meredith responded.

"James Hammond was an asshole who wanted to fuck anything that moved. He had his eyes on me ever since I started working here. It was a power thing. I can't tell you the number of times I had to tell him to back off."

"What happened at the Christmas party?" Meredith asked.

"Dammit, Theresa." Kristi sighed.

"Don't be pissed at her," Tyler said. "At least she's playing straight with us."

"You told her that it was consensual?" Meredith asked.

"Yeah."

"But you're telling us it wasn't?"

Kristi mirthlessly laughed. "James hit the booze way too hard at the Christmas party, like he always did. I was in a bad place. I had stepped down. Dougie wasn't doing well. James said he had an idea for how I could get my position back. He had a plan to oust Sean, and he wanted to explain it to me but didn't want anyone to overhear us, so we needed to go someplace private. Like an idiot, I believed him. The minute he closed the door, he started … kissing and groping … He said he was going to have me. Mumbled something about his ex-wife. He said he knew that I couldn't say no."

"Why not?" Tyler asked.

"Because of Dougie. I love my husband, unconditionally, but the health insurance of a freelance graphic designer isn't what you would call 'all encompassing.' But sure"—she sneered—"I could have said no. I could have fought him in court for a few months, but all the while Dougie would be dying. Even if I had won, it would have sent CashFlo under and Dougie would still be dead. Or, I could have just left and found a new job, but who knows how long that could have taken and what kind of insurance we could get. James would have had no problem with that. That's the kind of man he was … Theresa walked in and saw us and to add insult to injury, James told me to go sort it out with her like my job and my son's life depended on it, because it did."

Neither Meredith nor Tyler doubted her story, but Meredith still felt that it didn't excuse her lies.

"Does your husband know?" she asked.

Kristi hesitated. "You'll have to ask him."

"We're asking you," Tyler said.

"And I'm telling you, you'll have to ask him."

Tyler looked to Meredith, who was fed up.

"Why didn't you tell us about the assault?"

"Because you might waste your time thinking I killed him at my own son's goddamn birthday party!" She stopped herself and took a breath. "Don't get me wrong; I wish I had killed him. I wish I had taken that bat to his skull because I know for a fact that this world is better off without James Hammond in it."

Chapter 53

Meredith and Tyler sat at the bar, staring blankly over the tops of their beer bottles.

"You two all right?" the bartender asked.

"Yeah …" Tyler said. "We're dealin' with some stuff."

The bartender shrugged and moved on.

Tyler shook himself out of his stupor. "Okay. We got this. Sean Winston is still our guy, right? That parking garage footage showed a guy who was clearly being eaten up by guilt. He got in his fancy car and went on the run. He'll turn up. People like that don't do well trying to stay off the grid."

"And what do you make about this new development with Kristi Sanders?"

"It's messed up, but I get it. It would have been better if she had been up-front with us about it, but I understand why you wouldn't want to share that experience."

"She didn't 'share' it with us, Tyler. She confirmed it when we confronted her. It's not the same, and it opens up a whole new set of questions."

"Do you believe her when she says that it wasn't consensual?"

"I one hundred percent believe her, but now she has a pretty convincing motive."

"I get it," Tyler said.

"What do you mean, 'you get it'?"

"If someone tried to use Hannah's life to blackmail me like that, damn right I'm picking up that bat."

Meredith was stunned at Tyler's admission.

Tyler appeared to think nothing of it and took another swig of beer. "Okay. Let's play this out with Kristi Sanders as our killer. How does she do it? Because according to the timeline, James Hammond went into the backyard only a few minutes after the magic show started. Kristi Sanders didn't go inside the house until the end of the show. That means that she sent the text, which no one remembers seeing her do, and then James Hammond was in the backyard for like, twenty minutes, presumably standing around. Then, Kristi Sanders hustles back there, sneaks up behind him, smacks him in the back of the head, flips him over, puts the tablecloth on his face, goes to town, stages the fence thing, and then goes running back to the front yard, only to calmly lead everyone back there to find the body. I know we're spitballin' but that feels like a stretch."

"I know. None of this is making any sense." Meredith tapped her finger against the bottle. "We're going to need to talk to Kristi Sanders, again. I want to pin down everything she said."

"Copy that."

Tyler motioned to the bartender for the check.

"Tyler?"

"Yeah?"

"Did you mean what you said, that if someone did that to you, you would pick up the bat?"

"If someone tried to use my defenseless sister's life against me? Absolutely." There was not a hint of sarcasm or irony in Tyler's answer. The bartender placed his credit card and their tab in front of him. Tyler added a tip and scratched his name at the bottom of the receipt. He could sense Meredith's stare. "Look, Somerset, I ain't saying it's right. If Kristi Sanders is our killer, I'll still slap the cuffs on her. All I'm saying is that I just might shake her hand before I do it."

Chapter 54

He's still here, Meredith told herself as she sat in the chair in the spare bedroom and stared through the small space between the blinds to the street beyond.

She had left the lights on in the kitchen and living room of her apartment, hoping to convince her watcher that she was on her couch or at her kitchen table. Maybe he would relax and slip up, again, though it was a long shot after what had happened the previous night. If anything, he'd be even more cautious, but he wouldn't give up. He'd been watching her for years. His obsession had to match hers. He wouldn't look the same. He might have a different car or use a different method to stalk her, but he would definitely be back.

Meredith had already taken her nightly run but had gone slower than usual. She'd tried to take in every detail, every shadow, every other soul that was out and about that night. She'd even taken second glances at people she knew from the neighborhood. She had no doubt that this man knew everything about her and her surroundings, and he wouldn't be above taking on the appearance of someone she might recognize in passing to get closer to her.

Why is he doing this? she wondered.

To torture her? To get inside her head? Mission accomplished on both counts, but was it worth it? They were connected in a way that could only end with one of them destroying the other, but it must be worth it to him.

After her run, Meredith showered in record time, turned on her decoy lights in the living room and kitchen, and then went to the chair in the spare bedroom to watch the street. Occasionally, she would look over her shoulder and Alice would be standing next to her. Other times, she would turn around and Alice would be gone. Meredith tried to keep her eyes on the street as much as possible, but sitting in that chair for two hours straight was taking its toll on her muscles, which were already protesting from her run.

And she had other things she had to focus on, mainly Kristi Sanders.

Did this new revelation change anything?

Maybe, but with Sean Winston on the run, he was still the main suspect. Kristi Sanders had a clear motive, but Sean's actions had kept him at the head of the pack.

Maybe Nick killed James Hammond because of what he had done to his wife. It was a possibility, but then what was going on between him and Jessica? Would Nick kill his wife's attacker while sleeping with her attacker's wife? Or was Tyler right when he suggested that Nick had killed James to be with Jessica?

And that still left the bizarre Harold Mantelli.

Meredith sighed, rubbed her eyes, and stood. Her quads ached, but she needed to move. She needed to get out of that room and back to the case at hand.

But he might be out there, watching her.

She almost sat back down to watch the street, just for a little longer, but shook it off and walked out of the room and into the kitchen. She went to the fridge and grabbed the bottle of chilled rosé she had purchased on the drive home. She poured herself a glass, picked up her laptop from the kitchen table, and carried them both over to the couch. She was going to go over the photos and statements again. Maybe there was another lie, like the one Nick and Jessica had told them. Nothing would surprise her at this p—

Her phone began ringing. Pete was calling.

"Hey, Pete. What's going o—?"

"Is Allison with you?"

"What?"

"Allison?" he repeated, his voice tight. "Is she with you?"

"No. She's not here. Why? What happened?"

"We had a fight. We caught her planning to sneak out this weekend with her friends and all hell broke loose. She took my car and drove off."

"What?!" Meredith shot up from the couch, bumping the coffee table and knocking over the wine glass, sending the rosé down to the carpet. "Jesus, Pete."

"We thought she was upstairs in her room, and then I heard my car pull out of the driveway. I looked, and it was gone. We ran upstairs to Allison's room, and she wasn't there."

"How long ago?"

"It's been about twenty minutes. I've been trying to call her nonstop, but she won't answer. Heather's been trying Allison's friends, but they haven't seen her."

Meredith's police training had taught her to keep a cool head under pressure, to assess the situation and form a strategy, but this was her daughter, and it took a few seconds before she could think clearly.

"Okay. Okay. Let me call the precinct and see if they can relay a message to the highway patrol to keep a lookout for your car."

"I'll keep trying to call her."

"She's not going to answer you, and I'm not sure if we want her talking on the phone while she's driving."

Horrible images began racing through Meredith's mind: Allison slamming into someone on the interstate, Pete's car wrapped around a tree, and Allison's bloody, mangled body slumped over the wheel.

There was a pounding on her door.

Meredith raced across the apartment and threw it open.

There stood Allison, her eyes shimmering and bloodshot. She was carrying a gym bag.

"I'm staying with you," she said and walked past Meredith into the apartment.

Meredith took a series of deep breaths, trying to get her pulse under control.

She suddenly remembered the phone in her hand. "Pete?"

"Yeah?"

"It's okay. She's here."

"She's with you?"

"She just got here. She's fine."

"Thank God."

"I'll call you back, okay?"

"Yeah. Ugh. Dammit. Okay. Tell her I'm glad she's safe but between you and me—"

"I'll tell her," Meredith said and hung up the phone. She knew what was coming next and didn't blame him, but she needed to deal with Allison. She turned and stared at her daughter. "What the hell do you think you're doing, young lady?"

Fresh tears spilled from Allison's eyes. "They're being so unfair."

"I don't care. Do you realize you could have gotten yourself killed driving over here like that? Do you know what you just put me, your father, and Heather through?"

"See?! No one cares about how I feel. No one listens to me."

"We do. All of us care, but you just stole a car—"

"I didn't steal it. It's Dad's car."

"You took it without his permission. That's stealing."

"What? Is he going to press charges or something?"

Meredith held up her finger. "Watch it. I don't care what happened. It doesn't excuse you taking a car and driving off. You could have really hurt yourself or someone else."

Allison bit her lip. "I was just going to meet up with some

friends this weekend. That's all. I know Dad and Heather think that—"

"No. No, baby. We all need to talk about this together. We're going back to your dad's and Heather's and then we can—"

"No. I can't go back there. Why can't I stay here for a little while?"

"Baby, I'm sorry, but it's not a good time, right now."

"Please! I'll stay out of your way. I promise."

"It's not that. I don't have—"

"Please, Mom. Just for tonight. I'll stay in the guest room, like I used to." Allison began walking toward the door to the spare room.

Meredith was gripped with terror. "Allison. Sweetheart, don't—"

Allison pushed open the door, went in, and turned on the light.

Meredith raced into the room.

Allison was frozen. Her eyes were wide as she took in the photos, police reports, and handwritten notes that papered the walls. She finally came to a stop at the bathing suit and the note pinned to it.

She still misses you, Meredith.

Meredith grabbed her arm. "Come on."

Allison continued to stare at the walls. "Mom?"

"You shouldn't be in here," Meredith said and glanced up at the bathing suit.

Alice was there.

She was pinned to the wall, wearing the bathing suit. Water dripped from her hair, and she was staring angrily down at Allison.

"Let's go," Meredith commanded.

"Mom, what is—?"

Meredith yanked Allison's arm, hard. She pulled with such force that Allison stumbled through the door and back into the apartment. Meredith quickly closed the door behind them.

It was the most physical she had ever been with her daughter. Allison gaped at her, stunned and afraid.

"... Mom? What is going on?"

"You're going back to your father's."

Chapter 55

Once Allison was out of the room, all resistance to going back to her father's dropped. She wasn't happy about it, but Allison was too lost in thought to argue.

Meredith felt the same way. There was too much on her mind to address Allison taking Pete's car. Meredith didn't know what to say to her daughter, who sat silently in the passenger seat, her face turned to the window. Meredith wondered if she should try to explain, but there was no way to get it all out and answer any of Allison's questions before they arrived at Pete's.

And Pete. The idea of Allison telling Pete what she had seen filled Meredith with dread.

Other than Dr. Kaplan, Pete was the one person who knew how much Alice's disappearance continued to affect Meredith, but neither Pete nor Dr. Kaplan was aware of the floodgate that the bathing suit had opened in Meredith's life. If Allison told him what she saw, it could cause everything to blow up. He might even go to Sergeant Wheaton. Meredith at the very least would be put on leave or worse, fired for not being up-front about Alice's bathing suit. That one decision would cause everything else about her job to be called into question.

"Listen," Meredith said, finally ending the silence that had been riding with them. "Don't tell your father about what you saw, okay? It's something I've been working on for a case, but no one can know about it."

Meredith couldn't believe what she was saying. She was lying to her daughter.

No, it's not lying. It is for a case, she tried to tell herself, but stopped.

She stole a sideways glance at Allison, who continued to stare out the window at the other cars on the road.

*

Allison still had not said a word by the time they pulled into Pete's driveway.

Meredith killed the engine and turned to her daughter.

"Baby, before we go in, just tell me, are you okay?"

Allison nodded.

"Are you sure?"

"Yeah."

She was less than convincing, but Meredith didn't want to press her.

Pete and Heather stepped out of the front door onto the porch and waited.

"Come on," Meredith said. "Let's go."

Meredith and Allison got out of the car and walked up to them.

There was no fury. No rage. Neither Pete nor Heather angrily insisted that Allison "get in the house." Everyone was too exhausted.

Allison took one look at them, and then quietly went inside.

"Should we call her back down here and have a talk?" Pete asked wearily.

Meredith turned to Heather. "What do you think?"

Heather sighed. "I think it's late. I think there's been enough excitement for one night, and it might be better if we all got some sleep."

"I'm with you," Meredith said. "She's not off the hook, but it's not getting sorted tonight."

Pete nodded. "Are you going to be okay here while I drive Meredith back to her place?" he asked Heather.

"Yeah," Heather replied, turning to look at the now-lighted window in Allison's room. "I don't think she's coming out of her room tonight."

*

Like the drive to Heather and Pete's, the journey back to Meredith's was conducted in almost total silence.

They didn't want to discuss Allison's punishment without Heather present. Meredith didn't want to talk about her job at the moment, and Pete didn't want to talk about his stalled job search or the effect it was having on his relationship with Heather. That only left some half-hearted jokes about getting his car and their daughter back in one piece.

He dropped her off outside her apartment. They said their good-nights and agreed to work out a time that they would all sit down and talk with Allison.

As he drove away, Meredith did her best not to betray the fact that she was scanning the street, looking for her watcher.

She had to find him, now. Her secret was going to get out, and the only way to get rid of that room was to find the man who had taken Alice, the man she was certain was still nearby, watching her from the shadows.

Chapter 56

"One of your suspects was sexually assaulted by the victim. Now, you think that suspect's husband is having an affair with the victim's wife. Another suspect may have acted inappropriately with his daughter, which might have nothing to do with your case, and your prime suspect appears to have gone on the run? Do I have that about right?"

Meredith nodded.

"Guys. Come on," Sergeant Wheaton groaned from behind the desk. "I haven't even had my morning coffee. Why are you doing this to me?"

"We wanted to keep you up to speed, boss," Tyler said.

"What speed is this? I'm not even sure in what direction we're going."

"There are loose ends," Meredith conceded. "But Sean Winston is still our primary suspect."

"You're sure he's on the run?"

"It's conjecture based on what we know and what we saw on the security footage of him leaving his apartment."

"I hate conjecture."

"We've got everyone looking for him," Tyler said.

"And in the meantime?"

"We need to know one way or the other if there is a relationship between Jessica Hammond and Nick Sanders," Meredith said.

"There is," Tyler said.

"We're talking to him about it later today. We'll also ask if he knew of the sexual assault on his wife."

"Kristi Sanders wouldn't tell us if she had told him," Tyler added.

"You think she's covering for her husband because he might have killed the guy?" Sergeant Wheaton asked.

"It's possible, but if she is, I don't know why she would tell us to ask him," Tyler said.

"Be careful," Sergeant Wheaton said, still baffled. "And what about Mantelli's daughter? What's your plan there?"

"We were hoping you might help us with that," Meredith said.

Chapter 57

"I don't understand. Why can't I be in there with her?"

"Because, Mrs. Mantelli—"

"It's Lochmore. I told you that."

"I'm sorry, Mrs. Lochmore," Meredith said, gently. "We can't have you in there possibly coaxing your daughter's answers."

"But it's Harold you're interested in. Not me."

"Yes, but we need to eliminate the possibility of any bias you might have against your ex-husband."

Mrs. Lochmore turned back to the one-way glass that offered a view into the next room, through which they could see her daughter, Cybil, and Dr. Althouse, the social worker, sitting at a table.

While Sergeant Wheaton had given the go-ahead to set up the interview with Dr. Althouse, the entire situation wasn't ideal. Meredith and Tyler would have preferred that the interview take place somewhere more comfortable than a room usually reserved for questioning suspected felons, but with the disappearance of Sean Winston, the revelations about Kristi Sanders, and the lies of Nick Sanders and Jessica Hammond, things were moving fast.

To help them out, Sergeant Wheaton had asked the Cobb County Division of Family & Children's Services for their best, and they had called Dr. Sheldon Althouse, who could only meet them at the station. He was a busy man, and they were lucky to snag a half-hour window in his schedule for that afternoon.

Meredith argued that even if this had nothing to do with their case, they could still bust Harold Mantelli if he had abused his daughter or clear his ex-wife's mind, but instead, Mrs. Lochmore was surprisingly frustrated.

"I told you," Mrs. Lochmore said. "I have no idea what you think—"

"You seemed to have an idea that your husband may have done something to your daughter," Tyler said. "Until you suddenly had no idea what you were talking about."

"But you were asking about murder. I didn't—"

"Let's just see how this plays out, okay?" Tyler said. "Your daughter's safe. Dr. Althouse is a professional. A few minutes and this will all be sorted out."

Mrs. Lochmore was about to protest, but on the other side of the glass, Dr. Althouse began speaking.

"Are you ready, Cybil?" he asked. His voice was warm and gentle.

"I guess so."

"Good. My name is Dr. Althouse. How are you, today?"

"I'm fine." There was a hint of nervousness in her answer.

"Would you like a glass of water or something to eat? There's a vending machine with some candy bars down the hall," Dr. Althouse offered.

"No. I'm okay."

"Great. Just let me know if you get hungry or thirsty, all right?"

She nodded.

"How old are you, Cybil?"

"I'm eight."

"And what grade are you in?"

"Third."

"How do you like school?" Dr. Althouse asked. There was a pad of paper on the table in front of him, but he ignored it, giving her his undivided attention.

"I like it."

In the adjoining room, Mrs. Lochmore shook her head.

"Why is he asking her—?"

"He's establishing trust," Meredith said. "He's making her comfortable and asking easy questions that she can answer honestly in the hopes that she'll be honest when the hard questions come."

It was enough to silence Mrs. Lochmore.

"Do you have any favorite subjects?" Dr. Althouse asked.

"I like math."

Dr. Althouse smiled. "Really?"

Cybil nodded.

"What do you like about math?"

Her nervousness disappeared as she considered her answer.

"I like to figure stuff out."

Meredith and Tyler passed a thought between them: like father, like daughter.

"When I was your age, I didn't like math. I still don't," Dr. Althouse said.

"How come?" Cybil asked.

In a flash, Meredith saw what Dr. Althouse had done. It was so simple, and he had accomplished it so casually. He had gotten her to ask *him* a question, engaging her further.

"I'm no good with numbers, and with math, there's only one answer, you know? I like when you can look at something a lot of different ways."

Cybil thought it over and nodded. She understood and respected his answer.

"But that's great that you like math."

"I'm pretty good at it," Cybil answered confidently.

"She is," Mrs. Lochmore agreed.

"What do you like to do for fun?" Dr. Althouse asked.

"Ummmm … I like to ride my bike. I like to read."

"Me, too. Read, I mean. Not ride my bike. I used to like riding my bike, but I'm a little old, now. My knees aren't what they used to be. When I was your age, I used to ride my bike to the used bookstore near my house."

He was speaking to her as if they were equals or at least acquaintances.

"I like to play games, too," Cybil added.

"I love games. Who do you play games with?"

"My dad and I play games, sometimes."

"What kind of games?"

"He's trying to teach me how to play chess," Cybil said. Her tone implied that she wasn't a huge fan of chess.

"What else do you and your dad do for fun?" Dr. Althouse asked.

"We go see movies, sometimes."

"Do you like hanging out with your dad?"

Cybil shrugged. "Yeah. It's okay."

"Just okay?"

For the first time over the course of the last few questions, Cybil deliberately broke eye contact with Dr. Althouse. Mrs. Lochmore tensed.

"It's okay, Cybil," Dr. Althouse said, casually. "You can tell me."

"It's kind of … boring."

"Yeah?"

"Yeah. Sometimes we just watch TV or go for walks."

Dr. Althouse nodded. "Sometimes I'm not sure what to do with my daughters. We like different stuff."

Cybil looked at him sideways.

"That doesn't mean that we don't love each other. We love each other very much," Dr. Althouse added. "We just have our things that we like. They may have things they like that I don't even know about."

That brought Cybil back from the brink of shutting down.

"Does your dad ever ask you to keep secrets?"

Cybil froze.

Dr. Althouse's tone had been conversational enough. Somehow, he had made it sound like an extension of the discussion they had been having, but there was no mistaking that this was a different sort of question.

"No," Cybil answered, but her shrinking posture and wavering tone was her true answer.

"So, you're not a big fan of chess?"

Dr. Althouse seamlessly shifted back, like a boxer landing a sudden jab and retreating to see how his opponent reacted.

"Not really."

"Neither am I," Dr. Althouse continued. "Too many pieces, and they all move differently. It's kind of confusing."

"Yeah," Cybil replied.

"What games do you like?"

"I like checkers."

"Me, too. A lot simpler than chess. Are you any good at it?"

"Pretty good," Cybil answered.

"I'll bet. Any other games you like to play?"

Cybil scrunched up her brow.

"I like Go Fish ... I also like Trouble. Have you ever played Trouble?"

"Is that the one with the dice in the bubble in the middle of the board?"

Cybil nodded.

"I love that one," Dr. Althouse said. "I used to play that with my daughters when they were about your age."

"I beat my dad three times in a row the last time we played," Cybil proudly stated.

"You'd probably beat me, too."

Cybil beamed.

"Do you and your dad play any other games? Games that don't use dice, or cards, or boards or anything?"

She cocked her head. "What do you mean?"

Dr. Althouse shrugged. "Games that you and he came up with by yourselves. I used to play a game with my daughters called Animals on Parade. Someone would start by imitating something about one animal, like the trunk of an elephant. Then, the next person would have to do that, plus something from another animal, like the wing of a bird. We would keep adding stuff until it got really crazy."

Cybil laughed at the image in her head. "That sounds silly."

"It was really silly," Dr. Althouse confirmed. "Do you and your dad play any games like that?"

"No. Dad's not very good at playing make-believe stuff."

"I see." Dr. Althouse sat back and sighed. "Cybil, I'm going to ask you something very important, okay?" His tone was still gentle but somber.

Cybil nodded.

"Does your dad ever make you feel uncomfortable?"

"What?" she asked, confused.

"Does he ever make you feel, you know, icky?"

Cybil shook her head. "No."

She wasn't afraid or defensive.

Dr. Althouse smiled. "Good." He then stood from his chair. "I don't know about you, but I'm a little hungry. I'm going to go get a candy bar from the vending machine. Do you want one?"

"I'm supposed to ask my mom before I have candy."

"She told me it was okay," Dr. Althouse said.

Mrs. Lochmore straightened up. "I most certainly did not."

"Don't worry. I'm pretty sure he's doing a thing," Tyler said.

"Can I have a Snickers?" Cybil asked Dr. Althouse.

"You bet. I'll be right back."

Dr. Althouse stepped out of the interrogation room. A moment later, he joined Meredith, Tyler, and Mrs. Lochmore in the observation room.

"Well?" Mrs. Lochmore eagerly asked.

"My honest, professional opinion? Her father has not sexually abused her."

"How can you tell?"

"A couple things. I was pretty sure about halfway through the interview, but her reaction to me asking her point-blank sealed it. Her confusion was genuine, but there were other indications. She described her time with her father as 'boring.' Her hesitation proved she knew that 'boring' has a negative connotation. Most victims her age would be afraid to utter a bad word about their abuser for fear of being punished. She was comfortable enough to be honest. That was a good sign. She also said that she should ask you before having a candy bar. She respects parental authority, even when they're not in the room, and she was still honest in her answers, to the point that she admitted that she and her father don't entirely connect. It leads me to believe that she hasn't been sexually abused."

"What about the whole 'secrets' thing?" Meredith asked.

"That was the one red flag. Her answer and her body language suggest that her father may have asked her to keep a secret about something, but it might not be abusive in nature. I've seen it in plenty of similar instances. Most of the time it's when a parent slips up and does something embarrassing. The parent may have said something they shouldn't, a curse word or a derogatory remark, and they ask the child not to tell anyone about it. It normally happens when there's an ongoing custody battle, but my understanding is that's not the case here, correct?" he asked, turning to Mrs. Lochmore.

"No. It's not."

"May I ask why you suspected your husband may have been abusing your daughter?" Dr. Althouse asked.

Mrs. Lochmore looked embarrassed. "A few weeks ago, she returned home after spending some time with Harold, and she was behaving strangely. She was quiet. I was worried, but it seemed to pass. Then, when the police came asking about Harold, I started to worry, again."

"I see. There may have been something that happened, but from what I saw and heard in there, I don't think it had anything to do with abuse, but I'm more than happy to have a few more sessions so that we can be certain."

"Thank you, doctor." She let out a light laugh of relief. "It must have been difficult for your daughters, having a father who could practically read their every thought as they grew up."

"Oh. I don't have any children." Dr. Althouse turned to Meredith and Tyler. "Do either of you have change for the vending machine? I don't have any cash, and I don't want to go back in there empty-handed."

*

Meredith and Tyler watched as Mrs. Lochmore and Cybil walked across the parking lot to their car.

Cybil was contentedly munching on her Snickers bar.

"Don't worry," Meredith said. "I'm sure there's still plenty of dead ends left."

"That's easy for you to say. You're not out a buck fifty for a Snickers bar."

Meredith checked her phone. "Come one. We're going to be late for our next dead end, and there's something I need to talk to you about."

"Cool," Tyler replied, sourly. "But you're buying me a candy bar."

Chapter 58

"Would either of you like a glass of water or something?" Nick asked, sounding completely uninterested in getting them one.

"We're fine," Tyler said as he and Meredith sat on the couch in the Sanderses' living room.

"How's Dougie doing?" Meredith asked.

"We sent him to go stay at Kristi's parents for a few days."

"Why did you do that?" she asked.

"There's a lot going on," Nick said, tiredly. "We felt it was best for both Kristi and I to have one less thing to worry about for a little bit."

"What about his treatments?"

"He's in complete remission, which means that nothing is showing up on his tests. Hopefully, he doesn't need any more treatments."

"That's really great," Meredith replied, honestly. Even if his parents were murder suspects, a kid beating cancer was a good thing.

"It is," Nick said and sighed. "But I assume that's not why you're here this evening."

"No. It's not. Mr. Sanders, we need to know why you told us that you didn't see anyone inside while searching the house, but both you and Jessica changed your stories when we confronted you, and why they still don't match."

"Because Jessica Hammond and I have been having an affair."

Even though Meredith and Tyler had already heavily suspected it, Nick's frank confession still sucked the air out of the living room.

Nick sat back in the chair, staring up at the ceiling.

"It started a while ago. Kristi was always at work, even when she was physically here at home. I know it was horrible and selfish, since it was her job that was keeping us afloat and her insurance that was keeping Dougie alive, but I felt neglected, unattractive … impotent. And there was Jessica. James treated her like garbage with his constant sleeping around and then being jealous of any man who paid her any sort of attention. Jessica and I felt like we were stuck in the same situation. I guess that was enough. She made me feel alive, again … To answer your question, detective: no, Jessica didn't come inside to rest during the party. She came inside to find me. I'm pretty sure that at the time James Hammond was killed, she and I were in the closet in the master bedroom. We decided to join the party before anyone became suspicious." Nick huffed and shook his head. "Our brilliant plan was to come out separately so it wouldn't be obvious, so I left first. Do you need any more details than that?"

Between the two detectives, Meredith was the first to regain her power of speech.

"Does your wife know?"

"No. I would ask that you not tell her, but I assume that's out of the question?"

"Afraid so," Tyler said.

"Then would you allow me to tell her myself and also let Jessica know that our secret is out?"

"I don't see how we could stop you," Tyler said. "You'll probably call them as soon as we leave."

"I appreciate it," Nick said, utterly defeated. "I want them to hear it from me." He leaned forward and put his face in his palms. "This is going to be a nightmare, but at least you know that Jessica and I have alibis."

"Not exactly," Meredith said.

Nick's face snapped up from his palms. "What?"

"You and Mrs. Hammond could have killed James together and claimed that you were in the upstairs bedroom. Also, you said that you left first, but according to witnesses, you came out after her. The point is that you separated, and either one of you could have killed James Hammond on your own."

Nick's mouth hung open in disbelief. "In other words, I've told you everything, possibly ending my marriage, and I'm still a suspect?"

"Yes."

"But why would I kill him?"

Meredith heard Sergeant Wheaton's warning in her head but made a judgment call.

"Mr. Sanders, were you aware that James Hammond allegedly raped your wife?"

Nick's eyes darkened. "Yes. I am. She told me shortly after it *allegedly* happened. I wanted her to take action, but she wouldn't because of the insurance for Dougie. She couldn't do anything. We were already on the rocks, but after that, she wouldn't let me touch her and she wouldn't touch me. That's when Jessica and I started seeing each other."

Nick glared at Meredith with such loathing that Tyler tensed in his seat, ready to get between them if necessary.

"Is there anything else you'd like to know, detective?" Nick asked, coldly.

"Is there anything else you haven't told us?"

"Only my desire for you to get out of my house."

*

295

Tyler shut the car door and turned to Meredith.

"I don't get it. Why wouldn't Kristi just tell us that she told her husband about the assault?"

"She didn't want us to know that her husband had a motive to kill him."

"Who are these people, Somerset?"

*

Nick Sanders watched from the living-room window as the detectives drove away.

He knew he should have tried to lie about knowing. Kristi hadn't answered the detectives because she had wanted to protect him. That way Nick could make his own decision on how to handle it. If she had said that she hadn't told him and he couldn't convincingly lie, it would have only added to their rapidly mounting problems.

Besides, he didn't want to lie. He didn't want to pretend he was ignorant of what James Hammond had done to his family.

But he couldn't dwell on that now.

There were fires that needed to be put out.

*

Back at the office, Meredith and Tyler gave Sergeant Wheaton a rundown of what Nick Sanders had told them.

"This is one of the most bizarre cases I've ever seen," he said with a mirthless chuckle. "Suspects running while motives pile up on other suspects. Keep digging."

After more fruitless hours trying to track down Sean Winston, Meredith and Tyler headed out for the day.

Meredith had grown quiet as she thought about the eyes that might be waiting for her to return home.

"Hey," Tyler said as she split off for her car.

She turned to him.

"You good?"

"Yeah," she said.

Tyler smiled his trademark smirk. "Don't worry, Somerset. I got you," he said as he climbed into his car.

Meredith wished she shared his confidence.

*

Nick paced back and forth across the back patio as he spoke into the phone.

"It's going to be okay."

"But why did you tell them, Nick?" Jessica pleaded.

"Because they already knew, and I wanted to get ahead of it. Neither one of us killed him."

"But what are you going to tell Kristi? Do you want me to call her?"

"No. Do not do that," Nick insisted, masking his exasperation. "Let me handle this."

"Nick … are you going to do it? Are you going to leave her like you said you would?"

"Jessica."

"No. No. I'm sorry. I shouldn't have asked … I love you, Nick."

Only you, Jessica, Nick thought. *A few days past the murder of your husband, I tell you I'm going to confess our affair to my wife, and all you can think of is yourself.*

But Nick was able to choke down his anger. "I love you, too. I'll talk to you soon," he said and hung up the phone.

It took Nick several moments to wrangle his frustration.

Finally, he called Kristi.

"Nick?" she asked upon answering the phone.

"They know," he said.

*

Meredith hit the button on the remote to start the next episode of the show she wasn't really watching. She was biding her time. It had been a painful two hours. Outside, the sun had set. She should be working. She should have been trying to untangle the mystery surrounding who had killed James Hammond, but she—

Her phone lit up with a text.

I'm waiting for you.

Chapter 59

The man sitting behind the wheel of the gray Chevy Malibu kept his head low as he watched the door to Meredith's apartment.

He had underestimated her, and it had nearly cost him everything. She had caught a glimpse of him the night she was jogging, and then she had seen him the night Detective Foles was at her apartment. He should have never parked on that side street, so close to her front door. After all these years, he was getting sloppy. Thankfully, he had switched out the plates on the Nissan. That had to have been what saved him from being traced, but it had been a wake-up call nonetheless.

As soon as he made his escape that night, he'd ditched the Nissan and rented the Chevy. He made sure to pick one that had tinted windows, but not so tinted that it would attract attention. After everything that had happened, if Meredith had spotted a car with nearly blacked-out windows on her street, she most definitely would have run the plates or she might even have been brazen enough to walk up to the car and knock on the window.

He couldn't have that.

What intrigued him was that she hadn't called for backup. For someone who came off as a consummate professional, why hadn't she called for a patrol on her street? Why didn't she want anyone to know that she was being watched?

The man studied the glowing windows of Meredith's apartment. *What is she doing in there?* he wondered.

She spent an awful lot of time in that guest bedroom. He wanted to peek inside the window, but there was no way he was going to get that close. His curiosity burned, but he couldn't risk it. She also had a doorbell camera, and if he tried to look in that window, he would set it off. His only option was to watch and wait.

It was getting late. He was hoping that soon, Meredith would turn out the lights and go to bed. He could then say his good-night and leave.

It was humid inside the car, but he couldn't roll down a window. What would be the point of the tinted windows? A jogger might happen by and wonder who he was and what he was doing. The jogger might be a concerned, upstanding citizen and call the police. So, the man would suffer. He was used to it.

He lifted his head. The light in the guest bedroom had gone out. He breathed a sigh of relief. He'd give it thirty minutes. If all the lights stayed off, he would be on his way. He thought about turning on the radio, but the door to Meredith's apartment opened, and she stepped outside and walked with purpose down the pathway to her car.

The man was far enough away, and he trusted the tinting of the windows to conceal him, but he still involuntarily pressed himself lower into the seat as he watched.

Meredith appeared distracted and made no attempt to scan the street as before. Something was on her mind as she got in her car and pulled away.

The man let her go. He had to see where she was going, but no matter how distracted Meredith was, she would notice if he suddenly wheeled out of his spot to follow her.

Once she turned the corner, he started the car.

He made it to the intersection and looked to his left. Meredith was in the distance, but still in sight. He received a stroke of luck when a car shot past him in Meredith's direction. He used the car as cover to get closer and settled into a safe distance behind her as she pulled onto I-75.

They passed the I-285 perimeter, still heading north. The apartment complexes and buildings began to give way to dense pine forests.

He was alert and prepared in case Meredith attempted any sudden maneuvers to lose anyone that might be following her, but her speed was constant.

Where is she going? he thought.

He knew everything about Meredith, and he wasn't aware of any friends or family out here. Keeping one hand on the wheel, he got out his phone, pulled up the maps app, and zeroed in on their location. He then widened the map to show the surrounding businesses and locations of interest, hoping to see where she might be headed because he had absolutely no idea.

She exited at Wade Green Road in Kennesaw and took a left through the light.

The man followed, keeping a safe distance back, which caused him to barely make it through the light. Soon, they were on surface streets, cutting through fields and more forests. The gas stations and strip malls began to thin, until the only structures were rundown, cinderblock homes that occasionally littered the sides of the road.

It was now even more tricky to follow while remaining unnoticed. The man had to accept that he may lose her, and he'd have to come back and canvass the area tomorrow to see if he could figure out where she had gone.

Meredith was stopped at a four-way intersection about a hundred yards ahead. He was about to give up. It was too risky to get any closer. He had never been caught, and that wasn't about to change, now. He would turn around and go back to the Waffle House by the interstate and enjoy some hash browns, scattered, covered, and topped, and resume his vigil tomorrow, but when Meredith pulled through the intersection, she drove about another fifty yards and turned down a dirt drive.

His blood began pumping. His grip on the wheel tightened.

Maybe the night wasn't over just yet.

He pulled through the intersection and drove past the drive. There was a tall wooden post with a light mounted on it halfway down the dirt drive. Meredith drove through the circle of illumination it cast on the ground and stopped. At the end of the drive, he could make out a squat, elongated building. He continued on, over a short crest in the road. He descended on the other side, around an immediate bend, and pulled off to the side of the road. The hill he had descended was barely tall enough to hide his car from view, but that was all he needed. He pulled over as far as he could, hoping to hide the car as well. If a helpful cop came along and spotted it, they were sure to stop to lend a hand, which would lead to the discovery of his new set of false plates.

Couldn't have that.

He sat in the car, taking in the surroundings.

They were in the middle of nowhere.

He opened the door and stepped out onto the soft ground. His nostrils were assaulted with the dank, dusty stench of a chicken farm—of feed, feathers, and shit.

Staying low, he crossed the road and into the field of tall grass, which had been moistened by the recent rain, and made almost no sound as he crept up the short, gentle slope back toward the farm.

The drive came into view. Meredith was standing next to her car, a few feet beyond the pool of light. She was staring intently at the wooden building. She then began walking toward it and disappeared into the darkness.

The man crept forward, venturing up to the drive, but staying hidden in the grass. He studied the wooden building in the dim distance. There were no lights on inside and no sound.

302

What is she doing? Is she meeting someone? Does this have to do with her sister? It has to, he thought. *But alone? In the middle of nowhere? This doesn't make any sense.*

That's when he began to worry.

Had Meredith been so distracted that she hadn't worried about being followed? Was she really that absentminded? Or was it that she wanted him to—

There was a sound behind him. The same damp grass that had masked his approach had been used to someone else's advantage.

The man turned around and found himself staring straight down the barrel of Tyler's MP9.

"Hi," Tyler said with a smirk. "Who the fuck are you?"

The man released a volley of internal swearing at his sloppiness, but outwardly stayed calm and mute.

"I get it. The strong, silent type," Tyler said, unimpressed, and flicked the barrel of his gun in the direction of the light over the drive. "Let's go over here where it's a little brighter. Nice and slow and keep the hands up."

The man turned and started walking. Tyler followed.

"Stop," Tyler commanded once they were under the light. "Gonna need you to hug some dirt."

The man lowered himself to his knees, lay face down, and put his arms out to his sides.

"Glad you know the drill," Tyler said, extracting his cuffs. He put his knee squarely on the man's back and holstered his gun. He then pulled the man's wrists together and snapped on the cuffs. Tyler lifted him to his knees and then walked around to face him.

"Now, you wanna tell me who you are and what you're doing here?"

"Am I under arrest?" the man calmly asked.

"He does speak. Not yet, but I gotta think you're up to no good, snoopin' on my partner, using stolen plates. You tailing a cop is a really bad i—"

"Where is she?!"

Tyler turned to see Meredith coming back down the drive toward them.

As she drew nearer to the light, Tyler saw the rage in her face and, more troubling, the gun in her hand.

"Where is she?!" Meredith repeated.

Tyler stepped in front of the kneeling man, blocking Meredith's path.

"Whoa, whoa, whoa, Somerset. Take a second. He's cuffed. We got—"

To his shock, Meredith tried to get around him.

"What did you do to her?!" she spat. "Answer me!"

Tyler was able to get his arm out to keep her back, but he had never seen this from Meredith. There was none of the calm, analytical professional he knew.

She was pure, burning anger.

The man stared at her, trying to keep his cool exterior, but her intensity and Tyler's look of shock made him understand that the situation may not be as in control as he thought.

Meredith's adrenaline proved too much. She threw off Tyler's arm and got inches from the man's face.

"WHERE IS SHE?!"

The man swallowed hard but stayed silent.

Suddenly, Meredith raised her Sig Sauer and pressed it against his forehead.

Tyler stepped to her side, but made no effort to go for her gun, which would end the man's life.

"Somerset, what the fuck are you doing?"

Meredith was oblivious to Tyler.

"What did you do to her?" she asked.

The man's eyes bulged, but he didn't speak.

Meredith cocked the hammer.

"Somerset!" Tyler yelled.

The man's nerve broke. "Okay! Okay! Okay! Jesus Christ, lady!"

Tyler looked on in horror. Meredith was still tense with her finger on the trigger. Her world appeared to have been reduced to her and the man kneeling in front of her.

"Meredith ..."

Tyler rarely addressed her by her first name, only when he needed to reach her.

"Meredith, lower the gun."

Meredith relaxed a fraction while still focusing on the man's panicked expression, and slowly lowered her arm.

"Okay, listen," the man started. "Unless you are placing me under arrest, you have to let me go—"

The ear-splitting gunshot rang out across the field and a puff of dirt lifted from the ground by the man's knee where the bullet from Meredith's gun had buried itself.

In one swift motion, Tyler drew his weapon and pointed it at Meredith.

"GODDAMMIT, SOMERSET!"

Tyler couldn't believe what he was doing. He was pointing his weapon at his own partner, but that was what he was supposed to do and if she aimed her gun at the man again, a defenseless man who was kneeling in front of her with his hands cuffed behind his back, Tyler would be forced to pull the trigger.

"Holy shit, holy shit, holy shit ..." the man blubbered.

"What did you do to Alice?" Meredith asked.

"What?" the man squeaked.

"What did you do to her?"

Tyler's eyes widened, and his mouth fell open. "Alice? Alice?! Jesus, Somerset. You think that's what this is about?"

Meredith's rage remained locked on the man.

Tyler lowered his gun and got right next to Meredith's face. "You think this is the guy who took your sister? Are you out of your goddamn mind?"

She continued to stare, her nostrils flaring.

"Look at him," Tyler insisted. When Meredith showed no signs of backing down, Tyler turned to the kneeling figure. "How old are you?"

"Wh-what?"

"How. Old. Are. You? And now is the time to talk because I'm trying to save your life."

"I'm … I'm thirty-eight."

"Thirty-eight, Somerset."

"So?" she asked.

"So, you think he made off with your sister when he was what? Thirteen? Fourteen? This ain't the guy."

Meredith blinked but remained tense.

"It's not him … Stand down, Somerset," Tyler said, quietly but forcefully. "Holster the fucking gun."

It finally sank in for Meredith. She slid her gun back into the shoulder holster, turned, and stepped away.

Everyone took a moment to collect themselves.

"All right," Tyler said, turning toward the man in handcuffs. "I'm done doing you favors, man. It's time to talk."

"My name is Jeffrey Malcolm. I'm a private investigator," he said, trembling.

"A private investigator?" Tyler asked.

"Yeah."

"Who hired you?" Meredith asked.

Jeffrey searched the ground for a way out.

Tyler crouched and got in his face. "Listen, asshole, you ain't leaving here until you tell us everything. So, spit it out."

"… I was hired by Sean Winston."

Tyler straightened up and looked at Meredith.

"He hired you to follow me?" she asked.

Jeffrey nodded. "Whenever he wants to find out about a business rival or someone he might want to make a deal with, he comes to me. He's been hiring me for years."

"You knew that she was a cop?" Tyler asked.

"Yeah."

"That didn't trigger any flags?"

"He tripled my rate, and I'm pretty good at what I do, so I figured it wouldn't be a problem."

"How long have you been following me?" Meredith asked, back to the professional demeanor that Tyler recognized.

"About a week. Just after you interviewed Mr. Winston at CashFlo."

"And you've been feeding him information about what we've been doing this whole time?"

"Yeah."

"Do you know where he is? No one's been able to get a hold of him," Tyler said.

"I haven't heard from him either," Jeffrey said.

"What was the last thing you told him about the investigation?" Meredith asked.

"I followed you to Cellular Depot. After you left, I paid the guy there two hundred bucks to tell me what you were asking about. I called Mr. Winston and gave him the update. That's the last time I spoke to him."

Meredith motioned with her head, and she and Tyler stepped away toward the grass, leaving Jeffrey on his knees under the light.

"What do you think?" she asked, once they were alone.

"Sean Winston trying to put a tail on you doesn't speak very well of his innocence, no matter what's going on with the Sanderses or Harold Mantelli."

"I agree. If he's innocent, why do it?"

"You heard him back there. It might just be how Sean Winston operates. He likes to be in control of everything. He knew he was suspect, so I wouldn't put it past him, but going underground? That doesn't seem to fit."

"Unless he's trying to run."

"If this guy was feeding him info, then he knew we were looking at Mantelli. Why bolt if we're about to pop someone else?"

"Maybe Mantelli had something on Winston, and Winston assumed he would tell us."

"Maybe," Tyler said, running a hand through his hair. "We've got to find Winston and talk some more to Mantelli."

"What do you want to do with him?" Meredith asked, looking back at Jeffrey.

"Well, let's try not to kill him, okay, Somerset?" Tyler asked and walked off.

Under normal circumstances, it would have been a joke, but Tyler was not joking.

Meredith followed him back to the light.

"Okay, here's the deal," Tyler said, standing before him. "Your employment with Mr. Winston is officially over. If either me or my partner see you anywhere near us, I don't care if we happen to run into each other in the vegetable aisle at the store, you'll be arrested for interfering with an investigation."

"Actually, you don't have cause to arr—"

"This is not a negotiation," Tyler growled. "You're gonna sit this one out, and you are going to let us know the moment you hear from Sean Winston. You got it?"

Jeffrey hung his head. "Yeah."

"Say 'Yes, officer, I got it.'"

"Yes, officer. I got it."

"Good."

Meredith was about to protest. They already had enough to arrest him on the charge, but Tyler continued.

"I'm going to take the cuffs off, you're going to walk away, and we're never going to see each other or speak of this little date night, again." Tyler went around behind him and unlocked the cuffs. As he did, he whispered in Jeffrey's ear, "Seriously, stay away. Next time, I might not be able to save your life."

Jeffrey kept his eyes on Meredith.

Once Tyler was finished unlocking the cuffs, Jeffrey got to his feet, took one last look at Meredith, and began walking away down the drive, rubbing his wrists.

They watched him retreat into the darkness.

"We had enough to arrest him on interfering with an investigation," Meredith said. "Why did you let him go?"

"Because if we arrested him, he would get to tell his story about you putting a gun in his face and nearly blowing off his kneecap."

"I had it under control."

"That ain't what I saw," Tyler replied. "But we'll discuss it another time. We got work to do."

Chapter 60

"Are you telling me that this guy put a tail on my detectives and now he's making a run for it?"

Meredith had rarely seen Sergeant Wheaton so pissed, but he jealously guarded his officers, and even though she didn't like to admit it, he was especially protective of her. Sean Winston hiring a private eye to follow her had sent him through the roof.

"It would appear so," Tyler said.

Sergeant Wheaton's face tightened. "Find him and put his ass in this office. I want to have a little talk with him before Kelly informs him of the amount of time he's going to spend at Arrendale State Prison."

"We've already sent alerts to every precinct in a fifty-mile radius, and highway patrol is on the lookout for Sean Winston's car."

"Make it a hundred and fifty miles, and I'll talk to Georgia Highway Patrol to make sure they understand that we want this guy." Sergeant Wheaton continued to fume. "Did this private eye have any idea where Mr. Winston is? Is he feeding him updates?"

"It doesn't look that way," Meredith said. "At least according to the private eye. He claims he hasn't heard from him since Wednesday, which is the same night he left his apartment and never returned. He says the last thing he told Sean Winston about was that we had tracked the sale of the burner phone."

Sergeant Wheaton cocked his head. "He told you all of this?"

Meredith nodded.

"I've dealt with these private investigators before, and when they get caught, they don't tell the cops anything. My guess is that Sean Winston hired one of the better ones and yet you're saying he offered up all this info?"

Meredith grew quiet and then said, "… I'm sorry, Sergeant Wheaton. I didn't quite catch that last question."

Tyler's grip on the armrests of his seat tightened.

Meredith and Sergeant Wheaton had worked out their own little code long before Tyler became Meredith's partner. If it was better that Sergeant Wheaton didn't know the answer to a question so that he could plausibly deny knowledge of it later, Meredith would let him know by employing that response, "I'm sorry, Sergeant Wheaton, I didn't catch that last question."

Meredith could feel Tyler tense up sitting next to her. He knew of their system, and she knew he didn't approve. She also knew in this case, it was hard to defend. She and Sergeant Wheaton only used it in service to a case. She was using it now to cover for her own actions, but Sergeant Wheaton didn't know that.

"I asked, what's the plan for the investigation going forward?" Sergeant Wheaton asked without missing a beat. Either he was so used to their inside baseball, it barely registered, or he possibly didn't care how they got the information out of the private eye who had been messing with his favorite detective.

Meredith hesitated, giving Tyler a chance to add to the conversation, but he was staring down at his knees and his knuckles had gone pale on the armrests.

"We have an interview with Kristi Sanders later today at her office to find out more about what happened with James Hammond," Meredith said.

"Fine," Sergeant Wheaton said. "Wrap up all the loose ends

you can, but meanwhile, I want you two working on finding Sean Winston."

*

Halfway between Sergeant Wheaton's door and their desks, Meredith tapped Tyler on the shoulder.

He turned to face her.

"Hey. You okay?"

"Yeah. I'm solid."

"Listen, Tyler, I couldn't tell him what happened last night. There's enough going on, already. Once we're done with this, I'll tell him what happened."

"You sure?"

"What's that supposed to mean?"

Tyler exhaled. "Nothing. Let's go."

Chapter 61

Sergeant Wheaton took the lead on getting the word out to the Georgia Highway Patrol about Sean Winston's car, which left Meredith and Tyler to handle contacting the individual police departments in the surrounding counties.

Using downtown Atlanta as the epicenter, they drew a circle a hundred and fifty miles out. Interstate 20 cut the circle in half. Meredith took everything north of the line. Tyler took everything to the south.

They began their task with a sense of hopelessness that only increased as they made each call.

If Sean Winston was on the run, he was most likely already outside their search field. He might want to get as far away as possible without crossing a border, since he would have to show his ID. That meant places like Seattle or the northern tip of Maine would be looking pretty good. There was also the possibility that he would sell the Jag for cash and use the money to hide out in a densely populated place like New York or Chicago until things died down. On the other hand, he might decide the money could last longer if he lay low in the middle of nowhere, like Montana or the plains of Texas.

Or he could be doing something else, entirely.

Their search was a fool's errand, but it was the best they could do. If Sean Winston had chosen any of those options, he would have had to drive through their search area and maybe they would catch a lucky break that would tell them which direction he was going.

There was no harm in wishful thinking when the reality was bleak.

Meredith was slightly grateful for the tedium. It allowed her to think and observe Tyler. After last night, there was a wall between them. She didn't question Tyler's ability to focus on the task at hand for a second. They were partners. They had a case to solve and they could put their feelings aside, but he had never acted this way, before.

He had a right to be angry, and Meredith was already trying to lay out an explanation for her actions. She could try to make him understand that she had it under control but wondered how much she would have to tell him to make him see. How could she explain why she had suspected that the private eye had been the one who had taken Alice without revealing how completely obsessed she had become with her sister's disappearance? The line was the bathing suit. If she had to admit that she had been contacted by Alice's kidnapper and withheld evidence while opening her own investigation, she didn't know how he would react, but it wouldn't be pretty.

By the time she finished her share of the calls, she still didn't have a strategy, but Tyler was still dialing numbers.

Meredith was going over the case notes and trying to come up with questions for Kristi Sanders when he hung up the phone with an air of finality.

Meredith was prepared to give him a few moments to unwind before asking what kind of mood he was in for lunch before their interview with Kristi Sanders at CashFlo, but to her surprise, upon hanging up the phone, Tyler was immediately out of his chair and heading for the door.

"Where are you going?" she asked.

"Grab some food. I'll be back in time for us to make the interview."

Tyler was gone before Meredith could respond, leaving her momentarily stunned.

She and Tyler had lunch together every day. Sometimes, they worked while eating. Sometimes they talked about anything but the cases they were working on. Other times, they didn't talk at all. It was comforting to sit with someone and not feel the need to fill the time with inane chitchat. They would sit and eat in comfortable silence.

Meredith didn't dwell on it for too long. Tyler was his own guy. He could do what he wanted with his lunch hour, but the break in tradition was further proof that there was a growing divide between them.

She spent her lunch hour sitting at her desk, trying to focus on Sean Winston, and forgetting her growling stomach.

Sergeant Wheaton popped his head out of the office to let her know he had followed up with Georgia Highway Patrol, but there had been no sightings of Sean Winston's car. Meredith nodded her appreciation.

Tyler finally reappeared, cutting it dangerously close to the time they needed to leave to make the interview. He strode through the door, shoveling the last few bites of a burger into his mouth.

"Ready?" he asked through a mouthful of food.

"How was— How is lunch?"

"Great. Let's go talk to Kristi Sanders."

Chapter 62

"I really don't understand why you're questioning me about my rape, but I will thank you for forcing my husband to admit he was having an affair," Kristi said, sarcastically.

"You're welcome," Tyler said. "And if James Hammond were still alive, we'd be questioning him, too."

"I already told you that I wish I had killed him, but I didn't. I was too busy corralling children for my son's birthday party while my husband was getting his rocks off upstairs with someone I considered a friend."

"Believe me, Mrs. Sanders, I can sympathize—"

"No, detective. I don't think you can."

"And you could still be the one who killed him," Tyler said. "You admit to going back inside during the magic show for a few minutes, which was more than enough time to work his face over."

"I was taking a piss. Is your plan to keep us talking in circles while whoever killed James is probably enjoying a late lunch, right now?"

Meredith had remained largely silent since they had arrived in Kristi's office. Tyler had wanted to take the lead.

On the drive over, she and Tyler had slipped into business mode. There was no discussion of the night before, Meredith's deliberate omission about how close she came to potentially

316

killing someone, or Tyler's cold shoulder. It was Allison taking the car all over again; there would be a time to deal with it, but they had to focus on other things.

"So, when you went back inside, you didn't see anything?" Tyler asked for the third or fourth time. "You didn't happen to look toward the kitchen, through the sliding door, and into the backyard to see James Hammond lying there in the corner of the yard?"

"What can I say? My bladder was full, and I didn't stop to see if there was a dead body in my backyard."

Meredith was ready to call it, but with Tyler taking the lead, he was the one who got to decide when the curtain came down.

Meredith's phone chimed, alerting her that she had a new email.

"Excuse me for a sec," she said, rising from her seat in front of Kristi's desk and moving toward a corner of the office while they continued sparring.

The email was from Johnny Masten from Cellular Depot and contained numerous attachments. She opened the email, which took a few seconds to load.

I matched the sales records to the security footage. These are the people who bought that model phone. All paid in cash. I assume this makes us square and I don't have to worry about your assistance into the robberies at my store.

Meredith flicked her thumb up the screen to scroll through the attached images.

There had to be close to forty pictures. They were low resolution but clear enough.

The buyers were almost exclusively men in their teens or twenties, wearing sunglasses and ball caps in obvious attempts to conceal their identities.

Meredith zoomed in for a better look, expecting to come across Sean Winston, wearing a trench coat, sunglasses, and a fedora like a stereotypical spy, but there were only young men and the occasional woman, followed by more men, standing at the counter, handing over their cash.

Another man, then another, then another, and then …

Meredith stopped and zoomed in further.

"No way …" she whispered and then looked up. "Tyler?"

Tyler and Kristi halted their pleasantries.

Meredith went to Tyler and handed him the phone.

Despite the ball cap and baggy sweatshirt she was wearing, there was no mistaking the face of Cybil Mantelli.

"Son of a bitch," Tyler breathed, forgetting all about the presence of Kristi Sanders a few feet away. "He had his daughter buy the phone so no one would recognize him."

"And that was the secret he asked her to keep," Meredith said.

Tyler stood and began heading for the door. "We need to get over there, right now."

Meredith only remembered Kristi as she and Tyler exited the office.

"Thank you for your time," she said over her shoulder.

*

"You want me to call and make sure he's there?" Tyler asked, pressing the button on the elevator panel.

"No. I don't want him to have any warning. We're going to show him the photo without saying a word and see what he has to say. Based off that, we'll give Kelly a call about getting a warrant."

"Copy that," Tyler said.

The elevator doors slid closed.

*

Back in her office, Kristi's heart began pounding.

She had a decision to make, one upon which everything now rested, and she needed to make it fast.

Chapter 63

Meredith and Tyler parked in the street outside Harold Mantelli's house and walked across the lawn toward the front door. Tyler nodded to the car parked in the driveway.

It looked like Harold was home.

They quickened their stride. Meredith had the photo ready on her phone, and they were eager to pounce on what was hopefully the break that would unlock everything.

Meredith slowed as they neared the front porch.

"Tyler, look …"

The front door was open a few inches. They stopped outside the door and listened. A voice was coming from inside.

"Is someone there?!" Harold Mantelli faintly cried out. "Please! Please! Help me! I'm down here!"

Meredith and Tyler pulled their firearms.

"Mr. Mantelli?" she called.

"Please! Help me! Sean Winston was here! He tied me up! I'm in the basement!"

Tyler set his feet to cover Meredith and whispered, "Go."

Keeping low, Meredith slowly pushed open the door and aimed her gun down the hallway to the kitchen. Once she was certain it was clear, she nodded, and Tyler crossed the threshold behind her.

"Is someone there?" Harold called out, again. "Please! I'm down here!"

"We're here, Mr. Mantelli," Tyler yelled. "Stay c—"

"Help! Please!"

Meredith and Tyler moved down the hallway. They paused near the entrance and then stepped into the kitchen at the same time, standing back-to-back, their guns aimed in opposite directions.

Across the kitchen, the door to the basement was open. Meredith was suddenly aware of an acrid smell.

"Please! Help me!" Harold called from below.

Meredith and Tyler moved across the kitchen and took up spots on the sides of the door. Meredith silently motioned for Tyler to watch their backs.

Tyler nodded.

"Hello?!"

Meredith began cautiously descending the stairs, aiming her Sig Sauer. Tyler followed, staying as close to her as possible, keeping his gun trained back up toward the kitchen.

"Mr. Mantelli?" Meredith called out.

"I'm in the basement! He tied me up!"

Meredith and Tyler continued downward. The acrid smell grew to a point that Meredith's eyes began to water.

They arrived at the bottom of the stairs and moved into the basement, still back-to-back.

Meredith slowly lowered her gun. Tyler felt her movement and turned to look.

"What the fuck? ..." he whispered.

There was Harold's workstation in the corner with his tools mounted on the wall and bits of machinery scattered nearby. Other than that, the basement was empty, except for the portable Bluetooth speaker sitting in the middle of the carpeted floor, from which Harold's recorded voice emanated. "Please! Help! I'm down here!"

Meredith and Tyler stepped over. She picked up the speaker and hit the power button.

"Please! I'm tied u—" Harold's voice abruptly halted.

"… Somerset … look …"

Meredith turned and followed Tyler's gaze toward the open door, leading to a short hallway and a utility room beyond. A faint work light was on in the utility room, illuminating a large plastic vat. The crown of someone's head was sticking out of it.

Meredith once again raised her Sig Sauer, and she and Tyler carefully approached the short hallway.

Tyler watched behind them but couldn't help stealing glimpses over his shoulder as they neared the utility room. Both were forced to cover their noses as the smell intensified.

Tyler turned to face the room as they both stepped inside.

The vat was filled three-quarters of the way with a cloudy, scummy liquid.

The crown of the head, or what was left of it, belonged to the decomposing remains of Sean Winston. Half of his face was submerged in the acid, and his lips and cheeks were gone to reveal bone white teeth. His eyes were open, but one socket was empty.

"Jesus …" Tyler whispered, mesmerized by the sight and moving forward for a closer look.

Meredith glanced behind them to make sure no one was sneaking up and gasped.

She quickly turned.

"Tyler! Stop!"

It was too late.

He felt a slight resistance against his shin.

A thread snapped.

Meredith lunged at him, knocking him to the side, against the wall.

There was a sharp hiss, a *whooshing* sound, and Meredith's world went dark.

Chapter 64

Something popped in Tyler's ankle as all his weight came down on it sideways when Meredith slammed into him. He fell to the floor but quickly pulled himself into a sitting position against the wall.

Meredith was lying next to him, her eyes closed.

Tyler looked up.

The work light had kicked off, but there was enough illumination coming down the hall that he could see the metal rod swaying back and forth like a baseball bat, expending the last of its energy. It was attached to a thin pole that stood upright just inside the door. A canister on the floor had released a blast of air through a hose when the thread was snapped, which had violently swung the rod around the pole.

Meredith had saved him but had taken the hit.

"Somerset?!" he called out and cradled her head.

He pressed his fingers against the side of her neck, checking for a pulse. It was there, but it was weak. He brought his ear toward her mouth. She was faintly breathing. He quickly ran his fingers through her hair and found the rapidly expanding knot on the side of her head.

It had to have been a glancing blow. A direct hit would have killed her. He checked his hands and then Meredith's ears. There was no blood, which was good.

"Somerset? Can you hear me?"

She made no response.

Tyler got to his feet. His ankle cried out in agony, but it was the least of his concerns.

"Come on," he said, crouching down. "We gotta go."

It would have been best to carry her out, but that required both hands, and he needed to keep his weapon at the ready. He briefly considered trying to throw her over his shoulder, but there wasn't enough space in the small room. He would have to get her out into the larger room. He wrapped his arm across her chest and began dragging her backward into the short hallway.

Every stunted step brought a flash of pain that forked from his ankle throughout his body, but the thought of leaving Meredith there and going for backup never crossed his mind. He could call for backup now, but it was more important that they get out as soon as possible, and it would waste precious seconds if Mantelli was coming for them.

Just get to the main room, Tyler thought. There, he could get her over his shoulder and carry her upstairs while still being able to use his firearm.

They finally emerged from the hallway and into the larger room.

Tyler continued dragging her for a few more steps to get clear of the door. He then gently set Meredith down and moved behind her.

Tyler looked over Meredith's shoulder.

There, standing at the foot of the stairs was Harold Mantelli.

He wore something bulky on his head and watched Tyler with an amused expression. In one hand was a gun, and his other hand rested on the light switch.

"Shit!" Tyler hissed. He tried to aim his own weapon,

but Harold hit the switch, plunging the basement into total darkness.

It was then that Tyler recognized what Harold was wearing on his head: night-vision goggles.

Fumbling in the pitch black, Tyler sat on the floor behind Meredith. He pulled her up to a sitting position between his splayed legs, wrapped an arm over her shoulder, across her chest, and leaned forward, using his body to shield as much of Meredith as he could, and aimed over her shoulder into the darkness.

Tyler listened for Harold's movements, but the floor was carpeted, which would conceal Harold's footsteps. There was nothing but the pounding of Tyler's own blood in his ears and his ragged, shallow breathing.

He tried to remain perfectly still.

What is he waiting for? Tyler thought.

Tyler realized that this was no longer the timid, awkward Harold Mantelli they had met the day of James Hammond's murder. This was a guy who dissolved bodies in acid. A guy who set up boobytraps and used night-vision goggles. A guy who had outsmarted them.

This was a killer.

So, why hasn't he done it? Why hasn't he taken a shot?

Tyler put himself in Harold's position as he listened.

He pictured what Harold was seeing and the answer came to him.

Even though Tyler was shielding Meredith as much as he could with his own body, from where Harold was standing, Meredith was still between them. If Harold fired, he might hit Meredith, which would give away his position and leave Tyler to take his own shot.

He's getting behind me, Tyler thought.

It was the only explanation as to why the guy with night-vision goggles in his own basement hadn't fired.

And it was a smart decision.

Tyler held his breath and strained to listen. He could be wrong. There was no sound to let him know either way, but he quickly formed a plan.

It all came down to timing.

If he acted too early, Harold wouldn't be behind him, and it would be easy for Harold to take his shot after Tyler's miscalculation.

But if Tyler waited too long after Harold got behind him, he'd never have a chance to put his plan to work.

Tyler waited, still aiming over Meredith's shoulder. With his other arm wrapped across her chest, he could feel her heart beating. Tyler's cheek was pressed against hers, and he could hear her faint breath passing over her lips.

He had one chance or they were both dead.

The seconds it had been since Harold hit the lights felt like hours.

Now.

He had to act now, or he might never get the chance.

"I'm sorry about this, Meredith," he whispered into her ear.

In one fluid motion, Tyler shoved Meredith to the side as hard as he could, hoping to get her out of the line of fire while using the resistance to fling himself onto his back.

As he fell backward, a shot rang out from somewhere over his shoulder.

The bullet whizzed by Tyler's ear and ricocheted off the floor by his legs.

Tyler's back hit the floor. He aimed over his head into the darkness and squeezed off one shot.

He wasn't going for a lucky shot. He would take it, but he was after something else.

The gun kicked in Tyler's hand, and he got his wish.

The muzzle flash from his shot illuminated the space behind him in one staccato strobe.

In that fraction of a second, Tyler saw Harold Mantelli about ten feet away, just off to his left, gun raised, goggles on, and a startled expression on his face.

The room was thrown back into darkness.

Still on his back, gun aimed over his head, Tyler made the adjustment, and fired three shots in quick succession.

Chapter 65

Kristi Sanders was losing it, and there was nothing Nick could do but watch.

It had been two days since the detectives had left her office to go and talk to Harold about the cell phone, and she hadn't heard from Harold since. She hadn't heard from the detectives, either.

CashFlo was in a tailspin.

It could have survived the loss of James Hammond, but now Sean Winston was nowhere to be found, and every partner and associate was backing away. Kristi had become the de facto CEO. She had tried to hold everything together, but CashFlo was going under. She then told the staff to take the rest of the week off.

And incredibly that wasn't even their biggest problem.

She and Nick were in their bedroom, throwing clothes in a suitcase.

"I still don't think we should do this," Nick said. "It looks like we're going on the run."

"It's not going on the run," Kristi said, blindly grabbing clothes off the hangers in the closet. "We're getting a little distance. That way, if something happens, we'll see it coming. If it makes you feel any better, we'll tell the police where we're going."

"But Dougie—"

"Dougie is fine, Nick. My parents can take care of—"

Nick shook his head. "Kristi—"

Her phone, resting on the bed next to the suitcase, began to ring. She gave Nick the index finger in a gesture that said *wait* and answered.

"Hey, Spencer," she happily said, despite the fact that she was sweating. "… I appreciate that … No— … No, Spencer. CashFlo is fine. I promise. It's been a crazy couple of days, but I assure you that our partnership with your company is stronger tha— …" Kristi began pacing, and her face contorted in pain. "No. Spen— … Spencer? I promise you, it's going to be fine …"

She continued pacing and pleading.

Nick sat back, invisible and useless.

His own phone in his pocket pinged with a text.

He took it out and stared at the screen.

Meet me in the backyard.

He looked over at Kristi, who continued her tense conversation, oblivious to his presence.

He stood and walked out of the room.

Kristi's voice trailed off as he descended the stairs and worked his way down the hallway to the kitchen. He paused by the windowed patio door.

When he read the text, he hadn't fully believed it, but sure enough, it was true.

He opened the door and stormed across the lawn.

"Are you out of your goddamned mind?" he asked, fighting to keep his voice down.

Jessica looked up at him with shimmering eyes.

"I'm sorry, but I couldn't take it anymore, Nick. I had to see you. I haven't heard from you."

"Yeah," Nick replied, condescendingly. "Don't know if you've noticed, but there's a lot going on."

Jessica stared at him like a hurt, lost puppy, which enflamed him even more.

"You have to get out of here," he said. "And don't ever contact me, again."

"… What about us?"

"Are you—? Jesus Christ, are you serious, Jessica?"

"I just thought—"

"Are you kidding me?" Kristi spat as she emerged from the open door to the kitchen and into the backyard. "Are you fucking kidding me?!"

Jessica stumbled backward two steps with good reason. Kristi looked like she wanted to kill her.

Nick stepped in front of Kristi, but she blew past him and got in Jessica's face.

"What are you doing here?" she asked.

Jessica braced herself. "I'm sorry, Kristi. I'm so sorry. I didn't want you to find out like this."

"Find out what? What are you talking about?"

"Nick and I are in love."

Something inside Kristi snapped.

"No …" she said, shaking her head.

"I'm sorry, Kristi, but it's true."

Kristi began laughing. "I meant, 'No. There's no way you're that stupid. There's no way you're that naive.'"

Jessica blinked. "Kristi, you have to believe me; Nick and I are really in love." She turned to Nick. "Tell her."

It was Nick's turn to laugh. "You really are that stupid. I never loved you. You were a decent screw, but nothing compared to my wife."

Jessica stared in disbelief. "No. Nick, you said you loved me—"

"Stop! Stop embarrassing yourself."

Jessica stammered, trying to find something to say, but the looks on their faces said that they were together, and they were telling the truth.

She felt sick.

"Then … Why? Why, Nick?"

"Because your husband was one of the biggest pieces of shit to walk the earth. Because he was going to ruin all of our lives. But most of all, because he raped my wife and used our son's cancer to make *her* cover it up."

Jessica stared and began to shake her head. "No … No. James would never—"

"Oh, grow up! … You knew," Nick said. "You always knew, and she wasn't the first, and you turned a blind eye because you got the money, the clothes, the house, but you knew exactly who James was. How many times did you rationalize that it was okay that we were fucking because James was sleeping around? You're either a liar or an idiot."

"But if you didn't love me … why?" Jessica asked.

"It was the only way to get back at him. We were going to tell him, and you know how much that would have messed with his head. It would have driven him crazy and wrecked your sham of a marriage. Yeah, it was petty, but do you think I was going to sit by and let him do that to my family? To my wife?"

Kristi smiled. "When we told James, he would never fire me to get back at Nick. I knew where all of his skeletons were at CashFlo. He would be helpless, just like he made me feel. So, we were waiting. Then came Blackstone."

"What's Blackstone?"

Her ignorance caused their anger to double.

"He was going to sell the company and screw us over!" Kristi nearly screamed. "A guy from Blackstone got in touch with Harold to talk about it, not knowing Harold had nothing to do with CashFlo. Harold felt he was getting screwed over, again, and talked to Sean. Sean told us, and we all decided that James had to be stopped."

"Stopped?" Jessica asked.

Kristi and Nick continued to stare at her in disbelief at her failure to grasp the reality, but it finally seemed to dawn on her.

"Nick ... Please ... Tell me you weren't a part of James's death ..."

Nick looked to Kristi, who nodded.

"Jessica ... sweetheart ... we were all a part of it."

Jessica shook her head. "No ... No. That's not—"

"After I left you in the closet, I went to the backyard to wait for James. Harold sent the text message. We didn't want to include him, but if we killed James on our own, he would have known it was us. The only way to keep him in line was to make him just as guilty as the rest of us. I put the bat next to the door and waited for your husband. He came out, and I told him all about us, the motels, the afternoon delights. I left your lipstick on my face and told him it wasn't the only place on my body with your lipstick." Nick smirked. "You should have heard the names he called you. He was so caught up in cursing you, he didn't hear Harold and Sean come into the yard. Harold waited by the door as Sean picked up the bat ... The last thing your husband heard was me telling him that I was sleeping with his wife."

Jessica gagged.

"Harold took his turn with the bat as I staged it to look like someone hopped the fence," Nick said. "But he only tapped James's arm. Then, I went out front, which was Kristi's signal to come to the backyard."

He looked down at his wife with ultimate affection. Kristi returned his beaming grin and continued.

"I didn't care that he was already dead. I pulled the tablecloth over him and beat his face to a pulp ... That was me, and he deserved all of it."

Jessica began trembling. "Why? ... Why are you telling me all of this?"

"Because you deserve to know," Kristi said in equal parts sarcasm and menace.

Jessica looked between them in genuine fear. "I'll tell the police."

"They won't believe you," Kristi said. "Or maybe you'll never get the chance."

The gate to the backyard opened.

"She doesn't need to," Meredith said as she stepped onto the grass, accompanied by Tyler, Sheriff Howell, and three officers.

Kristi and Nick turned back to Jessica and stared in disbelief. There was still an element of fear but also anger in her face.

"If you haven't figured it out, yet," Tyler said, "she's with us."

Kristi was the first one to find her tongue.

"Listen, detectives, I don't know what you think you heard but it's our word against—"

Jessica reached under her shirt and pulled out the small wired microphone that had been taped to her skin. She handed it to Meredith without looking away from Nick.

"Harold Mantelli is the one you're after," Kristi stammered. "This doesn't mean that Nick and I—"

"Harold Mantelli was waiting for us," Tyler said, approaching Kristi with his slight limp. "Someone warned him we were coming. There was only one person in the world who knew we were heading his way and they knew that because we had just left her office. So, you probably want to stop talking now."

Kristi and Nick turned to Jessica.

"I loved you," Jessica said to Nick.

Nick took Kristi's hand.

"Well, I'm really glad you got to hear the truth from us," Nick said in a way that turned Meredith's blood to ice.

She thought that Jessica would collapse, but she kept her feet as Sheriff Howell and the officers joined Tyler.

Sheriff Howell snapped the cuffs on Nick while Tyler handled Kristi.

Tyler hesitated.

Meredith wondered if he was about to shake her hand, but instead, he put the cuffs on her as Jessica walked away, choking back tears.

Chapter 66

Meredith hated doing the postmortem on cases.

There was the high of solving a case, and then the crash when she stopped to wonder if anything had really changed. Sitting on her couch in her apartment, she wondered what would happen to Jessica and to Dani. She especially wondered what would happen to Dougie. He was with his grandparents and that might be where he stayed but—

The pounding on the door, accompanied by Tyler's voice, startled Meredith back to reality.

"Somerset? It's me. Open up."

Meredith got off the couch, went to the door, and threw it open. "Tyler, what are you doing h—?"

Without a word, he limped past her into the apartment.

"What are you doing?" she asked.

Tyler went straight to the closed door to the spare bedroom. "This it?" he asked.

"You can't just walk in here and—"

That was all Tyler needed. He opened the door and went inside. Meredith's annoyance at Tyler's unbidden visit turned to rage. "Wait!" she called, racing across the apartment.

She burst in to see Tyler standing in the middle of the

room, staring slack-jawed at the horrible mosaic spread across the walls.

"Somerset, what is this?"

"*This*," she said, crossing her arms and glaring at him, "is none of your damn business. You have no right—"

"Two years ago, you called me out when my 'personal business' nearly cost us a case and my job, and you were right. It saved my life, and now I'm repaying the favor."

"This is nothing like that, and how did you know about it?"

"Allison called me and I'm glad she did. She's terrified, Somerset."

"I'm fine. I do this on my own time and I—"

"Your own time?! Bullshit! You put a gun to a guy's head because you thought he had something to do with this," Tyler said, motioning around the room. "Somerset, I aimed my weapon at you, and I would have pulled the trigger if I had to. That's what this has done to you. Don't tell me that this doesn't interfere with your job."

"It was a one-time thing. I was on edge."

"One time?" Tyler asked, incredulously. "You're trying to tell me that this has affected your judgment just one time and that wasn't enough?"

Meredith didn't answer.

Tyler pointed to the bathing suit mounted on the wall with the note.

"That's your sister's, right? The asshole who took her sent that?"

Meredith nodded, not wanting to clarify that he hadn't sent it. He had left it on her doorstep.

"And you didn't tell anyone?"

"It's my sister's case. If I had told anyone, this guy would have gone to ground—"

"Title 16, Chapter 10, Subsection 94 of the Georgia Criminal Code. Any person who destroys, alters, or *conceals* physical evidence is guilty of a felony, punishable by not less than one year in prison. What you're doing is a crime, Somerset, and it won't stop at that. If this got out, every single one of your cases would be called into question."

Meredith wouldn't meet his glare. She wanted to be angry with him but knew he was right.

"I have to find him, Tyler. I couldn't tell anyone."

"You could have told me."

"What good would that have done?"

"We could have talked. I could have helped."

"I don't need help, Tyler."

Anger flared in Tyler's face as he motioned to the walls, again.

"Look at this and tell me that you don't need help. Tell me this isn't eating away at you. Tell me that this isn't infecting every part of your life, your relationships, and your work; and remember, I watched you almost kill someone."

Meredith could feel herself backed into a corner while Tyler rained down blows.

"I didn't turn the bathing suit over because it's worthless as evidence. I have this under control," she said.

"You're lying to yourself, and you know it."

"I'm the only one who can solve this. He's taunting me. 'She still misses you, Meredith.' Alice could still be out there, and yes, I had a momentary lapse in judgment, but that doesn't mean that I'll—"

Tyler had been shaking his head during her paltry explanations, his ire growing until he could no longer contain himself. He reached up, ripped the bathing suit from the wall, and brandished it toward Meredith.

"This ain't a fucking hobby, Somerset! This isn't some side project. This is an obsession." Tyler gripped the suit with both hands and ripped it in two.

"NO!!!" Meredith screamed. She rushed toward him and pulled the pieces from his hands.

"Oh …" he said. "I'm sorry. I thought you said that it was worthless as evidence and that it's not eating you up inside."

Meredith's eyes welled with tears. She took a few steps back until she was leaning against the wall and allowed herself to slide down until she was sitting on the floor, still holding the fabric in her hand.

Tyler stepped over and sat next to her.

"Obsession is just another word for addiction, Somerset. Believe me, I know, and this," he said with a nod toward the torn bathing suit, "this is your drug. I'm tired of losing people, Somerset. Friends, family, my mother ... I might lose Hannah ... I'm not going to lose you, Meredith ... I can't ... and neither can Allison."

She looked at him, tears spilling down her cheeks.

"What are you talking about? What do you mean you might lose Hannah?"

"She literally has a hole in her heart. It's a defect that happens in kids with Down syndrome. It normally develops when they're young and can be treated more easily, but when it happens later in life, it's a problem ... She might need a new heart." Tyler choked on the words. "So, no, Somerset. I'm not going to let you do this to yourself because I won't have any family left."

"Why didn't you tell me?"

"There was nothing you could do. There's nothing anyone could do, and I didn't want you feeling sorry for me. I needed our work as a distraction." He smiled at her. "Then you went and put your gun against that guy's head."

"Tyler, I'm so sorry."

"I appreciate that, but we're talking about you, okay?"

Meredith nodded and wiped her eyes. "Do you really know the wording to that law?"

"Nah," Tyler said. "I had to look that shit up."

They both laughed.

Meredith wiped her eyes. "I don't know what to do."

"From my extensive experience with this shit, I've got a good first step."

Chapter 67

Meredith and Allison stared at one another across the kitchen table, neither one sure of what came next.

Their excruciating awkwardness reached a point where Tyler, who was sitting off to the side, stepped in.

"You wanna do your intro thing?" he asked Allison.

"What?"

Tyler nodded to the microphone on the table in front of her.

"Oh," Allison blurted out, as if the microphone had materialized out of thin air. "Ummm ... This is Catching Evil, the podcast about, uh, people who commit evil and the people who catch them. I'm your host, Allison Somerset." The overly serious tone she had employed during Tyler's interview was gone. She sounded exactly like what she was, a nervous teenager embarking on a very awkward discussion with her mother. "I'm joined today by Meredith Somerset, a homicide detective with the Cobb County Police Department. Thank you for being here, detective."

"Thank you for having me," Meredith said, flatly. It wasn't out of disdain or indifference. She felt foolish saying it, but she wanted to treat this as seriously as possible. Tyler was right. She owed this to Allison, and she was going to be completely honest with her.

"In the interest of transparency, I need to point out that Detective Somerset is my mother," Allison said into the microphone.

Meredith forced a smile.

"How long have you been a homicide detective?"

"About fifteen years. I was an officer for a few years before that."

"And how many murder cases have you worked on?"

"I lost count a while ago."

"You don't remember?"

"I remember every single one of them. I just lost count."

"What's the worst case you ever worked on?"

"It depends on what you mean by 'the worst.'"

"Well, like, is there one that keeps you up at night?"

"Sure, but I wouldn't say it's just one case," Meredith answered after a moment. "It's a different case every night. The unsolved ones tend to haunt you the most. You think of something that you wish you would have done during the investigation and wonder if it would have caught the person who did it. Sometimes, even the ones you solved will keep you up at night."

"Why is that?"

"Because even if you do this job perfectly, the victims aren't coming back. There's still a hole where they used to be, and the next morning, you're going to get a call to another homicide. There's always another murder."

"Then why do you do it? My whole life, I've never seen you happy about your job, Mom."

Meredith and Allison were already so locked into one another that she was no longer Detective Somerset to Allison, but "Mom."

"Because the alternative is that the victim stays dead and the killer gets away. Even if things can never get back to 'even,' you have to do something. You can't let someone who does that get away with it."

"So … What made you want to be a detective?"

"When I was your age, my younger sister, Alice, was kidnapped from the local swimming pool while I was supposed to be watching her. We never heard from her or the person who took her, again."

"What happened after that?"

"It destroyed my family. Not knowing what had happened, living with the remote possibility that at any moment, we might find her alive or find her dead, made getting on with our lives impossible. My parents, your grandparents, ended up getting a divorce. Dad started drinking. Eventually, the drinking killed him. He died broke in a rundown one-bedroom apartment. My mother blamed me for Alice's disappearance. She blamed me for everything. She didn't need to. I blamed myself."

"You still blame yourself for your sister's kidnapping?"

"Every day."

"Not the person who actually took her?"

Meredith couldn't help but smile. "You should talk to Grandma."

"And that made you want to be a detective?"

"After a few months of false leads and no word from Alice's kidnapper, the head detective on the case, Detective Clayton Reed, took me aside and said that we were never going to find her. I hated him for that. It was like he was giving up, and at that point, finding Alice's dead body would have been better than nothing. At least we could have moved on, but the police, like everyone else, moved on. I was going to be a detective because I never wanted another family to go through that. I guess it also had a lot to do with my own guilt. I wanted to somehow make it up to my parents, and this was the only way I knew how to do it. As if one day, I might find Alice and make them proud. Dad loved cops. He taught me and Alice that cops were heroes, but he died before I became a detective."

"What about your mom?"

Meredith considered glossing over what had passed between them but decided against it. If Bethany, her mother, Allison's grandmother, wanted to tell her side of history, she could have been a part of Allison's life a long time ago.

"She still blamed me," Meredith said. "It rotted me inside because she was the only family that I had left. I still felt guilty about Alice, and when being a cop wasn't enough, I thought I might get over it by having a family of my own. I met your father. We got married and had you. I even named you after my sister in the hopes that my mother might forgive me. She didn't. In fact, she felt that it was a constant reminder of the fact that I was supposed to be watching Alice when she disappeared."

"You … You only had me to reconnect with your mother?"

Meredith shook her head. "No. No, your father and I wanted children. I picked the name, and it may have been a mistake. I don't know, but what I do know is that you are the best thing that's ever happened to me and the best thing I've ever done. When those cases come back to haunt me, the thought of you drives them away, because to me, you are everything that is good in this world, and I will never be able to express how much I love you and how proud I am of you."

Allison swallowed the lump in her throat.

"What happened with you and Dad? Why did you get a divorce? And if you loved me so much, why did you give up custody of me?"

Meredith tried to conceal the pain of the knife that had been plunged into her chest.

"I never processed the pain of my sister's kidnapping and everything that came afterwards. It affected my work. I thought that having a family would help me move on, but it didn't. I was angry and taking it out on everyone around me, including your father. It was ripping us apart, just like it had ripped my family apart when I was a kid. I didn't see it, but my boss, Sergeant Wheaton, did. He saw that I needed help. He had gone through something similar when he lost his wife and daughter to a drunk driver. He got me in touch with the doctor who helped him. She was able to see that I was in a lot of pain." Meredith's demeanor began to crack. "Working with her made me confront some

340

horrible truths. The hardest of which was that the best thing for you was to be with your father. It was the most painful decision I've ever had to make in my life, but I did it because it was the right thing for you, no matter what it meant for me. I've never told you that because I was worried that you wouldn't understand. I made the decision because I loved you so much and I wanted what was best for you. I wanted to be the best mother I could and the only way I could do that was to get help ... I can't explain it any plainer than that, and if you don't understand, that's okay. I only hope that one day you will."

Meredith was exhausted. That two-minute explanation had taken more out of her than she would have thought possible. Allison looked battered as well, but they had gone this far and Allison wanted to know more.

"You said your sister's disappearance affected your work as a homicide detective. How so?"

"I would see Alice's face on the faces of murder victims. The doctor helped me process my anger and grief. It got better."

"Do you still see your sister's face on murder victims?"

"Not for a while, but about two years ago, it started again when a girl who looked very similar to Alice was found strangled in the middle of a street. It started the visions all over again. And then, everything was made worse when the person who took Alice left her bathing suit, the one she was wearing the day she disappeared, on my doorstep."

"Did you tell anyone?"

"No."

"Why not?"

"Because I needed to catch him. I felt that the bathing suit was a personal invitation from Alice's kidnapper to find him. I started my own investigation. I collected everything I could from official reports to witness statements to recorded interrogations, even though it could cost me my career."

"Why would it cost you your career?"

"Because the rules of my job and the law dictate that I have to report the bathing suit."

"But it's an old case."

"Yes, but I'm a detective. If it got out that I didn't report a piece of critical evidence, it could call into question every decision I've made in every investigation I've ever been a part of. Dozens of murderers could be retried and set free."

"Did you know that when you decided not to report the bathing suit?"

"I suppose some part of me did, but I had over twenty years of regret and anger to rationalize my decision." Meredith then shook her head. "No ... I knew ... Of course, I knew it was wrong."

"Are you any closer to finding him?"

"I thought I was."

"What happened?"

Meredith nodded toward Tyler.

"Someone talked some sense into me."

"Are you still going to try to find him?"

"I have to," Meredith said.

"Why?"

"Because I just have to."

Allison pretended to consult her notes as she struggled before asking her next question.

"After not reporting the bathing suit, do you think you're a good detective?"

"Yes, I do, but ultimately, that's not up to me."

"I don't understand. Who is it up to?"

"It's up to those around me. Those who count on me to be a good detective."

Allison took it in and nodded.

Once Meredith felt that she understood her answer, she asked, "So, with that in mind, do you think I'm a good mother?"

The vulnerability with which Meredith had asked her daughter the question was gut-wrenching to Tyler. Meredith wasn't looking for validation. In much the same way that Allison had done an amazing job of asking questions from a dispassionate standpoint, Meredith had put her heart on the table.

She had asked the hardest question a parent could ask of their child.

Allison looked at her mother.

Meredith saw her grow years right before her eyes.

"You're amazing, Mom," Allison said.

Meredith nodded a silent acknowledgment and whispered, "Thank you."

Allison looked at the microphone in front of her and then off to the side at the screen of her laptop. She reached over and tapped a button, signaling that the recording was done.

"Is it true that if people heard this, you could lose your job?" she asked.

"Yeah."

Allison reached over again and tapped a few more keys before sitting back with a sigh.

"What did you do?" Meredith asked.

"I deleted it."

Chapter 68

Meredith stepped out of her apartment, turned, and locked the door. She was already prepping herself for what would be the toughest conversation of her professional life.

She had only taken a few steps down the path when she heard a door open behind her.

"Meredith!" a frail voice said.

Meredith turned to see Mrs. Johnson looking at her and waving.

"Good evening, Mrs. Johnson," Meredith said, returning her gesture with only a fraction of her enthusiasm, eager to get on with what had to be done.

To Meredith's surprise, Mrs. Johnson stepped out of her apartment, wearing a robe and house slippers, and carrying something in her hand.

"Meredith, sweetheart. How many times do I have to tell you to call me Mildred?" she asked, walking across the grass to meet her.

Meredith smiled. "One day I will."

"This was left on my doorstep, but someone messed up, because it's for you."

Mrs. Johnson extended her hand, in which she held a manila envelope with Meredith's name written on it in black marker.

Despite her best efforts to hide her shock, Meredith couldn't stop her eyes from widening.

"Is everything okay?" Mildred asked.

"Yes," Meredith managed to sputter. "Yes. Thank you, Mrs. Johnson."

"Mildred," she corrected.

"Mildred," Meredith repeated.

"Are you sure?"

"Yes. I'm fine," Meredith said.

Mrs. Johnson stared intently at her. "Hmmmm … No. No, you're not. I'm going to make some soup tonight and bring it to you tomorrow," she said, patting Meredith's arm. She turned, walked back to her apartment, stepped inside, and closed the door.

Meredith couldn't take her eyes from the envelope.

She knew who it was from.

Why had he left it on Mrs. Johnson's doorstep?

The answer was simple: to avoid the camera Meredith had installed on her door in case he ever decided to make another delivery.

Meredith hurried inside her apartment.

She didn't go to the kitchen. She stood right there in the entrance hall and ripped open the flap.

She reached in and pulled out a folded sheet of paper. She unfolded it and read the brief message. She then turned the envelope upside down.

A small plastic bag slid out into her palm.

Meredith began to hyperventilate.

She had to speak to Sergeant Wheaton, right now.

Chapter 69

Meredith sat at her desk, turning her badge over in her hands while she waited for Sergeant Wheaton and Kelly Yamara to finish their discussion in his office.

The district attorney was considering cutting a deal with the Sanderses, and Sergeant Wheaton was making his feelings known, arguing that Meredith and Tyler had done an exceptional job in getting a confession from the couple. Kelly said that she agreed, but the district attorney was the one who handled prosecutions and a deal was preferable to the chance that at the trial, the Sanders's attorney might seize on some stupid technicality, such as the questionable turning over of security footage by Cellular Depot, to acquit his clients. Kelly argued further that it was an incredibly complicated case that a jury might not completely understand, and it only took one confused juror for the Sanderses to walk.

As Meredith looked down at her badge, she wondered if she was going to lose her job.

She was a good detective. She knew that. Some of her colleagues had even called her great, but she felt that she wasn't leaving Sergeant Wheaton a choice.

She had withheld evidence. She had discharged her weapon to

intimidate a witness. She had pressed her gun against the man's head, nearly destroying the case that was her actual job, and as she had told Allison, it could have blown up her career. She had jeopardized her entire department. Every case she had ever worked on would be called into question. Sergeant Wheaton couldn't ignore that, no matter the strong paternal feelings he had for her.

She continued to stare at her badge, mindlessly turning it back and forth in her fingers, causing the light from the overhead halogen tubes to reflect across her face.

That badge meant everything to her.

It represented her promise to keep families from going through the same hell that had torn hers apart. It reflected her desire to win back her mother's favor for the crime she felt was her fault. Even though her father never lived to see her become a detective, she liked to think that he was somewhere watching, and felt a sense of pride, pride in the fact that she hadn't let the tragedy of Alice destroy her as it had him.

The job defined Meredith, and it was all there in that badge. In the eagle's wings that formed the upper half of the shield, above a blue ribbon that read "Cobb County" and the insignia of the Liberty Bell.

Outside of Allison, the badge meant the most to Meredith. It was a source of pride and power that she used to protect people she didn't even know.

But she had abused it.

She had used the badge to force a private investigation, and when it had gone wrong, she used it against the private detective to secure his silence.

She had used this gleaming, shiny emblem to—

Meredith stopped breathing.

Her eyes glassed over.

Sound ceased.

Everything fell into place.

Suddenly, she was propelled into action. She fired up the

computer and opened a browser. She logged in and went to the Dalton Police Department website, a website she had spent countless hours combing through over the past two decades while researching her sister's disappearance.

She began searching the records from 1992. Instead of going to the digitized case files, she pulled up the photos of the officers in the department at the time.

Just like every elementary, junior high, and high school, police precincts had "photo day," when officers had their photos taken, which were then put together and hung on the wall. Beginning in the nineties, they were also posted online.

She clicked a link and was treated to a page with rows and columns of men and women in uniform. She clicked on the first image. She didn't care about the face. That's not what she was after.

Not yet, at least.

The first photo was of an officer named Maria Atchison.

Meredith right-clicked the photo and saved it to the desktop. She then opened it in the photo-viewing application that came standard with the computer's operating system. Once it came up, she highlighted the area around Officer Atchison's badge and zoomed in.

Instead of the Liberty Bell found on the Cobb County badge, the police badges for Dalton displayed three rolls of fabric, honoring the town's textile-producing history, but the one thing that was identical between the two badges was the eagle with outstretched wings that formed the top-third of the badge.

Meredith kept the window open and began opening more web browsers.

She began researching surrounding towns and counties, repeating the process of finding department photos from 1992 and examining the badges. The insignias, like the Liberty Bell and rolls of fabric, changed according to the unique histories of the cities and counties, but the one thing that was universal was the eagle at the top of the badge.

Minutes later, Meredith had a screen full of silver eagles.

A screen full of "shiny birdies."

The door to Sergeant Wheaton's office suddenly opened, and Kelly Yamara walked out. She made her way past the empty desks and out the door without so much as a look in Meredith's direction.

Sergeant Wheaton appeared in his doorway.

Meredith quickly shut off her screen as he looked toward her. "Want to step inside?" he asked.

Chapter 70

Tyler snorted himself awake.

Is it storming? he wondered, still uncertain if he was dreaming.

It took a few seconds for him to shake it off and realize that someone was pounding on his door.

He picked up his phone from the nightstand and checked the time. 1:43 a.m.

The pounding continued.

"Yeah. I'm up. One second," he growled.

He threw off the covers and pulled on a T-shirt and jeans he found on the floor. He also unlocked the nightstand drawer and grabbed his MP9. Tyler believed his past was behind him, but someone pounding on his door at nearly two in the morning could be one of his old dealer associates coming to settle a score.

To his surprise, Tyler looked through the peephole and saw Meredith waiting, clutching some papers to her chest.

He threw back the bolt and opened the door.

"Somerset? What the hell are you—?"

"I need to talk to you," she said, pushing past him, seemingly oblivious to the fact that he was holding a gun.

"Yeah. Sure. Come on in," he replied, still shaking off sleep.

He left her in the living room while he went back to the bedroom to return the gun to the nightstand.

"What happened?" he asked upon returning to the living room. "Did you talk to Sergeant Wheaton?"

Meredith shook her head. "I told him that I needed a few more days."

"Somerset. That was the deal. Either you tell him or I do."

"The guy who took Alice, the guy who left the bathing suit? He left this for me." She held out the manila envelope with her name scrawled upon it.

Tyler took it and reached inside. He pulled out the letter and read the same brief message Meredith had read only a few hours ago.

Stop looking and move on with your life. There's only so many pieces I can mail to you.

Tyler tipped the envelope over and the small plastic bag slid out into his hand. Inside the bag was a lock of blond hair.

"Somerset …"

"Listen—"

"You didn't tell Sergeant Wheaton about this?"

"Tyler, I can't!"

The panic in her voice made him stop.

"Why not?"

"Because I think I figured it out. I figured out why Alice would trust this guy to walk away with him and why Wallace Hogan was so afraid and how this guy's been able to hide his tracks all these years."

"How?"

"Wallace Hogan kept saying that a man with a 'shiny birdie' threatened him. That the bird told him bad things would happen to him if he told anyone."

"Okay …"

351

Meredith went to the coffee table and began laying out the papers that she was carrying with her. There were roughly a dozen blown-up images she had printed at her apartment of police badges from Dalton and neighboring areas from 1992.

All of them had the silver eagle with the outstretched wings.

"It was a cop," Meredith said. "A cop took my sister. Maybe one who was involved in the investigation. My father taught us to revere cops. That's why Alice would have trusted him to leave the pool. It explains how he could avoid capture all these years. He knew how investigations worked. It's how he's stayed hidden. It's how he knew I was looking. Even if he's retired, he would still have connections in the Dalton Police Department who could tell him I was requesting records. That's why I couldn't tell Sergeant Wheaton. It can't get out because of that," she said, nodding to the bag with the lock of hair in his hand.

He looked at the bag.

"Tyler, a cop took my sister," Meredith said. "And I think she's still alive."